Anonymous

The Complete Works Of Mark Twain

In Defense Of Harriet Shelley

Anonymous

The Complete Works Of Mark Twain
In Defense Of Harriet Shelley

ISBN/EAN: 9783348008013

Printed in Europe, USA, Canada, Australia, Japan

Cover: Foto ©Andreas Hilbeck / pixelio.de

More available books at **www.hansebooks.com**

Gave It a Better Hold

American Artists Edition

THE COMPLETE
WORKS OF
MARK TWAIN

IN DEFENSE OF

HARRIET SHELLEY

HARPER & BROTHERS
NEW YORK

CONTENTS

Acknowledgment is hereby made to Harper & Brothers, The Century Company, The Cosmopolitan, and S. S. McClure & Co., for courtesy shown in allowing the reprint in this volume of a number of their articles.

LITERARY ESSAYS

IN DEFENSE OF HARRIET SHELLEY

I

I HAVE committed sins, of course; but I have not committed enough of them to entitle me to the punishment of reduction to the bread and water of ordinary literature during six years when I might have been living on the fat diet spread for the righteous in Professor Dowden's *Life of Shelley*, if I had been justly dealt with.

During these six years I have been living a life of peaceful ignorance. I was not aware that Shelley's first wife was unfaithful to him, and that that was why he deserted her and wiped the stain from his sensitive honor by entering into soiled relations with Godwin's young daughter. This was all new to me when I heard it lately, and was told that the proofs of it were in this book, and that this book's verdict is accepted in the girls' colleges of America and its view taught in their literary classes.

In each of these six years multitudes of young people in our country have arrived at the Shelley-reading age. Are these six multitudes unacquainted with this life of Shelley? Perhaps they are; indeed, one may feel pretty sure that the great bulk of them are. To these, then, I address myself, in the hope that some account of this romantic historical fable and the fabulist's manner of constructing and adorning it may interest them.

First, as to its literary style. Our negroes in America have several ways of entertaining themselves which are not found among the whites anywhere. Among these inventions of theirs is one which is particularly popular with them. It is a competition in elegant deportment. They hire a hall and bank the spectators' seats in rising tiers along the two sides, leaving all the middle stretch of the floor free. A cake is provided as a prize for the winner in the competition, and a bench of experts in deportment is appointed to award it. Sometimes there are as many as fifty contestants, male and female, and five hundred spectators. One at a time the contestants enter, clothed regardless of expense in what each considers the perfection of style and taste, and walk down the vacant central space and back again with that multitude of critical eyes on them. All that the competitor knows of fine airs and graces he throws into his carriage, all that he knows of seductive expression he throws into his countenance. He may use all the helps he can devise: watch-chain to twirl with his fingers, cane to do graceful things with, snowy handkerchief to flourish and get artful effects out of, shiny new stovepipe hat to assist in his courtly bows; and the colored lady may have a fan to work up *her* effects with, and smile over and blush behind, and she may add other helps, according to her judgment. When the review by individual detail is over, a grand review of all the contestants in procession follows, with all the airs and graces and all the bowings and smirkings on exhibition at once, and this enables the bench of experts to make the necessary comparisons and arrive at a verdict The successful competitor gets the prize which I have before mentioned, and an abundance of applause and envy along with it. The negroes have a name for this grave deportment tournament; a name taken from the prize contended for. They call it a Cake-Walk.

The Shelley biography is a literary cake-walk. The ordinary forms of speech are absent from it. All the pages, all the paragraphs, walk by sedately, elegantly, not to say mincingly, in their Sunday-best, shiny and sleek, perfumed, and with *boutonnières* in their buttonholes; it is rare to find even a chance sentence that has forgotten to dress. If the book wishes to tell us that Mary Godwin, child of sixteen, had known afflictions, the fact saunters forth in this nobby outfit: "Mary was herself not unlearned in the lore of pain"—meaning by that that she had not always traveled on asphalt; or, as some authorities would frame it, that she had "been there herself," a form which, while preferable to the book's form, is still not to be recommended. If the book wishes to tell us that Harriet Shelley hired a wet-nurse, that commonplace fact gets turned into a dancing-master, who does his professional bow before us in pumps and knee-breeches, with his fiddle under one arm and his crush-hat under the other, thus: "The beauty of Harriet's motherly relation to her babe was marred in Shelley's eyes by the introduction into his house of a hireling nurse to whom was delegated the mother's tenderest office."

This is perhaps the strangest book that has seen the light since Frankenstein. Indeed, it is a Frankenstein itself; a Frankenstein with the original infirmity supplemented by a new one; a Frankenstein with the reasoning faculty wanting. Yet it believes it can reason, and is always trying. It is not content to leave a mountain of fact standing in the clear sunshine, where the simplest reader can perceive its form, its details, and its relation to the rest of the landscape, but thinks it must help him examine it and understand it; so its drifting mind settles upon it with that intent, but always with one and the same result: there is a change of temperature and the mountain is hid in a fog. Every time it sets up a premise and starts to reason from it, there is a surprise in store for the reader. It is strangely near-sighted, cross-eyed, and purblind. Sometimes when a mastodon walks across the field of its vision it takes it for a rat; at other times it does not see it at all.

The materials of this biographical fable are facts, rumors, and poetry. They are connected together and harmonized by the help of suggestion, conjecture, innuendo, perversion, and semi-suppression.

The fable has a distinct object in view, but this object is not acknowledged in set words. Percy Bysshe Shelley has done something which in the case of other men is called a grave crime; it must be shown that in his case it is not that, because he does not think as other men do about these things.

Ought not that to be enough, if the fabulist is serious? Having proved that a crime is not a crime, was it worth while to go on and fasten the responsibility of a crime which was not a crime upon somebody else? What is the use of hunting down and holding to bitter account people who are responsible for other people's innocent acts?

Still, the fabulist thinks it a good idea to do that. In his view Shelley's first wife, Harriet, free of all offense as far as we have historical facts for guidance, must be held unforgivably responsible for her husband's innocent act in deserting her and taking up with another woman.

Any one will suspect that this task has its difficulties. Any one will divine that nice work is necessary here, cautious work, wily work, and that there is entertainment to be had in watching the magician do it. There is indeed entertainment in watching him. He arranges his facts, his rumors, and his poems on his table in full view of the house, and shows you that everything is there—no deception, everything fair and aboveboard. And this is apparently true, yet there is a defect, for some of his best stock is hid in an appendix-basket behind the door, and you do not come upon it until the exhibition is over and the enchantment of your mind accomplished—as the magician thinks.

There is an insistent atmosphere of candor and fairness about this book which is engaging at first, then a little burdensome, then a trifle fatiguing, then progressively suspicious, annoying, irritating, and oppressive. It takes one some little time to find out that phrases which seem intended to guide the reader aright are there to mislead him; that phrases which seem intended to throw light are there to throw darkness; that phrases which seem intended to interpret a fact are there to misinterpret it; that phrases which seem intended to forestall prejudice are there to create it; that phrases which seem antidotes are poisons in disguise. The naked facts arrayed in the book establish Shelley's guilt in that one episode which disfigures his otherwise superlatively lofty and beautiful life; but the historian's careful and methodical misinterpretation of them transfers the responsibility to the wife's shoulders—as he persuades himself. The few meager facts of Harriet Shelley's life, as furnished by the book, acquit her of offense; but by calling in the forbidden helps of rumor, gossip, conjecture, insinuation, and innuendo he destroys her character and rehabilitates Shelley's—as he believes. And in truth his unheroic work has not been barren of the results he aimed at; as witness the assertion made to me that girls in the colleges of America are taught that Harriet Shelley put a stain upon her husband's honor, and that that was what stung him into repurifying himself by deserting her and his child and entering into scandalous relations with a school-girl acquaintance of his.

If that assertion is true, they probably use a reduction of this work in those colleges, maybe only a sketch outlined from it. Such a thing as that could be harmful and misleading. They ought to cast it out and put the whole book in its place. It would not deceive. It would not deceive the janitor.

All of this book is interesting on account of the sorcerer's methods and the a tractiveness of some of his characters and the repulsveness of the rest, but no part of it is so much so as are the chapters wherein he tries to think he thinks he sets forth the causes which led to Shelley's desertion of his wife in 1814.

Harriet Westbrook was a school-girl sixteen years old. Shelley was teeming with advanced thought. He believed that Christianity was a degrading and selfish superstition, and he had a deep and sincere desire to rescue one of his sisters from it. Harriet was impressed by his various philosophies and looked upon him as an intellectual wonder—which indeed he was. He had an idea that she could give him valuable help in his scheme regarding his sister; therefore he asked her to correspond with him. She was quite willing. Shelley was not thinking of love, for he was just getting over a passion for his cousin, Harriet Grove, and just getting well steeped in one for Miss Hitchener, a school-teacher. What might happen to Harriet Westbrook before the letter-writing was ended did not enter his mind. Yet an older person could have made a good guess at it, for in person Shelley was as beautiful as an angel, he was frank, sweet, winning, unassuming, and so rich in unselfishness, generosities, and magnanimities that he made his whole generation seem poor in these great qualities by comparison. Besides, he was in distress. His college had expelled him for writing an atheistical pamphlet and afflicting the reverend heads of the university with it, his rich father and grandfather had closed their purses against him, his friends were cold. Necessarily, Harriet fell in love with him; and so deeply, indeed, that there was no way for Shelley to save her from suicide but to marry her. He believed himself to blame for this state of things, so the marriage took place. He was pretty fairly in love with Harriet, although he loved Miss Hitchener better. He wrote and explained the case to Miss Hitchener after the wedding, and he could not have been franker or more naïve and less stirred up about the circumstance if the matter in issue had been a commercial transaction involving thirty-five dollars.

Shelley was nineteen. He was not a youth, but a man. He had never had any youth. He was an erratic and fantastic child during eighteen years, then he stepped into manhood, as one steps over a door-sill. He was curiously mature at nineteen in his ability to do independent thinking on the deep questions of life and to arrive at sharply definite decisions regarding them, and stick to them—stick to them and stand by them at cost of bread, friendships, esteem, respect, and approbation.

For the sake of his opinions he was willing to sacrifice all these valuable things, and did sacrifice them; and went on doing it, too, when he could at any moment have made himself rich and supplied himself with friends and esteem by compromising with his father, at the moderate expense of throwing overboard one or two indifferent details of his cargo of principles.

DEFENSE OF HARRIET SHELLEY

He and Harriet eloped to Scotland and got married. They took lodgings in Edinburgh of a sort answerable to their purse, which was about empty, and there their life was a happy one and grew daily more so. They had only themselves for company, but they needed no additions to it. They were as cozy and contented as birds in a nest. Harriet sang evenings or read aloud; also she studied and tried to improve her mind, her husband instructing her in Latin. She was very beautiful, she was modest, quiet, genuine, and, according to her husband's testimony, she had no fine-lady airs or aspirations about her. In Matthew Arnold's judgment, she was "a pleasing figure."

The pair remained five weeks in Edinburgh, and then took lodgings in York, where Shelley's college-mate, Hogg, lived. Shelley presently ran down to London, and Hogg took this opportunity to make love to the young wife. She repulsed him, and reported the fact to her husband when he got back. It seems a pity that Shelley did not copy this creditable conduct of hers some time or other when under temptation, so that we might have seen the author of his biography hang the miracle in the skies and squirt rainbows at it.

At the end of the first year of marriage—the most trying year for any young couple, for then the mutual failings are coming one by one to light, and the necessary adjustments are being made in pain and tribulation—Shelley was able to recognize that his marriage venture had been a safe one. As we have seen, his love for his wife had begun in a rather

9

shallow way and with not much force, but now it was become deep and strong, which entitles his wife to a broad credit mark, one may admit. He addresses a long and loving poem to her, in which both passion and worship appear:

Exhibit A

O thou
Whose dear love gleamed upon the gloomy path
Which this lone spirit travelled,

. . . .

. . . wilt thou not turn
Those spirit-beaming eyes and look on me,
Until I be assured that Earth is Heaven
And Heaven is Earth?

. . . .

Harriet! let death all mortal ties dissolve,
But ours shall not be mortal.

Shelley also wrote a sonnet to her in August of this same year in celebration of her birthday:

Exhibit B

Ever as now with Love and Virtue's glow
May thy unwithering soul not cease to burn,
Still may thine heart with those pure thoughts o'erflow
Which force from mine such quick and warm return.

Was the girl of seventeen glad and proud and happy? We may conjecture that she was.

That was the year 1812. Another year passed—still happily, still successfully—a child was born in June, 1813, and in September, three months later, Shelley addresses a poem to this child, Ianthe, in which he points out just when the little creature is most particularly dear to him:

DEFENSE OF HARRIET SHELLEY

Exhibit C

Dearest when most thy tender traits express
The image of thy mother s loveliness.

Up to this point the fabulist counsel for Shelley
and prosecutor of his young wfe has had easy sailing,
but now his trouble begins, for Shelley is getting
ready to make some unpleasent history for himself,
and it will be necessary to put the blame of it on
the wife.

Shelley had made the acquaintance of a charming
gray-haired, young-hearted Mrs. Boinville, whose
face "retained a certain youthful beauty"; she lived
at Bracknell, and had a young daughter named
Cornelia Turner, who was equipped with many fascinations. Apparently these people were sufficiently
sentimental. Hogg says of Mrs. Boinville:

"The greater part of her associates were odious. I generally
found there two or three sentimental young butchers, an eminently philosophical tinker, and several very unsophisticated
medical practitioners or medical students, all of low origin and
vulgar and offensive manners. They sighed, turned up their
eyes, retailed philosophy, such as it was," etc.

Shelley moved to Bracknell, July 27th (this is
still 1813) purposely to be near this unwholesome
prairie-dogs' nest. The fabulist says: "It was the
entrance into a world more amiable and exquisite
than he had yet known."

"In this acquaintance the attraction was mutual"
—and presently it grew to be very mutual indeed,
between Shelley and Cornelia Turner, when they got
to studying the Italian poets together. Shelley,

"responding like a tremulous instrument to every breath of passion or of sentiment," had his chance here. It took only four days for Cornelia's attractions to begin to dim Harriet's. Shelley arrived on the 27th of July; on the 31st he wrote a sonnet to Harriet in which "one detects already the little rift in the lover's lute which had seemed to be healed or never to have gaped at all when the later and happier sonnet to Ianthe was written"—in September, we remember:

Exhibit D

EVENING. TO HARRIET

O thou bright Sun! Beneath the dark blue line
Of western distance that sublime descendest,
And, gleaming lovelier as thy beams decline,
Thy million hues to every vapor lendest,
And over cobweb, lawn, and grove, and stream
Sheddest the liquid magic of thy light,
Till calm Earth, with the parting splendor bright,
Shows like the vision of a beauteous dream;
What gazer now with astronomic eye
Could coldly count the spots within thy sphere?
Such were thy lover, Harriet, could he fly
The thoughts of all that makes his passion dear,
And turning senseless from thy warm caress
Pick flaws in our close-woven happiness.

I cannot find the "rift"; still it may be there. What the poem *seems* to say is, that a person would be coldly ungrateful who could consent to count and consider little spots and flaws in such a warm, great, satisfying sun as Harriet is. It is a "little rift which had seemed to be healed, *or* never to have gaped at all." That is, "one *detects*" a little rift which perhaps had never existed. How does one do that? How does one see the invisible? It is the fabulist's secret; he knows how to detect what does not exist, he knows how to see what is not seeable; it is his gift, and he works it many a time to poor dead Harriet Shelley's deep damage.

"As yet, however, if there was a speck upon Shelley's happiness it was no more than a speck" —meaning the one which one detects where "it may never have gaped at all"—"nor had Harriet cause for discontent."

Shelley's Latin instructions to his wife had ceased. "From a teacher he had now become a pupil." Mrs. Boinville and her young married daughter Cornelia were teaching him Italian poetry; a fact which warns one to receive with some caution that other statement that Harriet had no "cause for discontent."

Shelley had stopped instructing Harriet in Latin, as before mentioned. The biographer thinks that the busy life in London some time back, and the intrusion of the baby, account for this. These were hindrances, but were there no others? He is always overlooking a detail here and there that might be valuable in helping us understand a situation. For instance, when a man has been hard at work at the Italian poets with a pretty woman, hour after hour, and responding like a tremulous instrument to every breath of passion or of sentiment in the mean time, that man is dog-tired when he gets home, and he *can't* teach his wife Latin; it would be unreasonable to expect it.

Up to this time we have submitted to having Mrs. Boinville pushed upon us as ostensibly concerned in these Italian lessons, but the biographer drops her now, of his own accord. Cornelia "perhaps" is sole teacher. Hogg says she was a prey to a kind of sweet melancholy, arising from causes purely imaginary; she required consolation, and found it in Petrarch. He also says, "Bysshe entered at once fully into her views and caught the soft infection, breathing the tenderest and sweetest melancholy, as every true poet ought."

Then the author of the book interlards a most stately and fine compliment to Cornelia, furnished by a man of approved judgment who knew her well "in later years." It is a very good compliment indeed, and she no doubt deserved it in her "later years," when she had for generations ceased to be sentimental and lackadaisical, and was no longer engaged in enchanting young husbands and sowing sorrow for young wives. But why is that compliment to that old gentlewoman intruded there? Is it to make the reader believe she was well-chosen and safe society for a young, sentimental husband? The biographer's device was not well planned. That old person was not present—it was her other self that was there, her young, sentimental, melancholy, warm-blooded self, in those early sweet times before antiquity had cooled her off and mossed her back.

"In choosing for friends such women as Mrs. Newton, Mrs. Boinville, and Cornelia Turner, Shelley gave good proof of his insight and discrimination." That is the fabulist's opinion—Harriet Shelley's is not reported.

Early in August, Shelley was in London trying to raise money. In September he wrote the poem to the baby, already quoted from. In the first week of October Shelley and family went to Warwick, then to Edinburgh, arriving there about the middle of the month.

"Harriet was happy." Why? The author furnishes a reason, but hides from us whether it is history or conjecture; it is because "*the babe had borne the journey well.*" It has all the aspect of one of his artful devices—flung in in his favorite casual way—the way he has when he wants to draw one's attention away from an obvious thing and amuse it with some trifle that is less obvious but more useful —in a history like this. The obvious thing is, that Harriet was happy because there was much territory between her husband and Cornelia Turner now; and because the perilous Italian lessons were taking a rest; and because, if there chanced to be any respondings like a tremulous instrument to every breath of passion or of sentiment in stock in these days, she might hope to get a share of them herself; and because, with her husband liberated, now, from the fetid fascinations of that sentimental retreat so pitilessly described by Hogg, who also dubbed it "Shelley's paradise" later, she might hope to persuade him to stay away from it permanently; and because she might also hope that his brain would cool, now, and his heart become healthy, and both brain and heart consider the situation and resolve that it would be a right and manly thing to stand by this girl wife and her child and see that they were honorably dealt with, and cherished and protected and loved by the man that had promised these things, and so be made happy and kept so. And because, also—may we conjecture this?—we may hope for the privilege of taking up our cozy Latin lessons again, that used to be so pleasant, and brought us so near together—so near, indeed, that often our heads touched, just as heads do over Italian lessons; and our hands met in casual and unintentional, but still most delicious and thrilling little contacts and momentary clasps, just as they inevitably do over Italian lessons. Suppose one should say to any young wife: "I find that your husband is poring over the Italian poets and being instructed in the beautiful Italian language by the lovely Cornelia Robinson" —would that cozy picture fail to rise before her mind? would its possibilities fail to suggest themselves to her? would there be a pang in her heart and a blush on her face? or, on the contrary, would the remark give her pleasure, make her joyous and gay? Why, one needs only to make the experiment—the result will not be uncertain.

However, we learn—by authority of deeply reasoned and searching conjecture—that the baby bore the journey well, and that that was why the young wife was happy. That accounts for two per cent. of the happiness, but it was not right to imply that it accounted for the other ninety-eight also.

Peacock, a scholar, poet, and friend of the Shelleys, was of their party when they went away. He used dito laugh at the Boinville menagerie, and "was not a favorite." One of the Boinville group, writing to Hogg, said, "The Shelleys have made an addition to their party in the person of a cold scholar, who, I think, has neither taste nor feeling. This, Shelley will perceive sooner or later for his warm nature craves sympathy." True, and Shelley will fight his way back there to get it—there will be no way to head him off.

Toward the end of November it was necessary for Shelley to pay a business visit to London, and he conceived the project of leaving Harriet and the baby in Edinburgh with Harriet's sister, Eliza Westbrook, a sensible, practical maiden lady about thirty years old, who had spent a great part of her time with the family since the marriage. She was an estimable woman, and Shelley had had reason to like her, and did like her; but along about this time his feeling toward her changed. Part of Shelley's plan, as he wrote Hogg, was to spend his London evenings with the Newtons—members of the Boinville Hysterical Society. But, alas, when he arrived early in December, that pleasant game was partially blocked, for Eliza and the family arrived *with* him. We are left destitute of conjectures at this point by the biographer, and it is my duty to supply one. I chance the conjecture that it was Eliza who interfered with that game. I think she tried to do what she could toward modifying the Boinville connection, in the interest of her young sister's peace and honor.

If it was she who blocked that game, she was not

strong enough to block the next one. Before the month and year were out—no date given, let us call it Christmas—Shelley and family were nested in a furnished house in Windsor, "at no great distance from the Boinvilles"—these decoys still residing at Bracknell.

What we need, now, is a misleading conjecture. We get it with characteristic promptness and depravity:

> But Prince Athanase found not the aged Zonoras, the friend of his boyhood, in any wanderings to Windsor. Dr. Lind had died a year since, and with his death Windsor must have lost, for Shelley, its chief attraction.

Still, not to mention Shelley's wife, there was Bracknell, at any rate. While Bracknell remains, all solace is not lost. Shelley is represented by this biographer as doing a great many careless things, but to my mind this hiring a furnished house for three months in order to be with a man who has been dead a year, is the carelessest of them all. One feels for him—that is but natural, and does us honor besides—yet one is vexed, for all that. He could have written and asked about the aged Zonoras before taking the house. He may not have had the address, but that is nothing—any postman would know the aged Zonoras; a dead postman would remember a name like that.

And yet, why throw a rag like this to us ravening wolves? Is it seriously supposable that we will stop to chew it and let our prey escape? No, we are getting to expect this kind of device, and to give it merely a sniff for certainty's sake and then walk around it and leave it lying. Shelley was not after the aged Zonoras; he was pointed for Cornelia and the Italian lessons, for his warm nature was craving sympathy.

II

THE year 1813 is just ended now, and we step into 1814.

To recapitulate, how much of Cornelia's society has Shelley had, thus far? Portions of August and September, and four days of July. That is to say, he has had opportunity to enjoy it, more or less, during that brief period. Did he want some more of it? We must fall back upon history, and then go to conjecturing.

In the early part of the year 1814, Shelley was a frequent visitor at Bracknell.

"Frequent" is a cautious word, in this author's mouth; the very cautiousness of it, the vagueness of it, provokes suspicion; it makes one suspect that this frequency was more frequent than the mere common every-day kinds of frequency which one is in the habit of averaging up with the unassuming term "frequent." I think so because they fixed up a bedroom for him in the Boinville house. One doesn't need a bedroom if one is only going to run over now and then in a disconnected way to respond like a tremulous instrument to every breath of passion or of sentiment and rub up one's Italian poetry a little.

The young wife was not invited, perhaps. If she

was, she most certainly did not come, or she would have straightened the room up; the most ignorant of us knows that a wife would not endure a room in the condition in which Hogg found this one when he occupied it one night. Shelley was away—why, nobody can divine. Clothes were scattered about, there were books on every side: "Wherever a book could be laid was an open book turned down on its face to keep its place." It seems plain that the wife was not invited. No, not that; I think she was invited, but said to herself that she could not bear to go there and see another young woman touching heads with her husband over an Italian book and making thrilling hand-contacts with him accidentally.

As remarked, he was a frequent visitor there, "where he found an easeful resting-place in the house of Mrs. Boinville—the white-haired Maimuna —and of her daughter, Mrs. Turner." The aged Zonoras was deceased, but the white-haired Maimuna was still on deck, as we see. "Three charming ladies entertained the mocker (Hogg) with cups of tea, late hours, Wieland's Agathon, sighs and smiles, and the celestial manna of refined sentiment." "Such," says Hogg, "were the delights of Shelley's paradise in Bracknell."

The white-haired Maimuna presently writes to Hogg:

I will not have you despise home-spun pleasures. Shelley is making a trial of them with us—

A trial of them. It may be called that. It was March 11, and he had been in the house a month. She continues:

Shelley "likes them so well that he is resolved to leave off rambling—"

But he has *already* left it off.   He has been there a month.

"And begin a course of them hims·lf."

But he has already begun t.   He has been at it a *month*.   He likes it so well t iat he has forgotten all about his wife, as a letter ol his reveals.

Seriously, I think his mind and ɔody want rest.

Yet he has been resting both for a month, with Italian, and tea, and manna of sentiment, and late hours, and every restful thing a young husband could need for the refreshment of weary limbs and a sore conscience, and a nagging sense of shabbiness and treachery.

His journeys after what he has never found have racked his purse and his tranquillity.   He is resolved to take a little care of the former, in pity to the latter, which I applaud, and shall second with all my might.

But she does not say whether the young wife, a stranger and lonely yonder, wants another woman and her daughter Cornelia to be lavishing so much inflamed interest on her husband or not.   That young wife is always silent—we are never allowed to hear from her.   She must have opinions about such things, she cannot be indifferent, she must be approving or disapproving, surely she would speak if she were allowed—even to-day and from her grave she would, if she could, I think—but we get only the other side, they keep her silent always.

He has deeply interested us. In the course of your intimacy he must have made you feel what we now feel for him. He is seeking a house close to us—

Ah! he is not close enough yet, it seems—

and if he succeeds we shall have an additional motive to induce you to come among us in the summer.

The reader would puzzle a long time and not guess the biographer's comment upon the above letter. It is this:

These sound like words of a considerate and judicious friend.

That is what he thinks. That is, it is what he thinks he thinks. No, that is not quite it: it is what he thinks he can stupefy a particularly and unspeakably dull reader into thinking it is what he thinks. He makes that comment with the knowledge that Shelley is in love with this woman's daughter, and that it is because of the fascinations of these two that Shelley has deserted his wife—for this month, considering all the circumstances, and his new passion, and his employment of the time, amounted to desertion; that is its rightful name. We cannot know how the wife regarded it and felt about it; but if she could have read the letter which Shelley was writing to Hogg four or five days later, we could guess her thought and how she felt. Hear him:

.   .   .   .

I have been staying with Mrs. Boinville for the last month; I have escaped, in the society of all that philosophy and friendship combine, from the dismaying solitude of myself.

It is fair to conejcture that he was feeling ashamed.

They have revived in my heart the expiring flame of life. I have felt myself translated to a paradise which has nothing of mortality but its transitoriness; my heart sickens at the view of that necessity which will quickly divide me from the delightful tranquillity of this happy home— or it has become my home.

. . . .

Eliza is still with us—not here!—but will be with me when the infinite malice of destiny forces me to depart.

Eliza is she who blocked that game—the game in London—the one where we were purposing to dine every night with one of the "three charming ladies" who fed tea and manna and late hours to Hogg at Bracknell.

Shelley could send Eliza away, of course; could have cleared her out long ago if so minded, just as he had previously done with a predecessor of hers whom he had first worshiped and then turned against; but perhaps she was useful there as a thin excuse for staying away himself.

I am now but little inclined to contest this point. I certainly hate her with all my heart and soul. . . .

It is a sight which awakens an inexpressible sensation of disgust and horror, to see her caress my poor little Ianthe, in whom I may hereafter find the consolation of sympathy. I sometimes feel faint with the fatigue of checking the overflowings of my unbounded abhorrence for this miserable wretch. But she is no more than a blind and loathsome worm, that cannot see to sting.

I have begun to learn Italian again. . . . Cornelia assists me in this language. Did I not once tell you that I thought her cold and reserved? She is the reverse of this, as she is the reverse of everything bad. She inherits all the divinity of her mother. . . . I have sometimes forgotten that I am not an inmate of this delightful home—that a time will come which will cast me again into the boundless ocean of abhorred society.

MARK TWAIN

I have written nothing but one stanza, which has no meaning, and that I have only written in thought:

> Thy dewy looks sink in my breast;
>   Thy gentle words stir poison there;
> Thou hast disturbed the only rest
>   That was the portion of despair.
> Subdued to duty's hard control,
>   I could have borne my wayward lot:
> The chains that bind this ruined soul
>   Had cankered then, but crushed it not.

This is the vision of a delirious and distempered dream, which passes away at the cold clear light of morning. Its surpassing excellence and exquisite perfections have no more reality than the color of an autumnal sunset.

Then it did not refer to his wife. That is plain; otherwise he would have said so. It is well that he explained that it has no meaning, for if he had not done that, the previous soft references to Cornelia and the way he has come to feel about her now would make us think she was the person who had inspired it while teaching him how to read the warm and ruddy Italian poets during a month.

The biography observes that portions of this letter "read like the tired moaning of a wounded creature." Guesses at the nature of the wound are permissible; we will hazard one.

Read by the light of Shelley's previous history, his letter seems to be the cry of a tortured conscience. Until this time it was a conscience that had never felt a pang or known a smirch. It was the conscience of one who, until this time, had never done a dishonorable thing, or an ungenerous, or

24

cruel, or treacherous thing, but was now doing all of these, and was keenly aware of it. Up to this time Shelley had been master of his nature, and it was a nature which was as beautiful and as nearly perfect as any merely human nature may be. But he was drunk now, with a debasing passion, and was not himself. There is nothing in his previous history that is in character with the Shelley of this letter. He had done boyish things, foolish things, even crazy things, but never a thing to be ashamed of. He had done things which one might laugh at, but the privilege of laughing was limited always to the thing itself; you could not laugh at the motive back of it—that was high, that was noble. His most fantastic and quixotic acts had a purpose back of them which made them fine, often great, and made the rising laugh seem profanation and quenched it; quenched it, and changed the impulse to homage. Up to this time he had been loyalty itself, where his obligations lay—treachery was new to him; he had never done an ignoble thing—baseness was new to him; he had never done an unkind thing—that also was new to him.

This was the author of that letter, this was the man who had deserted his young wife and was lamenting, because he must leave another woman's house which had become a "home" to him, and go away. Is he lamenting *mainly* because he must go back to his wife and child? No, the lament is mainly for what he is to leave behind him. The physical comforts of the house? No, in his life he had never attached importance to such things.

Then the thing which he grieves to leave is narrowed down to a person—to the person whose "dewy looks" had sunk into his breast, and whose seducing words had "stirred poison there."

He was ashamed of himself, his conscience was upbraiding him. He was the slave of a degrading love; he was drunk with his passion, the real Shelley was in temporary eclipse. This is the verdict which his previous history must certainly deliver upon this episode, I think.

One must be allowed to assist himself with conjectures like these when trying to find his way through a literary swamp which has so many misleading finger-boards up as this book is furnished with.

We have now arrived at a part of the swamp where the difficulties and perplexities are going to be greater than any we have yet met with—where, indeed, the finger-boards are multitudinous, and the most of them pointing diligently in the wrong direction. We are to be told by the biography why Shelley deserted his wife and child and took up with Cornelia Turner and Italian. It was not on account of Cornelia's sighs and sentimentalities and tea and manna and late hours and soft and sweet and industrious enticements; no, it was because "his happiness in his home had been wounded and bruised almost to death."

It had been wounded and bruised almost to death in this way:

1st. Harriet persuaded him to set up a carriage.

2d. After the intrusion of the baby, Harriet stopped reading aloud and studying.

3d. Harriet's walks with Hogg "commonly conducted us to some fashionable bonnet-shop."

4th. Harriet hired a wet-nurse.

5th. When an operation was being performed upon the baby, "Harriet stood by, narrowly observing all that was done, but, to the astonishment of the operator, betraying not the smallest sign of emotion."

6th. Eliza Westbrook, sister-in-law, was still of the household.

The evidence against Harriet Shelley is all in; there is no more. Upon these six counts she stands indicted of the crime of driving her husband into that sty at Bracknell; and this crime, by these helps, the biographical prosecuting attorney has set himself the task of proving upon her.

Does the biographer *call* himself the attorney for the prosecution? No, only to himself, privately; publicly he is the passionless, disinterested, impartial judge on the bench. He holds up his judicial scales before the world, that all may see; and it all tries to look so fair that a blind person would sometimes fail to see him slip the false weights in.

Shelley's happiness in his home had been wounded and bruised almost to death, first, because Harriet had persuaded him to set up a carriage. I cannot discover that any evidence is offered that she asked him to set up a carriage. Still, if she did, was it a heavy offense? Was it unique? Other young wives had committed it before, others have committed it since. Shelley had dearly loved her in those London days; possibly he set up the carriage gladly to please her; affectionate young husbands do such things. When Shelley ran away with another girl, by and by, this girl persuaded him to pour the price of many carriages and many horses down the bottomless well of her father's debts, but this impartial judge finds no fault with that. Once she appeals to Shelley to raise money—necessarily by borrowing, there was no other way—to pay her father's debts with at a time when Shelley was in danger of being arrested and imprisoned for his own debts; yet the good judge finds no fault with her even for this.

First and last, Shelley emptied into that rapacious mendicant's lap a sum which cost him—for he borrowed it at ruinous rates—from eighty to one hundred thousand dollars. But it was Mary Godwin's papa, the supplications were often sent through Mary, the good judge is Mary's strenuous friend, so Mary gets no censures. On the Continent *Mary rode in her private carriage*, built, as Shelley boasts, "by one of the best makers in Bond Street," yet the good judge makes not even a passing comment on this iniquity. Let us throw out Count No. 1 against Harriet Shelley as being far-fetched and frivolous.

Shelley's happiness in his home had been wounded and bruised almost to death, secondly, because Harriet's studies "had dwindled away to nothing, Bysshe had ceased to express any interest in them." At what time was this? It was when Harriet "had fully recovered from the fatigue of her first effort of maternity, . . . and was now in full force, vigor, and effect." Very well, the baby was born two days before the close of June. It took the mother a month to get back her full force, vigor, and effect; this brings us to July 27th and the deadly Cornelia. If a wife of eighteen is studying with her husband and he gets smitten with another woman, isn't he likely to lose interest in his wife's studies for *that* reason, and is not his wife's interest n her studies likely to languish for the *same* reason? Would not the mere sight of those books of hers sharpen the pain that is in her heart? This sudden breaking down of a mutual intellectual interest of two years' standing is coincident with Shelley's re-encounter with Cornelia; and we are allowed to gather from that time forth for nearly two months he did all his studying in that person's society. We feel at liberty to rule out Count No. 2 from the indictment against Harriet.

Shelley's happiness in his home had been wounded and bruised almost to death, thirdly, because Harriet's walks with Hogg commonly led to some fashionable bonnet-shop. I offer no palliation; I only ask why the dispassionate, impartial judge did not offer one himself—merely, I mean, to offset his leniency in a similar case or two where the girl who ran away with Harriet's husband was the shopper. There are several occasions where she interested herself with shopping—among them being walks which ended at the bonnet-shop—yet in none of these cases does she get a word of blame from the good judge, while in one of them he covers the deed with a justifying remark, she doing the shopping that time to find easement for her mind, her child having died.

Shelley's happiness in his home had been wounded and bruised almost to death, fourthly, by the introduction there of a wet-nurse. The wet-nurse was introduced at the time of the Edinburgh sojourn, immediately after Shelley had been enjoying the two months of study with Cornelia which broke up his wife's studies and destroyed his personal interest in them. Why, by this time, nothing that Shelley's wife could do would have been satisfactory to him, for he was in love with another woman, and was never going to be contented again until he got back to her. If he had been still in love with his wife it is not easily conceivable that he would care much who nursed the baby, provided the baby was well nursed. Harriet's jealousy was assuredly voicing itself now, Shelley's conscience was assuredly nagging him, pestering him, persecuting him. Shelley needed excuses for his altered attitude toward his wife; Providence pitied him and sent the wet-nurse. If Providence had sent him a cotton doughnut it would have answered just as well; all he wanted was something to find fault with.

Shelley's happiness in his home had been wounded and bruised almost to death, fifthly, because Harriet narrowly watched a surgical operation which was being performed upon her child, and, "to the astonishment of the operator," who was watching Harriet instead of attending to his operation, she betrayed "not the smallest sign of emotion." The author of this biography was not ashamed to set down that exultant slander. He was apparently not aware that it was a small business to bring into his court a witness whose name he does not know, and whose character and veracity there is none to vouch for, and allow him to strike thi blow at the mother-heart of this friendless girl. The biographer says, "We may not infer from thi that Harriet did not feel"—why put it in, then—"but we learn that those about her could believe her to be hard and insensible." Who were those who were about her? Her husband? He hated her now, because he was in love elsewhere. Her sister Of course that is not charged. Peacock? Peacock does not testify. The wet-nurse? She does not testify. If any others were there we have no mention of them. "Those about her" are reduced to one person—her husband. Who reports the circumstance? It is Hogg. Perhaps he was there—we do not know. But if he was, he still got his information at second hand, as it was the operator who noticed Harriet's lack of emotion, not himself. Hogg is not given to saying kind things when Harriet is his subject. He may have said them the time that he tried to tempt her to soil her honor, but after that he mentions her usually with a sneer. "Among those who were about her" was one witness well equipped to silence all tongues, abolish all doubts, set our minds at rest; one witness, not called, and not callable, whose evidence, if we could but get it, would outweigh the oaths of whole battalions of hostile Hoggs and nameless surgeons—the baby. I wish we had the baby's testimony; and yet if we had it it would not do us any good—a furtive conjecture, a sly insinuation, a pious "if" or two, would be smuggled in, here and there, with a solemn air of judicial investigation, and its positiveness would wilt into dubiety.

The biographer says of Harriet, "If words of tender affection and motherly pride proved the reality of love, then undoubtedly she loved her first-born child." That is, if mere empty words can prove it, it stands proved—and in this way, without committing himself, he gives the reader a chance to infer that there isn't any extant evidence but words, and that he doesn't take much stock in them. How seldom he shows his hand! He is always lurking behind a non-committal "if" or something of that kind; always gliding and dodging around, distributing colorless poison here and there and everywhere, but always leaving himself in a position to say that his language will be found innocuous if taken to pieces and examined. He clearly exhibits a steady and never-relaxing purpose to make Harriet the scapegoat for her husband's first great sin—but it is in the general view that this is revealed, not in the details. His insidious literature is like blue water; you know what it is that makes it blue, but you cannot produce and verify any detail of the cloud of microscopic dust in it that does it. Your adversary can dip up a glassful and show you that it is pure white and you cannot deny it; and he can dip the lake dry, glass by glass, and show that every glassful is white, and prove it to any one's eye—and yet that lake *was* blue and you can swear it. This book is blue—with slander in solution.

Let the reader examine, for example, the paragraph of comment which immediately follows the

letter containing Shelley's self-exposure which we
have been considering. This is it. One should inspect the individual sentences as they go by, then
pass them in procession and review the cake-walk as
a whole:

Shelley's happiness in his home, as is evident from this
pathetic letter, had been fatally stricken; it is evident, also, that
he knew where duty lay; he felt that his part was to take up his
burden, silently and sorrowfully, and to bear it henceforth with
the quietness of despair. But we can perceive that he scarcely
possessed the strength and fortitude needful for success in such
an attempt. And clearly Shelley himself was aware how perilous
it was to accept that respite of blissful ease which he enjoyed in
the Boinville household; for gentle voices and dewy looks and
words of sympathy could not fail to remind him of an ideal of
tranquillity or of joy which could never be his, and which he
must henceforth sternly exclude from his imagination.

That paragraph commits the author in no way.
Taken sentence by sentence it *asserts* nothing against
anybody or in favor of anybody, pleads for nobody,
accuses nobody. Taken detail by detail, it is as
innocent as moonshine. And yet, taken as a whole,
it is a design against the reader; its intent is to remove the feeling which the letter must leave with
him if let alone, and put a different one in its place
—to remove a feeling justified by the letter and
substitute one not justified by it. The letter itself
gives you no uncertain picture—no lecturer is
needed to stand by with a stick and point out its
details and let on to explain what they mean. The
picture is the very clear and remorsefully faithful
picture of a fallen and fettered angel who is ashamed
of himself; an angel who beats his soiled wings and

cries, who complains to the woman who enticed him that he *could* have borne his wayward lot, he *could* have stood by his duty if it had not been for her beguilements; an angel who rails at the "boundless ocean of abhorred society," and rages at his poor judicious sister-in-law. If there is any dignity about this spectacle it will escape most people.

Yet when the paragraph of comment is taken as a whole, the picture is full of dignity and pathos; we have before us a blameless and noble spirit stricken to the earth by malign powers, but not conquered; tempted, but grandly putting the temptation away; enmeshed by subtle coils, but sternly resolved to rend them and march forth victorious, at any peril of life or limb. Curtain—slow music.

Was it the purpose of the paragraph to take the bad taste of Shelley's letter out of the reader's mouth? If that was not it, good ink was wasted; without that, it has no relevancy—the multiplication table would have padded the space as rationally.

We have inspected the six reasons which we are asked to believe drove a man of conspicuous patience, honor, justice, fairness, kindliness, and iron firmness, resolution, and steadfastness, from the wife whom he loved and who loved him, to a refuge in the mephitic paradise of Bracknell. These are six infinitely little reasons; but there were six colossal ones, and these the counsel for the destruction of Harriet Shelley persists in not considering very important.

Moreover, the colossal six preceded the little six, and had done the mischief before they were born.

DEFENSE OF HARRIET SHELLEY

Let us double-column the twelve; then we shall see at a glance that each little reason is in turn answered by a retorting reason of a size to overshadow it and make it insignificant:

1. Harriet sets up carriage.	1. CORNELIA TURNER.
2. Harriet stops studying.	2. CORNELIA TURNER.
3. Harriet goes to bonnet-shop.	3. CORNELIA TURNER.
4. Harriet takes a wet-nurse.	4. CORNELIA TURNER.
5. Harriet has too much nerve.	5. CORNELIA TURNER.
6. Detested sister-in-law.	6. CORNELIA TURNER.

As soon as we comprehend that Cornelia Turner and the Italian lessons happened *before* the little six had been discovered to be grievances, we understand why Shelley's happiness in his home had been wounded and bruised almost to death, and no one can persuade us into laying it on Harriet. Shelley and Cornelia are the responsible persons, and we cannot in honor and decency allow the cruelties which they practised upon the unoffending wife to be pushed aside in order to give us a chance to waste time and tears over six sentimental justifications of an offense which the six can't justify, nor even respectably assist in justifying.

Six? There were seven; but in charity to the biographer the seventh ought not to be exposed. Still, he hung it out himself, and not only hung it out, but thought it was a good point in Shelley's favor. For two years Shelley found sympathy and intellectual food and all that at home; there was enough for spiritual and mental support, but not enough for luxury; and so, at the end of the contented two years, this latter detail justifies him in

going bag and baggage over to Cornelia Turner and
supplying the rest of his need in the way of surplus
sympathy and intellectual pie unlawfully.   By the
same reasoning a man in merely comfortable circumstances may rob a bank without sin.

III

I⊤ is 1814, it is the 16th of March, Shelley had
written his letter, he has been in the Boinville
paradise a month, his deserted wife is in her hus-
bandless home.   Mischief has been wrought.   It is
the biographer who concedes this.   We greatly need
some light on Harriet's side of the case now; we
need to know how she enjoyed the month, but there
is no way to inform ourselves; there seems to be a
strange absence of documents and letters and diaries
on that side.   Shelley kept a diary, the approaching
Mary Godwin kept a diary, her father kept one, her
half-sister by marriage, adoption, and the dispensa-
tion of God kept one, and the entire tribe and all its
friends wrote and received letters, and the letters
were kept and are producible when this biography
needs them; but there are only three or four scraps
of Harriet's writing, and no diary.   Harriet wrote
plenty of letters to her husband—nobody knows
where they are, I suppose; she wrote plenty of
letters to other people—apparently they have disappeared, too.   Peacock says she wrote good letters,
but apparently interested people had sagacity enough
to mislay them in time.   After all her industry she
went down into her grave and lies silent there—

silent, when she has so much need to speak. We can only wonder at this mystery, not account for it.

No, there is no way of finding out what Harriet's state of feeling was during the month that Shelley was disporting himself in the Bracknell paradise. We have to fall back upon conjecture, as our fabulist does when he has nothing more substantial to work with. Then we easily conjecture that as the days dragged by Harriet's heart grew heavier and heavier under its two burdens—shame and resentment; the shame of being pointed at and gossiped about as a deserted wife, and resentment against the woman who had beguiled her husband from her and now kept him in a disreputable captivity. Deserted wives—deserted whether for cause or without cause—find small charity among the virtuous and the discreet. We conjecture that one after another the neighbors ceased to call; that one after another they got to being "engaged" when Harriet called; that finally they one after the other cut her dead on the street; that after that she stayed in the house daytimes, and brooded over her sorrows, and nighttimes did the same, there being nothing else to do with the heavy hours and the silence and solitude and the dreary intervals which sleep should have charitably bridged, but didn't.

Yes, mischief had been wrought. The biographer arrives at this conclusion, and it is a most just one. Then, just as you begin to half hope he is going to discover the cause of it and launch hot bolts of wrath at the guilty manufacturers of it, you have to turn away disappointed. You are disappointed, and you sigh. This is what he says—the italics are mine:

However the mischief may have been wrought—*and at this day no one can wish to heap blame on any buried head—*

So it is poor Harriet, after all. Stern justice must take its course—justice tempered with delicacy, justice tempered with compassion, justice that pities a forlorn dead girl and refuses to strike her. Except in the back. Will not be ignoble and *say* the harsh thing, but only insinuate it. Stern justice knows about the carriage and the wet-nurse and the bonnet-shop and the other dark things that caused this sad mischief, and may not, *must* not blink them; so it delivers judgment where judgment belongs, but softens the blow by not seeming to deliver judgment at all. To resume—the italics are mine:

However the mischief may have been wrought—and at this day no one can wish to heap blame on any buried head—*it is certain that some cause or causes of deep division between Shelley and his wife were in operation during the early part of the year 1814.*

This shows penetration. No deduction could be more accurate than this. There were indeed some causes of deep division. But next comes another disappointing sentence:

To guess at the precise nature of these causes, in the absence of definite statement, were useless.

Why, he has already been guessing at them for several pages, and we have been trying to outguess him, and now all of a sudden he is tired of it and won't play any more. It is not quite fair to us.

However, he will get over this by and by, when Shelley commits his next indiscretion and has to be guessed out of it at Harriet's expense.

"We may rest content with Shelley's own words" —in a Chancery paper drawn up by him three years later. They were these: "Delicacy forbids me to say more than that we were disunited by incurable dissensions."

As for me, I do not quite see why we should rest content with anything of the sort. It is not a very definite statement. It does not necessarily mean anything more than that he did not wish to go into the tedious details of those family quarrels. Delicacy could quite properly excuse him from saying, "I was in love with Cornelia all that time; my wife kept crying and worrying about it and upbraiding me and begging me to cut myself free from a connection which was wronging her and disgracing us both; and I being stung by these reproaches retorted with fierce and bitter speeches—for it is my nature to do that when I am stirred, especially if the target of them is a person whom I had greatly loved and respected before, as witness my various attitudes toward Miss Hitchener, the Gisbornes, Harriet's sister, and others—and finally I did not improve this state of things when I deserted my wife and spent a whole month with the woman who had infatuated me."

No, he could not go into those details, and we excuse him; but, nevertheless, we do not rest content with this bland proposition to puff away that whole long disreputable episode with a single meaningless remark of Shelley's.

We do admit that "it is certain that some cause or causes of deep division were in operation." We would admit it just the same if the grammar of the statement were as straight as a string, for we drift into pretty indifferent grammar ourselves when we are absorbed in historical work; but we have to decline to admit that we cannot guess those cause or causes.

But guessing is not really necessary. There is evidence attainable—evidence from the batch discredited by the biographer and set out at the back door in his appendix-basket; and yet a court of law would think twice before throwing it out, whereas it would be a hardy person who would venture to offer in such a place a good part of the material which is placed before the readers of this book as "evidence," and so treated by this daring biographer. Among some letters (in the appendix-basket) from Mrs. Godwin, detailing the Godwinian share in the Shelleyan events of 1814, she tells how Harriet Shelley came to her and her husband, agitated and weeping, to implore them to forbid Shelley the house, and prevent his seeing Mary Godwin.

She related that last November he had fallen in love with Mrs. Turner and paid her such marked attentions Mr. Turner, the husband, had carried off his wife to Devonshire.

The biographer finds a technical fault in this: "the Shelleys were in *Edinburgh* in November." What of that? The woman is recalling a conversation which is more than two months old; besides, she was probably more intent upon the central and important fact of it than upon its unimportant date.

Harriet's quoted statement has some sense in it; for that reason, if for no other, it ought to have been put in the body of the book. Still, that would not have answered; even the biographer's enemy could not be cruel enough to ask him to let this real grievance, this compact and substantial and picturesque figure, this rawhead-and-bloody-bones, come striding in there among those pale shams, those rickety specters labeled WET-NURSE, BONNET-SHOP, and so on—no, the father of all malice could not ask the biographer to expose his pathetic goblins to a competition like that.

The fabulist finds fault with the statement because it has a technical error in it; and he does this at the moment that he is furnishing us an error himself, and of a graver sort. He says:

> If Turner carried off his wife to Devonshire he brought her back, and Shelley was staying with her and her mother on terms of cordial intimacy in March, 1814.

We accept the "cordial intimacy"—it was the very thing Harriet was complaining of—but there is nothing to show that it was Turner who brought his wife back. The statement is thrown in as if it were not only true, but was proof that Turner was not uneasy. Turner's *movements* are proof of nothing. Nothing but a statement from Turner's mouth would have any value here, and he made none.

Six days after writing his letter Shelley and his wife were together again for a moment—to get remarried according to the rites of the English Church.

Within three weeks the new husband and wife

were apart again, and the former was back in his odorous paradise. This time it is the wife who does the deserting. She finds Cornelia too strong for her, probably. At any rate, she goes away with her baby and sister, and we have a playful fling at her from good Mrs. Boinville, the "mysterious spinner Maimuna"; she whose "face was as a damsel's face, and yet her hair was gray"; she of whom the biographer has said, "Shelley was indeed caught in an almost invisible thread spun around him, but unconsciously, by this subtle and benignant enchantress." The subtle and benignant enchantress writes to Hogg, April 18: "Shelley is again a widower; his beauteous half went to town on Thursday."

Then Shelley writes a poem—a chant of grief over the hard fate which obliges him now to leave his paradise and take up with his wife again. It seems to intimate that the paradise is cooling toward him; that he is warned off by acclamation; that he must not even venture to tempt with one last tear his friend Cornelia's ungentle mood, for her eye is glazed and cold and dares not entreat her lover to stay:

Exhibit E

Pause not! the time is past! Every voice cries "Away!"
Tempt not with one last tear thy friend's ungentle mood;
Thy lover's eye, so glazed and cold, dares not entreat thy stay:
Duty and dereliction guide thee back to solitude.

Back to the solitude of his now empty home, that is!

Away! away! to thy sad and silent home;
Pour bitter tears on its desolated hearth.

. . . .

DEFENSE OF HARRIET SHELLEY

But he will have rest in the grave by and by. Until that time comes, the charms of Bracknell will remain in his memory, along with Mrs. Boinville's voice and Cornelia Turner's smile:

Thou in the grave shalt rest—yet, till the phantoms flee
  Which that house and hearth and garden made dear to thee
    erewhile,
Thy remembrance and repentance and deep musings are not free
  From the music of two voices and the light of one sweet
    smile.

We *cannot* wonder that Harriet could not stand it. Any of us would have left. We would not even stay with a cat that was in this condition. Even the Boinvilles could not endure it; and so, as we have seen, they gave this one notice.

Early in May, Shelley was in London. He did not yet despair of reconciliation with Harriet, nor had he ceased to love her.

Shelley's poems are a good deal of trouble to his biographer. They are constantly inserted as "evidence," and they make much confusion. As soon as one of them has proved one thing, another one follows and proves quite a different thing. The poem just quoted shows that he was in love with Cornelia, but a month later he is in love with Harriet again, and there is a poem to prove it.

In this piteous appeal Shelley declares that he has now no grief but one—the grief of having known and lost his wife's love.

Exhibit F
Thy look of love has power to calm
The stormiest passion of my soul.

But without doubt she had been reserving her looks of love a good part of the time for ten months, now—ever since he began to lavish his own on Cornelia Turner at the end of the previous July. He does really seem to have already forgotten Cornelia's merits in one brief month, for he eulogizes Harriet in a way which rules all competition out:

> Thou only virtuous, gentle, kind,
> Amid a world of hate.

He complains of her hardness, and begs her to make the concession of a "slight endurance"—of his waywardness, perhaps—for the sake of "a fellow-being's lasting weal." But the main force of his appeal is in his closing stanza, and is strongly worded:

> O trust for once no erring guide!
>   Bid the remorseless feeling flee;
> 'Tis malice, 'tis revenge, 'tis pride,
>   'Tis anything but thee;
> O deign a nobler pride to prove,
> And pity if thou canst not love.

This is in May—apparently toward the end of it. Harriet and Shelley were corresponding all the time. Harriet got the poem—a copy exists in her own handwriting; she being the only gentle and kind person amid a world of hate, according to Shelley's own testimony in the poem, we are permitted to think that the daily letters would presently have melted that kind and gentle heart and brought about the reconciliation, if there had been time—but there wasn't; for in a very few days—in fact, before the 8th of June—Shelley was in love with *another* woman.

And so—perhaps while Harriet was walking the floor nights, trying to get *her* poem by heart—her husband was doing a fresh one—for the other girl —Mary Wollstonecraft Godwin—with sentiments like these in it:

Exhibit G

> To spend years thus nd be rewarded,
> As thou, sweet love, r quited me
> When none were near
> . . . thy lips did meet
> Mine tremblingly; . . .
>
> Gentle and good and mild thou art,
> Nor can I live if thou appear
> Aught but thyself. . . .

And so on. "Before the close of June it was known and felt by Mary and Shelley that each was inexpressibly dear to the other." Yes, Shelley had found this child of sixteen to his liking, and had wooed and won her in the graveyard. But that is nothing; it was better than wooing her in her nursery, at any rate, where it might have disturbed the other children.

However, she was a child in years only. From the day that she set her masculine grip on Shelley he was to frisk no more. If she had occupied the only kind and gentle Harriet's place in March it would have been a thrilling spectacle to see her invade the Boinville rookery and read the riot act. That holiday of Shelley's would have been of short duration, and Cornelia's hair would have been as gray as her mother's when the services were over.

Hogg went to the Godwin residence in Skinner

Street with Shelley on that 8th of June. They passed through Godwin's little debt-factory of a book-shop and went up-stairs hunting for the proprietor. Nobody there. Shelley strode about the room impatiently, making its crazy floor quake under him. Then a door "was partially and softly opened. A thrilling voice called, 'Shelley!' A thrilling voice answered, 'Mary!' And he darted out of the room like an arrow from the bow of the far-shooting King. A very young female, fair and fair-haired, pale, indeed, and with a piercing look, wearing a frock of tartan, an unusual dress in London at that time, had called him out of the room."

This is Mary Godwin, as described by Hogg. The thrill of the voices shows that the love of Shelley and Mary was already upward of a fortnight old; therefore it had been born within the month of May— born while Harriet was still trying to get her poem by heart, we think. I must not be asked how I know so much about that thrill; it is my secret. The biographer and I have private ways of finding out things when it is necessary to find them out and the customary methods fail.

Shelley left London that day, and was gone ten days. The biographer conjectures that he spent this interval with Harriet in Bath. It would be just like him. To the end of his days he liked to be in love with two women at once. He was more in love with Miss Hitchener when he married Harriet than he was with Harriet, and told the lady so with simple and unostentatious candor. He was more in love with Cornelia than he was with Harriet in the end of 1813 and the beginning of 1814, yet he supplied both of them with love poems of an equal temperature meantime; he loved Mary and Harriet in June, and while getting ready to run off with the one, it is conjectured that he put in his odd time trying to get reconciled to the other; by and by, while still in love with Mary, he will make love to her half-sister by marriage, adoption, and the visitation of God, through the medium of clandestine letters, and she will answer with letters that are for no eye but his own.

When Shelley encountered Mary Godwin he was looking around for another paradise. He had tastes of his own, and there were features about the Godwin establishment that strongly recommended it. Godwin was an advanced thinker and an able writer. One of his romances is still read, but his philosophical works, once so esteemed, are out of vogue now; their authority was already declining when Shelley made his acquaintance—that is, it was declining with the public, but not with Shelley. They had been his moral and political Bible, and they were that yet. Shelley the infidel would himself have claimed to be less a work of God than a work of Godwin. Godwin's philosophies had formed his mind and interwoven themselves into it and become a part of its texture; he regarded himself as Godwin's spiritual son. Godwin was not without self-appreciation; indeed, it may be conjectured that from his point of view the last syllable of his name was surplusage. He lived serene in his lofty world of philosophy, far above the mean interests that

47

absorbed smaller men, and only came down to the ground at intervals to pass the hat for alms to pay his debts with, and insult the man that relieved him. Several of his principles were out of the ordinary. For example, he was opposed to marriage. He was not aware that his preachings from this text were but theory and wind; he supposed he was in earnest in imploring people to live together without marrying, until Shelley furnished him a working model of his scheme and a practical example to analyze, by applying the principle in his own family; the matter took a different and surprising aspect then. The late Matthew Arnold said that the main defect in Shelley's make-up was that he was destitute of the sense of humor. This episode must have escaped Mr. Arnold's attention.

But we have said enough about the head of the new paradise. Mrs. Godwin is described as being in several ways a terror; and even when her soul was in repose she wore green spectacles. But I suspect that her main unattractiveness was born of the fact that she wrote the letters that are out in the appendix-basket in the back yard—letters which are an outrage and wholly untrustworthy, for they say some kind things about poor Harriet and tell some disagreeable truths about her husband; and these things make the fabulist grit his teeth a good deal.

Next we have Fanny Godwin—a Godwin by courtesy only; she was Mrs. Godwin's natural daughter by a former friend. She was a sweet and winning girl, but she presently wearied of the Godwin paradise, and poisoned herself.

Last in the list is Jane (or Claire, as she preferred to call herself) Clairmont, daughter of Mrs. Godwin by a former marriage. She was very young and pretty and accommodating, and always ready to do what she could to make things pleasant. After Shelley ran off with her par -sister Mary, she became the guest of the pair, and contributed a natural child to their nursery—Allegra. Lord Byron was the father.

We have named the several members and advantages of the new paradise in Skinner Street, with its crazy book-shop underneath. Shelley was all right now, this was a better place than the other; more variety anyway, and more different kinds of fragrance. One could turn out poetry here without any trouble at all.

The way the new love-match came about was this: Shelley told Mary all his aggravations and sorrows and griefs, and about the wet-nurse and the bonnet-shop and the surgeon and the carriage, and the sister-in-law that blocked the London game, and about Cornelia and her mamma, and how they had turned him out of the house after making so much of him; and how he had deserted Harriet and then Harriet had deserted him, and how the reconciliation was working along and Harriet getting her poem by heart; and still he was not happy, and Mary pitied him, for she had had trouble herself. But I am not satisfied with this. It reads too much like statistics. It lacks smoothness and grace, and is too earthy and business-like. It has the sordid look of a trades-union procession out on strike. That is not the right form for it. The book does it better; we will fall back on the book and have a cake-walk:

It was easy to divine that some restless grief possessed him; Mary herself was not unlearned in the lore of pain. His generous zeal in her father's behalf, his spiritual sonship to Godwin, his reverence for her mother's memory, were guarantees with Mary of his excellence.[1] The new friends could not lack subjects of discourse, and underneath their words about Mary's mother, and "Political Justice," and "Rights of Woman," were two young hearts, each feeling toward the other, each perhaps unaware, trembling in the direction of the other. The desire to assuage the suffering of one whose happiness has grown precious to us may become a hunger of the spirit as keen as any other, and this hunger now possessed Mary's heart; when her eyes rested unseen on Shelley, it was with a look full of the ardor of a "soothing pity."

Yes, that is better and has more composure. That is just the way it happened. He told her about the wet-nurse, she told him about political justice; he told her about the deadly sister-in-law, she told him about her mother; he told her about the bonnet-shop, she murmured back about the rights of woman; then he assuaged her, then she assuaged him; then he assuaged her some more, next she assuaged him some more; then they both assuaged one another simultaneously; and so they went on by the hour assuaging and assuaging and assuaging, until at last what was the result? They were in love. It will happen so every time.

He had married a woman who, as he now persuaded himself, had never truly loved him, who loved only his fortune and his rank, and who proved her selfishness by deserting him in his misery.

[1] What she was after was guarantees of his excellence. That he stood ready to desert his wife and child was one of them, apparently.

DEFENSE OF HARRIET SHELLEY

I think that that is not quite fair to Harriet. We have no certainty that she knew Cornelia had turned him out of the house. He went back to Cornelia, and Harriet may have supposed that he was as happy with her as ever. Still, it was judicious to begin to lay on the whitewash, for Shelley is going to need many a coat of it now, and the sooner the reader becomes used to the intrusion of the brush the sooner he will get reconciled to it and stop fretting about it.

After Shelley's (conjectured) visit to Harriet at Bath—8th of June to 18th—"it seems to have been arranged that Shelley should henceforth join the Skinner Street household each day at dinner."

Nothing could be handier than this; things will swim along now.

Although now Shelley was coming to believe that his wedded union with Harriet was a thing of the past, he had not ceased to regard her with affectionate consideration; he wrote to her frequently, and kept her informed of his whereabouts.

We must not get impatient over these curious inharmoniousnesses and irreconcilabilities in Shelley's character. You can see by the biographer's attitude toward them that there is nothing objectionable about them. Shelley was doing his best to make two adoring young creatures happy: he was regarding the one with affectionate consideration by mail, and he was assuaging the other one at home.

Unhappy Harriet, residing at Bath, had perhaps never desired that the breach between herself and her husband should be irreparable and complete.

51

I find no fault with that sentence except that the "perhaps" is not strictly warranted. It should have been left out. In support—or shall we say extenuation?—of this opinion I submit that there is not sufficient evidence to warrant the uncertainty which it implies. The only "evidence" offered that Harriet was hard and proud and standing out against a reconciliation is a poem—the poem in which Shelley beseeches her to "bid the remorseless feeling flee" and "pity" if she "cannot love." We have just that as "evidence," and out of its meager materials the biographer builds a cobhouse of conjectures as big as the Coliseum; conjectures which convince him, the prosecuting attorney, but ought to fall far short of convincing any fair-minded jury.

Shelley's love poems may be very good evidence, but we know well that they are "good for this day and train only." We are able to believe that they spoke the truth for that one day, but we know by experience that they could not be depended on to speak it the next. The very supplication for a re-warming of Harriet's chilled love was followed so suddenly by the poet's plunge into an adoring passion for Mary Godwin that if it had been a check it would have lost its value before a lazy person could have gotten to the bank with it.

Hardness, stubbornness, pride, vindictiveness—these may sometimes reside in a young wife and mother of nineteen, but they are not charged against Harriet Shelley outside of that poem, and one has no right to insert them into her character on such shadowy "evidence" as that. Peacock knew Harriet well, and she has a flexible and persuadable look, as painted by him:

Her manners were good, and her whole aspect and demeanor such manifest emanations of pure and truthful nature that to be once in her company was to know her thoroughly. She was fond of her husband, and accommodated herself in every way to his tastes. If they mixed in society, she adorned it; if they lived in retirement, she was satisfied; if they traveled, she enjoyed the change of scene.

"Perhaps" she had never desired that the breach should be irreparable and complete. The truth is, we do not even know that there was any breach at all at this time. We know that the husband and wife went before the altar and took a new oath on the 24th of March to love and cherish each other until death—and this may be regarded as a sort of reconciliation itself, and a wiping out of the old grudges. Then Harriet went away, and the sister-in-law removed herself from her society. That was in April. Shelley wrote his "appeal" in May, but the corresponding went right along afterward. We have a right to doubt that the subject of it was a "reconciliation," or that Harriet had any suspicion that she needed to be reconciled and that her husband was trying to persuade her to it—as the biographer has sought to make us believe, with his Coliseum of conjectures built out of a waste-basket of poetry. For we have "evidence" now—not poetry and conjecture. When Shelley had been dining daily in the Skinner Street paradise fifteen days and continuing the love-match which was already a fortnight old twenty-five days earlier, he forgot to write Harriet; forgot it the next day and the next. During four days Harriet got no letter from him. Then her fright and anxiety rose to expression-heat, and she wrote a letter to Shelley's publisher which seems to reveal to us that Shelley's letters to her had been the customary affectionate letters of husband to wife, and had carried no appeals for reconciliation and had not needed to:

BATH (postmark July 7, 1814).

MY DEAR SIR,—You will greatly oblige me by giving the inclosed to Mr. Shelley. I would not trouble you, but it is now four days since I have heard from him, which to me is an age. Will you write by return of post and tell me what has become of him? as I always fancy something dreadful has happened if I do not hear from him. If you tell me that he is well I shall not come to London, but if I do not hear from you or him I shall certainly come, as I cannot endure this dreadful state of suspense. You are his friend and you can feel for me.
I remain yours truly,

H. S.

Even without Peacock's testimony that "her whole aspect and demeanor were manifest emanations of a pure and truthful nature," we should hold this to be a truthful letter, a sincere letter, a loving letter; it bears those marks; I think it is also the letter of a person accustomed to receiving letters from her husband frequently, and that they have been of a welcome and satisfactory sort, too, this long time back—ever since the solemn remarriage and reconciliation at the altar most likely.

The biographer follows Harriet's letter with a conjecture. He conjectures that she "would now

gladly have retraced her steps." Which means that
it is proven that she had steps to retrace—proven
by the poem. Well, if the poem is better evidence
than the letter, we must let t stand at that.

Then the biographer att icks Harriet Shelley's
honor—by authority of rand)m and unverified gossip scavengered from a grou) of people whose very
names make a person shudd« r: Mary Godwin, mistress of Shelley; her part-si ter, discarded mistress
of Lord Byron; Godwin, tl e philosophical tramp,
who gathers his share of it from a shadow—that is
to say, from a person whom he shirks out of naming.
Yet the biographer dignifies this sorry rubbish with
the name of "evidence."

Nothing remotely resembling a distinct charge
from a named person professing to know is offered
among this precious "evidence."

1. "Shelley *believed*" so and so.

2. Byron's discarded mistress says that Shelley
told Mary Godwin so and so, and *Mary* told *her*.

3. "Shelley said" so and so—and later "admitted over and over again that he had been in
error."

4. The unspeakable Godwin "wrote to Mr. Bax-
ter" that he knew so and so "from unquestionable
authority"—name not furnished.

How any man in his right mind could bring himself to defile the grave of a shamefully abused and
defenseless girl with these baseless fabrications, this
manufactured filth, is inconceivable. How any man,
in his right mind or out of it, could sit down and
coldly try to persuade anybody to believe it, or

listen patiently to it, or, indeed, do anything but scoff at it and deride it, is astonishing.

The charge insinuated by these odious slanders is one of the most difficult of all offenses to prove; it is also one which no man has a right to mention even in a whisper about any woman, living or dead, unless he knows it to be true, and not even then unless he can also *prove* it to be true. There is no justification for the abomination of putting this stuff in the book.

Against Harriet Shelley's good name there is not one scrap of tarnishing evidence, and not even a scrap of evil gossip, that comes from a source that entitles it to a hearing.

On the credit side of the account we have strong opinions from the people who knew her best. Peacock says:

I feel it due to the memory of Harriet to state my most decided conviction that her conduct as a wife was as pure, as true, as absolutely faultless, as that of any who for such conduct are held most in honor.

Thornton Hunt, who had picked and published slight flaws in Harriet's character, says, as regards this alleged large one:

There is not a trace of evidence or a whisper of scandal against her before her voluntary departure from Shelley.

Trelawney says:

I was assured by the evidence of the few friends who knew both Shelley and his wife—Hookham, Hogg, Peacock, and one of the Godwins—that Harriet was perfectly innocent of all offense.

DEFENSE OF HARRIET SHELLEY

What excuse was there for raking up a parcel of foul rumors from malicious and discredited sources and flinging them at this dead girl's head? Her very defenselessness should have been her protection. The fact that all letters to her or about her, with almost every scrap of her own writing, had been diligently mislaid, leaving her case destitute of a voice, while every pen-stroke which could help her husband's side had been is diligently preserved, should have excused her from being brought to trial. Her witnesses have all disappeared, yet we see her summoned in her grave-clothes to plead for the life of her character, without the help of an advocate, before a disqualified judge and a packed jury.

Harriet Shelley wrote her distressed letter on the 7th of July. On the 28th her husband ran away with Mary Godwin and her part-sister Claire to the Continent. He deserted his wife when her confinement was approaching. She bore him a child at the end of November, his mistress bore him another one something over two months later. The truants were back in London before either of these events occurred.

On one occasion, presently, Shelley was so pressed for money to support his mistress with that he went to his wife and got some money of his that was in her hands—twenty pounds. Yet the mistress was not moved to gratitude; for later, when the wife was troubled to meet her engagements, the mistress makes this entry in her diary:

Harriet sends her creditors here; nasty woman. Now we shall have to change our lodgings.

57

The deserted wife bore the bitterness and obloquy of her situation two years and a quarter; then she gave up, and drowned herself. A month afterward the body was found in the water. Three weeks later Shelley married his mistress.

I must here be allowed to italicize a remark of the biographer's concerning Harriet Shelley:

That no act of Shelley's during the two years which immediately preceded her death tended to cause the rash act which brought her life to its close seems certain.

Yet her husband had deserted her and her children, and was living with a concubine all that time! Why should a person attempt to write biography when the simplest facts have no meaning to him? This book is littered with as crass stupidities as that one—deductions by the page which bear no discoverable kinship to their premises.

The biographer throws off that extraordinary remark without any perceptible disturbance to his serenity; for he follows it with a sentimental justification of Shelley's conduct which has not a pang of conscience in it, but is silky and smooth and undulating and pious—a cake-walk with all the colored brethren at their best. There may be people who can read that page and keep their temper, but it is doubtful.

Shelley's life has the one indelible blot upon it, but is otherwise worshipfully noble and beautiful. It even stands out indestructibly gracious and lovely from the ruck of these disastrous pages, in spite of the fact that they expose and establish his responsibility for his forsaken wife's pitiful fate—a responsibility which he himself tacitly admits in a letter to Eliza Westbrook, wherein he refers to his taking up with Mary Godwin as an act which Eliza "might excusably regard as the cause of her sister's ruin."

FENIMORE COOPER'S LITERARY OFFENSES

The Pathfinder and *The Deerslayer* stand at the head of Cooper's novels as artistic creations. There are others of his works which contain parts as perfect as are to be found in these, and scenes even more thrilling. Not one can be compared with either of them as a finished whole.

The defects in both of these tales are comparatively slight. They were pure works of art.—*Prof. Lounsbury.*

The five tales reveal an extraordinary fullness of invention.

. . . One of the very greatest characters in fiction, Natty Bumppo. . . .

The craft of the woodsman, the tricks of the trapper, all the delicate art of the forest, were familiar to Cooper from his youth up.—*Prof. Brander Matthews.*

Cooper is the greatest artist in the domain of romantic fiction yet produced by America.—*Wilkie Collins.*

IT seems to me that it was far from right for the Professor of English Literature in Yale, the Professor of English Literature in Columbia, and Wilkie Collins to deliver opinions on Cooper's literature without having read some of it. It would have been much more decorous to keep silent and let persons talk who have read Cooper.

Cooper's art has some defects. In one place in *Deerslayer*, and in the restricted space of two-thirds of a page, Cooper has scored 114 offenses against literary art out of a possible 115. It breaks the record.

COOPER'S LITERARY OFFENSES

There are nineteen rules governing literary art in the domain of romantic fiction—some say twenty-two. In *Deerslayer* Cooper violated eighteen of them. These eighteen require:

1. That a tale shall accomplish something and arrive somewhere. But the *Deerslayer* tale accomplishes nothing and arrives in the air.

2. They require that the episodes of a tale shall be necessary parts of the tale, and shall help to develop it. But as the *Deerslayer* tale is not a tale, and accomplishes nothing and arrives nowhere, the episodes have no rightful place in the work, since there was nothing for them to develop.

3. They require that the personages in a tale shall be alive, except in the case of corpses, and that always the reader shall be able to tell the corpses from the others. But this detail has often been overlooked in the *Deerslayer* tale.

4. They require that the personages in a tale, both dead and alive, shall exhibit a sufficient excuse for being there. But this detail also has been overlooked in the *Deerslayer* tale.

5. They require that when the personages of a tale deal in conversation, the talk shall sound like human talk, and be talk such as human beings would be likely to talk in the given circumstances, and have a discoverable meaning, also a discoverable purpose, and a show of relevancy, and remain in the neighborhood of the subject in hand, and be interesting to the reader, and help out the tale, and stop when the people cannot think of anything more to say. But this requirement has been ignored from

61

the beginning of the *Deerslayer* tale to the end of it.

6. They require that when the author describes the character of a personage in his tale, the conduct and conversation of that personage shall justify said description. But this law gets little or no attention in the *Deerslayer* tale, as Natty Bumppo's case will amply prove.

7. They require that when a personage talks like an illustrated, gilt-edged, tree-calf, hand-tooled, seven-dollar Friendship's Offering in the beginning of a paragraph, he shall not talk like a negro minstrel in the end of it. But this rule is flung down and danced upon in the *Deerslayer* tale.

8. They require that crass stupidities shall not be played upon the reader as "the craft of the woodsman, the delicate art of the forest," by either the author or the people in the tale. But this rule is persistently violated in the *Deerslayer* tale.

9. They require that the personages of a tale shall confine themselves to possibilities and let miracles alone; or, if they venture a miracle, the author must so plausibly set it forth as to make it look possible and reasonable. But these rules are not respected in the *Deerslayer* tale.

10. They require that the author shall make the reader feel a deep interest in the personages of his tale and in their fate; and that he shall make the reader love the good people in the tale and hate the bad ones. But the reader of the *Deerslayer* tale dislikes the good people in it, is indifferent to the others, and wishes they would all get drowned together.

11. They require that the characters in a tale shall be so clearly defined that the reader can tell beforehand what each will do in a g ven emergency. But in the *Deerslayer* tale th s rule is vacated.

In addition to these large rules there are some little ones. These require tha the author shall

12. *Say* what he is proposi g to say, not merely come near it.

13. Use the right word, no its second cousin.

14. Eschew surplusage.

15. Not omit necessary details.

16. Avoid slovenliness of form.

17. Use good grammar.

18. Employ a simple and straightforward style.

Even these seven are coldly and persistently violated in the *Deerslayer* tale.

Cooper's gift in the way of invention was not a rich endowment; but such as it was he liked to work it, he was pleased with the effects, and indeed he did some quite sweet things with it. In his little box of stage-properties he kept six or eight cunning devices, tricks, artifices for his savages and woodsmen to deceive and circumvent each other with, and he was never so happy as when he was working these innocent things and seeing them go. A favorite one was to make a moccasined person tread in the tracks of the moccasined enemy, and thus hide his own trail. Cooper wore out barrels and barrels of moccasins in working that trick. Another stage-property that he pulled out of his box pretty frequently was his broken twig He prized his broken twig above all the rest of his effects, and worked it the hardest. It is a restful chapter in any book of his when somebody doesn't step on a dry twig and alarm all the reds and whites for two hundred yards around. Every time a Cooper person is in peril, and absolute silence is worth four dollars a minute, he is sure to step on a dry twig. There may be a hundred handier things to step on, but that wouldn't satisfy Cooper. Cooper requires him to turn out and find a dry twig; and if he can't do it, go and borrow one. In fact, the Leatherstocking Series ought to have been called the Broken Twig Series.

I am sorry there is not room to put in a few dozen instances of the delicate art of the forest, as practised by Natty Bumppo and some of the other Cooperian experts. Perhaps we may venture two or three samples. Cooper was a sailor—a naval officer; yet he gravely tells us how a vessel, driving toward a lee shore in a gale, is steered for a particular spot by her skipper because he knows of an *undertow* there which will hold her back against the gale and save her. For just pure woodcraft, or sailorcraft, or whatever it is, isn't that neat? For several years Cooper was daily in the society of artillery, and he ought to have noticed that when a cannon-ball strikes the ground it either buries itself or skips a hundred feet or so; skips again a hundred feet or so—and so on, till finally it gets tired and rolls. Now in one place he loses some "females" —as he always calls women—in the edge of a wood near a plain at night in a fog, on purpose to give Bumppo a chance to show off the delicate art of the forest before the reader. These mislaid people are hunting for a fort. They hear a cannon-blast, and a cannon-ball presently comes rolling into the wood and stops at their feet. To the females this suggests nothing. The case is very different with the admirable Bumppo. I wish I may never know peace again if he doesn t strike out promptly and *follow the track* of that cannon-ball across the plain through the dense fog and find the fort. Isn't it a daisy? If Cooper had any real knowledge of Nature's ways of doing things, he had a most delicate art in concealing the fact. For instance: one of his acute Indian experts, Chingachgook (pronounced Chicago, I think), has lost the trail of a person he is tracking through the forest. Apparently that trail is hopelessly lost. Neither you nor I could ever have guessed out the way to find it. It was very different with Chicago. Chicago was not stumped for long. He turned a running stream out of its course, and there, in the slush in its old bed, were that person's moccasin tracks. The current did not wash them away, as it would have done in all other like cases—no, even the eternal laws of Nature have to vacate when Cooper wants to put up a delicate job of woodcraft on the reader.

We must be a little wary when Brander Matthews tell us that Cooper's books "reveal an extraordinary fullness of invention." As a rule, I am quite willing to accept Brander Matthews's literary judgments and applaud his lucid and graceful phrasing of them; but that particular statement needs to be taken with a few tons of salt. Bless your heart,

Cooper hadn't any more invention than a horse; and I don't mean a high-class horse, either; I mean a clothes-horse. It would be very difficult to find a really clever "situation" in Cooper's books, and still more difficult to find one of any kind which he has failed to render absurd by his handling of it. Look at the episodes of "the caves"; and at the celebrated scuffle between Maqua and those others on the table-land a few days later; and at Hurry Harry's queer water-transit from the castle to the ark; and at Deerslayer's half-hour with his first corpse; and at the quarrel between Hurry Harry and Deerslayer later; and at—but choose for yourself; you can't go amiss.

If Cooper had been an observer his inventive faculty would have worked better; not more interestingly, but more rationally, more plausibly. Cooper's proudest creations in the way of "situations" suffer noticeably from the absence of the observer's protecting gift. Cooper's eye was splendidly inaccurate. Cooper seldom saw anything correctly. He saw nearly all things as through a glass eye, darkly. Of course a man who cannot see the commonest little every-day matters accurately is working at a disadvantage when he is constructing a "situation." In the *Deerslayer* tale Cooper has a stream which is fifty feet wide where it flows out of a lake; it presently narrows to twenty as it meanders along for no given reason, and yet when a stream acts like that it ought to be required to explain itself. Fourteen pages later the width of the brook's outlet from the lake has suddenly shrunk thirty feet, and become "the narrowest part of the stream." This shrinkage is not accounted for. The stream has bends in it, a sure indication that it has alluvial banks and cuts them; yet these bends are only thirty and fifty feet long. If Cooper had been a nice and punctilious observer he would have noticed that the bends were oftener nine hundred feet long than short of it.

Cooper made the exit of that stream fifty feet wide, in the first place, for no particular reason; in the second place, he narrowed it to less than twenty to accommodate some Indians. He bends a "sapling" to the form of an arch over this narrow passage, and conceals six Indians in its foliage. They are "laying" for a settler's scow or ark which is coming up the stream on its way to the lake; it is being hauled against the stiff current by a rope whose stationary end is anchored in the lake; its rate of progress cannot be more than a mile an hour. Cooper describes the ark, but pretty obscurely. In the matter of dimensions "it was little more than a modern canal-boat." Let us guess, then, that it was about one hundred and forty feet long. It was of "greater breadth than common." Let us guess, then, that it was about sixteen feet wide. This leviathan had been prowling down bends which were but a third as long as itself, and scraping between banks where it had only two feet of space to spare on each side. We cannot too much admire this miracle. A low-roofed log dwelling occupies "two-thirds of the ark's length"—a dwelling ninety feet long and sixteen feet wide, let us say—a kind of vestibule train. The dwelling has two rooms—each forty-five feet long and sixteen feet wide, let us guess. One of them is the bedroom of the Hutter girls, Judith and Hetty; the other is the parlor in the day-time, at night it is papa's bedchamber. The ark is arriving at the stream's exit now, whose width has been reduced to less than twenty feet to accommo-date the Indians—say to eighteen. There is a foot to spare on each side of the boat. Did the Indians notice that there was going to be a tight squeeze there? Did they notice that they could make money by climbing down out of that arched sapling and just stepping aboard when the ark scraped by? No, other Indians would have noticed these things, but Cooper's Indians never notice anything. Cooper thinks they are marvelous creatures for noticing, but he was almost always in error about his Indians. There was seldom a sane one among them.

The ark is one hundred and forty-feet long; the dwelling is ninety feet long. The idea of the Indians is to drop softly and secretly from the arched sap-ling to the dwelling as the ark creeps along under it at the rate of a mile an hour, and butcher the family. It will take the ark a minute and a half to pass under. It will take the ninety-foot dwelling a minute to pass under. Now, then, what did the six Indians do? It would take you thirty years to guess, and even then you would have to give it up, I believe. Therefore, I will tell you what the Indians did. Their chief, a person of quite extraordinary intellect for a Cooper Indian, warily watched the canal-boat as it squeezed along under him, and when he had got his calculations fined down to exactly the right shade, as he judged, he let go and dropped. And *missed the house!* That is actually what he did. He missed the house, and landed n the stern of the scow. It was not much of a fall, y t it knocked him silly. He lay there unconscious. If the house had been ninety-seven feet long he wo ld have made the trip. The fault was Cooper's, not h s. The error lay in the construction of the house. Cooper was no architect.

There still remained in the roost five Indians. The boat has passed under and is now out of their reach. Let me explain what the five did—you would not be able to reason it out for yourself. No. 1 jumped for the boat, but fell in the water astern of it. Then No. 2 jumped for the boat, but fell in the water still farther astern of it. Then No. 3 jumped for the boat, and fell a good way astern of it. Then No. 4 jumped for the boat, and fell in the water *away* astern. Then even No. 5 made a jump for the boat—for he was a Cooper Indian. In the matter of intellect, the difference between a Cooper Indian and the Indian that stands in front of the cigar-shop is not spacious. The scow episode is really a sublime burst of invention; but it does not thrill, because the inaccuracy of the details throws a sort of air of fictitiousness and general improbability over it. This comes of Cooper's inadequacy as an observer.

The reader will find some examples of Cooper's high talent for inaccurate observation in the account of the shooting-match in *The Pathfinder*.

A common wrought nail was driven lightly into the target, its head having been first touched with paint.

The color of the paint is not stated—an important omission, but Cooper deals freely in important omissions. No, after all, it was not an important omission; for this nail-head is *a hundred yards from* the marksmen, and could not be seen by them at that distance, no matter what its color might be. How far can the best eyes see a common house-fly? A hundred yards? It is quite impossible. Very well; eyes that cannot see a house-fly that is a hundred yards away cannot see an ordinary nail-head at that distance, for the size of the two objects is the same. It takes a keen eye to see a fly or a nail-head at fifty yards—one hundred and fifty feet. Can the reader do it?

The nail was lightly driven, its head painted, and game called. Then the Cooper miracles began. The bullet of the first marksman chipped an edge of the nail-head; the next man's bullet drove the nail a little way into the target—and removed all the paint. Haven't the miracles gone far enough now? Not to suit Cooper; for the purpose of this whole scheme is to show off his prodigy, Deerslayer-Hawkeye - Long - Rifle - Leatherstocking - Pathfinder-Bumppo before the ladies.

"Be all ready to clench it, boys!" cried out Pathfinder, stepping into his friend's tracks the instant they were vacant. "Never mind a new nail; I can see that, though the paint is gone, and what I can see I can hit at a hundred yards, though it were only a mosquito's eye. Be ready to clench!"

The rifle cracked, the bullet sped its way, and the head of the nail was buried in the wood, covered by the piece of flattened lead.

There, you see, is a man who could hunt flies

with a rifle, and command a ducal salary in a Wild West show to-day if we had him back with us.

The recorded feat is certainly surprising just as it stands; but it is not surprising enough for Cooper. Cooper adds a touch. He has made Pathfinder do this miracle with another man's rifle; and not only that, but Pathfinder did not have even the advantage of loading it himself. He had everything against him, and yet he made that impossible shot; and not only made it, but did it with absolute confidence, saying, "Be ready to clench." Now a person like that would have undertaken that same feat with a brickbat, and with Cooper to help he would have achieved it, too.

Pathfinder showed off handsomely that day before the ladies. His very first feat was a thing which no Wild West show can touch. He was standing with the group of marksmen, observing—a hundred yards from the target, mind; one Jasper raised his rifle and drove the center of the bull's-eye. Then the Quartermaster fired. The target exhibited no result this time. There was a laugh. "It's a dead miss," said Major Lundie. Pathfinder waited an impressive moment or two; then said, in that calm, indifferent, know-it-all way of his, "No, Major, he has covered Jasper's bullet, as will be seen if any one will take the trouble to examine the target."

Wasn't it remarkable! How *could* he see that little pellet fly through the air and enter that distant bullet-hole? Yet that is what he did; for nothing is impossible to a Cooper person. Did any of those people have any deep-seated doubts about this thing?

No; for that would imply sanity, and these were all Cooper people.

The respect for Pathfinder's skill and for his *quickness and accuracy of sight* [the italics are mine] was so profound and general, that the instant he made this declaration the spectators began to distrust their own opinions, and a dozen rushed to the target in order to ascertain the fact. There, sure enough, it was found that the Quartermaster's bullet had gone through the hole made by Jasper's, and that, too, so accurately as to require a minute examination to be certain of the circumstance, which, however, was soon clearly established by discovering one bullet over the other in the stump against which the target was placed.

They made a "minute" examination; but never mind, how could they know that there were two bullets in that hole without digging the latest one out? for neither probe nor eyesight could prove the presence of any more than one bullet. Did they dig? No; as we shall see. It is the Pathfinder's turn now; he steps out before the ladies, takes aim, and fires.

But, alas! here is a disappointment; an incredible, an unimaginable disappointment—for the target's aspect is unchanged; there is nothing there but that same old bullet-hole!

"If one dared to hint at such a thing," cried Major Duncan, "I should say that the Pathfinder has also missed the target!"

As nobody had missed it yet, the "also" was not necessary; but never mind about that, for the Pathfinder is going to speak.

"No, no, Major," said he, confidently, "that *would* be a risky declaration. I didn't load the piece, and can't say what was in it; but if it was lead, you will find t 1e bullet driving down those of the Quartermaster and Jasper, else is not my name Pathfinder."

A shout from the target announced the truth of this assertion.

Is the miracle sufficient as it stands? Not for Cooper. The Pathfinder speaks again, as he "now slowly advances toward the stage occupied by the females":

" That's not all, boys, that's not all; if you find the target touched at all, I'll own to a miss. The Quartermaster cut the wood, but you'll find no wood cut by that last messenger."

The miracle is at last complete. He knew—doubtless *saw*—at the distance of a hundred yards —that his bullet had passed into the hole *without fraying the edges*. There were now three bullets in that one hole—three bullets embedded processionally in the body of the stump back of the target. Everybody knew this—somehow or other—and yet nobody had dug any of them out to make sure. Cooper is not a close observer, but he is interesting. He is certainly always that, no matter what happens. And he is more interesting when he is not noticing what he is about than when he is. This is a considerable merit.

The conversations in the Cooper books have a curious sound in our modern ears. To believe that such talk really ever came out of people's mouths would be to believe that there was a time when time was of no value to a person who thought he had something to say; when it was the custom to spread a two-minute remark out to ten; when a man's mouth was a rolling-mill, and busied itself all day long in turning four-foot pigs of thought into thirty-foot bars of conversational railroad iron by attenuation; when subjects were seldom faithfully stuck to, but the talk wandered all around and arrived nowhere; when conversations consisted mainly of irrelevancies, with here and there a relevancy, a relevancy with an embarrassed look, as not being able to explain how it got there.

Cooper was certainly not a master in the construction of dialogue. Inaccurate observation defeated him here as it defeated him in so many other enterprises of his. He even failed to notice that the man who talks corrupt English six days in the week must and will talk it on the seventh, and can't help himself. In the *Deerslayer* story he lets Deerslayer talk the showiest kind of book-talk sometimes, and at other times the basest of base dialects. For instance, when some one asks him if he has a sweetheart, and if so, where she abides, this is his majestic answer:

" She's in the forest—hanging from the boughs of the trees, in a soft rain—in the dew on the open grass—the clouds that float about in the blue heavens—the birds that sing in the woods —the sweet springs where I slake my thirst—and in all the other glorious gifts that come from God's Providence!"

And he preceded that, a little before, with this:

"It consarns me as all things that touches a fri'nd consarns a fri'nd."

And this is another of his remarks:

"If I was Injin born, now, I might tell of this, or carry in the scalp and boast of the expl'ite afore the whole tribe; or if my inimy had only been a bear "—[and so on].

COOPER'S LITERARY OFFENSES

We cannot imagine such a thing as a veteran Scotch Commander-in-Chief comporting himself in the field like a windy melodramatic actor, but Cooper could. On one occasion Alice and Cora were being chased by the French through a fog in the neighborhood of their father's fort:

> "*Point de quartier aux coquins!*" cried an eager pursuer, who seemed to direct the operations of the enemy.
> "Stand firm and be ready, my gallant 60ths!" suddenly exclaimed a voice above them; "wait to see the enemy; fire low, and sweep the glacis."
> "Father! father" exclaimed a piercing cry from out the mist; "it is I! Alice! thy own Elsie! spare, O! save your daughters!"
> "Hold!" shouted the former speaker, in the awful tones of parental agony, the sound reaching even to the woods, and rolling back in solemn echo. "'Tis she! God has restored me my children! Throw open the sally-port; to the field, 60ths, to the field! pull not a trigger, l st ye kill my lambs! Drive off these dogs of France with your steel!"

Cooper's word-sense was singularly dull. When a person has a poor ear for music he will flat and sharp right along without knowing it. He keeps near the tune, but it is *not* the tune. When a person has a poor ear for words, the result is a literary flatting and sharping; you perceive what he is intending to say, but you also perceive that he doesn't *say* it. This is Cooper. He was not a word-musician. His ear was satisfied with the *approximate* word. I will furnish some circumstantial evidence in support of this charge. My instances are gathered from half a dozen pages of the tale called *Deerslayer*. He uses "verbal" for "oral"; "precision" for "facility"; "phenomena" for "marvels"; "necessary" for "predetermined"; "unsophisticated" for "primitive"; "preparation" for "expectancy"; "rebuked" for "subdued"; "dependent on" for "resulting from"; "fact" for "condition"; "fact" for "conjecture"; "precaution" for "caution"; "explain" for "determine"; "mortified" for "disappointed"; "meretricious" for "factitious"; "materially" for "considerably"; "decreasing" for "deepening"; "increasing" for "disappearing"; "embedded" for "inclosed"; "treacherous" for "hostile"; "stood" for "stooped"; "softened" for "replaced"; "rejoined" for "remarked"; "situation" for "condition"; "different" for "differing"; "insensible" for "unsentient"; "brevity" for "celerity"; "distrusted" for "suspicious"; "mental imbecility" for "imbecility"; "eyes" for "sight"; "counteracting" for "opposing"; "funeral obsequies" for "obsequies."

There have been daring people in the world who claimed that Cooper could write English, but they are all dead now—all dead but Lounsbury. I don't remember that Lounsbury makes the claim in so many words, still he makes it, for he says that *Deerslayer* is a "pure work of art." Pure, in that connection, means faultless—faultless in all details— and language is a detail. If Mr. Lounsbury had only compared Cooper's English with the English which he writes himself—but it is plain that he didn't; and so it is likely that he imagines until this day that Cooper's is as clean and compact as his own. Now I feel sure, deep down in my heart, that Cooper wrote about the poorest English that exists in our language, and that the English of *Deerslayer* is the very worst that even Cooper ever wrote.

I may be mistaken, but it does seem to me that *Deerslayer* is not a work of art in any sense; it does seem to me that it is destitu e of every detail that goes to the making of a wo k of art; in truth, it seems to me that *Deerslayer* i. just simply a literary *delirium tremens*.

A work of art? It has n(invention; it has no order, system, sequence, or result; it has no life-likeness, no thrill, no stir, no seeming of reality; its characters are confusedly drawn, and by their acts and words they prove that they are not the sort of people the author claims that they are; its humor is pathetic; its pathos is funny; its conversations are —oh! indescribable; its love-scenes odious · its English a crime against the language.

Counting these out, what is left is Art. I think we must all admit that.

TRAVELING WITH A REFORMER

L AST spring I went out to Chicago to see the Fair, and although I did not see it my trip was not wholly lost—there were compensations. In New York I was introduced to a major in the regular army who said he was going to the Fair, and we agreed to go together. I had to go to Boston first, but that did not interfere; he said he would go along, and put in the time. He was a handsome man, and built like a gladiator. But his ways were gentle, and his speech was soft and persuasive. He was companionable, but exceedingly reposeful. Yes, and wholly destitute of the sense of humor. He was full of interest in everything that went on around him, but his serenity was indestructible; nothing disturbed him, nothing excited him.

But before the day was done I found that deep down in him somewhere he had a passion, quiet as he was—a passion for reforming petty public abuses. He stood for citizenship—it was his hobby. His idea was that every citizen of the republic ought to consider himself an unofficial policeman, and keep unsalaried watch and ward over the laws and their execution. He thought that the only effective way of preserving and protecting public rights was for each citizen to do his share in preventing or punishing such infringements of them as came under his personal notice.

It was a good scheme, but I thought it would keep a body in trouble all he time; it seemed to me that one would be alwa᾿s trying to get offending little officials discharge᾿ , and perhaps getting laughed at for all reward. But he said no, I had the wrong idea; that there vas no occasion to get anybody discharged; that i꜀ fact you *mustn't* get anybody discharged; that ꞏhat would itself be a failure; no, one must reform the man—reform him and make him useful where he was.

"Must one report the offender and then beg his superior not to discharge him, but reprimand him and keep him?"

"No, that is not the idea; you don't report him at all, for then you risk his bread and butter. You can act as if you are *going* to report him—when nothing else will answer. But that's an extreme case. That is a sort of *force*, and force is bad. Diplomacy is the effective thing. Now if a man has tact—if a man will exercise diplomacy—"

For two minutes we had been standing at a telegraph wicket, and during all this time the Major had been trying to get the attention of one of the young operators, but they were all busy skylarking. The Major spoke now, and asked one of them to take his telegram. He got for reply:

"I reckon you can wait a minute, can't you?" and the skylarking went on.

The Major said yes, he was not in a hurry. Then he wrote another telegram:

MARK TWAIN

Come and dine with me this evening. I can tell you how business is conducted in one of your branches.

Presently the young fellow who had spoken so pertly a little before reached out and took the telegram, and when he read it he lost color and began to apologize and explain. He said he would lose his place if this deadly telegram was sent, and he might never get another. If he could be let off this time he would give no cause of complaint again. The compromise was accepted.

As we walked away, the Major said:

"Now, you see, that was diplomacy—and you see how it worked. It wouldn't do any good to bluster, the way people are always doing—that boy can always give you as good as you send, and you'll come out defeated and ashamed of yourself pretty nearly always. But you see he stands no chance against diplomacy. Gentle words and diplomacy—those are the tools to work with."

"Yes, I see; but everybody wouldn't have had your opportunity. It isn't everybody that is on those familiar terms with the president of the Western Union."

"Oh, you misunderstand. I don't know the president—I only used him diplomatically. It is for his good and for the public good. There's no harm in it."

I said, with hesitation and diffidence:

"But is it ever right or noble to tell a lie?"

He took no note of the delicate self-righteousness of the question, but answered, with undisturbed gravity and simplicity:

"Yes, sometimes. Lies told to injure a person, and lies told to profit yourself are not justifiable, but lies told to help another person, and lies told in the public interest—oh, well, that is quite another matter. Anybody knows hat. But never mind about the methods: you see the result. That youth is going to be useful now, and well behaved. He had a good face. He was worth saving. Why, he was worth saving on his mo her's account if not his own. Of course, he has a mother—sisters, too. Damn those people who are always forgetting that! Do you know, I've never fought a duel in my life— never once—and yet have been challenged, like other people. I could always see the other man's unoffending women folks or his little children standing between him and me. *They* hadn't done anything—I couldn't break *their* hearts, you know."

He corrected a good many little abuses in the course of the day, and always without friction— always with a fine and dainty "diplomacy" which left no sting behind; and he got such happiness and such contentment out of these performances that I was obliged to envy him his trade—and perhaps would have adopted it if I could have managed the necessary deflections from fact as confidently with my mouth as I believe I could with a pen, behind the shelter of print, after a little practice.

Away late that night we were coming up-town in a horse-car when three boisterous roughs got aboard, and began to fling hilarious obscenities and profanities right and left among the timid passengers, some of whom were women and children. Nobody resisted or retorted; the conductor tried soothing words and moral suasion, but the roughs only called him names and laughed at him. Very soon I saw that the Major realized that this was a matter which was in his line; evidently he was turning over his stock of diplomacy in his mind and getting ready. I felt that the first diplomatic remark he made in this place would bring down a landslide of ridicule upon him and maybe something worse; but before I could whisper to him and check him he had begun, and it was too late. He said, in a level and dispassionate tone:

"Conductor, you must put these swine out. I will help you."

I was not looking for that. In a flash the three roughs plunged at him. But none of them arrived. He delivered three such blows as one could not expect to encounter outside the prize-ring, and neither of the men had life enough left in him to get up from where he fell. The Major dragged them out and threw them off the car, and we got under way again.

I was astonished; astonished to see a lamb act so; astonished at the strength displayed, and the clean and comprehensive result; astonished at the brisk and business-like style of the whole thing. The situation had a humorous side to it, considering how much I had been hearing about mild persuasion and gentle diplomacy all day from this pile-driver, and I would have liked to call his attention to that feature and do some sarcasms about it; but when I looked at him I saw that it would be of no use—his placid and contented face had no ray of humor in it; he would not have understood. When we left the car, I said:

"That was a good stroke of diplomacy—three good strokes of diplomacy, in fact."

"*That?* That wasn't diplomacy. You are quite in the wrong. Diplomacy is a wholly different thing. One cannot apply it to that sort; they would not understand it. No, that was not diplomacy; it was force."

"Now that you mention it, I—yes, I think perhaps you are right."

"Right? Of course I am right. It was just force."

"I think, myself, it had the outside aspect of it. Do you often have to reform people in that way?"

"Far from it. It hardly ever happens. Not oftener than once in half a year, at the outside."

"Those men will get well?"

"Get well? Why, certainly they will. They are not in any danger. I know how to hit and where to hit. You noticed that I did not hit them under the jaw. That would have killed them."

I believed that. I remarked—rather wittily, as I thought—that he had been a lamb all day, but now had all of a sudden developed into a ram—battering-ram; but with dulcet frankness and simplicity he said no, a battering-ram was quite a different thing and not in use now. This was maddening, and I came near bursting out and saying he had no more appreciation of wit than a jackass—in fact, I had it right on my tongue, but did not say it, knowing there was no hurry and I could say it just as well some other time over the telephone.

We started to Boston the next afternoon. The smoking-compartment in the parlor-car was full, and we went into the regular smoker. Across the aisle in the front seat sat a meek, farmer-looking old man with a sickly pallor in his face, and he was holding the door open with his foot to get the air. Presently a big brakeman came rushing through, and when he got to the door he stopped, gave the farmer an ugly scowl, then wrenched the door to with such energy as to almost snatch the old man's boot off. Then on he plunged about his business. Several passengers laughed, and the old gentleman looked pathetically shamed and grieved.

After a little the conductor passed along, and the Major stopped him and asked him a question in his habitually courteous way:

"Conductor, where does one report the misconduct of a brakeman? Does one report to you?"

"You can report him at New Haven if you want to. What has he been doing?"

The Major told the story. The conductor seemed amused. He said, with just a touch of sarcasm in his bland tones:

"As I understand you, the brakeman didn't *say* anything."

"No, he didn't say anything."

"But he scowled, you say."

"Yes."

"And snatched the door loose in a rough way."

"Yes."

"That's the whole business, is it?"

"Yes, that is the whole of it."

The conductor smiled pleasantly, and said:

"Well, if you want to report him, all right, but I don't quite make out what it's going to amount to. You'll say—as I understand you—that the brakeman insulted this old gentleman. They'll ask you what he *said*. You'll say he didn't say anything at all. I reckon they'll say, how are you going to make out an insult when you acknowledge yourself that he didn't say a word."

There was a murmur of applause at the conductor's compact reasoning, and it gave him pleasure—you could see it in his face. But the Major was not disturbed. He said:

"There—now you have touched upon a crying defect in the complaint system. The railway officials—as the public think and as you also seem to think—are not aware that there are any kind of insults except *spoken* ones. So nobody goes to headquarters and reports insults of manner, insults of gesture, look, and so forth; and yet these are sometimes harder to bear than any words. They are bitter hard to bear because there is nothing tangible to take hold of; and the insulter can always say, if called before the railway officials, that he never dreamed of intending any offense. It seems to me that the officials ought to specially and urgently request the public to report *unworded* affronts and incivilities."

The conductor laughed, and said:

"Well, that *would* be trimming it pretty fine, sure!"

"But not too fine, I think. I will report this

matter at New Haven, and I have an idea that I'll be thanked for it."

The conductor's face lost something of its complacency; in fact, it settled to a quite sober cast as the owner of it moved away. I said:

"You are not really going to bother with that trifle, are you?"

"It isn't a trifle. Such things ought always to be reported. It is a public duty, and no citizen has a right to shirk it. But I sha'n't have to report this case."

"Why?"

"It won't be necessary. Diplomacy will do the business. You'll see."

Presently the conductor came on his rounds again, and when he reached the Major he leaned over and said:

"That's all right. You needn't report him. He's responsible to me, and if he does it again I'll give him a talking to."

The Major's response was cordial:

"Now that is what I like! You mustn't think that I was moved by any vengeful spirit, for that wasn't the case. It was duty—just a sense of duty, that was all. My brother-in-law is one of the directors of the road, and when he learns that you are going to reason with your brakeman the very next time he brutally insults an unoffending old man it will please him, you may be sure of that."

The conductor did not look as joyous as one might have thought he would, but on the contrary looked sickly and uncomfortable. He stood around a little; then said:

"I think something ought to be done to him *now*. I'll discharge him."

"Discharge him? What good would that do? Don't you think it would be better wisdom to teach him better ways and keep him?"

"Well, there's something in that. What would you suggest?"

"He insulted the old gentleman in presence of all these people. How would it do to have him come and apologize in their presence?"

"I'll have him here right off. And I want to say this: If people would do as you've done, and report such things to me instead of keeping mum and going off and blackguarding the road, you'd see a different state of things pretty soon. I'm much obliged to you."

The brakeman came and apologized. After he was gone the Major said:

"Now, you see how simple and easy that was. The ordinary citizen would have accomplished nothing—the brother-in-law of a director can accomplish anything he wants to."

"But are you really the brother-in-law of a director?"

"Always. Always when the public interests require it. I have a brother-in-law on all the boards—everywhere. It saves me a world of trouble."

"It is a good wide relationship."

"Yes. I have over three hundred of them."

"Is the relationship never doubted by a conductor?"

"I have never met with a case. It is the honest truth—I never have."

"Why didn't you let him go ahead and discharge the brakeman, in spite of your favorite policy? You know he deserved it."

The Major answered with something which really had a sort of distant resemblance to impatience:

"If you would stop and think a moment you wouldn't ask such a question as that. Is a brakeman a dog, that nothing but dog's methods will do for him? He is a man, and has a man's fight for life. And he always has a sister, or a mother, or wife and children to support. Always—there are no exceptions. When you take his living away from him you take theirs away too—and what have they done to you?. Nothing. And where is the profit in discharging an uncourteous brakeman and hiring another just like him? It's unwisdom. Don't you see that the rational thing to do is to *reform* the brakeman and keep him? Of course it is."

Then he quoted with admiration the conduct of a certain division superintendent of the Consolidated road, in a case where a switchman of two years' experience was negligent once and threw a train off the track and killed several people. Citizens came in a passion to urge the man's dismissal, but the superintendent said:

"No, you are wrong. He has learned his lesson, he will throw no more trains off the track. He is twice as valuable as he was before. I shall keep him."

We had only one more adventure on the trip. Between Hartford and Springfield the train-boy came shouting in with an armful of literature and dropped a sample into a slumbering gentleman's lap, and the man woke up with a start. He was very angry, and he and a couple of friends discussed the outrage with much heat. They sent 'or the parlor-car conductor and described the matter, and were determined to have the boy expel ed from his situation. The three complainants were wealthy Holyoke merchants, and it was evident th it the conductor stood in some awe of them. He tried to pacify them, and explained that the boy was not under his authority, but under that of one of the news companies; but he accomplished nothing.

Then the Major volunteered some testimony for the defense. He said:

"I saw it all. You gentlemen have not meant to exaggerate the circumstances, but still that is what you have done. The boy has done nothing more than all train-boys do. If you want to get his ways softened down and his manners reformed, I am with you and ready to help, but it isn't fair to get him discharged without giving him a chance."

But they were angry, and would hear of no compromise. They were well acquainted with the president of the Boston & Albany, they said, and would put everything aside next day and go up to Boston and fix that boy.

The Major said he would be on hand too, and would do what he could to save the boy. One of the gentlemen looked him over, and said:

"Apparently it is going to be a matter of who can wield the most influence with the president. Do you know Mr. Bliss personally?"

The Major said, with composure:

"Yes; he is my uncle."

The effect was satisfactory. There was an awkward silence for a minute or more; then the hedging and the half-confessions of overhaste and exaggerated resentment began, and soon everything was smooth and friendly and sociable, and it was resolved to drop the matter and leave the boy's bread-and-butter unmolested.

It turned out as I had expected: the president of the road was not the Major's uncle at all—except by adoption, and for this day and train only.

We got into no episodes on the return journey. Probably it was because we took a night train and slept all the way.

We left New York Saturday night by the Pennsylvania road. After breakfast the next morning we went into the parlor-car, but found it a dull place and dreary. There were but few people in it and nothing going on. Then we went into the little smoking-compartment of the same car and found three gentlemen in there. Two of them were grumbling over one of the rules of the road—a rule which forbade card-playing on the trains on Sunday. They had started an innocent game of high-low-jack and been stopped. The Major was interested. He said to the third gentleman:

"Did you object to the game?"

"Not at all. I am a Yale professor and a religious man, but my prejudices are not extensive."

Then the Major said to the others:

"You are at perfect liberty to resume your game, gentlemen; no one here objects."

One of them declined the risk, but the other one said he would like to begin again if the Major would join him. So they spread an overcoat over their knees and the game proceeded. Pretty soon the parlor-car conductor arrived, and said brusquely:

"There, there, gentlemen, that won't do. Put up the cards—it's not allowed."

The Major was shuffling. He continued to shuffle, and said:

"By whose order is it forbidden?"

"It's my order. I forbid it."

The dealing began. The Major asked:

"Did you invent the idea?"

"What idea?"

"The idea of forbidding card-playing on Sunday."

"No—of course not."

"Who did?"

"The company."

"Then it isn't your order, after all, but the company's. Is that it?"

"Yes. But you don't stop playing; I have to require you to stop playing immediately."

"Nothing is gained by hurry, and often much is lost. Who authorized the company to issue such an order?"

"My dear sir, that is a matter of no consequence to me, and—"

"But you forget that you are not the only person concerned. It may be a matter of consequence to me. It is indeed a matter of very great importance to me. I cannot violate a legal requirement of my country without dishonoring myself; I cannot allow any man or corporation to hamper my liberties with illegal rules—a thing which railway companies are always trying to do — without dishonoring my citizenship. So I come back to that question: By whose authority has the company issued this order?"

"I don't *know*. That's *their* affair."

"Mine, too. I doubt if the company has any right to issue such a rule. This road runs through several states. Do you know what state we are in now, and what its laws are in matters of this kind?"

"Its laws do not concern me, but the company's orders do. It is my duty to stop this game, gentlemen, and it *must* be stopped."

"Possibly; but still there is no hurry. In hotels they post certain rules in the rooms, but they always quote passages from the state laws as authority for these requirements. I see nothing posted here of this sort. Please produce your authority and let us arrive at a decision, for you see yourself that you are marring the game."

"I have nothing of the kind, but I have my orders, and that is sufficient. They must be obeyed."

"Let us not jump to conclusions. It will be better all around to examine into the matter without heat or haste, and see just where we stand before either of us makes a mistake—for the curtailing of the liberties of a citizen of the United States is a much more serious matter than you and the railroads seem to think, and it cannot be done in my person until the curtailer proves his right to do so. Now—"

"My dear sir, *will* you put down those cards?"

"All in good time, perhaps. It depends. You say this order must be obeyed. *Must.* It is a strong word. You see yourself how strong it is. A wise company would not arm you with so drastic an order as this, of *course*, without appointing a penalty for its infringement. Otherwise it runs the risk of being a dead letter and a thing to laugh at. What is the appointed penalty for an infringement of this law?"

"Penalty? I never heard of any."

"Unquestionably you must be mistaken. Your company orders you to come here and rudely break up an innocent amusement, and furnishes you no way to enforce the order? Don't you see that that is nonsense? What do you *do* when people refuse to obey this order? Do you take the cards away from them?"

"No."

"Do you put the offender off at the next station?"

"Well, no—of course we couldn't if he had a ticket."

"Do you have him up before a court?"

The conductor was silent and apparently troubled. The Major started a new deal, and said:

"You see that you are helpless, and that the company has placed you in a foolish position. You are furnished with an arrogant order, and you deliver it in a blustering way, and when you come to look into the matter you find you haven't any way of enforcing obedience."

The conductor said, with chill dignity:

"Gentlemen, you have heard the order, and my duty is ended. As to obeying it or not, you will do as you think fit." And he turned to leave.

"But wait. The matter is not yet finished. I think you are mistaken about your duty being ended; but if it really is, I myself have a duty to perform yet."

"How do you mean?"

"Are you going to report my disobedience at headquarters in Pittsburg?"

"No. What good would that do?"

"You must report me, or I will report you."

"Report me for what?"

"For disobeying the company's orders in not stopping this game. As a citizen it is my duty to help the railway companies keep their servants to their work."

"Are you in earnest?"

"Yes, I am in earnest. I have nothing against you as a man, but I have this against you as an officer—that you have not carried out that order, and if you do not report me I must report you. And I will."

The conductor looked puzzled, and was thoughtful a moment; then he burst out with:

"I seem to be getting *myself* into a scrape! It's all a muddle; I can't make head or tail of it; it's never happened before; they always knocked under and never said a word, and so *I* never saw how ridiculous that stupid order with no penalty is. *I* don't want to report anybody, and I don't want to *be* reported—why, it might do me no end of harm!

Now *do* go on with the game—play the whole day if you want to—and don't let's have any more trouble about it!"

"No, I only sat down here to establish this gentleman's rights—he can have his place now. But before you go won't you tell me what you think the company made this rule for? Can you imagine an excuse for it? I mean a rational one—an excuse that is not on its face silly, and the invention of an idiot?"

"Why, surely I can. The reason it was made is plain enough. It is to save the feelings of the other passengers—the religious ones among them, I mean. They would not like it, to have the Sabbath desecrated by card-playing on the train."

"I just thought as much. They are willing to desecrate it themselves by traveling on Sunday, but they are not willing that other people—"

"By gracious, you've hit it! I never thought of that before. The fact is, it *is* a silly rule when you come to look into it."

At this point the train-conductor arrived, and was going to shut down the game in a very high-handed fashion, but the parlor-car conductor stopped him and took him aside to explain. Nothing more was heard of the matter.

I was ill in bed eleven days in Chicago and got no glimpse of the Fair, for I was obliged to return east as soon as I was able to travel. The Major secured and paid for a stateroom in a sleeper the day before we left, so that I could have plenty of room and be comfortable; but when we arrived at the station a mistake had been made and our car had not been put on. The conductor had reserved a section for us—it was the best he could do, he said. But the Major said we were not in a hurry, and would wait for the car to be put on. The conductor responded, with pleasant irony:

"It may be that *you* are not in a hurry, just as you say, but we *are*. Come, get aboard, gentlemen, get aboard—don't keep us waiting."

But the Major would not get aboard himself nor allow me to do it. He wanted his car, and said he must have it. This made the hurried and perspiring conductor impatient, and he said:

"It's the best we can *do*—we can't do impossibilities. You will take the section or go without. A mistake has been made and can't be rectified at this late hour. It's a thing that happens now and then, and there is nothing for it but to put up with it and make the best of it. Other people do."

"Ah, that is just it, you see. If they had stuck to their rights and enforced them you wouldn't be trying to trample mine under foot in this bland way now. I haven't any disposition to give you unnecessary trouble, but it is my duty to protect the next man from this kind of imposition. So I must have my car. Otherwise I will wait in Chicago and sue the company for violating its contract."

"Sue the company?—for a thing like that!"

"Certainly."

"Do you really mean that?"

"Indeed, I do."

TRAVELING WITH A REFORMER

The conductor looked the Major over wonderingly, and then said:

"It beats me—it's bran-new—I've never struck the mate to it before. But I swear I think you'd do it. Look here, I'll send 'or the station-master."

When the station-master car ie he was a good deal annoyed—at the Major, not a the person who had made the mistake. He was rather brusque, and took the same position which the conductor had taken in the beginning; but he failed to move the soft-spoken artilleryman, who still insisted that he must have his car. However, it was plain that there was only one strong side in this case, and that that side was the Major's. The station-master banished his annoyed manner, and became pleasant and even half apologetic. This made a good opening for a compromise, and the Major made a concession. He said he would give up the engaged stateroom, but he must have *a* stateroom. After a deal of ransacking, one was found whose owner was persuadable; he exchanged it for our section, and we got away at last. The conductor called on us in the evening, and was kind and courteous and obliging, and we had a long talk and got to be good friends. He said he wished the public would make trouble oftener—it would have a good effect. He said that the railroads could not be expected to do their whole duty by the traveler unless the traveler would take some interest in the matter himself.

I hoped that we were done reforming for the trip now, but it was not so. In the hotel-car, in the morning, the Major called for broiled chicken. The waiter said:

"It's not in the bill of fare, sir; we do not serve anything but what is in the bill."

"That gentleman yonder is eating a broiled chicken."

"Yes, but that is different. He is one of the superintendents of the road."

"Then all the more must I have broiled chicken. I do not like these discriminations. Please hurry—bring me a broiled chicken."

The waiter brought the steward, who explained in a low and polite voice that the thing was impossible—it was against the rule, and the rule was rigid.

"Very well, then, you must either apply it impartially or break it impartially. You must take that gentleman's chicken away from him or bring me one."

The steward was puzzled, and did not quite know what to do. He began an incoherent argument, but the conductor came along just then, and asked what the difficulty was. The steward explained that here was a gentleman who was insisting on having a chicken when it was dead against the rule and not in the bill. The conductor said:

"Stick by your rules—you haven't any option. Wait a moment—is this the gentleman?" Then he laughed and said: "Never mind your rules—it's my advice, and sound; give him anything he wants—don't get him started on his rights. Give him whatever he asks for; and if you haven't got it, stop the train and get it."

TRAVELING WITH A REFORMER

The Major ate the chicken, but said he did it from a sense of duty and to establish a principle, for he did not like chicken.

I missed the Fair, it is true, but I picked up some diplomatic tricks which I and the reader may find handy and useful as we go along.

PRIVATE HISTORY OF THE "JUMPING FROG" STORY

FIVE or six years ago a lady from Finland asked me to tell her a story in our negro dialect, so that she could get an idea of what that variety of speech was like. I told her one of Hopkinson Smith's negro stories, and gave her a copy of *Harper's Monthly* containing it. She translated it for a Swedish newspaper, but by an oversight named me as the author of it instead of Smith. I was very sorry for that, because I got a good lashing in the Swedish press, which would have fallen to his share but for that mistake; for it was shown that Boccaccio had told that very story, in his curt and meager fashion, five hundred years before Smith took hold of it and made a good and tellable thing out of it.

I have always been sorry for Smith. But my own turn has come now. A few weeks ago Professor Van Dyke, of Princeton, asked this question:

"Do you know how old your Jumping Frog story is?"

And I answered:

"Yes—forty-five years. The thing happened in Calaveras County in the spring of 1849."

"No; it happened earlier—a couple of thousand years earlier; it is a Greek story."

I was astonished—and hurt. I said:

THE "JUMPING FROG"

"I am willing to be a literary thief if it has been so ordained; I am even willing to be caught robbing the ancient dead alongside of Hopkinson Smith, for he is my friend and a good fellow, and I think would be as honest as any one if he could do it without occasioning remark; but I am not willing to antedate his crimes by fifteen hundred years. I must ask you to knock off part of that."

But the professor was not chaffing; he was in earnest, and could not abate a century. He named the Greek author, and offered to get the book and send it to me and the college text-book containing the English translation also. I thought I would like the translation best, because Greek makes me tired. January 30th he sent me the English version, and I will presently insert it in this article. It is my Jumping Frog tale in every essential. It is not strung out as I have strung it out, but it is all there.

To me this is very curious and interesting. Curious for several reasons. For instance:

I heard the story told by a man who was not telling it to his hearers as a thing new to them, but as a thing which *they had witnessed and would remember.* He was a dull person, and ignorant; he had no gift as a story-teller, and no invention; in his mouth this episode was merely history—history and statistics; and the gravest sort of history, too; he was entirely serious, for he was dealing with what to him were austere facts, and they interested him solely because they *were* facts; he was drawing on his memory, not his mind; he saw no humor in his tale, neither did his listeners; neither he nor they ever smiled or laughed; in my time I have not attended a more solemn conference. To him and to his fellow gold-miners there were just two things in the story that were worth considering. One was the smartness of the stranger in taking in its hero, Jim Smiley, with a loaded frog; and the other was the stranger's deep knowledge of a frog's nature— for he knew (as the narrator asserted and the listeners conceded) that a frog *likes shot* and is always ready to eat it. Those men discussed those two points, and those only. They were hearty in their admiration of them, and none of the party was aware that a first-rate story had been told in a first-rate way, and that it was brimful of a quality whose presence they never suspected—humor.

Now, then, the interesting question is, *did* the frog episode happen in Angel's Camp in the spring of '49, as told in my hearing that day in the fall of 1865? I am perfectly sure that it did. I am also sure that its duplicate happened in Bœotia a couple of thousand years ago. I think it must be a case of history actually repeating itself, and not a case of a good story floating down the ages and surviving because too good to be allowed to perish.

I would now like to have the reader examine the Greek story and the story told by the dull and solemn Californian, and observe how exactly alike they are in essentials.

[*Translation*]

THE ATHENIAN AND THE FROG [1]

An Athenian once fell in with a Bœotian who was sitting by the roadside looking at a frog. Seeing the other approach, the

[1] Sidgwick, *Greek Prose Composition*, page 116.

Bœotian said his was a remarkable frog, and asked if he would agree to start a contest of frogs, on condition that he whose frog jumped farthest should receive a large sum of money. The Athenian replied that he would if the other would fetch him a frog, for the lake was near. To this he agreed, and when he was gone the Athenian took the frog, and, opening its mouth, poured some stones into its stomach so that it did not indeed seem larger than before, but could not jump. The Bœotian soon returned with the other frog, and the contest began. The second frog first was pinched, and jumped moderately; then they pinched the Bœotian frog. And he gathered himself for a leap, and used the utmost effort, but he could not move his body the least. So the Athenian departed with the money. When he was gone the Bœotian, wondering what was the matter with the frog, lifted him up and examined him. And being turned upside down, he opened his mouth and vomited out the stones.

And here is the way it happened in California:

FROM "THE CELEBRATED JUMPING FROG OF CALAVERAS COUNTY"

Well, thish-yer Smiley had rat-tarriers, and chicken cocks, and tom-cats, and all them kind of things, till you couldn't rest, and you couldn't fetch nothing for him to bet on but he'd match you. He ketched a frog one day, and took him home, and said he cal'lated to educate him; and so he never done nothing for three months but set in his back yard and learn that frog to jump. And you bet you he *did* learn him, too. He'd give him a little punch behind, and the next minute you'd see that frog whirling in the air like a doughnut—see him turn one summerset, or maybe a couple if he got a good start, and come down flat-footed and all right, like a cat. He got him up so in the matter of ketching flies, and kep' him in practice so constant, that he'd nail a fly every time as fur as he could see him. Smiley said all a frog wanted was education, and he could do 'most anything—and I believe him. Why, I've seen him set Dan'l Webster down here on this floor—Dan'l Webster was the name of the frog—and sing out "Flies, Dan'l, flies!" and quicker'n you could wink he'd spring straight up and snake a fly off'n the counter there, and flop down on the floor ag'in as solid as a gob of mud, and fall to scratching the side of his head with his hind foot as indifferent as if he hadn't no idea he'd been doin' any more'n any frog might do. You never see a frog so modest and straightfor'ard as he was, for all he was so gifted. And when it come to fair and square jumping on a dead level, he could get over more ground at one straddle than any animal of his breed you ever see. Jumping on a dead level was his strong suit, you understand; and when it came to that, Smiley would ante up money on him as long as he had a red. Smiley was monstrous proud of his frog, and well he might be, for fellers that had traveled and been everywheres all said he laid over any frog that ever *they* see.

Well, Smiley kep' the beast in a little lattice box, and he used to fetch him down-town sometimes and lay for a bet. One day a feller—a stranger in the camp, he was—come acrost him with his box, and says:

"What might it be that you've got in the box?"

And Smiley says, sorter indifferent-like, "It might be a parrot, or it might be a canary, maybe, but it ain't—it's only just a frog."

And the feller took it, and looked at it careful, and turned it round this way and that, and says, "H'm—so 'tis. Well, what's *he* good for?"

"Well," Smiley says, easy and careless, "he's good enough for *one* thing, I should judge—he can outjump any frog in Calaveras County."

The feller took the box again and took another long, particular look, and gave it back to Smiley, and says, very deliberate, "Well," he says, "I don't see no p'ints about that frog that's any better'n any other frog."

"Maybe you don't," Smiley says. "Maybe you understand frogs and maybe you don't understand 'em; maybe you've had experience, and maybe you ain't only a amature, as it were. Anyways, I've got *my* opinion, and I'll resk forty dollars that he can outjump any frog in Calaveras County."

And the feller studies a minute, and then says, kinder sad-like, "Well, I'm only a stranger here, and I ain't got no frog, but if I had a frog I'd bet you."

And then Smiley says: "That's all right—that's all right—if you'll hold my box a minute, I'll go and get you a frog." And so the feller took the box and put up his forty dollars along with Smiley's and set down to wait.

So he set there a good while thinking and thinking to hisself, and then he got the frog out and prized his mouth open and took a teaspoon and filled him full of quail-shot—filled him pretty near up to his chin—and set him on the floor. Smiley he went to the swamp and slopped around in the mud for a long time, and finally he ketched a frog and fetched him in and give him to this feller, and says:

"Now, if you're ready, set him alongside of Dan'l, with his fore paws just even with Dan'l's, and 'll give the word." Then he says, "One—two—three—*git!*" and him and the feller touched up the frogs from behind, and the new frog hopped off lively; but Dan'l give a heave, and hysted up his shoulders—so—like a Frenchman, but it warn't no use—he couldn't budge; he was planted as solid as a church, and he couldn't no more stir than if he was anchored out. Smiley was a good deal surprised, and he was disgusted, too, but he didn't have no idea what the matter was, of course.

The feller took the money and started away; and when he was going out at the door he sorter jerked his thumb over his shoulder—so—at Dan'l, and says again, very deliberate: "Well," he says, "*I* don't see no p'ints about that frog that's any better'n any other frog."

Smiley he stood scratching his head and looking down at Dan'l a long time, and at last he says, "I do wonder what in the nation that frog throw'd off for—I wonder if there ain't something the matter with him—he 'pears to look mighty baggy, somehow." And he ketched Dan'l by the nap of the neck, and hefted him, and says, "Why, blame my cats if he don't weigh five pound!" and turned him upside down, and he belched out a double handful of shot. And then he see how it was, and he was the maddest man—he set the frog down and took out after that feller, but he never ketched him.

The resemblances are deliciously exact. There you have the wily Bœotian and the wily Jim Smiley waiting—two thousand years apart—and waiting, each equipped with his frog and "laying" for the stranger. A contest is proposed—for money. The Athenian would take a chance "if the other would fetch him a frog"; the Yankee says: "I'm only a stranger here, and I ain't got no frog; but if I had a frog I'd bet you." The wily Bœotian and the wily Californian, with that vast gulf of two thousand years between, retire eagerly and go frogging in the marsh; the Athenian and the Yankee remain behind and work a base advantage, the one with pebbles, the other with shot. Presently the contest began. In the one case "they pinched the Bœotian frog"; in the other, "him and the feller touched up the frogs from behind." The Bœotian frog "gathered himself for a leap" (you can just *see* him!), "but could not move his body in the least"; the Californian frog "give a heave, but it warn't no use— he couldn't budge." In both the ancient and the modern cases the strangers departed with the money. The Bœotian and the Californian wonder what is the matter with their frogs; they lift them and examine; they turn them upside down and out spills the informing ballast.

Yes, the resemblances are curiously exact. I used to tell the story of the Jumping Frog in San Francisco, and presently Artemus Ward came along and wanted it to help fill out a little book which he was about to publish; so I wrote it out and sent it to his publisher, Carleton; but Carleton thought the book had enough matter in it, so he gave the story to Henry Clapp as a present, and Clapp put it in his *Saturday Press*, and it killed that paper with a suddenness that was beyond praise. At least the paper died with that issue, and none but envious people have ever tried to rob me of the honor and credit of killing it. The "Jumping Frog" was the first piece of writing of mine that spread itself through the newspapers and brought me into public notice. Consequently, the *Saturday Press* was a cocoon and I the worm in it; also, I was the gay-colored literary moth which its death set free. This simile has been used before.

Early in '66 the "Jumping Frog" was issued in book form, with other sketches of mine. A year or two later Madame Blanc translated it into French and published it in the *Revue des Deux Mondes*, but the result was not what should have been expected, for the *Revue* struggled along and pulled through, and is alive yet. I think the fault must have been in the translation. I ought to have translated it myself. I think so because I examined into the matter and finally retranslated the sketch from the French back into English, to see what the trouble was; that is, to see just what sort of a focus the French people got upon it. Then the mystery was explained. In French the story is too confused, and chaotic, and unreposeful, and ungrammatical, and insane; consequently it could only cause grief and sickness—it could not kill. A glance at my re-translation will show the reader that this must be true.

[*My Retranslation*]

THE FROG JUMPING OF THE COUNTY OF CALAVERAS

Eh bien! this Smiley nourished some terriers à rats, and some cocks of combat, and some cats, and all sort of things; and with his rage of betting one no had more of repose. He trapped one day a frog and him imported with him (*et l'emporta chez lui*) saying that he pretended to make his education. You me believe if you will, but during three months he not has nothing done but to him apprehend to jump (*apprendre à sauter*) in a court retired of her mansion (*de sa maison*). And I you respond that he have succeeded. He him gives a small blow by behind, and the instant after you shall see the frog turn in the air like a grease-biscuit, make one summersault, sometimes two, when she was well started, and re-fall upon his feet like a cat. He him had accomplished in the art of to gobble the flies (*gober des mouches*), and him there exercised continually—so well that a fly at the most far that she appeared was a fly lost. Smiley had custom to say that all which lacked to a frog it was the education, but with the education she could do nearly all—and I him believe. *Tenez*, I him have seen pose Daniel Webster there upon this plank—Daniel Webster was the name of the frog—and to him sing, "Some flies, Daniel, some flies!"—in a flash of the eye Daniel had bounded and seized a fly here upon the counter, then jumped anew at the earth, where he rested truly to himself scratch the head with his behind-foot, as if he no had not the least idea of his superiority. Never you not have seen frog as modest, as natural, sweet as she was. And when he himself agitated to jump purely and simply upon plain earth, she does more ground in one jump than any beast of his species than you can know.

To jump plain—this was his strong. When he himself agitated for that Smiley multiplied the bets upon her as long as there to him remained a red. It must to know, Smiley was monstrously proud of his frog, and he of it was right, for some men who were traveled, who had all seen, said that they to him would be injurious to him compare to another frog. Smiley guarded Daniel in a little box latticed which he carried by times to the village for some bet.

One day an individual stranger at the camp him arrested with his box and him said:

"What is this that you have then shut up there within?"

Smiley said, with an air indifferent:

"That could be a paroquet, or a syringe (*ou un serin*), but this no is nothing of such, it not is but a frog."

The individual it took, it regarded with care, it turned from one side and from the other, then he said:

"*Tiens!* in effect!—At what is she good?"

"My God!" respond Smiley, always with an air disengaged, "she is good for one thing, to my notice (*à mon avis*), she can batter in jumping (*elle peut batter en sautant*) all frogs of the county of Calaveras."

THE "JUMPING FROG"

The individual re-took the box, it examined of new longly, and it rendered to Smiley in saying with an air deliberate:

"*Eh bien!* I no saw not that that frog had nothing of better than each frog." (*Je ne vois pas que ette grenouille ait rien de mieux qu'aucune grenouille.*) [If that isn't grammar gone to seed, then I count myself no judge.—M. T.]

"Possible that you not it saw not " said Smiley, "possible that you—you comprehend frogs; possi le that you not you there comprehend nothing; possible that yo1 had of the experience, and possible that you not be but an amateur. Of all manner (*De toute manière*) I bet forty dollars t at she batter in jumping no matter which frog of the county of Calaveras."

The individual reflected a second, and said like sad:

"I not am but a stranger here, I no have not a frog; but if I of it had one, I would embrace the bet."

"Strong, well!" respond Smiley; "nothing of more facility. If you will hold my box a minute, I go you to search a frog (*j'irai vous chercher*)."

Behold, then, the individual, who guards the box, who puts his forty dollars upon those of Smiley, and who attends (*et qui attend*). He attended enough longtimes, reflecting all solely. And figure you that he takes Daniel, him opens the mouth by force and with a teaspoon him fills with shot of the hunt, even him fills just to the chin, then he him puts by the earth. Smiley during these times was at slopping in a swamp. Finally he trapped (*attrape*) a frog, him carried to that individual, and said:

"Now if you be ready, put him all against Daniel, with their before-feet upon the same line, and I give the signal"—then he added: "One, two, three—advance!"

Him and the individual touched their frogs by behind, and the frog new put to jump smartly, but Daniel himself lifted ponderously, exalted the shoulders thus, like a Frenchman—to what good? he could not budge, he is planted solid like a church, he not advance no more than if one him had put at the anchor.

Smiley was surprised and disgusted, but he not himself doubted not of the turn being intended (*mais il ne se doutait pas du tour bien entendu*). The individual empocketed the silver, himself with it went, and of it himself in going is that he no gives not a jerk of thumb over the shoulder—like that—at the poor Daniel, in saying with his air deliberate—(*L'individu empoche l'argent s'en va et en s'en allant est ce qu'il ne donne pas un coup de pouce par-dessus l'épaule, comme ça, au pauvre Daniel, en disant de son air délibéré.)*

"Eh bein! I no see not that that frog has nothing of better than another."

Smiley himself scratched longtimes the head, the eyes fixed upon Daniel, until that which at last he said:

"I me demand how the devil it makes itself that this beast has refused. Is it that she had something? One would believe that she is stuffed."

He grasped Daniel by the skin of the neck, him lifted and said:

"The wolf me bite if he no weigh not five pounds."

He him reversed and the unhappy belched two handfuls of shot (*et le malheureux*, etc.).—When Smiley recognized how it was, he was like mad. He deposited his frog by the earth and ran after the individual, but he not him caught never.

It may be that there are people who can translate better than I can, but I am not acquainted with them.

So ends the private and public history of the Jumping Frog of Calaveras County, an incident which has this unique feature about it—that it is both old and new, a "chestnut" and not a "chestnut"; for it was original when it happened two thousand years ago, and was again original when it happened in California in our own time.

MENTAL TELEGRAPHY

A MANUSCRIPT WITH A HISTORY

NOTE TO THE EDITOR.—By glancing over the inclosed bundle of rusty old manuscript, you will perceive that I once made a great discovery: the discovery that certain sorts of thing which, from the beginning of the world, had always been regarded as merely "curious coincidences"—that is to say, accidents—were no more accidental than is the sending and receiving of a telegram an accident. I made this discovery sixteen or seventeen years ago, and gave it a name—"Mental Telegraphy." It is the same thing around the outer edges of which the Psychical Society of England began to group (and play with) four or five years ago, and which they named "Telepathy." Within the last two or three years they have penetrated toward the heart of the matter, however, and have found out that mind can act upon mind in a quite detailed and elaborate way over vast stretches of land and water. And they have succeeded in doing, by their great credit and influence, what I could never have done—they have convinced the world that mental telegraphy is not a jest, but a fact, and that it is a thing not rare, but exceedingly common. They have done our age a service—and a very great service, I think.

In this old manuscript you will find mention of an extraordinary experience of mine in the mental telegraphic line, of date about the year 1874 or 1875—the one concerning the Great Bonanza book. It was this experience that called my attention to the matter under consideration. I began to keep a record, after that, of such experiences of mine as seemed explicable by the theory that minds telegraph thoughts to each other. In 1878 I went to Germany and began to write the book called *A Tramp Abroad*. The bulk of this old batch of manuscript was written at that time and for that book. But I removed it when

III

I came to revise the volume for the press; for I feared that the public would treat the thing as a joke and throw it aside, whereas I was in earnest.

At home, eight or ten years ago, I tried to creep in under shelter of an authority grave enough to protect the article from ridicule—*The North American Review*. But Mr Metcalf was too wary for me. He said that to treat these mere "coincidences" seriously was a thing which the *Review* couldn't dare to do; that I must put either my name or my *nom de plume* to the article, and thus save the *Review* from harm. But I couldn't consent to that; it would be the surest possible way to defeat my desire that the public should receive the thing seriously, and be willing to stop and give it some fair degree of attention. So I pigeonholed the MS., because I could not get it published anonymously.

Now see how the world has moved since then. These small experiences of mine, which were too formidable at that time for admission to a grave magazine—if the magazine must allow them to appear as something above and beyond "accidents" and "coincidences"—are trifling and commonplace now, since the flood of light recently cast upon mental telegraphy by the intelligent labors of the Psychical Society. But I think they are worth publishing, just to show what harmless and ordinary matters were considered dangerous and incredible eight or ten years ago.

As I have said, the bulk of this old manuscript was written in 1878; a later part was written from time to time two, three, and four years afterward. The "Postscript" I add to-day.

MAY, '78.—Another of those apparently trifling things has happened to me which puzzle and perplex all men every now and then, keep them thinking an hour or two, and leave their minds barren of explanation or solution at last. Here it is—and it looks inconsequential enough, I am obliged to say. A few days ago I said: "It must be that Frank Millet doesn't know we are in Germany, or he would have written long before this. I have been on the point of dropping him a line at least a dozen times during the past six weeks, but I always decided to wait a day or two longer, and see if we shouldn't hear from him. Bt t now I *will* write." And so I did. I directed the letter to Paris, and thought, "*Now* we shall hear from him before this letter is fifty miles from Feidelberg—it always happens so."

True enough; but *why* sho ıld it? That is the puzzling part of it. We are ılways talking about letters "crossing" each other, :or that is one of the very commonest accidents of this life. We call it "accident," but perhaps we misname it. We have the instinct a dozen times a year that the letter we are writing is going to "cross" the other person's letter; and if the reader will rack his memory a little he will recall the fact that this presentiment had strength enough to it to make him cut his letter down to a decided briefness, because it would be a waste of time to write a letter which was going to "cross," and hence be a useless letter. I think that in my experience this instinct has generally come to me in cases where I had put off my letter a good while in the hope that the other person would write.

Yes, as I was saying, I had waited five or six weeks; then I wrote but three lines, because I felt and seemed to know that a letter from Millet would cross mine. And so it did. He wrote the same day that I wrote. The letters crossed each other. His letter went to Berlin, care of the American minister, who sent it to me. In this letter Millet said he had been trying for six weeks to stumble upon somebody who knew my German addres, and at last the idea had occured to him that a letter sent to the care of the embassy at Berlin might possibly find me.

Maybe it was an "accident" that he finally determined to write me at the same moment that I finally determined to write him, but I think not.

With me the most irritating thing has been to wait a tedious time in a purely business matter, hoping that the other party will do the writing, and then sit down and do it myself, perfectly satisfied that that other man is sitting down at the same moment to write a letter which will "cross" mine. And yet one must go on writing, just the same; because if you get up from your table and postpone, that other man will do the same thing, exactly as if you two were harnessed together like the Siamese twins, and must duplicate each other's movements.

Several months before I left home a New York firm did some work about the house for me, and did not make a success of it, as it seemed to me. When the bill came, I wrote and said I wanted the work perfected before I paid. They replied that they were very busy, but that as soon as they could spare the proper man the thing should be done. I waited more than two months, enduring as patiently as possible the companionship of bells which would fire away of their own accord sometimes when nobody was touching them, and at other times wouldn't ring though you struck the button with a sledge-hammer. Many a time I got ready to write and then postponed it; but at last I sat down one evening and poured out my grief to the extent of a page or so, and then cut my letter suddenly short, because a strong instinct told me that the firm had begun to move in the matter. When I came down to breakfast next morning the postman had not yet taken my letter away, but the electrical man had been there, done his work, and was gone again! He had received his orders the previous evening from his employers, and had come up by the night train.

If that was an "accident," it took about three months to get it up in good shape.

One evening last summer I arrived in Washington, registered at the Arlington Hotel, and went to my room. I read and smoked until ten o'clock; then, finding I was not yet sleepy, I thought I would take a breath of fresh air. So I went forth in the rain, and tramped through one street after another in an aimless and enjoyable way. I knew that Mr. O——, a friend of mine, was in town, and I wished I might run across him; but I did not propose to hunt for him at midnight, especially as I did not know where he was stopping. Toward twelve o'clock the streets had become so deserted that I felt lonesome; so I stepped into a cigar shop far up the avenue, and remained there fifteen minutes, listening to some bummers discussing national politics. Suddenly the spirit of prophecy came upon me, and I said to myself, "Now I will go out at this door, turn to the left, walk ten steps, and meet Mr. O—— face to face." I did it, too! I could not see his face, because he had an umbrella before it, and it was pretty dark anyhow, but he interrupted the man he was walking and talking with, and I recognized his voice and stopped him.

That I should step out there and stumble upon Mr. O—— was nothing, but that I should know beforehand that I was going to do it was a good deal. It is a very curious thing when you come to look at it. I stood far within the cigar shop when I delivered my prophecy; I walked about five steps to the door, opened it, closed it after me, walked down a flight of three steps to the sidewalk, then turned to the left and walked four or five more, and found my man. I repeat that in itself the thing was nothing; but to know it would happen so *beforehand*, wasn't that really curious?

I have criticized absent people so often, and then discovered, to my humiliation, that I was talking with their relatives, that I have grown superstitious about that sort of thing and dropped it. How like an idiot one feels after a blunder like that!

We are always mentioning people, and in that very instant they appear before us. We laugh, and say, "Speak of the devil," and so forth, and there we drop it, considering it an "accident." It is a cheap and convenient way of disposing of a grave and very puzzling mystery. The fact is, it does seem to happen too often to be an accident.

Now I come to the oddest thing that ever happened to me. Two or three years ago I was lying in bed, idly musing, one morning—it was the 2d of March—when suddenly a red-hot new idea came whistling down into my camp, and exploded with such comprehensive effectiveness as to sweep the vicinity clean of rubbishy reflections and fill the air with their dust and flying fragments. This idea, stated in simple phrase, was that the time was ripe and the market ready for a certain book; a book which ought to be written at once; a book which must command attention and be of peculiar interest —to wit, a book about the Nevada silver-mines. The "Great Bonanza" was a new wonder then, and everybody was talking about it. It seemed to me that the person best qualified to write this book was Mr. William H. Wright, a journalist of Virginia, Nevada, by whose side I had scribbled many months when I was a reporter there ten or twelve years before. He might be alive still; he might be dead; I could not tell; but I would write him, anyway. I began by merely and modestly suggesting that he make such a book; but my interest grew as I went on, and I ventured to map out what I thought ought to be the plan of the work, he being an old friend, and not given to taking good intentions for ill. I even dealt with details, and suggested the order and sequence which they should follow. I was about to put the manuscript in an envelope, when the thought occurred to me that if this book should be written at my suggestion, and then no publisher happened to want it, I should feel uncomfortable; so I con- cluded to keep my letter back until I should have secured a publisher. I pigeonholed my document, and dropped a note to my own publisher, asking him to name a day for a business consultation. He was out of town on a far journey.

My note remained unanswered, and at the end

of three or four days the whole matter had passed out of my mind. On the 9th of March the postman brought three or four letters, and among them a thick one whose superscription was in a hand which seemed dimly familiar to me. I could not "place" it at first, but presently I succeeded. Then I said to a visiting relative who was present:

"Now I will do a miracle. I will tell you everything this letter contains—date, signature, and all—without breaking the seal. It is from a Mr. Wright, of Virginia, Nevada, and is dated the 2d of March—seven days ago. Mr. Wright proposes to make a book about the silver-mines and the Great Bonanza, and asks what I, as a friend, think of the idea. He says his subjects are to be so and so, their order and sequence so and so, and he will close with a history of the chief feature of the book, the Great Bonanza."

I opened the letter, and showed that I had stated the date and the contents correctly. Mr. Wright's letter simply contained what my own letter, written on the same date, contained, and mine still lay in its pigeonhole, where it had been lying during the seven days since it was written.

There was no clairvoyance about this, if I rightly comprehend what clairvoyance is. I think the clairvoyant professes to actually *see* concealed writing, and read it off word for word. This was not my case. I only seemed to know, and to know absolutely, the contents of the letter in detail and due order, but I had to *word* them myself. I translated them, so to speak, out of Wright's language into my own.

MENTAL TELEGRAPHY

Wright's letter and the one which I had written to him but never sent were in substance the same.

Necessarily this could not come by accident; such elaborate accidents cannot happen. Chance might have duplicated one or two of the details, but she would have broken down on the rest. I could not doubt—there was no tenable reason for doubting—that Mr. Wright's mind and mine had been in close and crystal-clear communication with each other across three thousand miles of mountain and desert on the morning of the 2d of March. I did not consider that both minds *originated* that succession of ideas, but that one mind originated it, and simply telegraphed it to the other. I was curious to know which brain was the telegrapher and which the receiver, so I wrote and asked for particulars. Mr. Wright's reply showed that his mind had done the originating and telegraphing, and mine the receiving. Mark that significant thing now; consider for a moment how many a splendid "original" idea has been unconsciously stolen from a man three thousand miles away! If one should question that this is so, let him look into the cyclopedia and con once more that curious thing in the history of inventions which has puzzled every one so much—that is, the frequency with which the same machine or other contrivance has been invented at the same time by several persons in different quarters of the globe. The world was without an electric telegraph for several thousand years; then Professor Henry, the American, Wheatstone in England, Morse on the sea, and a German in Munich, all invented it at the same time. The discovery of certain ways of applying steam was made in two or three countries in the same year. Is it not possible that inventors are constantly and unwittingly stealing each other's ideas whilst they stand thousands of miles asunder?

Last spring a literary friend of mine,[1] who lived a hundred miles away, paid me a visit, and in the course of our talk he said he had made a discovery —conceived an entirely new idea—one which certainly had never been used in literature. He told me what it was. I handed him a manuscript, and said he would find substantially the same idea in that—a manuscript which I had written a week before. The idea had been in my mind since the previous November; it had only entered his while I was putting it on paper, a week gone by. He had not yet written his; so he left it unwritten, and gracefully made over all his right and title in the idea to me.

The following statement, which I have clipped from a newspaper, is true. I had the facts from Mr. Howells's lips when the episode was new:

A remarkable story of a literary coincidence is told of Mr. Howells's *Atlantic Monthly* serial, "Dr. Breen's Practice." A lady of Rochester, New York, contributed to the magazine after "Dr. Breen's Practice" was in type, a short story which so much resembled Mr. Howells's that he felt it necessary to call upon her and explain the situation of affairs in order that no charge of plagiarism might be preferred against him. He showed her the proof-sheets of his story, and satisfied her that the similarity between her work and his was one of those strange coincidences which have from time to time occurred in the literary world.

[1] W. D. Howells.

MENTAL TELEGRAPHY

I had read portions of Mr. Howells's story, both in MS. and in proof, before the lady offered her contribution to the magazine.

Here is another case. I clip it from a newspaper:

The republication of Miss Alcott s novel *Moods* recalls to a writer in the Boston *Post* a singu ar coincidence which was brought to light before the book v as first published: "Miss Anna M. Crane, of Baltimore, pt blished *Emily Chester*, a novel which was pronounced a very striking and strong story. A comparison of this book with *Moods* showed that the two writers, though entire strangers to each other, and living hundreds of miles apart, had both chosen the same subject for their novels, had followed almost the same line of treatment up to a certain point, where the parallel ceased, and the dénouements were entirely opposite. And even more curious, the leading characters in both books had identically the same names, so that the names in Miss Alcott's novel had to be changed. Then the book was published by Loring."

Four or five times within my recollection there has been a lively newspaper war in this country over poems whose authorship was claimed by two or three different people at the same time. There was a war of this kind over "Nothing to Wear," "Beautiful Snow," "Rock me to Sleep, Mother," and also over one of Mr. Will Carleton's early ballads, I think. These were all blameless cases of unintentional and unwitting mental telegraphy, I judge.

A word more as to Mr. Wright. He had had his book in mind some time; consequently he, and not I, had originated the idea of it. The subject was entirely foreign to my thoughts; I was wholly absorbed in other things. Yet this friend, whom I had not seen and had hardly thought of for eleven years, was able to shoot his thoughts at me across three thousand miles of country, and fill my head with them, to the exclusion of every other interest, in a single moment. He had begun his letter after finishing his work on the morning paper—a little after three o'clock, he said. When it was three in the morning in Nevada it was about six in Hartford, where I lay awake thinking about nothing in particular; and just about that time his ideas came pouring into my head from across the continent, and I got up and put them on paper, under the impression that they were my own original thoughts.

I have never seen any mesmeric or clairvoyant performances or spiritual manifestations which were in the least degree convincing—a fact which is not of consequence, since my opportunities have been meager; but I am forced to believe that one human mind (still inhabiting the flesh) can communicate with another, over any sort of a distance, and without any *artificial* preparation of "sympathetic conditions" to act as a transmitting agent. I suppose that when the sympathetic conditions happen to exist the two minds communicate with each other, and that otherwise they don't; and I suppose that if the sympathetic conditions could be kept up right along, the two minds would continue to correspond without limit as to time.

Now there is that curious thing which happens to everybody: suddenly a succession of thoughts or sensations flocks in upon you, which startles you with the weird idea that you have ages ago experienced just this succession of thoughts or sensations in a previous existence. The previous existence is possible, no doubt, but I am persuaded that the solution of this hoary mystery lies not there, but in the fact that some far-off stranger has been telegraphing his thoughts and sensations into your consciousness, and that he stopped because some counter-current or other obstruction intruded and broke the line of communication. Perhaps they seem repetitions to you because they *are* repetitions, got at second hand from the other man. Possibly Mr. Brown, the "mind-reader," reads other people's minds, possibly he does not; but I know of a surety that I have read another man's mind, and therefore I do not see why Mr. Brown shouldn't do the like also.

I wrote the foregoing about three years ago, in Heidelberg, and laid the manuscript aside, purposing to add to it instances of mind-telegraphing from time to time as they should fall under my experience. Meantime the "crossing" of letters has been so frequent as to become monotonous. However, I have managed to get something useful out of this hint; for now, when I get tired of waiting upon a man whom I very much wish to hear from, I sit down and *compel* him to write, whether he wants to or not; that is to say, I sit down and write him, and then tear my letter up, satisfied that my act has forced him to write me at the same moment. I do not need to mail my letter—the writing it is the only essential thing.

Of course I have grown superstitious about this letter-crossing business — this was natural. We stayed awhile in Venice after leaving Heidelberg.

One day I was going down the Grand Canal in a gondola, when I heard a shout behind me, and looked around to see what the matter was; a gondola was rapidly following, and the gondolier was making signs to me to stop. I did so, and the pursuing boat ranged up alongside. There was an American lady in it—a resident of Venice. She was in a good deal of distress. She said:

"There's a New York gentleman and his wife at the Hotel Britannia who arrived a week ago, expecting to find news of their son, whom they have heard nothing about during eight months. There was no news. The lady is down sick with despair; the gentleman can't sleep or eat. Their son arrived at San Francisco eight months ago, and announced the fact in a letter to his parents the same day. That is the last trace of him. The parents have been in Europe ever since; but their trip has been spoiled, for they have occupied their time simply in drifting restlessly from place to place, and writing letters everywhere and to everybody, begging for news of their son; but the mystery remains as dense as ever. Now the gentleman wants to stop writing and go calling. He wants to cable San Francisco. He has never done it before, because he is afraid of— of he doesn't know what—death of his son, no doubt. But he wants somebody to *advise* him to cable; wants me to do it. Now I simply can't; for if no news came, that mother yonder would die. So I have chased you up in order to get you to support me in urging him to be patient, and put the thing off a week or two longer; it may be the saving of this lady. Come along; let's not lose any time."

So I went along, but I had a program of my own. When I was introduced to the gentleman I said: "I have some supersti ions, but they are worthy of respect. If you will cable San Francisco immediately, you will hear news of your son inside of twenty-four hours. I don't know that you will get the news from San Franci: co, but you will get it from somewhere. The only necessary thing is to *cable* — that is all. The news will come within twenty-four hours. Cable Peking, if you prefer; there is no choice in this matter. This delay is all occasioned by your not cabling long ago, when you were first moved to do it."

It seems absurd that this gentleman should have been cheered up by this nonsense, but he was; he brightened up at once, and sent his cablegram; and next day, at noon, when a long letter arrived from his lost son, the man was as grateful to me as if I had really had something to do with the hurrying up of that letter. The son had shipped from San Francisco in a sailing-vessel, and his letter was written from the first port he touched at, months afterward.

This incident argues nothing, and is valueless. I insert it only to show how strong is the superstition which "letter-crossing" has bred in me. I was so sure that a cablegram sent to any place, no matter where, would defeat itself by "crossing" the incoming news, that my confidence was able to raise up a hopeless man and make him cheery and hopeful.

But here are two or three incidents which come

strictly under the head of mind-telegraphing. One Monday morning, about a year ago, the mail came in, and I picked up one of the letters and said to a friend: "Without opening this letter I will tell you what it says. It is from Mrs. ——, and she says she was in New York last Saturday, and was purposing to run up here in the afternoon train and surprise us, but at the last moment changed her mind and returned westward to her home."

I was right; my details were exactly correct. Yet we had had no suspicion that Mrs. —— was coming to New York, or that she had even a remote intention of visiting us.

I smoke a good deal—that is to say, all the time—so, during seven years, I have tried to keep a box of matches handy, behind a picture on the mantelpiece; but I have had to take it out in trying, because George (colored), who makes the fires and lights the gas, always uses my matches and never replaces them. Commands and persuasions have gone for nothing with him all these seven years. One day last summer, when our family had been away from home several months, I said to a member of the household:

"Now, with all this long holiday, and nothing in the way to interrupt—"

"I can finish the sentence for you," said the member of the household.

"Do it, then," said I.

"George ought to be able, by practising, to learn to let those matches alone."

It was correctly done. That was what I was

going to say. Yet until that moment George and the matches had not been in my mind for three months, and it is plain that the part of the sentence which I uttered offers not the least cue or suggestion of what I was purposing to follow it with.

My mother[1] is descended from the younger of two English brothers named Lambton, who settled in this country a few generations ago. The tradition goes that the elder of the two eventually fell heir to a certain estate in England (now an earldom), and died right away. This has always been the way with our family. They always die when they could make anything by not doing it. The two Lambtons left plenty of Lambtons behind them; and when at last, about fifty years ago, the English baronetcy was exalted to an earldom, the great tribe of American Lambtons began to bestir themselves—that is, those descended from the elder branch. Ever since that day one or another of these has been fretting his life uselessly away with schemes to get at his "rights." The present "rightful earl"—I mean the American one—used to write me occasionally, and try to interest me in his projected raids upon the title and estates by offering me a share in the latter portion of the spoil; but I have always managed to resist his temptations.

Well, one day last summer I was lying under a tree, thinking about nothing in particular, when an absurd idea flashed into my head, and I said to a member of the household, "Suppose I should live to be ninety-two, and dumb and blind and toothless,

[1] She was still living when this was written.

and just as I was gasping out what was left of me on my death-bed—"

"Wait, I will finish the sentence," said a member of the household.

"Go on," said I.

"Somebody should rush in with a document, and say, 'All the other heirs are dead, and you are the Earl of Durham!'"

That is truly what I was going to say. Yet until that moment the subject had not entered my mind or been referred to in my hearing for months before. A few years ago this thing would have astounded me, but the like could not much surprise me now, though it happened every week; for I think I *know* now that mind can communicate accurately with mind without the aid of the slow and clumsy vehicle of speech.

This age does seem to have exhausted invention nearly; still, it has one important contract on its hands yet—the invention of the *phrenophone;* that is to say, a method whereby the communicating of mind with mind may be brought under command and reduced to certainty and system. The telegraph and the telephone are going to become too slow and wordy for our needs. We must have the *thought* itself shot into our minds from a distance; then, if we need to put it into words, we can do that tedious work at our leisure. Doubtless the something which conveys our thoughts through the air from brain to brain is a finer and subtler form of electricity, and all we need do is to find out how to capture it and how to force it to do its work, as we have had to do in the case of the electric currents. Before the day of telegraphs neither one of these marvels would have seemed any easier to achieve than the other.

While I am writing this, doubtless somebody on the other side of the globe is writing it, too. The question is, am I inspiring him or is he inspiring me? I cannot answer that; but that these thoughts have been passing through somebody else's mind all the time I have been setting them down I have no sort of doubt.

I will close this paper with a remark which I found some time ago in Boswell's *Johnson:*

> "Voltaire's *Candide* is wonderfully similar in its plan and conduct to Johnson's *Rasselas;* insomuch that I have heard Johnson say that if they had not been published so closely one after the other that there was not time for imitation, *it would have been in vain to deny that the scheme of that which came latest was taken from the other.*"

The two men were widely separated from each other at the time, and the sea lay between them.

POSTSCRIPT

In the *Atlantic* for June, 1882, Mr. John Fiske refers to the often-quoted Darwin-and-Wallace "coincidence":

> I alluded, just now, to the "unforeseen circumstance" which led Mr. Darwin in 1859 to break his long silence, and to write and publish the *Origin of Species.* This circumstance served, no less than the extraordinary success of his book, to show how ripe the minds of men had become for entertaining such views as

those which Mr. Darwin propounded. In 1858 Mr. Wallace, who was then engaged in studying the natural history of the Malay Archipelago, sent to Mr. Darwin (as the man most likely to understand him) a paper in which he sketched the outlines of a theory identical with that upon which Mr. Darwin had so long been at work. The same sequence of observed facts and inferences that had led Mr. Darwin to the discovery of natural selection and its consequences had led Mr. Wallace to the very threshold of the same discovery; but in Mr. Wallace's mind the theory had by no means been wrought out to the same degree of completeness to which it had been wrought in the mind of Mr. Darwin. In the preface to his charming book on Natural Selection, Mr. Wallace, with rare modesty and candor, acknowledges that whatever value his speculations may have had, they have been utterly surpassed in richness and cogency of proof by those of Mr. Darwin. This is no doubt true, and Mr. Wallace has done such good work in further illustration of the theory that he can well afford to rest content with the second place in the first announcement of it.

The coincidence, however, between Mr. Wallace's conclusions and those of Mr. Darwin was very remarkable. But, after all, coincidences of this sort have not been uncommon in the history of scientific inquiry. Nor is it at all surprising that they should occur now and then, when we remember that a great and pregnant discovery must always be concerned with some question which many of the foremost minds in the world are busy thinking about. It was so with the discovery of the differential calculus, and again with the discovery of the planet Neptune. It was so with the interpretation of the Egyptian hieroglyphics, and with the establishment of the undulatory theory of light. It was so, to a considerable extent, with the introduction of the new chemistry, with the discovery of the mechanical equivalent of heat, and the whole doctrine of the correlation of forces. It was so with the invention of the electric telegraph and with the discovery of spectrum analysis. And it is not at all strange that it should have been so with the doctrine of the origin of species through natural selection.

He thinks these "coincidences" were apt to happen because the matters from which they sprang were matters which many of the foremost minds in the world were busy thinking about. But perhaps *one* man in each case did the telegraphing to the others. The aberrations which gave Leverrier the idea that there must be a planet of such and such mass and such and such orbit hidden from sight out yonder in the remote abysses of space were not new; they had been noticed by astronomers for generations. Then why should it happen to occur to three people, widely separated—Leverrier, Mrs. Somerville, and Adams—to suddenly go to worrying about those aberrations all at the same time, and set themselves to work to find out what caused them, and to measure and weigh an invisible planet, and calculate its orbit, and hunt it down and catch it?— a strange project which nobody but they had ever thought of before. If one astronomer had invented that odd and happy project fifty years before, don't you think he would have telegraphed it to several others without knowing it?

But now I come to a puzzler. How is it that *inanimate* objects are able to affect the mind? They seem to do that. However, I wish to throw in a parenthesis first—just a reference to a thing everybody is familiar with—the experience of receiving a clear and particular *answer* to your telegram before your telegram has reached the sender of the answer. That is a case where your telegram has gone straight from your brain to the man it was meant for, far outstripping the wire's slow electricity, and it is an exercise of mental telegraphy which is as common as dining. To return to the influence of inanimate things. In the cases of non-professional clairvoyance examined by the Psychical Society the clairvoyant has usually been blindfolded, then some object which has been touched or worn by a person is placed in his hand; the clairvoyant immediately describes that person, and goes on and gives a history of some event with which the text object has been connected. If the inanimate object is able to affect and inform the clairvoyant's mind, maybe it can do the same when it is working in the interest of mental telegraphy. Once a lady in the West wrote me that her son was coming to New York to remain three weeks, and would pay me a visit if invited, and she gave me his address. I mislaid the letter, and forgot all about the matter till the three weeks were about up. Then a sudden and fiery irruption of remorse burst up in my brain that illuminated all the region round about, and I sat down at once and wrote to the lady and asked for that lost address. But, upon reflection, I judged that the stirring up of my recollection had not been an accident, so I added a postscript to say, never mind, I should get a letter from her son before night. And I did get it; for the letter was already in the town, although not delivered yet. It had influenced me somehow. I have had so many experiences of this sort—a dozen of them at least—that I am nearly persuaded that inanimate objects do not confine their activities to helping the clairvoyant, but do every now and then give the mental telegraphist a lift.

The case of mental telegraphy which I am coming to now comes under I don't exactly know what head. I clipped it from one of our local papers six or eight years ago. I know the details to be right and true, for the story was told to me in the same form by one of the two persons concerned (a clergyman of Hartford) at the time that the curious thing happened:

A REMARKABLE COINCIDENCE.— Strange coincidences make the most interesting of stories and most curious of studies. Nobody can quite say how they come about, but everybody appreciates the fact when they do come, and it is seldom that any more complete and curious coincidence is recorded of minor importance than the following, which is absolutely true and occurred in this city.

At the time of the building of one of the finest residences of Hartford, which is still a very new house, a local firm supplied the wall-paper for certain rooms, contracting both to furnish and to put on the paper. It happened that they did not calculate the size of one room exactly right, and the paper of the design selected for it fell short just half a roll. They asked for delay enough to send on to the manufacturers for what was needed, and were told that there was no especial hurry. It happened that the manufacturers had none on hand, and had destroyed the blocks from which it was printed. They wrote that they had a full list of the dealers to whom they had sold that paper, and that they would write to each of these and get from some of them a roll. It might involve a delay of a couple of weeks, but they would surely get it.

In the course of time came a letter saying that, to their great surprise, they could not find a single roll. Such a thing was very unusual, but in this case it had so happened. Accordingly the local firm asked for further time, saying they would write to their own customers who had bought of that pattern, and would get the piece from them. But to their surprise, this effort also failed. A long time had now elapsed, and there was no use of delaying any longer. They had contracted to paper the room, and their only course was to take off that which was insufficient and put on some other of which there was enough to go around. Accordingly at length a man was sent out to remove the paper. He got his apparatus ready, and was about to begin to work, under the direction of the owner of the building, when the latter was for the moment called away. The house was large and very interesting, and so many people had rambled about it that finally admission had been refused by a sign at the door. On the occasion, however, when a gentleman had knocked and asked for leave to look about, the owner, being on the premises, had been sent for to reply to the request in person. That was the call that for the moment delayed the final preparations. The gentleman went to the door and admitted the stranger, saying he would show him about the house, but first must return for a moment to that room to finish his directions there, and he told the curious story about the paper as they went on. They entered the room together, and the first thing the stranger, who lived fifty miles away, said on looking about was, "Why, I have that very paper on a room in my house, and I have an extra roll of it laid away, which is at your service." In a few days the wall was papered according to the original contract. Had not the owner been at the house, the stranger would not have been admitted; had he called a day later, it would have been too late; had not the facts been almost accidentally told to him, he would probably have said nothing of the paper, and so on. The exact fitting of all the circumstances is something very remarkable, and makes one of those stories that seem hardly accidental in their nature.

Something that happened the other day brought my hoary MS. to mind, and that is how I came to dig it out from its dusty pigeonhole grave for publication. The thing that happened was a question. A lady asked: "Have you ever had a vision —when awake?" I was about to answer promptly, when the last two words of the question began to grow and spread and swell, and presently they attained to vast dimensions. She did not know that they were important; and I did not at first, but I soon saw that they were putting me on the track of the solution of a mystery which had perplexed me a good deal. You will see what I mean when I get down to it. Ever since the English Society for Psychical Research began its investigations of ghost stories, haunted houses, and apparitions of the living and the dead, I have read their pamphlets with avidity as fast as they arrived. Now one of their commonest inquiries of a dreamer or a vision-seer is, "Are you sure you were awake at the time?" If the man can't say he is sure he was awake, a doubt falls upon his tale right there. But if he is positive he was awake, and offers reasonable evidence to substantiate it, the fact counts largely for the credibility of his story. It does with the society, and it did with me until that lady asked me the above question the other day.

The question set me to considering, and brought me to the conclusion that you can be asleep—at least, wholly unconscious—for a time, and not suspect that it has happened, and not have any way to prove that it *has* happened. A memorable case was in my mind. About a year ago I was standing on the porch one day, when I saw a man coming up the walk. He was a stranger, and I hoped he would ring and carry his business into the house without stopping to argue with me; he would have to pass the front door to get to me, and I hoped he wouldn't take the trouble; to help, I tried to look like a stranger myself—it often works. I was looking straight at that man; he had got to within ten feet of the door and within twenty-five feet of me—and suddenly he disappeared. It was as astounding as if a church should vanish from before your face and leave nothing behind it but a vacant lot. I was unspeakably delighted. I had seen an apparition at last, with my own eyes, in broad daylight. I made up my mind to write an account of it to the society. I ran to where the specter had been, to make sure he was playing fair, then I ran to the other end of the porch, scanning the open grounds as I went. No, everything was perfect; he couldn't have escaped without my seeing him; he was an apparition, without the slightest doubt, and I would write him up before he was cold. I ran, hot with excitement, and let myself in with a latch-key. When I stepped into the hall my lungs collapsed and my heart stood still. For there sat that same apparition in a chair all alone, and as quiet and reposeful as if he had come to stay a year! The shock kept me dumb for a moment or two then I said, "Did you come in at that door?"

"Yes."

"Did *you* open it, or did you ring?"

"I rang, and the colored man opened it."

I said to myself: "This is astonishing. It takes George all of two minutes to answer the door-bell when he is in a hurry, and I have never seen him in a hurry. How *did* this man stand two minutes at that door, within five steps of me, and I did not see him?"

I should have gone to my grave puzzling over that riddle but for that lady's chance question last week: "Have you ever had a vision—when awake?" It stands explained now. During at least sixty seconds that day I was asleep, or at least totally unconscious, without suspecting it. In that interval the man came to my immediate vicinity, rang, stood there and waited, then entered and closed the door, and I did not see him and did not hear the door slam.

If he had slipped around the house in that interval and gone into the cellar—he had time enough—I should have written him up for the society, and magnified him, and gloated over him, and hurrahed about him, and thirty yoke of oxen could not have pulled the belief out of me that I was of the favored ones of the earth, and had seen a vision—while wide awake.

Now how are you to tell when you are awake? What are you to go by? People bite their fingers to find out. Why, you can do that in a dream.

MENTAL TELEGRAPHY AGAIN

I HAVE three or four curious incidents to tell about. They seem to come under the head of what I named "Mental Telegraphy" in a paper written seventeen years ago, and published long afterward.

Several years ago I made a campaign on the platform with Mr. George W. Cable. In Montreal we were honored with a reception. It began at two in the afternoon in a long drawing-room in the Windsor Hotel. Mr. Cable and I stood at one end of this room, and the ladies and gentlemen entered it at the other end, crossed it at that end, then came up the long left-hand side, shook hands with us, said a word or two, and passed on, in the usual way. My sight is of the telescopic sort, and I presently recognized a familiar face among the throng of strangers drifting in at the distant door, and I said to myself, with surprise and high gratification, "That is Mrs. R.; I had forgotten that she was a Canadian." She had been a great friend of mine in Carson City, Nevada, in the early days. I had not seen her or heard of her for twenty years; I had not been thinking about her; there was nothing to suggest her to me, nothing to bring her to my mind; in fact, to me she had long ago ceased to exist, and had disappeared from my consciousness. But I knew her instantly; and I saw her so clearly that I was able to note some of the particulars of her dress, and did note them, and they remained in my mind. I was impatient for her to come. In t ic midst of the handshakings I snatched glimpses of her and noted her progress with the slow-moving ile across the end of the room; then I saw her start ip the side, and this gave me a full front view of her face. I saw her last when she was within twenty-five feet of me. For an hour I kept thinking she must still be in the room somewhere and would come at last, but I was disappointed.

When I arrived in the lecture-hall that evening some one said: "Come into the waiting-room; there's a friend of yours there who wants to see you. You'll not be introduced—you are to do the recognizing without help if you can."

I said to myself: "It is Mrs. R.; I sha'n't have any trouble."

There were perhaps ten ladies present, all seated. In the midst of them was Mrs. R., as I had expected. She was dressed exactly as she was when I had seen her in the afternoon. I went forward and shook hands with her and called her by name, and said:

"I knew you the moment you appeared at the reception this afternoon."

She looked surprised, and said: "But I was not at the reception. I have just arrived from Quebec, and have not been in town an hour."

It was my turn to be surprised now. I said:
"I can't help it. I give you my word of honor that
it is as I say. I saw you at the reception, and you
were dressed precisely as you are now. When they
told me a moment ago that I should find a friend in
this room, your image rose before me, dress and all,
just as I had seen you at the reception."

Those are the facts. She was not at the reception
at all, or anywhere near it; but I saw her there nevertheless, and most clearly and unmistakably. To that
I could make oath. How is one to explain this? I
was not thinking of her at the time; had not thought
of her for years. But she had been thinking of me,
no doubt; did her thoughts flit through leagues of
air to me, and bring with it that clear and pleasant
vision of herself? I think so. That was and remains
my sole experience in the matter of apparitions—I
mean apparitions that come when one is (ostensibly)
awake. I could have been asleep for a moment;
the apparition could have been the creature of a
dream. Still, that is nothing to the point; the
feature of interest is the happening of the thing
just at that time, instead of at an earlier or later
time, which is argument that its origin lay in
thought-transference.

My next incident will be set aside by most persons
as being merely a "coincidence," I suppose. Years
ago I used to think sometimes of making a lecturing
trip through the antipodes and the borders of the
Orient, but always gave up the idea, partly because
of the great length of the journey and partly because
my wife could not well manage to go with me.

Toward the end of last January that idea, after an interval of years, came suddenly into my head again —forcefully, too, and without any apparent reason. Whence came it? What suggested it? I will touch upon that presently.

I was at that time where I am now—in Paris. I wrote at once to Henry M. Stanley (London), and asked him some questions about his Australian lecture tour, and inquired who had conducted him and what were the terms. After a day or two his answer came. It began:

> The lecture agent for Australia and New Zealand is *par excellence* Mr. R. S. Smythe, of Melbourne.

He added his itinerary, terms, sea expenses, and some other matters, and advised me to write Mr. Smythe, which I did—February 3d. I began my letter by saying in substance that, while he did not know me personally, we had a mutual friend in Stanley, and that would answer for an introduction. Then I proposed my trip, and asked if he would give me the same terms which he had given Stanley.

I mailed my letter to Mr. Smythe February 6th, and three days later I got a letter from the selfsame Smythe, dated Melbourne, December 17th. I would as soon have expected to get a letter from the late George Washington. The letter began somewhat as mine to him had begun—with a self-introduction:

> DEAR MR. CLEMENS.—It is so long since Archibald Forbes and I spent that pleasant afternoon in your comfortable house at Hartford that you have probably quite forgotten the occasion.

In the course of his letter this occurs:

I am willing to give you [here he named the terms which he had given Stanley] for an antipodean tour to last, say, three months.

Here was the single essential detail of my letter answered three days after I had mailed my inquiry. I might have saved myself the trouble and the postage—and a few years ago I would have done that very thing, for I would have argued that my sudden and strong impulse to write and ask some questions of a stranger on the under side of the globe meant that the impulse came from that stranger, and that he would answer my questions of his own motion if I would let him alone.

Mr. Smythe's letter probably passed under my nose on its way to lose three weeks traveling to America and back, and gave me a whiff of its contents as it went along. Letters often act like that. Instead of the *thought* coming to you in an instant from Australia, the (apparently) unsentient letter imparts it to you as it glides invisibly past your elbow in the mail-bag.

Next incident. In the following month—March —I was in America. I spent a Sunday at Irvington-on-the-Hudson with Mr. John Brisben Walker, of the *Cosmopolitan* magazine. We came into New York next morning, and went to the Century Club for luncheon. He said some praiseful things about the character of the club and the orderly serenity and pleasantness of its quarters, and asked if I had never tried to acquire membership in it. I said I had not, and that New York clubs were a continuous expense to the country members without being of frequent use or benefit to them.

"And now I've got an idea'" said I. "There's the Lotos—the first New York club I was ever a member of—my very earliest love in that line. I have been a member of it for considerably more than twenty years, yet have seldom had a chance to look in and see the boys. They turn gray and grow old while I am not watching. And *my dues go on.* I am going to Hartford this afternoon for a day or two, but as soon as I get back I will go to John Elderkin very privately and say: 'Remember the veteran and confer distinction upon him, for the sake of old times. Make me an honorary member and abolish the tax. If you haven't any such thing as honorary membership, all the better—create it for my honor and glory.' That would be a great thing; I will go to John Elderkin as soon as I get back from Hartford."

I took the last express that afternoon, first telegraphing Mr. F. G. Whitmore to come and see me next day. When he came he asked:

"Did you get a letter from Mr. John Elderkin, secretary of the Lotos Club, before you left New York?"

"No."

"Then it just missed you. If I had known you were coming I would have kept it. It is beautiful, and will make you proud. The Board of Directors, by unanimous vote, have made your a life member, and *squelched those dues;* and you are to be on hand

and receive your distinction on the night of the 30th, which is the twenty-fifth anniversary of the founding of the club, and it will not surprise me if they have some great times there."

What put the honorary membership in my head that day in the Century Club? for I had never thought of it before. I don't know what brought the thought to me at *that* particular time instead of earlier, but I am well satisfied that it originated with the Board of Directors, and had been on its way to my brain through the air ever since the moment that saw their vote recorded.

Another incident. I was in Hartford two or three days as a guest of the Rev. Joseph H. Twichell. I have held the rank of Honorary Uncle to his children for a quarter of a century, and I went out with him in the trollery-car to visit one of my nieces, who is at Miss Porter's famous school in Farmington. The distance is eight or nine miles. On the way, talking, I illustrated something with an anecdote. This is the anecdote:

Two years and a half ago I and the family arrived at Milan on our way to Rome, and stopped at the Continental. After dinner I went below and took a seat in the stone-paved court, where the customary lemon trees stand in the customary tubs, and said to myself, "Now *this* is comfort, comfort and repose, and nobody to disturb it; I do not know anybody in Milan."

Then a young gentleman stepped up and shook hands, which damaged my theory. He said, in substance:

"You won't remember me, Mr. Clemens, but I remember you very well. I was a cadet at West Point when you and Rev. Joseph H. Twichell came there some years ago and talked to us on a Hundredth Night. I am a lieutenant in the regular army now, and my name is H. I am in Europe, all alone, for a modest little tour, my regiment is in Arizona."

We became friendly and sociable, and in the course of the talk he told me of an adventure which had befallen him—about to this effect:

"I was at Bellagio, stopping at the big hotel there, and ten days ago I lost my letter of credit. I did not know what in the world to do. I was a stranger; I knew no one in Europe; I hadn't a penny in my pocket; I couldn't even send a telegram to London to get my lost letter replaced; my hotel bill was a week old, and the presentation of it imminent—so imminent that it could happen at any moment now. I was so frightened that my wits seemed to leave me. I tramped and tramped, back and forth, like a crazy person. If anybody approached me I hurried away, for no matter what a person looked like, I took him for the head waiter with the bill.

"I was at last in such a desperate state that I was ready to do any wild thing that promised even the shadow of help, and so this is the insane thing that I did. I saw a family lunching at a small table on the veranda, and recognized their nationality—Americans—father, mother, and several young daughters—young, tastefully dressed, and pretty—the rule with our people. I went straight there in my civilian costume, named my name, said I was a lieutenant in the army, and told my story and asked for help.

"What do you suppose the gentleman did? But you would not guess in twenty years. He took out a handful of go d coin and told me to help myself—freely. That is what he did."

The next morning the lieutenant told me his new letter of credit had arrived in the night, so we strolled to Cook's to draw money to pay back the benefactor with. We got it, and then went strolling through the great arcade. Presently he said, "Yonder they are; come and be introduced." I was introduced to the parents and the young ladies; then we separated, and I never saw him or them any m—

"Here we are at Farmington," said Twichell, interrupting.

We left the trolley-car and tramped through the mud a hundred yards or so to the school, talking about the time we and Warner walked out there years ago, and the pleasant time we had.

We had a visit with my niece in the parlor, then started for the trolley again. Outside the house we encountered a double rank of twenty or thirty of Miss Porter's young ladies arriving from a walk, and we stood aside, ostensibly to let them have room to file past, but really to look at them. Presently one of them stepped out of the rank and said:

"You don't know me, Mr. Twichell, but I know your daughter and that gives me the privilege of shaking hands with you."

Then she put out her hand to me, and said:

MENTAL TELEGRAPHY AGAIN

"And I wish to shake hands with you too, Mr. Clemens. You don't remember me, but you were introduced to me in the arcade in Milan two years and a half ago by Lieutenant H."

What had put that story in o my head after all that stretch of time? Was it ust the proximity of that young girl, or was it merely an odd accident?

WHAT PAUL BOURGET THINKS
OF US

HE reports the American joke correctly. In Boston they ask, How much does he know? in New York, How much is he worth? in Philadelphia, Who were his parents? And when an alien observer turns his telescope upon us—advertisedly in our own special interest—a natural apprehension moves us to ask, What is the diameter of his reflector?

I take a great interest in M. Bourget's chapters, tor I know by the newspapers that there are several Americans who are expecting to get a whole education out of them; several who foresaw, and also foretold, that our long night was over, and a light almost divine about to break upon the land.

His utterances concerning us are bound to be weighty and well timed.
He gives us an object-lesson which should be thoughtfully and profitably studied.

These well-considered and important verdicts were of a nature to restore public confidence, which had been disquieted by questionings as to whether so young a teacher would be qualified to take so large a class as seventy million, distributed over so extensive a school-house as America, and pull it through without assistance.

I was even disquieted myself, although I am of a cold, calm temperament, and not easily disturbed. I feared for my country. And I was not wholly tranquilized by the verdicts rendered as above. It seemed to me that there was still room for doubt. In fact, in looking the ground over I became more disturbed than I was before. Many worrying questions came up in my mind. Two were prominent. Where had the teacher gotten his equipment? What was his method?

He had gotten his equipment in France.

Then as to his method! I saw by his own intimations that he was an Observer, and had a System —that used by naturalists and other scientists. The naturalist collects many bugs and reptiles and butterflies and studies their ways a long time patiently. By this means he is presently able to group these creatures into families and subdivisions of families by nice shadings of differences observable in their characters. Then he labels all those shaded bugs and things with nicely descriptive group names, and is now happy, for his great work is completed, and as a result he intimately knows every bug and shade of a bug there, inside and out. It may be true, but a person who was not a naturalist would feel safer about it if he had the opinion of the bug. I think it is a pleasant System, but subject to error.

The Observer of Peoples has to be a Classifier, a Grouper, a Deducer, a Generalizer, a Psychologizer; and, first and last, a Thinker. He has to be all these, and when he is at home, observing his own folk, he is often able to prove competency. But history has shown that when he is abroad observing unfamiliar peoples the chances are heavily against him. He is then a naturalist observing a bug, with no more than a naturalist's chance of being able to tell the bug anything new about itself, and no more than a naturalist's chance of being able to teach it any new ways which it will prefer to its own.

To return to that first question. M. Bourget, as teacher, would simply be France teaching America. It seemed to me that the outlook was dark—almost Egyptian, in fact. What would the new teacher, representing France, teach us? Railroading? No. France knows nothing valuable about railroading. Steamshipping? No. France has no superiorities over us in that matter. Steamboating? No. French steamboating is still of Fulton's date—1809. Postal service? No. France is a back number there. Telegraphy? No, we taught her that ourselves. Journalism? No. Magazining? No, that is our own specialty. Government? No; Liberty, Equality, Fraternity, Nobility, Democracy, Adultery—the system is too variegated for our climate. Religion? No, not variegated enough for our climate. Morals? No, we cannot rob the poor to enrich ourselves. Novel-writing? No. M. Bourget and the others know only one plan, and when that is expurgated there is nothing left of the book.

I wish I could think what he is going to teach us. Can it be Deportment? But he experimented in that at Newport and failed to give satisfaction, except to a few. Those few are pleased. They are enjoying their joy as well as they can. They confess their happiness to the interviewer. They feel pretty striped, but they remember with reverent recognition that they had sugar between the cuts. True, sugar with sand in it, but sugar. And true, they had some trouble to tell which was sugar and which was sand, because the sugar itself looked just like the sand, and also had a gravelly taste; still, they knew that the sugar was there, and would have been very good sugar indeed if t had been screened. Yes, they are pleased; not noisily so, but pleased; invaded, or streaked, as one may say, with little recurrent shivers of joy—subdued joy, so to speak, not the overdone kind. And they commune together, these, and massage each other with comforting sayings, in a sweet spirit of resignation and thankfulness, mixing these elements in the same proportions as the sugar and the sand, as a memorial, and saying, the one to the other, and to the interviewer: "It was severe—yes, it was bitterly severe; but oh, how true it was; and it will do us so much good!"

If it isn't Deportment, what is left? It was at this point that I seemed to get on the right track at last. M. Bourget would teach us to know ourselves; that was it: he would reveal us to ourselves. That would be an education. He would explain us to ourselves. Then we should understand ourselves; and after that be able to go on more intelligently.

It seemed a doubtful scheme. He could explain *us* to *him*self—that would be easy. That would be the same as the naturalist explaining the bug to himself. But to explain the bug to the bug—that is quite a different matter. The bug may not know himself perfectly, but he knows himself better than the naturalist can know him, at any rate.

A foreigner can photograph the exteriors of a nation, but I think that that is as far as he can get. I think that no foreigner can report its interior—its soul, its life, its speech, its thought. I think that a knowledge of these things is acquirable in only one way—not two or four or six—*absorption;* years and years of unconscious absorption; years and years of intercourse with the life concerned; of living it, indeed; sharing personally in its shames and prides, its joys and griefs, its loves and hates, its prosperities and reverses, its shows and shabbinesses, its deep patriotisms, its whirlwinds of political passion, its adorations—of flag, and heroic dead, and the glory of the national name. Observation? Of what real value is it? One learns peoples through the heart, not the eyes or the intellect.

There is only one expert who is qualified to examine the souls and the life of a people and make a valuable report—the native novelist. This expert is so rare that the most populous country can never have fifteen conspicuously and confessedly competent ones in stock at one time. This native specialist is not qualified to begin work until he has been absorbing during twenty-five years. How much of his competency is derived from conscious "observation"? The amount is so slight that it counts for next to nothing in the equipment. Almost the whole capital of the novelist is the slow accumulation of *un*conscious observation—absorption. The native expert's intentional observation of manners, speech, character, and ways of life can have value, for the native knows what they mean without having to cipher out the meaning. But I should be astonished to see a foreigner get at the right meanings, catch the elusive shades of these subtle things. Even the native novelist becomes a foreigner, with a foreigner's limitations, when he steps from the state whose life is familiar to h m into a state whose life he has not lived. Bret Harte got his California and his Californians by unconscious absorption, and put both of them into his tales alive. But when he came from the Pacific to the Atlantic and tried to do Newport life from study—conscious observation —his failure was absolutely monumental. Newport is a disastrous place for the unacclimated observer, evidently.

To return to novel-building. Does the native novelist try to generalize the nation? No, he lays plainly before you the ways and speech and life of a few people grouped in a certain place—his own place—and that is one book. In time he and his brethren will report to you the life and the people of the whole nation—the life of a group in a New England village; in a New York village; in a Texan village; in an Oregon village; in villages in fifty states and territories; then the farm-life in fifty states and territories; a hundred patches of life and groups of people in a dozen widely separated cities. And the Indians will be attended to; and the cowboys; and the gold and silver miners; and the negroes; and the Idiots and Congressmen; and the Irish, the

Germans, the Italians, the Swedes, the French, the Chinamen, ' the Greasers; and the Catholics, the Methodists, the Presbyterians, the Congregationalists, the Baptists, the Spiritualists, the Mormons, the Shakers, the Quakers, the Jews, the Campbellites, the infidels, the Christian Scientists, the Mind-Curists, the Faith-Curists, the train-robbers, the White Caps, the Moonshiners. And when a thousand able novels have been written, *there* you have the soul of the people, the life of the people, the speech of the people; and not anywhere else can these be had. And the shadings of character, manners, feelings, ambitions, will be infinite.

The nature of a people is always of a similar shade in its vices and its virtues, in its frivolities and in its labor. *It is this physiognomy which it is necessary to discover*, and every document is good, from the hall of a casino to the church, from the foibles of a fashionable woman to the suggestions of a revolutionary leader. I am therefore quite sure that this *American soul*, the principal interest and the great object of my voyage, appears behind the records of Newport for those who choose to see it.—*M. Paul Bourget.*

[The italics are mine.] It is a large contract which he has undertaken. "Records" is a pretty poor word there, but I think the use of it is due to hasty translation. In the original the word is *fastes.* I think M. Bourget meant to suggest that he expected to find the great "American soul" secreted behind the *ostentations* of Newport; and that he was going to get it out and examine it, and generalize it, and psychologize it, and make it reveal to him its hidden vast mystery: "the nature of the people" of the United States of America. We have been accused of being a nation addicted to inventing wild schemes. I trust that we shall be allowed to retire to second place now.

There isn't a single human characteristic that can be safely labeled "American." There isn't a single human ambition, or religious trend, or drift of thought, or peculiarity of education, or code of principles, or breed of folly, or style of conversation, or preference for a particular subject for discussion, or form of legs or trunk or head or face or expression or complexion, or gait, or dress, or manners, or disposition, or any other human detail, inside or outside, that can rationally be generalized as "American."

Whenever you have found what seems to be an "American" peculiarity, you have only to cross a frontier or two, or go down or up in the social scale, and you perceive that it has disappeared. And you can cross the Atlantic and find it again. There may be a Newport religious drift, or sporting drift, or conversational style or complexion, or cut of face, but there are entire empires in America, north, south, east, and west, where you could not find your duplicates. It is the same with everything else which one might propose to call "American." M. Bourget thinks he has found the American Coquette. If he had really found her he would also have found, I am sure, that she was not new, that she exists in other lands in the same forms, and with the same frivolous heart and the same ways and impulses. I think this because I have seen our coquette; I have seen her in life; better still, I have seen her in our novels, and seen her twin in foreign novels. I wish M. Bourget had seen ours. He thought he saw her. And so he applied his System to her. She was a Species. So he gathered a number of samples of what seemed to be her, and put them under his glass, and divided them into groups which he calls "types," and labeled them in his usual scientific way with "formulas"—brief, sharp descriptive flashes that make a person blink, sometimes, they are so sudden and vivid. As a rule they are pretty far-fetched, but that is not an important matter; they surprise, they compel admiration, and I notice by some of the comments which his efforts have called forth that they deceive the unwary. Here are a few of the coquette variants which he has grouped and labeled:

THE COLLECTOR.

THE EQUILIBREE.

THE PROFESSIONAL BEAUTY.

THE BLUFFER.

THE GIRL-BOY.

If he had stopped with describing these characters we should have been obliged to believe that they exist; that they exist, and that he has seen them and spoken with them. But he did not stop there; he went further and furnished to us light-throwing samples of their behavior, and also light-throwing samples of their speeches. He entered those things in his note-book without suspicion, he takes them out and delivers them to the world with a candor and simplicity which show that he believed them

genuine. They throw altogether too much light.
They reveal to the native the origin of his find. I
suppose he knows how he came to make that novel
and captivating discovery, by this time. If he does
not, any American can tell him—any American
to whom he will show his anecdotes. It was "put
up" on him, as we say. It was a jest—to be plain,
it was a series of frauds. To my mind it was a poor
sort of jest, witless and contemptible. The players
of it have their reward, such as it is; they have
exhibited the fact that whatever they may be they
are not ladies. M. Bourget did not discover a type
of coquette; he merely discovered a type of practical joker. One may say *the* type of practical
joker, for these people are exactly alike all over the
world. Their equipment is always the same: a
vulgar mind, a puerile wit, a cruel disposition as a
rule, and always the spirit of treachery.

In his Chapter IV. M. Bourget has two or three
columns gravely devoted to the collating and examining and psychologizing of these sorry little
frauds. One is not moved to laugh. There is nothing
funny in the situation; it is only pathetic. The
stranger gave those people his confidence, and they
dishonorably treated him in return.

But one must be allowed to suspect that M.
Bourget was a little to blame himself. Even a
practical joker has some little judgment. He has
to exercise some degree of sagacity in selecting his
prey if he would save himself from getting into
trouble. In my time I have seldom seen such daring
things marketed at any price as these conscienceless

folk have worked off at par on this confiding observer. It compels the conviction that there was
something about him that bred in those speculators
a quite unusual sense of safety, and encouraged
them to strain their powers in his behalf. They
seem to have satisfied themselves that all he wanted
was "significant" facts, and that he was not accustomed to examine the source whence they proceeded. It is plain that there was a sort of conspiracy against him almost from the start — a
conspiracy to freight him up with all the strange
extravagances those people's decayed brains could
invent.

The lengths to which they went are next to
incredible. They told him things which surely would
have excited any one else's suspicion, but they did
not excite his. Consider this:

There is not in all the United States an entirely nude statue.

If an angel should come down and say such a
thing about heaven, a reasonably cautious observer
would take that angel's number and inquire a little
further before he added it to his catch. What does
the present observer do? Adds it. Adds it at once.
Adds it, and labels it with this innocent comment:

This small fact is strangely significant.

It does seem to me that this kind of observing is
defective.

Here is another curiosity which some liberal
person made him a present of. I should think it
ought to have disturbed the deep slumber of his

WHAT BOURGET THINKS OF US

suspicion a little, but it didn't. It was a note from a fog-horn for strenuousness, it seems to me, but the doomed voyager did not catch it. If he had but caught it, it would have saved him from several disasters:

If the American knows that you ar traveling to take notes, he is interested in it, and at the same time rejoices in it, as in a tribute.

Again, this is defective obser vation. It is human to like to be praised; one can even notice it in the French. But it is not human to like to be ridiculed, even when it comes in the form of a "tribute." I think a little psychologizing ought to have come in there. Something like this: A dog does not like to be ridiculed, a redskin does not like to be ridiculed, a negro does not like to be ridiculed, a Chinaman does not like to be ridiculed; let us deduce from these significant facts this formula: the American's grade being higher than these, and the chain of argument stretching unbroken all the way up to him, there is room for suspicion that the person who said the American likes to be ridiculed, and regards it as a tribute, is not a capable observer.

I feel persuaded that in the matter of psychologizing, a professional is too apt to yield to the fascinations of the loftier regions of that great art, to the neglect of its lowlier walks. Every now and then, at half-hour intervals, M. Bourget collects a hatful of airy inaccuracies and dissolves them in a panful of assorted abstractions, and runs the charge into a mold and turns you out a compact principle which will explain an American girl, or an Amer-

159

ican woman, or why new people yearn for old things, or any other impossible riddle which a person wants answered.

It seems to be conceded that there are a few human peculiarities that can be generalized and located here and there in the world and named by the name of the nation where they are found. I wonder what they are. Perhaps one of them is temperament. One speaks of French vivacity and German gravity and English stubbornness. There is no American temperament. The nearest that one can come at it is to say there are two—the composed Northern and the impetuous Southern; and both are found in other countries. Morals? Purity of women may fairly be called universal with us, but that is the case in some other countries. We have no monopoly of it; it cannot be named American. I think that there is but a single specialty with us, only one thing that can be called by the wide name "American." That is the national devotion to ice-water. All Germans drink beer, but the British nation drinks beer, too; so neither of those peoples is *the* beer-drinking nation. I suppose we do stand alone in having a drink that nobody likes but ourselves. When we have been a month in Europe we lose our craving for it, and we finally tell the hotel folk that they needn't provide it any more. Yet we hardly touch our native shore again, winter or summer, before we are eager for it. The reasons for this state of things have not been psychologized yet. I drop the hint and say no more.

It is my belief that there are some "national"

traits and things scattered about the world that are
mere superstitions, frauds that have lived so long
that they have the solid look of facts. One of them
is the dogma that the French are the only chaste
people in the world. Ever since I arrived in France
this last time I have been accumulating doubts about
that; and before I leave this sunny land again I will
gather in a few random statistics and psychologize
the plausibilities out of it. If people are to come
over to America and find fault with our girls and
our women, and psychologize every little thing they
do, and try to teach them how to behave, and how
to cultivate themselves up to where one cannot tell
them from the French model, I intend to find out
whether those missionaries are qualified or not. A
nation ought always to examine into this detail
before engaging the teacher for good. This last one
has let fall a remark which renewed those doubts of
mine when I read it:

> In our high Parisian existence, for instance, we find applied
> to arts and luxury, and to debauchery, all the powers and all
> the weaknesses of the French soul.

You see, it amounts to a trade with the French
soul; a profession; a science; the serious business of
life, so to speak, in our high Parisian existence. I
do not quite like the look of it. I question if it can
be taught with profit in our country, except, of
course, to those pathetic, neglected minds that are
waiting there so yearningly for the education which
M. Bourget is going to furnish them from the serene
summits of our high Parisian life.

I spoke a moment ago of the existence of some superstitions that have been parading the world as facts this long time. For instance, consider the Dollar. The world seems to think that the love of money is "American"; and that the mad desire to get suddenly rich is "American." I believe that both of these things are merely and broadly human, not American monopolies at all. The love of money is natural to all nations, for money is a good and strong friend. I think that this love has existed everywhere, ever since the Bible called it the root of all evil.

I think that the reason why we Americans seem to be so addicted to trying to get rich suddenly is merely because the *opportunity* to make promising efforts in that direction has offered itself to us with a frequency out of all proportion to the European experience. For eighty years this opportunity has been offering itself in one new town or region after another straight westward, step by step, all the way from the Atlantic coast to the Pacific. When a mechanic could buy ten town lots on tolerably long credit for ten months' savings out of his wages, and reasonably expect to sell them in a couple of years for ten times what he gave for them, it was human for him to try the venture, and he did it no matter what his nationality was. He would have done it in Europe or China if he had had the same chance.

In the flush times in the silver regions a cook or any other humble worker stood a very good chance to get rich out of a trifle of money risked in a stock deal; and that person promptly took that risk, no matter what his or her nationality might be. I was there, and saw it.

But these opportunities have not been plenty in our Southern states; so there you have a prodigious region where the rush for sudden wealth is almost an unknown thing—and has been, rom the beginning.

Europe has offered few opp rtunities for poor Tom, Dick, and Harry; but w en she has offered one, there has been no noticeabl difference between European eagerness and Ameri an. England saw this in the wild days of the Railroad King; France saw it in 1720—time of Law and the Mississippi Bubble. I am sure I have never seen in the gold and silver mines any madness, fury, frenzy to get suddenly rich which was even remotely comparable to that which raged in France in the Bubble day. If I had a cyclopedia here I could turn to that memorable case, and satisfy nearly anybody that the hunger for the sudden dollar is no more "American" than it is French. And if I could furnish an American opportunity to staid Germany, I think I could wake her up like a house afire.

But I must return to the Generalizations, Psychologizings, Deductions. When M. Bourget is exploiting these arts, it is then that he is peculiarly and particularly himself. His ways are wholly original when he encounters a trait or a custom which is new to him. Another person would merely examine the find, verify it, estimate its value, and let it go; but that is not sufficient for M. Bourget: he always wants to know *why* that thing exists, he wants to know how it came to happen; and he will not let go of it until he has found out. And in every instance he will find that reason where no one but himself would have thought of looking for it. He does not seem to care for a reason that is not picturesquely located; one might almost say picturesquely and impossibly located.

He found out that in America men do not try to hunt down young married women. At once, as usual, he wanted to know *why*. Any one could have told him. He could have divined it by the lights thrown by the novels of the country. But no, he preferred to find out for himself. He has a trustfulness as regards men and facts which is fine and unusual; he is not particular about the source of a fact, he is not particular about the character and standing of the fact itself; but when it comes to pounding out the reason for the existence of the fact, he will trust no one but himself.

In the present instance here was his fact: American young married women are not pursued by the corrupter; and here was the question: What is it that protects her?

It seems quite unlikely that that problem could have offered difficulties to any but a trained philosopher. Nearly any person would have said to M. Bourget: "Oh, that is very simple. It is very seldom in America that a marriage is made on a commercial basis; our marriages, from the beginning, have been made for love; and where love is there is no room for the corrupter."

Now, it is interesting to see the formidable way in which M. Bourget went at that poor, humble little thing. He moved upon it in column—three columns—and with artillery.

"Two reasons of a very different kind explain"—that fact.

And now that I have got so far, I am almost afraid to say what his two reasons are, lest I be charged with inventing them. But I will not retreat now; I will condense them and print them, giving my word that I am honest and not trying to deceive any one.

1. Young married women are protected from the approaches of the seducer in New England and vicinity by the diluted remains of a prudence created by a Puritan law of two hundred years ago, which for a while punished adultery with death.

2. And young married women of the other forty or fifty states are protected by laws which afford extraordinary facilities for divorce.

If I have not lost my mind I have accurately conveyed those two Vesuvian irruptions of philosophy. But the reader can consult Chapter IV. of *Outre-Mer*, and decide for himself. Let us examine this paralyzing Deduction or Explanation by the light of a few sane facts.

1. This universality of "protection" has existed in our country *from the beginning;* before the death-penalty existed in New England, and during all the generations that have dragged by since it was annulled.

2. Extraordinary facilities for divorce are of such recent creation that any middle-aged American can remember a time when such things had not yet been thought of.

Let us suppose that the first easy divorce law went

into effect forty years ago, and got noised around and fairly started in business thirty-five years ago, when we had, say, 25,000,000 of white population. Let us suppose that among 5,000,000 of them the young married women were "protected" by the surviving shudder of that ancient Puritan scare—what is M. Bourget going to do about those who lived among the 20,000,000? They were clean in their morals, they were pure, yet there was no easy divorce law to protect them.

Awhile ago I said that M. Bourget's method of truth-seeking—hunting for it in out-of-the-way places—was new; but that was an error. I remember that when Leverrier discovered the Milky Way, he and the other astronomers began to theorize about it in substantially the same fashion which M. Bourget employs in his reasonings about American social facts and their origin. Leverrier advanced the hypothesis that the Milky Way was caused by gaseous protoplasmic emanations from the field of Waterloo, which, ascending to an altitude determinable by their own specific gravity, became luminous through the development and exposure—by the natural processes of animal decay—of the phosphorus contained in them.

This theory was warmly complimented by Ptolemy, who, however, after much thought and research, decided that he could not accept it as final. His own theory was that the Milky Way was an emigration of lightning-bugs; and he supported and reinforced this theorem by the well-known fact that the locusts do like that in Egypt.

WHAT BOURGET THINKS OF US

Giordano Bruno also was outspoken in his praises of Leverrier's important contribution to astronomical science, and was at first inclined to regard it as conclusive; but later, conceiving it to be erroneous, he pronounced against it, and advanced the hypothesis that the Milky Way was a detachment or corps of stars which became arrested and held in *suspenso suspensorum* by refraction of gravitation while on the march to join their several constellations; a proposition for which he was afterward burned at the stake in Jacksonville, Illinois.

These were all brilliant and picturesque theories, and each was received with enthusiasm by the scientific world; but when a New England farmer, who was not a thinker, but only a plain sort of person who tried to account for large facts in simple ways, came out with the opinion that the Milky Way was just common, ordinary stars, and was put where it was because God "wanted to hev it so," the admirable idea fell perfectly flat.

As a literary artist, M. Bourget is as fresh and striking as he is as a scientific one. He says, "Above all, I do not believe much in anecdotes." Why? "In history they are all false"—a sufficiently broad statement—"in literature all libelous"—also a sufficiently sweeping statement, coming from a critic who notes that we are a people who are peculiarly extravagant in our language—"and when it is a matter of social life, almost all biased." It seems to amount to stultification, almost. He has built two or three breeds of American coquettes out of anecdotes—mainly "biased" ones, I suppose; and,

167

as they occur "in literature," furnished by his pen,
they must be "all libelous." Or did he mean not
in literature or anecdotes *about* literature or literary people? I am not able to answer that. Perhaps
the original would be clearer, but I have only the
translation of this instalment by me. I think the
remark had an intention; also that this intention
was booked for the trip; but that either in the hurry
of the remark's departure it got left, or in the confusion of changing cars at the translator's frontier it
got side-tracked.

"But on the other hand I believe in statistics;
and those on divorces appear to me to be most conclusive." And he sets himself the task of explaining—in a couple of columns—the process by which
Easy-Divorce conceived, invented, originated, developed, and perfected an empire-embracing condition
of sexual purity in the States. *In forty years.* No,
he doesn't state the interval. With all his passion
for statistics he forgot to ask how long it took to
produce this gigantic miracle.

I have followed his pleasant but devious trail
through those columns, but I was not able to get
hold of his argument and find out what it was. I
was not even able to find out where it left off. It
seemed to gradually dissolve and flow off into other
matters. I followed it with interest, for I was
anxious to learn how easy-divorce eradicated adultery in America, but I was disappointed; I have no
idea yet how it did it. I only know it didn't. But
that is not valuable; I knew it before.

Well, humor is the great thing, the saving thing,

after all. The minute it crops up, all our hardnesses yield, all our irritations and resentments flit away, and a sunny spirit takes their place. And so, when M. Bourget said that bright th ng about our grandfathers, I broke all up. I ren ember exploding its American countermine once, ur der that grand hero, Napoleon. He was only First Consul then, and I was Consul-General—for the United States, of course; but we were very intim ate, notwithstanding the difference in rank, for I waived that. One day something offered the opening, and he said:

"Well, General, I suppose life can never get entirely dull to an American, because whenever he can't strike up any other way to put in his time he can always get away with a few years trying to find out who his grandfather was!"

I fairly shouted, for I had never heard it sound better; and then I was back at him as quick as a flash:

"Right, your Excellency! But I reckon a Frenchman's got *his* little stand-by for a dull time, too; because when all other interests fail he can turn in and see if he can't find out who his father was!"

Well, you should have heard him just whoop, and cackle, and carry on! He reached up and hit me one on the shoulder, and says:

"Land, but it's good! It's im-mensely good! I'George, I never heard it said so good in my life before! Say it again."

So I said it again, and he said his again, and I said mine again, and then he did, and then I did, and then he did, and we kept on doing it, and doing

it, and I *never* had such a good time, and he said the
same. In my opinion there isn't anything that is
as killing as one of those dear old ripe pensioners
if you know how to snatch it out in a kind of a
fresh sort of original way.

But I wish M. Bourget had read more of our
novels before he came. It is the only way to thoroughly understand a people. When I found I war-
coming to Paris, I read *La Terre*.

A LITTLE NOTE TO M. PAUL BOURGET

[The preceding squib was assailed in *The North American Review* in an article entitled "Mark Twain and Paul Bourget," by Max O'Rell. The following little note is a Rejoinder to that article. It is possible that the position assumed here—that M. Bourget dictated the O'Rell article himself—is untenable.]

YOU have every right, my dear M. Bourget, to retort upon me by dictation, if you prefer that method to writing at me with your pen; but if I may say it without hurt—and certainly I mean no offense—I believe you would have acquitted yourself better with the pen. With the pen you are at home; it is your natural weapon; you use it with grace, eloquence, charm, persuasiveness, when men are to be convinced, and with formidable effect when they have earned a castigation. But I am sure I see signs in the above article that you are either unaccustomed to dictating or are out of practice. If you will reread it you will notice, yourself, that it lacks definiteness; that it lacks purpose; that it lacks coherence; that it lacks a subject to talk about; that it is loose and wabbly; that it wanders around; that it loses itself early and does not find itself any more. There are some other defects, as you will notice, but I think I have named the main ones. I feel sure that they are all due to your lack of practice in dictating.

Inasmuch as you had not signed it I had the impression at first that you had not dictated it. But only for a moment. Certain quite simple and definite facts reminded me that the article *had* to come from you, for the reason that it could not come from any one else without a specific invitation from you or from me. I mean, it could not except as an intrusion, a transgression of the law which forbids strangers to mix into a private dispute between friends, unasked.

Those simple and definite facts were these: I had published an article in this magazine, with you for my subject; just you yourself; I stuck strictly to that one subject, and did not interlard any other. No one, of course, could call me to account but you alone, or your authorized representative. I asked some questions—asked them of myself. I answered them myself. My article was thirteen pages long, and all devoted to you; devoted to you, and divided up in this way: one page of guesses as to what sub- jects you would instruct us in, as teacher; one page of doubts as to the effectiveness of your method of examining us and our ways; two or three pages of criticism of your method, and of certain results which it furnished you; two or three pages of at- tempts to show the justness of these same criticisms; half a dozen pages made up of slight fault-findings with certain minor details of your literary work- manship, of extracts from your *Outre-Mer* and com- ments upon them; then I closed with an anecdote. I repeat—for certain reasons—that *I closed with an anecdote.*

NOTE TO M. PAUL BOURGET

When I was asked by this magazine if I wished to "answer" a "reply" to that article of mine, I said "yes," and waited in Paris for the proof-sheets of the "reply" to come. I already knew, by the cablegram, that the "reply" would not be signed by you, but upon reflection I knew it would be dictated by you, because no volunteer would feel himself at liberty to assume your championship in a private dispute, unasked, in view of the fact that you are quite well able to take care of your matters of that sort yourself and are not in need of any one's help. No, a volunteer could not make such a venture. It would be too immodest. Also too gratuitously generous. And a shade too self-sufficient. No, he could not venture it. It would look too much like anxiety to get in at a feast where no plate had been provided for him. In fact he could not get in at all, except by the back way, and with a false key; that is to say, a pretext—a pretext invented for the occasion by putting into my mouth words which I did not use, and by wresting sayings of mine from their plain and true meaning. Would he resort to methods like those to get in? No; there are no people of that kind. So then I knew for a certainty that you dictated the Reply yourself. I knew you did it to save yourself manual labor.

And you had the right, as I have already said; and I am content—perfectly content. Yet it would have been little trouble to you, and a great kindness to me, if you had written your Reply all out with your own capable hand.

Because then it would have replied—and that is

really what a Reply is for. Broadly speaking, its function is to refute—as you will easily concede. That leaves something for the other person to take hold of: he has a chance to reply to the Reply, he has a chance to refute the refutation. This would have happened if you had written it out instead of dictating. Dictating is nearly sure to unconcentrate the dictator's mind, when he is out of practice, confuse him, and betray him into using one set of literary rules when he ought to use a quite different set. Often it betrays him into employing the RULES FOR CONVERSATION BETWEEN A SHOUTER AND A DEAF PERSON—as in the present case—when he ought to employ the RULES FOR CONDUCTING DISCUSSION WITH A FAULT-FINDER. The great foundation-rule and basic principle of discussion with a fault-finder is relevancy and concentration upon the subject; whereas the great foundation-rule and basic principle governing conversation between a shouter and a deaf person is irrelevancy and persistent desertion of the topic in hand. If I may be allowed to illustrate by quoting example IV., section 7, from chapter ix of "Revised Rules for Conducting Conversation between a Shouter and a Deaf Person," it will assist us in getting a clear idea of the difference between the two sets of rules:

Shouter. Did you say his name is WETHERBY?

Deaf Person. Change? Yes, I think it will. Though if it should clear off I—

Shouter. It's his NAME I want—his NAME.

Deaf Person. Maybe so, maybe so; but it will only be a shower, I think.

NOTE TO M. PAUL BOURGET

Shouter. No, no, *no!* — you have quite misunderSTOOD me. If—

Deaf Person. Ah! GOOD morning; I am sorry you must go. But call again, and let me continue to be of assistance to you in every way I can.

You see it is a perfect kodak of the article you have dictated. It is really curious and interesting when you come to compare it with yours; in detail, with my former article to which it is a Reply in your hand. I talk twelve pages about your American instruction projects, and your doubtful scientific system, and your painstaking classification of non-existent things, and your diligence and zeal and sincerity, and your disloyal attitude toward anecdotes, and your undue reverence for unsafe statistics and for facts that lack a pedigree; and you turn around and come back at me with eight pages of weather.

I do not see how a person can act so. It is good of you to repeat, with change of language, in the bulk of your rejoinder, so much of my own article, and adopt my sentiments, and make them over, and put new buttons on; and I like the compliment, and am frank to say so; but *agreeing* with a person cripples controversy and ought not to be allowed. It is weather; and of almost the worst sort. It pleases me greatly to hear you discourse with such approval and expansiveness upon my text:

"A foreigner can photograph the exteriors of a nation, but I think that is as far as he can get. I think that no foreigner can report its interior;"[1]

---

[1] And you say: "A man of average intelligence, who has passed six months among a people, cannot express opinions that are worth

which is a quite clear way of saying that a foreigner's report is only valuable when it restricts itself to *impressions*. It pleases me to have you follow my lead in that glowing way, but it leaves me nothing to combat. You should give me something to deny and refute; I would do as much for you.

It pleases me to have you playfully warn the public against taking one of your books seriously.[1] Because I used to do that cunning thing myself in earlier days. I did it in a prefatory note to a book of mine called *Tom Sawyer*.

NOTICE

Persons attempting to find a motive in this narrative will be prosecuted; persons attempting to find a moral in it will be banished; persons attempting to find a plot in it will be shot.

BY ORDER OF THE AUTHOR,

PER G. G., CHIEF OF ORDNANCE.

The kernel is the same in both prefaces, you see—the public must not take us too seriously. If we remove that kernel we remove the life-principle, and the preface is a corpse. Yes, it pleases me to have you use that idea, for it is a high compliment. But it leaves me nothing to combat; and that is damage to me.

jotting down, but he can form impressions that are worth repeating. For my part, I think that foreigners' impressions are more interesting than native opinions. After all, such impressions merely mean 'how the country *struck* the foreigner.'"

[1]When I published *Jonathan and His Continent*, I wrote in a preface addressed to Jonathan: "If ever you should insist on seeing in this little volume a serious study of your country and of your countrymen, I warn you that your world-wide fame for humor will be exploded."

NOTE TO M. PAUL BOURGET

Am I seeming to say that your Reply is not a reply at all, M. Bourget? If so, I must modify that; it is too sweeping. For you have furnished a general answer to my inquiry as to what France—through you—can teach us.[1] It is a good answer. It relates to manners, customs and morals—three things concerning which we can never have exhaustive and determinate statistics, and so the verdicts delivered upon them must always lack conclusiveness and be subject to revision; but you have stated the truth, possibly, as nearly as any one could do it, in the circumstances. But why did you choose a detail of my question which could be answered only with vague hearsay evidence, and go

---

[1] "What could France teach America?" exclaims Mark Twain. France can teach America all the higher pursuits of life, and there is more artistic feeling and refinement in a street of French workingmen than in many avenues inhabited by American millionaires. She can teach her, not perhaps how to work, but how to rest, how to live, how to be happy. She can teach her that the aim of life is not money-making, but that money-making is only a means to obtain an end. She can teach her that wives are not expensive toys, but useful partners, friends, and confidants, who should always keep men under their wholesome influence by their diplomacy, their tact, their common sense, without bumptiousness. These qualities, added to the highest standard of morality (not angular and morose, but cheerful morality), are conceded to Frenchwomen by whoever knows something of French life outside of the Paris boulevards, and Mark Twain's ill-natured sneer cannot even so much as stain them.
I might tell Mark Twain that in France a man who was seen tipsy in his club would immediately see his name canceled from membership. A man who had settled his fortune on his wife to avoid meeting his creditors would be refused admission into any decent society. Many a Frenchman has blown his brains out rather than declare himself a bankrupt. Now would Mark Twain remark to this: "An American is not such a fool: when a creditor stands in his way he closes his doors, and reopens them the following day. When he has been a bankrupt three times he can retire from business"?

right by one which could have been answered with deadly facts?—facts in everybody's reach, facts which none can dispute. I asked what France could teach us about government. I laid myself pretty wide open, there; and I thought I was handsomely generous, too, when I did it. France can teach us how to levy village and city taxes which distribute the burden with a nearer approach to perfect fairness than is the case in any other land; and she can teach us the wisest and surest system of collecting them that exists. She can teach us how to elect a President in a sane way; and also how to do it without throwing the country into earthquakes and convulsions that cripple and embarrass business, stir up party hatred in the hearts of men, and make peaceful people wish the term extended to thirty years. France can teach us—but enough of that part of the question. And what else can France teach us? She can teach us all the fine arts—and does. She throws open her hospitable art academies, and says to us, "Come"—and we come, troops and troops of our young and gifted; and she sets over us the ablest masters in the world and bearing the greatest names; and she teaches us all that we are capable of learning, and persuades us and encourages us with prizes and honors, much as if we were somehow children of her own; and when this noble education is finished and we are ready to carry it home and spread its gracious ministries abroad over our nation, and we come with homage and gratitude and ask France for the bill—*there is nothing to pay*. And in return for this imperial generosity, what does America do? She charges a duty on French works of art!

I wish I had your end of this dispute; I should have something worth talking about. If you would only furnish me something to argue, something to refute—but you persistently won't. You leave good chances unutilized and spend your strength in proving and establishing unimportant things. For instance, you have proven and established these eight facts here following—a good score as to number, but not worth while:

Mark Twain is—

1. "Insulting."

2. (Sarcastically speaking) "This refined humorist."

3. Prefers the manure-pile to the violets.

4. Has uttered "an ill-natured sneer."

5. Is "nasty."

6. Needs a "lesson in politeness and good manners."

7. Has published a "nasty article."

8. Has made remarks "unworthy of a gentleman." [1]   These are all true, but really they are not

---

[1] "It is more funny than his [Mark Twain's] anecdote, and would have been less insulting."

A quoted remark of mine "is a gross insult to a nation friendly to America."

"He has read *La Terre*, this refined humorist."

"When Mark Twain visits a garden . . . he goes in the far-away corner where the soil is prepared."

"Mark Twain's ill-natured sneer cannot so much as stain them" (the Frenchwomen).

"When he [Mark Twain] takes his revenge he is unkind, unfair, bitter, nasty."

valuable; no one cares much for such finds. In our American magazines we recognize this and suppress them. We avoid naming them. American writers never allow themselves to name them. It would look as if they were in a temper, and we hold that exhibitions of temper in public are not good form—except in the very young and inexperienced. And even if we had the disposition to name them, in order to fill up a gap when we were short of ideas and arguments, our magazines would not allow us to do it, because they think that such words sully their pages. This present magazine is particularly strenuous about it. Its note to me announcing the forwarding of your proof-sheets to France closed thus —for your protection:

"*It is needless to ask you to avoid anything that he might consider as personal.*"

It was well enough, as a measure of precaution, but really it was not needed. You can trust me implicitly, M. Bourget; I shall never call you any names in print which I should be ashamed to call you with your unoffending and dearest ones present.

Indeed, we are reserved, and particular in America to a degree which you would consider exaggerated. For instance, we should not write notes like that one of yours to a lady for a small fault—or a large one.[1] We should not think it kind. No matter

---

"But not even your nasty article on my country, Mark," etc.

"Mark might certainly have derived from it [M. Bourget's book] a lesson in politeness and good manners."

A quoted remark of mine is "unworthy of a gentleman."

[1] When M. Paul Bourget indulges in a little chaffing at the expense, of the Americans, "who can always get away with a few years'

how much we might have associated with kings and
nobilities, we should not think it right to crush her
with it and make her ashamed of her lowlier walk in

trying to find out who their grandfathers were,' he merely makes
an allusion to an American foible; but, forsooth, what a kind man,
what a humorist Mark Twain is when he retorts by calling France
a nation of bastards! How the American of culture and refinement
will admire him for thus speaking in their name!

Snobbery. . . . I could give Mark Twain an example of the
American specimen. It is a piquant story. I never published it
because I feared my readers might think that I was giving them
a typical illustration of American character instead of a rare ex-
ception.

I was once booked by my manager to give a *causerie* in the drawing-
room of a New York millionaire. I accepted with reluctance. I do
not like private engagements. At five o'clock on the day the
causerie was to be given, the lady sent to my manager to say that
she would expect me to arrive at nine o'clock and to speak for
about an hour. Then she wrote a postcript. Many women are
unfortunate there. Their minds are full of afterthoughts, and the
most important part of their letters is generally to be found after
their signature. This lady's P.S. ran thus: "I suppose he will not
expect to be entertained after the lecture."

I fairly shouted, as Mark Twain would say, and then, indulging
myself in a bit of snobbishness, I was back at her as quick as a
flash—

"Dear Madam: As a literary man of some reputation, I have
many times had the pleasure of being entertained by the members
of the old aristocracy of France. I have also many times had the
pleasure of being entertained by the members of the old aristocracy
of England. If it may interest you, I can even tell you that I have
several times had the honor of being entertained by royalty; but
my ambition has never been so wild as to expect that one day I
might be entertained by the aristocracy of New York. No, I do
not expect to be entertained by you, nor do I want you to expect me
to entertain you and your friends to-night, for I decline to keep the
engagement."

Now, I could fill a book on America with reminiscences of this
sort, adding a few chapters on bosses and boodlers, on New York
chronique scandaleuse, on the tenement houses of the large cities,
on the gambling-hells of Denver, and the dens of San Francisco, and
what not! But not even your nasty article on my country, Mark,
will make me do it.

life; for we have a saying, "Who humiliates my mother includes his own."

Do I seriously imagine you to be the author of that strange letter, M. Bourget? Indeed I do not. I believe it to have been surreptitiously inserted by your amanuensis when your back was turned. I think he did it with a good motive, expecting it to add force and piquancy to your article, but it does not reflect your nature, and I know it will grieve you when you see it. I also think he interlarded many other things which you will disapprove of when you see them. I am certain that all the harsh names discharged at me come from him, not you. No doubt you could have proved me entitled to them with as little trouble as it has cost him to do it, but it would have been your disposition to hunt game of a higher quality.

Why, I even doubt if it is you who furnish me all that excellent information about Balzac and those others.[1] All this in simple justice to you—and to

---

[1] "Now the style of M. Bourget and many other French writers is apparently a closed letter to Mark Twain; but let us leave that alone. Has he read Erckmann-Chatrian, Victor Hugo, Lamartine, Edmond About, Cherbuliez, Renan? Has he read Gustave Droz's *Monsieur, Madame, et Bébé*, and those books which leave for a long time a perfume about you? Has he read the novels of Alexandre Dumas, Eugène Sue, George Sand, and Balzac? Has he read Victor Hugo's *Les Misérables* and *Notre Dame de Paris*? Has he read or heard the plays of Sandeau, Augier, Dumas, and Sardou, the works of those Titans of modern literature, whose names will be household words all over the world for hundreds of years to come? He has read *La Terre*—this kind-hearted, refined humorist! When Mark Twain visits a garden does he smell the violets, the roses, the jasmine, or the honeysuckle? No, he goes in the far-away corner where the soil is prepared. Hear what he says: 'I wish M. Paul Bourget had

me; for, to gravely accept those interlardings as yours would be to wrong your head and heart, and at the same time convict myself of being equipped with a vacancy where my penetration ought to be lodged.

And now finally I must uncover the secret pain, the wee sore from which the Reply grew—*the anecdote which closed my recent article*—and consider how it is that this pimple has spread to these cancerous dimensions. If any but you had dictated the Reply, M. Bourget, I would know that that anecdote was twisted around and its intention magnified some hundreds of times, in order that it might be used as a pretext to creep in the back way. But I accuse you of nothing—nothing but error. When you say that I "retort by calling France a nation of bastards," it is an error. And not a small one, but a large one. I made no such remark, nor anything resembling it. Moreover, the magazine would not have allowed me to use so gross a word as that.

You told an anecdote. A funny one—I admit that. It hit a foible of our American aristocracy, and it stung me—I admit that; it stung me sharply. It was like this: You found some ancient portraits of French kings in the gallery of one of our aristocracy, and you said:

"He has the Grand Monarch, but *where is the portrait of his grandfather?*" That is, the American aristocrat's grandfather.

read more of our novels before he came. It is the only way to thoroughly understand a people. When I found I was coming to Paris I read *La Terre*.'"

MARK TWAIN

Now that hits only a few of us, I grant—just the upper crust only—but it hits exceedingly hard.

I wondered if there was any way of getting back at you. In one of your chapters I found this chance:

"In our high Parisian existence, for instance, we find applied to arts and luxury, and to debauchery, all the powers and all the weaknesses of the French soul."

You see? Your "higher Parisian" class—not everybody, not the nation, but only the *top crust* of the nation—*applies to debauchery all the powers of its soul.*

I argued to myself that that energy must produce results. So I built an anecdote out of your remark. In it I make Napoleon Bonaparte say to me—but see for yourself the anecdote (ingeniously clipped and curtailed) in paragraph eleven of your Reply.[1]

---

[1] So, I repeat, Mark Twain does not like M. Paul Bourget's book. So long as he makes light fun of the great French writer he is at home, he is pleasant, he is the American humorist we know. When he takes his revenge (and where is the reason for taking a revenge?) he is unkind, unfair, bitter, nasty.

For example:

See his answer to a Frenchman who jokingly remarks to him:

"I suppose life can never get entirely dull to an American, because whenever he can't strike up any other way to put in his time, he can always get away with a few years trying to find out who his grandfather was."

Hear the answer:

"I reckon a Frenchman's got *his* little standby for a dull time, too; because when all other interests fail, he can turn in and see if he can't find out who his father was."

The first remark is a good-humored bit of chaffing on American snobbery. I may be utterly destitute of humor, but I call the second remark a gratuitous charge of immorality hurled at the French women—a remark unworthy of a man who has the ear of the public, unworthy of a gentleman, a gross insult to a nation

184

NOTE TO M. PAUL BOURGET

Now, then, your anecdote about the grandfathers hurt me. Why? Because it had a *point*. It wouldn't have hurt me if it hadn't had point. You wouldn't have wasted space on it if it hadn't had point.

My anecdote has hurt you. Why? Because it had point, I suppose. It wouldn't have hurt you if it hadn't had point. I judged from your remark about the diligence and industry of the high Parisian upper crust that it would have some point, but really I had no idea what a gold-mine I had struck. I never suspected that the point was going to stick into the entire nation; but of course you know your nation better than I do, and if you think it punctures them all, I have to yield to your judgment. But you are to blame, your own self. Your remark misled me. I supposed the industry was confined to that little unnumerous upper layer.

Well, now that the unfortunate thing has been done, let us do what we can to undo it. There must be a way, M. Bourget, and I am willing to do anything that will help; for I am as sorry as you can be yourself.

I will tell you what I think will be the very thing. We will *swap anecdotes*. I will take your anecdote

friendly to America, a nation that helped Mark Twain's ancestors in their struggle for liberty, a nation where to-day it is enough to say that you are American to see every door open wide to you.

If Mark Twain was hard up in search of a French "chestnut," I might have told him the following little anecdote. It is more funny than his, and would have been less insulting: Two little street boys are abusing each other. "Ah, hold your tongue," says one, "you ain't got no father."

"Ain't got no father!" replied the other; "I've got more fathers than you."

and you take mine. I will say to the dukes and counts and princes of the ancient nobility of France: "Ha, ha! You must have a pretty hard time trying to find out who your grandfathers were?"

They will merely smile indifferently and not feel hurt, because they can trace their lineage back through centuries.

And you will hurl mine at every individual in the American nation, saying:

"And *you* must have a pretty hard time trying to find out who your *fathers* were." They will merely smile indifferently, and not feel hurt, because they haven't any difficulty in finding their fathers.

Do you get the idea? The whole harm in the anecdotes is in the *point*, you see; and when we swap them around that way, they *haven't* any.

That settles it perfectly and beautifully, and I am glad I thought of it. I am very glad indeed, M. Bourget; for it was just that little wee thing that caused the whole difficulty and made you dictate the Reply, and your amanuensis call me all those hard names which the magazines dislike so. And I did it all in fun, too, trying to cap your funny anecdote with another one—on the give-and-take principle, you know—which is American. *I* didn't know that with the French it was all give and no take, and you didn't tell me. But now that I have made everything comfortable again, and fixed both anecdotes so they can never have any point any more, I know you will forgive me.

THE INVALID'S STORY

I SEEM sixty and married, but these effects are due to my condition and sufferings, for I am a bachelor, and only forty-one. It will be hard for you to believe that I, who am now but a shadow, was a hale, hearty man two short years ago—a man of iron, a very athlete!—yet such is the simple truth. But stranger still than this fact is the way in which I lost my health. I lost it through helping to take care of a box of guns on a two-hundred-mile railway journey one winter's night. It is the actual truth, and I will tell you about it.

I belong in Cleveland, Ohio. One winter's night, two years ago, I reached home just after dark, in a driving snow-storm, and the first thing I heard when I entered the house was that my dearest boyhood friend and schoolmate, John B. Hackett, had died the day before, and that his last utterance had been a desire that I would take his remains home to his poor old father and mother in Wisconsin. I was greatly shocked and grieved, but there was no time to waste in emotions; I must start at once. I took the card, marked "Deacon Levi Hackett, Bethlehem, Wisconsin," and hurried off through the whistling storm to the railway-station. Arrived there I found the long white-pine box which had been described to me, I fastened the card to it with some tacks, saw it put safely aboard the express-car, and then ran into the eating-room to provide myself with a sandwich and some cigars. When I returned, presently, there was my coffin-box *back again*, apparently, and a young fellow examining around it, with a card in his hands, and some tacks and a hammer! I was astonished and puzzled. He began to nail on his card, and I rushed out to the express-car, in a good deal of a state of mind, to ask for an explanation. But no—there was my box, all right, in the express-car; it hadn't been disturbed. [The fact is that without my suspecting it a prodigious mistake had been made. I was carrying off a box of *guns* which that young fellow had come to the station to ship to a rifle company in Peoria, Illinois, and *he* had got my corpse!] Just then the conductor sang out "All aboard," and I jumped into the express-car and got a comfortable seat on a bale of buckets. The expressman was there, hard at work—a plain man of fifty, with a simple, honest, good-natured face, and a breezy, practical heartiness in his general style. As the train moved off a stranger skipped into the car and set a package of peculiarly mature and capable Limburger cheese on one end of my coffin-box—I mean my box of guns. That is to say, I know *now* that it was Limburger cheese, but at that time I never had heard of the article in my life, and of course was wholly ignorant of its character. Well, we sped through the wild night, the bitter storm raged on, a cheerless misery stole over me, my heart went down, down, down! The old expressman made a brisk remark or two about the tempest and the arctic weather, slammed his sliding doors to, and bolted them, closed his window down tight, and then went bustling around, here and there and yonder, setting things to rights and all the time contentedly humming "Sweet By and By," in a low tone, and flatting a good deal. Presently I began to detect a most evil and searching odor stealing about on the frozen air. This depressed my spirits still more, because of course I attributed it to my poor departed friend. There was something infinitely saddening about his calling himself to my remembrance in this dumb, pathetic way, so it was hard to keep the tears back. Moreover, it distressed me on account of the old expressman, who, I was afraid, might notice it. However, he went humming tranquilly on, and gave no sign; and for this I was grateful. Grateful, yes, but still uneasy; and soon I began to feel more and more uneasy every minute, for every minute that went by that odor thickened up the more, and got to be more and more gamey and hard to stand. Presently, having got things arranged to his satisfaction, the expressman got some wood and made up a tremendous fire in his stove. This distressed me more than I can tell, for I could not but feel that it was a mistake. I was sure that the effect would be deleterious upon my poor departed friend. Thompson—the expressman's name was Thompson, as I found out in the course of the night—now went poking around his car, stopping up whatever stray cracks he could find, remarking that it didn't make any difference what kind of a night it was outside, he calculated to make *us* comfortable, anyway. I said nothing, but I believed he was not choosing the right way. Meantime he was humming to himself just as before; and meantime, too, the stove was getting hotter and hotter, and the place closer and closer. I felt myself growing pale and qualmish, but grieved in silence and said nothing. Soon I noticed that the "Sweet By and By" was gradually fading out; next it ceased altogether, and there was an ominous stillness. After a few moments Thompson said—

"Pfew! I reckon it ain't no cinnamon 't I've loaded up thish-yer stove with!"

He gasped once or twice, then moved toward the cof—gun-box, stood over that Limburger cheese part of a moment, then came back and sat down near me, looking a good deal impressed. After a contemplative pause, he said, indicating the box with a gesture—

"Friend of yourn?"

"Yes," I said with a sigh.

"He's pretty ripe, *ain't* he!"

Nothing further was said for perhaps a couple of minutes, each being busy with his own thoughts; then Thompson said, in a low, awed voice—

"Sometimes it's uncertain whether they're really gone or not—*seem* gone, you know—body warm, joints limber—and so, although you *think* they're gone, you don't really know. I've had cases in my car. It's perfectly awful, becuz *you* don't know what minute they'll rise up and look at you!" Then, after a pause, and slightly lifting his elbow toward the box,—"But *he* ain't in no trance! No, sir, I go bail for *him!*"

We sat some time, in meditative silence, listening to the wind and the roar of the train; then Thompson said, with a good deal of feeling:

"Well-a-well, we've all got to go, they ain't no getting around it. Man that is born of woman is of few days and far between, as Scriptur' says. Yes, you look at it any way you want to, it's awful solemn and cur'us: they ain't *nobody* can get around it; *all's* got to go—just *everybody*, as you may say. One day you're hearty and strong"—here he scrambled to his feet and broke a pane and stretched his nose out at it a moment or two, then sat down again while I struggled up and thrust my nose out at the same place, and this we kept on doing every now and then—"and next day he's cut down like the grass, and the places which knowed him then knows him no more forever, as Scriptur' says. Yes'ndeedy, it's awful solemn and cur'us; but we've all got to go, one time or another; they ain't no getting around it."

There was another long pause; then—

"What did he die of?"

I said I didn't know.

"How long has he ben dead?"

It seemed judicious to enlarge the facts to fit the probabilities; so I said:

"Two or three days."

But it did no good; for Thompson received it with an injured look which plainly said, "Two or three *years*, you mean." Then he went right along, placidly ignoring my statement, and gave his views at considerable length upon the unwisdom of putting off burials too long. Then he lounged off toward the box, stood a moment, then came back on a sharp trot and visited the broken pane, observing:

"'Twould 'a' ben a dum sight better, all around, if they'd started him along last summer."

Thompson sat down and buried his face in his red silk handkerchief, and began to slowly sway and rock his body like one who is doing his best to endure the almost unendurable. By this time the fragrance—if you may call it fragrance—was just about suffocating, as near as you can come at it. Thompson's face was turning gray; I knew mine hadn't any color left in it. By and by Thompson rested his forehead in his left hand, with his elbow on his knee, and sort of waved his red handkerchief toward the box with his other hand, and said:

"I've carried a many a one of 'em—some of 'em considerable overdue, too—but, lordy, he just lays over 'em all!—and does it *easy*. Cap, they was heliotrope to *him!*"

This recognition of my poor friend gratified me, in spite of the sad circumstances, because it had so much the sound of a compliment.

Pretty soon it was plain that something had got to be done. I suggested cigars. Thompson thought it was a good idea. He said:

"Likely it'll modify him some."

We puffed gingerly along for a while, and tried hard to imagine that things were improved. But it wasn't any use. Before very long, and without any consultation, both cigars were quietly dropped from our nerveless fingers at the same moment. Thompson said, with a sigh:

"No, Cap, it don't modify him worth a cent. Fact is, it makes him worse,)ecuz it appears to stir up his ambition. What do) ou reckon we better do, now?"

I was not able to suggest anyı hing; indeed, I had to be swallowing and swallowiı g all the time, and did not like to trust myself tо speak. Thompson fell to maundering, in a desultory and low-spirited way, about the miserable experiences of this night; and he got to referring to my poor friend by various titles—sometimes military ones, sometimes civil ones; and I noticed that as fast as my poor friend's effectiveness grew, Thompson promoted him accordingly—gave him a bigger title. Finally he said:

"I've got an idea. Suppos'n' we buckle down to it and give the Colonel a bit of a shove toward t'other end of the car?—about ten foot, say. He wouldn't have so much influence, then, don't you reckon?"

I said it was a good scheme. So we took in a good fresh breath at the broken pane, calculating to hold it till we got through; then we went there and bent over that deadly cheese and took a grip on the box. Thompson nodded "All ready," and then we threw ourselves forward with all our might; but Thompson slipped, and slumped down with his nose on the cheese, and his breath got loose. He gagged and gasped, and floundered up and made a break for the door, pawing the air and saying hoarsely, "Don't hender me!—gimme the road! I'm a-dying; gimme the road!" Out on the cold platform I sat down and held his head awhile, and he revived. Presently he said:

"Do you reckon we started the Gen'rul any?"

I said no; we hadn't budged him.

"Well, then, *that* idea's up the flume. We got to think up something else. He's suited wher' he is, I reckon; and if that's the way he feels about it, and has made up his mind that he don't wish to be disturbed, you bet he's a-going to have his own way in the business. Yes, better leave him right wher' he is, long as he wants it so; becuz he holds all the trumps, don't you know, and so it stands to reason that the man that lays out to alter his plans for him is going to get left."

But we couldn't stay out there in that mad storm; we should have frozen to death. So we went in again and shut the door, and began to suffer once more and take turns at the break in the window. By and by, as we were starting away from a station where we had stopped a moment Thompson pranced in cheerily, and exclaimed:

"We're all right, now! I reckon we've got the Commodore this time. I judge I've got the stuff here that'll take the tuck out of him."

It was carbolic acid. He had a carboy of it. He sprinkled it all around everywhere; in fact he drenched everything with it, rifle-box, cheese and all. Then we sat down, feeling pretty hopeful. But it wasn't for long. You see the two perfumes began to mix, and then—well, pretty soon we made a break for the door; and out there Thompson swabbed his face with his bandanna and said in a kind of disheartened way:

"It ain't no use. We can't buck agin *him*. He just utilizes everything we put up to modify him with, and gives it his own flavor and plays it back on us. Why, Cap, don't you know, t's as much as a hundred times worse in there now than it was when he first got a-going. I never *did* see one of 'em warm up to his work so, and take such a dumnation interest in it. No, sir, I never did, as long as I've ben on the road; and I've carried a many a one of 'em, as I was telling you."

We went in again after we were frozen pretty stiff; but my, we couldn't *stay* in, now. So we just waltzed back and forth, freezing, and thawing, and stifling, by turns. In about an hour we stopped at another station; and as we left it Thompson came in with a bag, and said—

"Cap, I'm a-going to chance him once more—just this once; and if we don't fetch him this time, the thing for us to do, is to just throw up the sponge and withdraw from the canvass. That's the way *I* put it up."

He had brought a lot of chicken feathers, and dried apples, and leaf tobacco, and rags, and old shoes, and sulphur, and asafetida, and one thing or another; and he piled them on a breadth of sheet iron in the middle of the floor, and set fire to them.

When they got well started, I couldn't see, myself, how even the corpse could stand it. All that went before was just simply poetry to that smell—but mind you, the original smell stood up out of it just as sublime as ever—fact is, these other smells just seemed to give it a better hold; and my, how rich it was! I didn't make these reflections there—there wasn't time—made them on the platform. And breaking for the platform, Thompson got suffocated and fell; and before I got him dragged out, which I did by the collar, I was mighty near gone myself. When we revived, Thompson said dejectedly:

"We got to stay out here, Cap. We got to do it. They ain't no other way. The Governor wants to travel alone, and he's fixed so he can outvote us."

And presently he added:

"And don't you know, we're *pisoned*. It's *our* last trip, you can make up your mind to it. Typhoid fever is what's going to come of this. I feel it a-coming right now. Yes, sir, we're elected, just as sure as you're born."

We were taken from the platform an hour later, frozen and insensible, at the next station, and I went straight off into a virulent fever, and never knew anything again for three weeks. I found out, then, that I had spent that awful night with a harmless box of rifles and a lot of innocent cheese; but the news was too late to save *me;* imagination had done its work, and my health was permanently shattered; neither Bermuda nor any other land can ever bring it back to me. This is my last trip; I am on my way home to die.

STIRRING TIMES IN AUSTRIA

I. THE GOVERNMENT IN THE FRYING-PAN

HERE in Vienna in these closing days of 1897 one's blood gets no chance to stagnate. The atmosphere is brimful of political electricity. All conversation is political; every man is a battery, with brushes overworn, and gives out blue sparks when you set him going on the common topic. Everybody has an opinion, and lets you have it frank and hot, and out of this multitude of counsel you get merely confusion and despair. For no one really understands this political situation, or can tell you what is going to be the outcome of it.

Things have happened here recently which would set any country but Austria on fire from end to end, and upset the government to a certainty; but no one feels confident that such results will follow here. Here, apparently, one must wait and see what will happen, then he will know, and not before; guessing is idle; guessing cannot help the matter. This is what the wise tell you; they all say it; they say it every day, and it is the sole detail upon which they all agree.

There is some approach to agreement upon another point: that there will be no revolution. Men say: "Look at our history—revolutions have not been in our line; and look at our political map —its construction is unfavorable to an organized uprising, and without unity what could a revolt accomplish? It is *dis*union which has held our empire together for centuries, and what it has done in the past it may continue to do now and in the future."

The most intelligible sketch I have encountered of this unintelligible arrangement of things was contributed to the *Travelers Record* by Mr. Forrest Morgan, of Hartford, three years ago. He says:

The Austro-Hungarian Monarchy is the patchwork quilt, the Midway Plaisance, the national chain-gang of Europe; a state that is not a nation but a collection of nations, some with national memories and aspirations and others without, some occupying distinct provinces almost purely their own, and others mixed with alien races, but each with a different language, and each mostly holding the others foreigners as much as if the link of a common government did not exist. Only one of its races even now comprises so much as *one-fourth* of the whole, and not another so much as *one-sixth;* and each has remained for ages as unchanged in isolation, however mingled together in locality, as globules of oil in water. There is nothing else in the modern world that is nearly like it, though there have been plenty in past ages; it seems unreal and impossible even though we know it is true; it violates all our feeling as to what a country should be in order to have a right to exist; and it seems as though it was too ramshackle to go on holding together any length of time. Yet it has survived, much in its present shape, two centuries of storms that have swept perfectly unified countries from existence and others that have brought it to the verge of ruin, has survived formidable European coalitions to dismember it, and has steadily gained force after each; forever changing in its exact make-up, losing in the West but gaining in the East, the changes leave the structure as firm as ever, like the dropping off and adding on of logs in a raft, its mechanical union of pieces showing all the vitality of genuine national life.

That seems to confirm and justify the prevalent Austrian faith that in this confusion of unrelated and irreconcilable elements, this condition of incurable disunion, there is strength—for the government. Nearly every day some one explains to me that a revolution would not succeed here. "It couldn't, you know. Broadly speaking, all the nations in the empire hate the government—but they all hate each other, too, and with devoted and enthusiastic bitterness; no two of them can combine; the nation that rises must rise alone; then the others would joyfully join the government against her, and she would have just a fly's chance against a combination of spiders. This government is entirely independent. It can go its own road, and do as it pleases; it has nothing to fear. In countries like England and America, where there is one tongue and the public interests are common, the government must take account of public opinion; but in Austria-Hungary there are nineteen public opinions—one for each state. No—two or three for each state, since there are two or three nationalities in each. A government cannot satisfy all these public opinions; it can only go through the motions of trying. This government does that. It goes through the motions, and they do not succeed; but that does not worry the government much."

The next man will give you some further information. "The government has a policy—a wise one

—and sticks steadily to it. This policy is—*tranquillity:* keep this hive of excitable nations as quiet as possible; encourage them to amuse themselves with things less inflammatory than politics.   To this end it furnishes them an abundance of Catholic priests to teach them to be docile and obedient, and to be diligent in acquiring ignorance about things here below, and knowledge about the kingdom of heaven, to whose historic delights they are going to add the charm of their society by and by; and further—to this same end—it cools off the newspapers every morning at five o'clock, whenever warm events are happening."   There is a censor of the press, and apparently he is always on duty and hard at work. A copy of each morning paper is brought to him at five o'clock. His official wagons wait at the doors of the newspaper offices and scud to him with the first copies that come from the press. His company of assistants read every line in these papers, and mark everything which seems to have a dangerous look; then he passes final judgment upon these markings. Two things conspire to give to the results a capricious and unbalanced look: his assistants have diversified notions as to what is dangerous and what isn't; he can't get time to examine their criticisms in much detail; and so sometimes the very same matter which is suppressed in one paper fails to be damned in another one, and gets published in full feather and unmodified. Then the paper in which it was suppressed blandly copies the forbidden matter into its evening edition—provokingly giving credit and detailing all the circumstances in courteous and inoffensive language--and of course the censor cannot say a word.

Sometimes the censor sucks all the blood out of a newspaper and leaves it colorless and inane; sometimes he leaves it undisturbed, and lets it talk out its opinions with a frankness and vigor hardly to be surpassed, I think, in the journals of any country. Apparently the censor sometimes revises his verdicts upon second thought, for several times lately he has suppressed journals after their issue and partial distribution. The distributed copies are then sent for by the censor and destroyed. I have two of these, but at the time they were sent for I could not remember what I had done with them.

If the censor did his work before the morning edition was printed, he would be less of an inconvenience than he is; but of course the papers cannot wait many minutes after five o'clock to get his verdict; they might as well go out of business as do that; so they print, and take the chances. Then, if they get caught by a suppression, they must strike out the condemned matter and print the edition over again. That delays the issue several hours, and is expensive besides. The government gets the suppressed edition for nothing. If it bought it, that would be joyful, and would give great satisfaction. Also, the edition would be larger. Some of the papers do not replace the condemned paragraphs with other matter; they merely snatch them out and leave blanks behind—mourning blanks, marked "*Confiscated.*"

The government discourages the dissemination of

newspaper information in other ways. For instance, it does not allow newspapers to be sold on the streets; therefore the newsboy is unknown in Vienna. And there is a stamp duty of nearly a cent upon each copy of a newspaper's issue. Every American paper that reaches me has a stamp upon it, which has been pasted there in the post-office or down-stairs in the hotel office; but no matter who put it there, I have to pay for it, and that is the main thing. Sometimes friends send me so many papers that it takes all I can earn that week to keep this government going.

I must take passing notice of another point in the government's measures for maintaining tranquillity. Everybody says it does not like to see any individual attain to commanding influence in the country, since such a man can become a disturber and an inconvenience. "We have as much talent as the other nations," says the citizen, resignedly, and without bitterness, "but for the sake of the general good of the country we are discouraged from making it overconspicuous; and not only discouraged, but tactfully and skillfully prevented from doing it, if we show too much persistence. Consequently we have no renowned men; in centuries we have seldom produced one—that is, seldom allowed one to produce himself. We can say to-day what no other nation of first importance in the family of Christian civilizations can say: that there exists no Austrian who has made an enduring name for himself which is familiar all around the globe."

Another helper toward tranquillity is the army. It is as pervasive as the atmosphere. It is everywhere. All the mentioned creators, promoters, and preservers of the public tranquility do their several shares in the quieting work. They make a restful and comfortable serenity and re osefulness. This is disturbed sometimes for a littl : while: a mob assembles to protest against some thing; it gets noisy —noisier—still noisier—finally *oo* noisy; then the persuasive soldiery come char; ing down upon it, and in a few minutes all is quie, again, and there is no mob.

There is a Constitution and there is a Parliament. The House draws its membership of 425 deputies from the nineteen or twenty states heretofore mentioned. These men represent peoples who speak eleven languages. That means eleven distinct varieties of jealousies, hostilities, and warring interests. This could be expected to furnish forth a parliament of a pretty inharmonious sort, and make legislation difficult at times—and it does that. The parliament is split up into many parties—the Clericals, the Progressists, the German Nationalists, the Young Czechs, the Social Democrats, the Christian Socialists, and some others—and it is difficult to get up working combinations among them. They prefer to fight apart sometimes.

The recent troubles have grown out of Count Badeni's necessities. He could not carry on his government without a majority vote in the House at his back, and in order to secure it he had to make a trade of some sort. He made it with the Czechs—the Bohemians. The terms were not easy for him: he must pass a bill making the Czech tongue the official language in Bohemia in place of the German. This created a storm. All the Germans in Austria were incensed. In numbers they form but a fourth part of the empire's population, but they urge that the country's public business should be conducted in one common tongue, and that tongue a world language—which German is.

However, Badeni secured his majority. The German element in parliament was apparently become helpless. The Czech deputies were exultant.

Then the music began. Badeni's voyage, instead of being smooth, was disappointingly rough from the start. The government must get the *Ausgleich* through. It must not fail. Badeni's majority was ready to carry it through; but the minority was determined to obstruct it and delay it until the obnoxious Czech-language measure should be shelved.

The *Ausgleich* is an Adjustment, Arrangement, Settlement, which holds Austria and Hungary together. It dates from 1867, and has to be renewed every ten years. It establishes the share which Hungary must pay toward the expenses of the imperial government. Hungary is a kingdom (the Emperor of Austria is its King), and has its own parliament and governmental machinery. But it has no foreign office, and it has no army—at least its army is a part of the imperial army, is paid out of the imperial treasury, and is under the control of the imperial war office.

The ten-year rearrangement was due a year ago, but failed to connect. At least completely. A year's compromise was arranged. A new arrange-

STIRRING TIMES IN AUSTRIA

ment must be effected before the last day of this
year. Otherwise the two countries become separate
entities. The Emperor woul l still be King of
Hungary—that is, King of an independent foreign
country. There would be Hung arian custom-houses
on the Austrian frontier, and th re would be a Hungarian army and a Hungarian oreign office. Both
countries would be weakened l y this, both would
suffer damage.

The Opposition in the House, although in the
minority, had a good weapon to fight with in the
pending *Ausgleich*. If it could delay the *Ausgleich*
a few weeks, the government would doubtless have
to withdraw the hated language bill or lose Hungary.

The Opposition began its fight. Its arms were the
Rules of the House. It was soon manifest that by
applying these Rules ingeniously it could make the
majority helpless, and keep it so as long as it pleased.
It could shut off business every now and then with
a motion to adjourn. It could require the ayes and
noes on the motion, and use up thirty minutes on
that detail. It could call for the reading and verifi-
cation of the minutes of the preceding meeting, and
use up half a day in that way. It could require that
several of its members be entered upon the list of
permitted speakers previously to the opening of a
sitting; and as there is no time limit, further delays
could thus be accomplished.

These were all lawful weapons, and the men of
the Opposition (technically called the Left) were
within their rights in using them. They used them
to such dire purpose that all parliamentary business

was paralyzed. The Right (the government side) could accomplish nothing. Then it had a saving idea. This idea was a curious one. It was to have the President and the Vice-Presidents of the parliament trample the Rules under foot upon occasion!

This, for a profoundly embittered minority constructed out of fire and gun-cotton! It was time for idle strangers to go and ask leave to look down out of a gallery and see what would be the result of it.

II. A MEMORABLE SITTING

And now took place that memorable sitting of the House which broke two records. It lasted the best part of two days and a night, surpassing by half an hour the longest sitting known to the world's previous parliamentary history, and breaking the long-speech record with Dr. Lecher's twelve-hour effort, the longest flow of unbroken talk that ever came out of one mouth since the world began.

At 8.45, on the evening of the 28th of October, when the House had been sitting a few minutes short of ten hours, Dr. Lecher was granted the floor. It was a good place for theatrical effects. I think that no other Senate House is so shapely as this one, or so richly and showily decorated. Its plan is that of an opera-house. Up toward the straight side of it—the stage side—rise a couple of terraces of desks for the ministry, and the official clerks or secretaries —terraces thirty feet long, and each supporting about half a dozen desks with spaces between them. Above these is the President's terrace, against the wall. Along it are distributed the proper accommodations for the presiding officer and his assistants. The wall is of richly colored marble highly polished, its paneled sweep relieved by fluted columns and pilasters of distinguished grace and dignity, which glow softly and frostily in the electric light. Around the spacious half-circle of the floor bends the great two-storied curve of the boxes, it frontage elaborately ornamened and sumptuously gilded. On the floor of the House the four hundred and twenty-five desks radiate fanwise from the President's tribune.

The galleries are crowded on this particular evening, for word has gone about that the *Ausgleich* is before the House; that the President, Ritter von Abrahamowicz, has been throttling the Rules; that the Opposition are in an inflammable state in consequence, and that the night session is likely to be of an exciting sort.

The gallery guests are fashionably dressed, and the finery of the women makes a bright and pretty show under the strong electric light. But down on the floor there is no costumery.

The deputies are dressed in day clothes; some of the clothes neat and trim, others not; there may be three members in evening dress, but not more. There are several Catholic priests in their long black gowns, and with crucifixes hanging from their necks. No member wears his hat. One may see by these details that the aspects are not those of an evening sitting of an English House of Commons, but rather those of a sitting of our House of Representatives.

In his high place sits the President, Abraham-

owicz, object of the Opposition's limitless hatred.
He is sunk back in the depths of his arm-chair, and
has his chin down. He brings the ends of his spread
fingers together in front of his breast, and reflectively
taps them together, with the air of one who would
like to begin business, but must wait, and be as
patient as he can. It makes you think of Richelieu.
Now and then he swings his head up to the left or
to the right and answers something which some one
has bent down to say to him. Then he taps his
fingers again. He looks tired, and maybe a trifle
harassed. He is a gray-haired, long, slender man,
with a colorless long face, which, in repose, suggests
a death-mask; but when not in repose is tossed and
rippled by a turbulent smile which washes this way
and that, and is not easy to keep up with—a pious
smile, a holy smile, a saintly smile, a deprecating
smile, a beseeching and supplicating smile; and when
it is at work the large mouth opens and the flexible
lips crumple, and unfold, and crumple again, and
move around in a genial and persuasive and angelic
way, and expose large glimpses of the teeth; and
that interrupts the sacredness of the smile and gives
it momentarily a mixed worldly and political and
satanic cast. It is a most interesting face to watch.
And then the long hands and the body—they furnish great and frequent help to the face in the
business of adding to the force of the statesman's
words.

To change the tense. At the time of which I
have just been speaking the crowds in the galleries
were gazing at the stage and the pit with rapt in-

terest and expectancy. One half of the great fan of desks was in effect empty, vacant; in the other half several hundred members were bunched and jammed together as solidly as the bristles in a brush; and they also were waiting and expecting. Presently the Chair delivered this utterance:

"Dr. Lecher has the floor."

Then burst out such another wild and frantic and deafening clamor as has not been heard on this planet since the last time the Comanches surprised a white settlement at midnight. Yells from the Left, counter-yells from the Right, explosions of yells from all sides at once, and all the air sawed and pawed and clawed and cloven by a writhing confusion of gesturing arms and hands. Out of the midst of this thunder and turmoil and tempest rose Dr. Lecher, serene and collected, and the providential length of him enabled his head to show out above it. He began his twelve-hour speech. At any rate, his lips could be seen to move, and that was evidence. On high sat the President imploring order, with his long hands put together as in prayer, and his lips visibly but not hearably speaking. At intervals he grasped his bell and swung it up and down with vigor, adding its keen clamor to the storm weltering there below.

Dr. Lecher went on with his pantomime speech, contented, untroubled. Here and there and now and then powerful voices burst above the din, and delivered an ejaculation that was heard. Then the din ceased for a moment or two, and gave opportunity to hear what the Chair might answer; then the noise broke out again. Apparently the President was being charged with all sorts of illegal exercises of power in the interest of the Right (the government side): among these, with arbitrarily closing an Order of Business before it was finished; with an unfair distribution of the right to the floor; with refusal of the floor, upon quibble and protest, to members entitled to it; with stopping a speaker's speech upon quibble and protest; and with other transgressions of the Rules of the House. One of the interrupters who made himself heard was a young fellow of slight build and neat dress, who stood a little apart from the solid crowd and leaned negligently, with folded arms and feet crossed, against a desk. Trim and handsome, strong face and thin features; black hair roughed up; parsimonious mustache; resonant great voice, of good tone and pitch. It is Wolf, capable and hospitable with sword and pistol; fighter of the recent duel with Count Badeni, the head of the government. He shot Badeni through the arm, and then walked over in the politest way and inspected his game, shook hands, expressed regret, and all that. Out of him came early this thundering peal, audible above the storm:

"I demand the floor. I wish to offer a motion."

In the sudden lull which followed, the President answered, "Dr. Lecher has the floor."

Wolf. "I move the close of the sitting!"

P. "Representative Lecher has the floor." (Stormy outburst from the Left—that is, the Opposition.]

Wolf. "I demand the floor for the introduction

of a formal motion. [Pause.] Mr. President, are you going to grant it, or not? [Crash of approval from the Left.] I will keep on demanding the floor till I get it."

P. "I call Representative Wolf to order. Dr. Lecher has the floor."

Wolf. "Mr. President, are you going to observe the Rules of this House?" [Tempest of applause and confused ejaculations from the Left—a boom and roar which long endured, and stopped all business for the time being.]

Dr. von Pessler. "By the Rules motions are in order, and the Chair *must* put them to vote."

For answer the President (who is a Pole—I make this remark in passing) began to jangle his bell with energy at the moment that that wild pandemonium of voices burst out again.

Wolf (hearable above the storm). "Mr. President, I demand the floor. We intend to find out, here and now, which is the hardest, *a Pole's skull or a German's!*"

This brought out a perfect cyclone of satisfaction from the Left. In the midst of it some one again moved an adjournment. The President blandly answered that Dr. Lecher had the floor. Which was true; and he was speaking, too, calmly, earnestly, and argumentatively; and the official stenographers had left their places and were at his elbows taking down his words, he leaning and orating into their ears—a most curious and interesting scene.

Dr. von Pessler (to the Chair). "Do not drive us to extremities!"

The tempest burst out again; yells of approval from the Left, catcalls, an ironical laughter from the Right. At this point a new and most effective noise-maker was pressed into service. Each desk has an extension, consisting of a removable board eighteen inches long, six wide, and a half-inch thick. A member pulled one of these out and began to belabor the top of his desk with it. Instantly other members followed suit, and perhaps you can imagine the result. Of all conceivable rackets it is the most ear-splitting, intolerable, and altogether fiendish.

The persecuted President leaned back in his chair, closed his eyes, clasped his hands in his lap, and a look of pathetic resignation crept over his long face. It is the way a country schoolmaster used to look in days long past when he had refused his school a holiday and it had risen against him in ill-mannered riot and violence and insurrection. Twice a motion to adjourn had been offered—a motion always in order in other Houses, and doubtless so in this one also. The President had refused to put these motions. By consequence, he was not in a pleasant place now, and was having a right hard time. Votes upon motions, whether carried or defeated, could make endless delay, and postpone the *Ausgleich* to next century.

In the midst of these sorrowful circumstances and this hurricane of yells and screams and satanic clatter of desk-boards, Representative Dr. Kronawetter unfeelingly reminds the Chair that a motion has been offered, and adds: "Say yes, or no! What do you sit there for, and give no answer?"

P. "After I have given a speaker the floor, I cannot give it to another. After Dr. Lecher is through, I will put your motion." [Storm of indignation from the Left.]

Wolf (to the Chair). "Thunder and lightning! look at the Rule governing the case!"

Kronawetter. "I move the close of the sitting! And I demand the ayes and noes!"

Dr. Lecher. "Mr. President, have I the floor?"

P. "You have the floor."

Wolf (to the Chair, in a stentorian voice which cleaves its way through the storm). "It is by such brutalities as these that you drive us to extremities! Are you waiting till some one shall throw into your face the word that shall describe what you are bringing about?[1] [Tempest of insulted fury from the Right.] *Is that what you are waiting for, old Grayhead?*" [Long-continued clatter of desk-boards from the Left, with shouts of "The vote! the vote!" An ironical shout from the Right, "Wolf is boss!"]

Wolf keeps on demanding the floor for his motion. At length:

P. "I call Representative Wolf to order! Your conduct is unheard-of, sir! You forget that you are in a parliament; you must remember where you are, sir." [Applause from the Right. Dr. Lecher is still peacefully speaking, the stenographers listening at his lips.]

Wolf (banging on his desk with his desk-board). "I demand the floor for my motion! I won't stand this trampling of the Rules under foot—no, not if

[1] That is, *revolution.*

I die for it! I will never yield! You have got to stop me by force. Have I the floor?"

P. "Representative Wolf, what kind of behavior is this? I call you to order again. You should have some regard for your dignity."

Dr. Lecher speaks on. Wolf turns upon him with an offensive innuendo.

Dr. Lecher. "Mr. Wolf, I beg you to refrain from that sort of suggestions." [Storm of hand-clapping from the Right.]

This was applause from the enemy, for Lecher himself, like Wolf, was an Obstructionist.

Wolf growls to Lecher: "You can scribble that applause in your album!"

P. "Once more I call Representative Wolf to order! Do not forget that you are a Representative, sir!"

Wolf (slam-banging with his desk-board). "I will force this matter! Are you going to grant me the floor, or not?"

And still the sergeant-at-arms did not appear. It was because there wasn't any. It is a curious thing, but the Chair has no effectual means of compelling order.

After some more interruptions:

Wolf (banging with his board). "I demand the floor. I will not yield!"

P. "I have no recourse against Representative Wolf. In the presence of behavior like this it is to be regretted that such is the case." [A shout from the Right, "Throw him out!"]

It is true, he had no effective recourse. He had

STIRRING TIMES IN AUSTRIA

an official called an "Ordner," whose help he could invoke in desperate cases, but apparently the Ordner is only a persuader, not a compeller. Apparently he is a sergeant-at-arms who is not loaded; a good enough gun to look at, but not valuable for business.

For another twenty or thirty minutes Wolf went on banging with his board and demanding his rights; then at last the weary President threatened to summon the dread order-maker. But both his manner and his words were reluctant. Evidently it grieved him to have to resort to this dire extremity. He said to Wolf, "If this goes on, I shall feel obliged to summon the Ordner, and beg him to restore order in the House."

Wolf. "I'd like to see you do it! Suppose you fetch in a few policemen, too! [Great tumult.] Are you going to put my motion to adjourn, or not?"

Dr. Lecher continues his speech. Wolf accompanies him with his board-clatter.

The President despatches the Ordner, Dr. Lang (himself a deputy), on his order-restoring mission. Wolf, with his board uplifted for defense, confronts the Ordner with a remark which Boss Tweed might have translated into "Now let's see what you are going to do about it!" [Noise and tumult all over the House.]

Wolf stands upon his rights, and says he will maintain them till he is killed in his tracks. Then he resumes his banging, the President jangles his bell and begs for order, and the rest of the House augments the racket the best it can.

Wolf. "I require an adjournment, because I find

215

myself personally threatened. [Laughter from the Right.] Not that I fear for myself; I am only anxious about what will happen to the man who touches me."

The Ordner. "I am not going to fight with you."

Nothing came of the efforts of the angel of peace, and he presently melted out of the scene and disappeared. Wolf went on with his noise and with his demands that he be granted the floor, resting his board at intervals to discharge criticisms and epithets at the Chair. Once he reminded the Chairman of his violated promise to grant him (Wolf) the floor, and said, "Whence I came, we call promise-breakers rascals!" And he advised the Chairman to take his conscience to bed with him and use it as a pillow. Another time he said that the Chair was making itself ridiculous before all Europe. In fact, some of Wolf's language was almost unparliamentary. By and by he struck the idea of beating out a *tune* with his board. Later he decided to stop asking for the floor, and to confer it upon himself. And so he and Dr. Lecher now spoke at the same time, and mingled their speeches with the other noises, and nobody heard either of them. Wolf rested himself now and then from speech-making by reading, in his clarion voice, from a pamphlet.

I will explain that Dr. Lecher was not making a twelve-hour speech for pastime, but for an important purpose. It was the government's intention to push the *Ausgleich* through its preliminary stages in this one sitting (for which it was the Order of the Day), and then by vote refer it to a select committee.

It was the Majority's scheme—as charged by the Opposition—to drown debate upon the bill by pure noise—drown it out and stop it The debate being thus ended, the vote upon the reference would follow —with victory for the government. But into the government's calculations had not entered the possibility of a single-barreled speech which should occupy the entire time-limit of he sitting, and also get itself delivered in spite of a l the noise. Goliah was not expecting David. But David was there; and during twelve hours he tranquilly pulled statistical, historical, and argumentative pebbles out of his scrip and slung them at the giant; and when he was done he was victor, and the day was saved.

In the English House an obstructionist has held the floor with Bible-readings and other outside matters; but Dr. Lecher could not have that restful and recuperative privilege—he must confine himself strictly to the subject before the House. More than once, when the President could not hear him because of the general tumult, he sent persons to listen and report as to whether the orator was speaking to the subject or not.

The subject was a peculiarly difficult one, and it would have troubled any other deputy to stick to it three hours without exhausting his ammunition, because it required a vast and intimate knowledge— detailed and particularized knowledge—of the commercial, railroading, financial, and international banking relations existing between two great sovereignties, Hungary and the Empire. But Dr. Lecher is President of the Board of Trade of his city of

Brünn, and was master of the situation. His speech was not formally prepared. He had a few notes jotted down for his guidance; he had his facts in his head; his heart was in his work; and for twelve hours he stood there, undisturbed by the clamor around him, and with grace and ease and confidence poured out the riches of his mind, in closely reasoned arguments, clothed in eloquent and faultless phrasing.

He is a young man of thirty-seven. He is tall and well proportioned, and has cultivated and fortified his muscle by mountain-climbing. If he were a little handsomer he would sufficiently reproduce for me the Chauncey Depew of the great New England dinner nights of some years ago; he has Depew's charm of manner and graces of language and delivery.

There was but one way for Dr. Lecher to hold the floor—he must stay on his legs. If he should sit down to rest a moment, the floor would be taken from him by the enemy in the Chair. When he had been talking three or four hours he himself proposed an adjournment, in order that he might get some rest from his wearing labors; but he limited his motion with the condition that if it was lost he should be allowed to continue his speech, and if it carried he should have the floor at the next sitting. Wolf was now appeased, and withdrew his own thousand-times offered motion, and Dr. Lecher's was voted upon—and lost. So he went on speaking.

By one o'clock in the morning, excitement and noise-making had tired out nearly everybody but the orator. Gradually the seats of the Right underwent depopulation; the occupants had slipped out to the refreshment-rooms to eat and drink, or to the corridors to chat. Some one remarked that there was no longer a quorum present, and moved a call of the House. The Chair (Vice-President Dr. Kramarz) refused to put it to a vote. There was a small dispute over the legality of this ruling, but the Chair held its ground.

The Left remained on the battle-field to support their champion. He went steadily on with his speech; and always it was strong, virile, felicitous, and to the point. He was earning applause, and this enabled his party to turn that fact to account. Now and then they applauded him a couple of minutes on a stretch, and during that time he could stop speaking and rest his voice without having the floor taken from him.

At a quarter to two a member of the Left demanded that Dr. Lecher be allowed a recess for rest, and said that the Chairman was "heartless." Dr. Lecher himself asked for ten minutes. The Chair allowed him five. Before the time had run out Dr. Lecher was on his feet again.

Wolf burst out again with a motion to adjourn. Refused by the Chair. Wolf said the whole parliament wasn't worth a pinch of powder. The Chair retorted that that was true in a case where a single member was able to make all parliamentary business impossible. Dr. Lecher continued his speech.

The members of the Majority went out by detachments from time to time and took naps upon sofas in the reception-rooms; and also refreshed themselves with food and drink—in quantities nearly unbelievable—but the Minority stayed loyally by their champion. Some distinguished deputies of the Majority stayed by him, too, compelled thereto by admiration of his great performance. When a man has been speaking eight hours, is it conceivable that he can still be interesting, still fascinating? When Dr. Lecher had been speaking eight hours he was still compactly surrounded by friends who would not leave him and by foes (of all parties) who *could* not; and all hung enchanted and wondering upon his words, and all testified their admiration with constant and cordial outbursts of applause. Surely this was a triumph without precedent in history.

During the twelve-hour effort friends brought to the orator three glasses of wine, four cups of coffee, and one glass of beer — a most stingy reinforcement of his wasting tissues, but the hostile Chair would permit no addition to it. But no matter, the Chair could not beat that man. He was a garrison holding a fort, and was not to be starved out.

When he had been speaking eight hours his pulse was seventy-two; when he had spoken twelve, it was one hundred.

He finished his long speech in these terms, as nearly as a permissibly free translation can convey them:

"I will now hasten to close my examination of the subject. I conceive that we of the Left have made it clear to the honorable gentlemen of the other side of the House that we are stirred by no intemperate enthusiasm for this measure in its present shape. . . .

"What we require, and shall fight for with all lawful weapons, is a formal, comprehensive, and definitive solution and settlement of these vexed matters. We desire the restoration of the earlier condition of things; the cancellation of all this incapable government's pernicious trades with Hungary; and then—release from the sorry burden of the Badeni ministry!

"I voice the hope—I know not if it will be fulfilled—I voice the deep and sincere and patriotic hope that the committee into whose hands this bill will eventually be committed will take its stand upon high ground, and will return the *Ausgleich-Provisorium* to this House in a form which shall make it the protector and promoter alike of the great interests involved and of the honor of our fatherland." After a pause, turning toward the government benches: "But in any case, gentlemen of the Majority, make sure of this: henceforth, as before, you will find us at our post. The Germans of Austria will neither surrender nor die!"

Then burst a storm of applause which rose and fell, rose and fell, burst out again and again and again, explosion after explosion, hurricane after hurricane, with no apparent promise of ever coming to an end; and meantime the whole Left was surging and weltering about the champion, all bent upon wringing his hand and congratulating him and glorifying him.

Finally he got away, and went home and ate five loaves and twelve baskets of fishes, read the morning papers, slept three hours, took a short drive, then returned to the House and sat out the rest of the thirty-three-hour session.

To merely *stand up* in one spot twelve hours on a stretch is a feat which very few men could achieve; to add to the task the utterance of a hundred thousand words would be beyond the possibilities of the most of those few; to superimpose the requirement that the words should be put into the form of a compact, coherent, and symmetrical oration would probably rule out the rest of the few, bar Dr. Lecher.

III. CURIOUS PARLIAMENTARY ETIQUETTE

In consequence of Dr. Lecher's twelve-hour speech and the other obstructions furnished by the Minority, the famous thirty-three-hour sitting of the House accomplished nothing. The government side had made a supreme effort, assisting itself with all the helps at hand, both lawful and unlawful, yet had failed to get the *Ausgleich* into the hands of a committee. This was a severe defeat. The Right was mortified, the Left jubilant.

Parliament was adjourned for a week—to let the members cool off, perhaps—a sacrifice of precious time, for but two months remained in which to carry the all-important *Ausgleich* to a consummation.

If I have reported the behavior of the House intelligibly, the reader has been surprised at it, and has wondered whence these lawmakers come and what they are made of; and he has probably supposed that the conduct exhibited at the Long Sitting was far out of the common, and due to special excitement and irritation. As to the make-up of the House, it is this: the deputies come from all the walks of life and from all the grades of society There are princes, counts, barons, priests, peasants, mechanics, laborers, lawyers, judges, physicians, professors, merchants, bankers, shopkeepers. They are religious men, they are earnest, sincere, devoted, and they hate the Jews. The title of Doctor is so common in the House that one may almost say that the deputy who does not bear it is by that reason conspicuous. I am assured that it is not a self-granted title, and not an honorary one, but an *earned* one; that in Austria it is very seldom conferred as a mere compliment; that in Austria the degrees of Doctor of Music, Doctor of Philosophy, and so on, are not conferred by the seats of learning; and so, when an Austrian is called Doctor it means that he is either a lawyer or a physician, and that he is not a self-educated man, but is college-bred, and has been diplomaed for merit.

That answers the question of the constitution of the House. Now as to the House's curious manners. The manners exhibited by this convention of Doctors were not at that time being tried as a wholly new experiment. I will go back to a previous sitting in order to show that the deputies had already had some practice.

There had been an incident. The dignity of the House had been wounded by improprieties indulged in in its presence by a couple of the members. This matter was placed in the hands of a committee to determine where the guilt lay, and the degree of it, and also to suggest the punishment. The chairman of the committee brought in his report. By this it appeared that, in the course of a speech, Deputy Schrammel said that religion had no proper place in the public schools—it was a private matter. Whereupon Deputy Gregorig shouted, "How about free love!"

To this, Deputy Iro flung out this retort: "Soda-water at the Wimberger!"

This appeared to deeply offend Deputy Gregorig, who shouted back at Iro, "You cowardly blather-skite, say that again!"

The committee had sat three hours. Gregorig had apologized; Iro had explained. Iro explained that he didn't say anything about soda-water at the Wimberger. He explained in writing, and was very explicit: "I declare *upon my word of honor* that I did not say the words attributed to me."

Unhappily for his word of honor, it was proved by the official stenographers and by the testimony of several deputies that he *did* say them.

The committee did not officially know why the apparently inconsequential reference to soda-water at the Wimberger should move Deputy Gregorig to call the utterer of it a cowardly blatherskite; still, after proper deliberation, it was of the opinion that the House ought to formally censure the whole business. This verdict seems to have been regarded as sharply severe. I think so because Deputy Dr. Lueger, Bürgermeister of Vienna, felt it a duty to soften the blow to his friend Gregorig by showing that the soda-water remark was not so innocuous as it might look; that indeed Gregorig's tough retort was justifiable—and he proceeded to explain why. He read a number of scandalous post-cards which he intimated had proceeded from Iro, as indicated by the handwriting, though they were anonymous. Some of them were posted to Gregorig at his place of business, and could have been read by all his subordinates; the others were posted *to Gregorig's wife.* Lueger did not say—but everybody knew—that the cards referred to a matter of town gossip which made Mr. Gregorig a chief actor in a tavern scene where siphon-squirting played a prominent and humorous part, and wherein women had a share.

There were several of the cards; more than several, in fact; no fewer than five were sent in one day, Dr. Lueger read some of them, and described others. Some of them had pictures on them; one a picture of a hog with a monstrous snout, and beside it a squirting soda-siphon; below it some sarcastic doggerel.

Gregorig deals in shirts, cravats, etc. One of the cards bore these words: "Much respected Deputy and collar-sewer—or *stealer.*"

Another: "Hurrah for the Christian-Social work among the women assemblages! Hurrah for the soda-squirter!" Comment by Dr. Lueger: "I cannot venture to read the rest of that one, nor the signature, either."

Another: "Would you mind telling me if . . ."

Comment by Dr. Lueger: "The rest of it is not properly readable."

To Deputy Gregorig's wife: "Much respected Madam Gregorig,— The undersigned desires an invitation to the next soda-squirt." Comment by Dr. Lueger: "Neither the rest of the card nor the signature can I venture to read to the House, so vulgar are they."

The purpose of this card—to expose Gregorig to his family—was repeated in others of these anonymous missives.

The House, by vote, censured the two improper deputies.

This may have had a modifying effect upon the phraseology of the membership for a while, and upon its general exuberance also, but it was not for long. As has been seen, it had become lively once more on the night of the Long Sitting. At the next sitting after the long one there was certainly no lack of liveliness. The President was persistently ignoring the Rules of the House in the interest of the government side, and the Minority were in an unappeasable fury about it. The ceaseless din and uproar, the shouting and stamping and desk-banging, were deafening, but through it all burst voices now and then that made themselves heard. Some of the remarks were of a very candid sort, and I believe that if they had been uttered in our House of Representatives they would have attracted attention. I will insert some samples here. Not in their order, but selected on their merits:

Dr. Mayreder (to the President). "You have lied! You conceded the floor to me; make it good, or you have lied!"

Mr. Glöckner (to the President). "Leave! Get out!"

Wolf (indicating the President). "There sits a man to whom a certain title belongs!"

Unto Wolf, who is continuously reading, in a powerful voice, from a newspaper, arrive these personal remarks from the Majority: "Oh, shut your mouth!" "Put him out!" "Out with him!" Wolf stops reading a moment to shout at Dr. Lueger, who has the floor, but cannot get a hearing, "Please, Betrayer of the People, begin!"

Dr. Lueger. "Meine Herren--" ["Oho!" and groans.]

Wolf. "*That's* the holy light of the Christian Socialists!"

Mr. Kletzenbauer (Christian Socialist). "Damnation! are you ever going to quiet down?"

Wolf discharges a galling remark at Mr. Wohlmeyer.

Wohlmeyer (responding). "You Jew, you!"

There is a moment's lull, and Dr. Lueger begins his speech. Graceful, handsome man, with winning manners and attractive bearing, a bright and easy speaker, and is said to know how to trim his political sails to catch any favoring wind that blows. He manages to say a few words, then the tempest overwhelms him again.

Wolf stops reading his paper a moment to say a drastic thing about Lueger and his Christian-Social pieties, which sets the C. S.'s in a sort of frenzy.

Mr. Vielohlawek. "You leave the Christian Socialists alone, you word-of-honor-breaker! Obstruct all you want to, but you leave *them* alone! You've no business in this House; you belong in a gin-mill!"

Mr. Prochazka. "In a lunatic asylum, you mean!"

Vielohlawek. "It's a pity that such a man should be leader of the Germans; he disgraces the German name!"

Dr. Scheicher. "It's a shame that the like of him should insult us."

Strohback (to Wolf). "Contemptible cub—we will bounce thee out of this!" [It is inferable that the "thee" is not intended to indicate affection this time, but to reinforce and emphasize Mr. Strohbach's scorn.]

Dr. Scheicher. "His insults are of no consequence. He wants his ears boxed."

Dr. Lueger (to Wolf). "You'd better worry a trifle over your Iro's word of honor. You are behaving like a street arab."

Dr. Scheicher. "It's infamous!"

Dr. Lueger. "And *these* shameless creatures are the leaders of the German People's Party!"

Meantime Wolf goes whooping along with his newspaper-readings in great contentment.

Dr. Pattai. "Shut up! Shut up! Shut *up!* You haven't the floor!"

Strohbach. "The miserable cub!"

Dr. Lueger (to Wolf, raising his voice strenuously above the storm). "You are a wholly honorless street brat!" [A voice, "Fire the rapscallion out!" But Wolf's soul goes marching noisily on, just the same.]

Schönerer (vast and muscular, and endowed with the most powerful voice in the Reichsrath; comes plowing down through the standing crowds, red,

and choking with anger; halts before Deputy Wohlmeyer, grabs a rule and smashes it with a blow upon
a desk, threatens Wohlmeyer's face with his fist,
and bellows out some personalities, and a promise).
"Only you wait—we'll teach you!" [A whirlwind
of offensive retorts assails him from the band of
meek and humble Christian Socialists compacted
around their leader, that distinguished religious expert, Dr. Lueger, Bürgermeister of Vienna. Our
breath comes in excited gasps now, and we are
full of hope. We imagine that we are back fifty
years ago in the Arkansas Legislature, and we
think we know what is going to happen, and are
glad we came, and glad we are up in the gallery,
out of the way, where we can see the whole thing
and yet not have to supply any of the material for
the inquest. However, as it turns out, our confidence is abused, our hopes are misplaced.]

Dr. Pattai (wildly excited). "You quiet down, or
we shall turn ourselves loose! There will be a cuff-
ing of ears!"

Prochazka (in a fury). "No—*not* ear-boxing, but
genuine *blows!*"

Vielohlawek. "I would rather take my hat off to
a Jew than to Wolf!"

Strohbach (to Wolf). "Jew-flunky! Here we have
been fighting the Jews for ten years, and now you
are helping them to power again. How much do
you get for it?"

Holansky. "What he wants is a strait-jacket!"

Wolf continues his readings. It is a market report now.

MARK TWAIN

Remark flung across the House to Schönerer: *"Die Grossmutter auf dem Misthaufen erzeugt worden!"*

It will be judicious not to translate that. Its flavor is pretty high, in any case, but it becomes particularly gamey when you remember that the first gallery was well stocked with ladies.

Apparently it was a great hit. It fetched thunders of joyous enthusiasm out of the Christian Socialists, and in their rapture they flung biting epithets with wasteful liberality at specially detested members of the Opposition; among others, this one at Schönerer: *"Bordell in der Krugerstrasse!"* Then they added these words, which they whooped, howled, and also even sang, in a deep-voiced chorus: *"Schmul Leeb Kohn! Schmul Leeb Kohn! Schmul Leeb Kohn!"* and made it splendidly audible above the banging of desk-boards and the rest of the roaring cyclone of fiendish noises. [A gallery witticism comes flitting by from mouth to mouth around the great curve: "The swan-song of Austrian representative government!" You can note its progress by the applausive smiles and nods it gets as it skims along.]

Kletzenbauer. "Holofernes, where is Judith?" [Storm of laughter.]

Gregorig (the shirt-merchant). "This Wolf-Theater is costing six thousand florins!"

Wolf (with sweetness). "Notice him, gentlemen; it is Mr. Gregorig." [Laughter.]

Vielohlawek (to Wolf). "You Judas!"

Schneider. "Brothel-Knight!"

Chorus of Voices. "East-German offal-tub!"

And so the war of epithets crashes along, with never-diminishing energy, for a couple of hours.

The ladies in the gallery were learning. That was well; for by and by ladies will form a part of the membership of all the legislatures in the world; as soon as they can prove competency they will be admitted. At present, men only are competent to legislate; therefore they look down upon women, and would feel degraded if they had to have them for colleagues in their high calling.

Wolf is yelling another market report now.

Gessman. "Shut up, infamous louse-brat!"

During a momentary lull Dr. Lueger gets a hearing for three sentences of his speech. They demand and require that the President shall suppress the four noisiest members of the Opposition.

Wolf (with a that-settles-it toss of the head). "The shifty trickster of Vienna has spoken!"

Iro belonged to Schönerer's party. The word-of-honor incident has given it a new name. Gregorig is a Christian Socialist, and hero of the post-cards and the Wimberger soda-squirting incident. He stands vast and conspicuous, and conceited and self-satisfied, and roosterish and inconsequential, at Lueger's elbow, and is proud and cocky to be in such great company. He looks very well indeed; really majestic, and aware of it. He crows out his little empty remark, now and then, and looks as pleased as if he had been delivered of the *Ausgleich.* Indeed, he does look notably fine. He wears almost the only dress vest on the floor: it exposes a continental spread of white shirt-front; his hands are posed at ease in the lips of his trousers pockets; his head is tilted back complacently; he is attitudinizing; he is playing to the gallery. However, they are all doing that. It is curious to see. Men who only vote, and can't make speeches, and don't know how to invent witty ejaculations, wander about the vacated parts of the floor, and stop in a good place and strike attitudes—attitudes suggestive of weighty thought, mostly—and glance furtively up at the galleries to see how it works; or a couple will come together and shake hands in an artificial way, and laugh a gay manufactured laugh, and do some constrained and self-conscious attitudinizing; and *they* steal glances at the galleries to see if they are getting notice. It is like a scene on the stage—by-play by minor actors at the back while the stars do the great work at the front. Even Count Badeni attitudinizes for a moment; strikes a reflective Napoleonic attitude of fine picturesqueness—but soon thinks better of it and desists. There are two who do not attitudinize—poor harried and insulted President Abrahamowicz, who seems wholly miserable, and can find no way to put in the dreary time but by swinging his bell and by discharging occasional remarks which nobody can hear; and a resigned and patient priest, who sits lonely in a great vacancy on Majority territory and munches an apple.

Schönerer uplifts his fog-horn of a voice and shakes the roof with an insult discharged at the Majority.

Dr. Lueger. "The Honorless Party would better keep still here!"

Gregroig (the echo, swelling out his shirt-front).
"Yes, keep quiet, pimp!"

Schönerer (to Lueger). "Political mountebank!"

Prochazka (to Schönerer). "Drunken clown!"

During the final hour of the sitting many happy
phrases were distributed through the proceedings.
Amóng them were these—and hey are strikingly
good ones:

Blatherskite!

Blackguard!

Scoundrel!

Brothel-daddy!

This last was the contribution of Dr. Gessman,
and gave great satisfaction. And deservedly. It
seems to me that it was one of the most sparkling
things that was said during the whole evening.

At half-past two in the morning the House adjourned. The victory was with the Opposition.
No; not quite that. The effective part of it was
snatched away from them by an unlawful exercise
of Presidential force—another contribution toward
driving the mistreated Minority out of their minds.

At other sittings of the parliament, gentlemen of
the Opposition, shaking their fists toward the President, addressed him as "Polish Dog." At one sitting an angry deputy turned upon a colleague and
shouted:

"— — — — —!"

You must try to imagine what it was. If I should
offer it even in the original it would probably not get
by the Magazine editor's blue pencil; to offer a
translation would be to waste my ink, of course.

This remark was frankly printed in its entirety by one of the Vienna dailies, but the others disguised the toughest half of it with stars.

If the reader will go back over this chapter and gather its array of extraordinary epithets into a bunch and examine them, he will marvel at two things: how this convention of gentlemen could consent to use such gross terms; and why the users were allowed to get out of the place alive. There is no way to understand this strange situation. If every man in the House were a professional blackguard, and had his home in a sailor boarding-house, one could still not understand it; for although that sort do use such terms, they never *take* them. These men are not professional blackguards; they are mainly gentlemen, and educated; yet they use the terms, and take them, too. They really seem to attach no consequence to them. One cannot say that they act like school-boys; for that is only almost true, not entirely. School-boys blackguard each other fiercely, and by the hour, and one would think that nothing would ever come of it but noise; but that would be a mistake. Up to a certain limit the result would be noise only, but that limit overstepped, trouble would follow right away. There are certain phrases —phrases of a peculiar character—phrases of the nature of that reference to Schönerer's grandmother, for instance, which not even the most spiritless school-boy in the English-speaking world would allow to pass unavenged. One difference between school-boys and the lawmakers of the Reichsrath seems to be that the lawmakers have no limit, no danger-line. Apparently they may call each other what they please, and go home unmutilated.

Now, in fact, they did have a scuffle on two occasions, but it was not on account of names called. There has been no scuffle where *that* was the cause.

It is not to be inferred that the House lacks a sense of honor because it lacks delicacy. That would be an error. Iro was caught in a lie, and it profoundly disgraced him. The House cut him, turned its back upon him. He resigned his seat; otherwise he would have been expelled. But it was lenient with Gregorig, who had called Iro a cowardly blatherskite in debate. It merely went through the form of mildly censuring him. That did not trouble Gregorig.

The Viennese say of themselves that they are an easy-going, pleasure-loving community, making the best of life, and not taking it very seriously. Nevertheless, they are grieved about the ways of their parliament, and say quite frankly that they are ashamed. They claim that the low condition of the parliament's manners is new, not old. A gentleman who was at the head of the government twenty years ago confirms this, and says that in his time the parliament was orderly and well behaved. An English gentleman of long residence here indorses this, and and says that a low order of politicians originated the present forms of questionable speech on the stump some years ago, and imported them into the parliament.[1] However, some day there will be a

[1] In that gracious bygone time when a mild and good-tempered spirit was the atmosphere of our House, when the manner of our

Minister of Etiquette and a sergeant-at-arms, and then things will go better. I mean if parliament and the Constitution survive the present storm.

IV. THE HISTORIC CLIMAX

During the whole of November things went from bad to worse. The all-important *Ausgleich* remained hard aground, and could not be sparred off. Badeni's government could not withdraw the Language Ordinance and keep its majority, and the Opposition could not be placated on easier terms. One night, while the customary pandemonium was crashing and thundering along at its best, a fight broke out. It was a surging, struggling, shoulder-to-shoulder scramble. A great many blows were struck. Twice Schönerer lifted one of the heavy ministerial fauteuils —some say with one hand—and threatened members of the Majority with it, but it was wrenched away from him; a member hammered Wolf over the head with the President's bell, and another member choked him; a professor was flung down and belabored with fists and choked; he held up an open penknife as a defense against the blows; it was snatched from him and flung to a distance; it hit a peaceful Christian Socialist who wasn't doing anything, and brought blood from his hand. This was the only blood drawn. The men who got hammered and choked looked sound and well next day. The fists and the

speakers was studiously formal and academic, and the storms and explosions of to-day were wholly unknown," etc.—*Translation of the opening remark of an editorial in this morning's Neue Freie Presse, December 1.*

bell were not properly handled, or better results would have been apparent. I am quite sure that the fighters were not in earnest.

On Thanksgiving day the sitting was a history-making one. On that day the harried, bedeviled, and despairing government went insane. In order to free itself from the thraldom of the Opposition it committed this curiously juvenile crime: it moved an important change of the Rules of the House, forbade debate upon the motion, put it to a stand-up vote instead of ayes and noes, and then gravely claimed that it had been adopted; whereas, to even the dullest witness—if I without immodesty may pretend to that place—it was plain that nothing legitimately to be called a vote had been taken at all.

I think that Saltpeter never uttered a truer thing than when he said, "Whom the gods would destroy they first make mad."

Evidently the government's mind was tottering when this bald insult to the House was the best way it could contrive for getting out of the frying-pan.

The episode would have been funny if the matter at stake had been a trifle; but in the circumstances it was pathetic. The usual storm was raging in the House. As usual, many of the Majority and the most of the Minority were standing up—to have a better chance to exchange epithets and make other noises. Into this storm Count Falkenhayn entered, with his paper in his hand; and at once there was a rush to get near him and hear him read his motion. In a moment he was walled in by listeners. The several clauses of his motion were loudly applauded by these allies, and as loudly disapplauded—if I may invent a word—by such of the Opposition as could hear his voice. When he took his seat the President promptly put the motion—persons desiring to vote in the affirmative, *stand up!* The House was already standing up; had been standing for an hour; and before a third of it had found out what the President had been saying, he had proclaimed the adoption of the motion! And only a few heard *that*. In fact, when that House is legislating you can't tell it from artillery practice.

You will realize what a happy idea it was to side-track the lawful ayes and noes and substitute a stand-up vote by this fact: that a little later, when a deputation of deptuties waited upon the President and asked him if he was actually willing to claim that that measure had been passed, he answered, "Yes—and *unanimously*." It shows that in effect the whole house was on its feet when that trick was sprung.

The "Lex Falkenhayn," thus strangely born, gave the President power to suspend for three days any deputy who should continue to be disorderly after being called to order twice, and it also placed at his disposal such force as might be necessary to make the suspension effective. So the House had a sergeant-at-arms at last, and a more formidable one, as to power, than any other legislature in Christendom had ever possessed. The Lex Falkenhayn also gave the House itself authority to suspend members for *thirty* days.

On these terms the *Ausgleich* could be put through

in an hour—apparently. The Opposition would have to sit meek and quiet, and stop obstructing, or be turned into the street, deputy after deputy, leaving the Majority an unvexed field for its work.

Certainly the thing looked well. The government was out of the frying-pan at last. It congratulated itself, and was almost girlishly happy. Its stock rose suddenly from less than nothing to a premium. It confessed to itself, with pride, that its Lex Falkenhayn was a master-stroke—a work of genius.

However, there were doubters; men who were troubled, and believed that a grave mistake had been made. It might be that the Opposition was crushed, and profitably for the country, too; but the *manner* of it—the *manner* of it! That was the serious part. It could have far-reaching results; results whose gravity might transcend all guessing. It might be the initial step toward a return to government by force, a restoration of the irresponsible methods of obsolete times.

There were no vacant seats in the galleries next day. In fact, standing-room outside the building was at a premium. There were crowds there, and a glittering array of helmeted and brass-buttoned police, on foot and on horseback, to keep them from getting too much excited. No one could guess what was going to happen, but every one felt that *something* was going to happen, and hoped he might have a chance to see it, or at least get the news of it while it was fresh.

At noon the House was empty—for I do not count myself. Half an hour later the two galleries were solidly packed, the floor still empty. Another half-hour later Wolf entered and passed to his place; then other deputies began to stream in, among them many forms and faces grown familiar of late. By one o'clock the membership was present in full force. A band of Socialists stood grouped against the ministerial desks, in the shadow of the Presidential tribune. It was observable that these official strongholds were now protected against rushes by bolted gates, and that these were in ward of servants wearing the House's livery. Also the removable desk-boards had been taken away, and nothing left for disorderly members to slat with.

There was a pervading, anxious hush—at least what stood very well for a hush in that house. It was believed by many that the Opposition was cowed, and that there would be no more obstruction, no more noise. That was an error.

Presently the President entered by the distant door to the right, followed by Vice-President Fuchs, and the two took their way down past the Polish benches toward the tribune. Instantly the customary storm of noises burst out, and rose higher and higher, and wilder and wilder, and really seemed to surpass anything that had gone before it in that place. The President took his seat, and begged for order, but no one could hear him. His lips moved—one could see that; he bowed his body forward appealingly, and spread his great hand eloquently over his breast— one could see that; but as concerned his uttered words, he probably could not hear them himself. Below him was that crowd of two dozen Socialists glaring up at him, shaking their fists at him, roaring imprecations and insulting epithets at him. This went on for some time. Suddenly the Socialists burst through the gates and stormed up through the ministerial benches, and a man in a red cravat reached up and snatched the documents that lay on the President's desk and flung them abroad. The next moment he and his allies were struggling and fighting with the half-dozen uniformed servants who were there to protect the new gates. Meantime a detail of Socialists had swarmed up the side-steps and overflowed the President and the Vice, and were crowding and shouldering and shoving them out of the place. They crowded them out, and down the steps and across the House, past the Polish benches; and all about them swarmed hostile Poles and Czechs, who resisted them. One could see fists go up and come down, with other signs and shows of a heady fight; then the President and the Vice disappeared through the door of entrance, and the victorious Socialists turned and marched back, mounted the tribune, flung the President's bell and his remaining papers abroad, and then stood there in a compact little crowd, eleven strong, and held the place as if it were a fortress. Their friends on the floor were in a frenzy of triumph, and manifested it in their deafening way. The whole House was on its feet, amazed and wondering.

It was an astonishing situation, and imposingly dramatic. Nobody had looked for this. The unexpected had happened. What next? But there *can* be no next; the play is over; the grand climax is reached; the possibilities are exhausted: ring down the curtain.

Not yet. That distant door opens again. And now we see what history will be talking of five centuries hence: a uniformed and helmeted battalion of bronzed and stalwart men marching in double file down the floor of the House—a free parliament 'profaned by an invasion of brute force.

It was an odious spectacle—odious and awful. For one moment it was an unbelievable thing— thing beyond all credibility; it must be a delusion, dream, a nightmare. But no, it was real—pitifully real, shamefully real, hideously real. These sixty policemen had been soldiers, and they went at their work with the cold unsentimentality of their trade. They ascended the steps of the tribune, laid their hands upon the inviolable persons of the representatives of a nation, and dragged and tugged and hauled them down the steps and out at the door; then ranged themselves in stately military array in front of the ministerial *estrade*, and so stood.

It was a tremendous episode. The memory of it will outlast all the thrones that exist to-day. In the whole history of free parliaments the like of it had been seen but three times before. It takes its imposing place among the world's unforgetable things. I think that in my lifetime I have not twice seen abiding history made before my eyes, but I know that I have seen it once.

Some of the results of this wild freak followed instantly. The Badeni government came down with a crash; there was a popular outbreak or two in

Vienna; there were three or four days of furious rioting in Prague, followed by the establishing there of martial law; the Jews and Germans were harried and plundered, and their houses destroyed; in other Bohemian towns there was rioting—in some cases the Germans being the rioters in others the Czechs —and in all cases the Jew had to roast, no matter which side he was on. We are well along in December now;[1] the new Minister-President has not been able to patch up a peace among the warring factions of the parliament, therefore there is no use in calling it together again for the present; public opinion believes that parliamentary government and the Constitution are actually threatened with extinction, and that the permanency of the monarchy itself is a not absolutely certain thing!

Yes, the Lex Falkenhayn was a great invention, and did what was claimed for it—it got the government out of the frying-pan.

[1] It is the 9th.—M. T.

THE GERMAN CHICAGO

I FEEL lost in Berlin. It has no resemblance to
the city I had supposed it was. There was once
a Berlin which I would have known, from descrip-
tions in books—the Berlin of the last century and the
beginning of the present one: a dingy city in a marsh,
with rough streets, muddy and lantern - lighted,
dividing straight rows of ugly houses all alike, compacted into blocks as square and plain and uniform
and monotonous and serious as so many dry-goods
boxes. But that Berlin has disappeared. It seems
to have disappeared totally, and left no sign. The
bulk of the Berlin of to-day has about it no suggestion of a former period. The site it stands on has
traditions and a history, but the city itself has no
traditions and no history. It is a new city; the
newest I have ever seen. Chicago would seem
venerable beside it; for there are many old-looking
districts in Chicago, but not many in Berlin. The
main mass of the city looks as if it had been built
last week, the rest of it has a just perceptibly graver
tone, and looks as if it might be six or even eight
months old.

The next feature that strikes one is the spaciousness, the roominess of the city. There is no other
city, in any country, whose streets are so generally

wide. Berlin is not merely a city of wide streets, it is *the* city of wide streets. As a wide-street city it has never had its equal, in any age of the world. "Unter den Linden" is three streets in one; the Potsdamerstrasse is bordered on both sides by side-walks which are themselves wider than some of the historic thoroughfares of the old European capitals; there seem to be no lanes or alleys; there are no short cuts; here and there, where several important streets empty into a common center, that center's circumference is of a magnitude calculated to bring that word spaciousness into your mind again. The park in the middle of the city is so huge that it calls up that expression once more.

The next feature that strikes one is the straightness of the streets. The short ones haven't so much as a waver in them; the long ones stretch out to pro-digious distances and then tilt a little to the right or left, then stretch out on another immense reach as straight as a ray of light. A result of this arrange-ment is, that at night Berlin is an inspiring sight to see. Gas and the electric light are employed with a wasteful liberality, and so, wherever one goes, he has always double ranks of brilliant lights stretching far down into the night on every hand, with here and there a wide and splendid constellation of them spread out over an intervening "Platz"; and be-tween the interminable double procession of street lamps one has the swarming and darting cab lamps, a lively and pretty addition to the fine spectacle, for they counterfeit the rush and confusion and sparkle of an invasion of fireflies.

There is one other noticeable feature—the absolutely level surface of the site of Berlin. Berlin—to recapitulate—is newer to the eye than is any other city, and also blonder of complexion and tidier; no other city has such an air of roominess, freedom from crowding; no other city has so many straight streets; and with Chicago it contests the chrome for flatness of surface and for phenomenal swiftness of growth. Berlin is the European Chicago. The two cities have about the same population—say a million and a half. I cannot speak in exact terms, because I only know what Chicago's population was week before last; but at that time it was about a million and a half. Fifteen years ago Berlin and Chicago were large cities, of course, but neither of them was the giant it now is.

But now the parallels fail. Only parts of Chicago are stately and beautiful, whereas all of Berlin is stately and substantial, and it is not merely in parts but uniformly beautiful. There are buildings in Chicago that are architecturally finer than any in Berlin, I think, but what I have just said above is still true. These two flat cities would lead the world for phenomenal good health if London were out of the way. As it is, London leads by a point or two. Berlin's death rate is only nineteen in the thousand. Fourteen years ago the rate was a third higher.

Berlin is a surprise in a great many ways—in a multitude of ways, to speak strongly and be exact. It seems to be the most governed city in the world, but one must admit that it also seems to be the best governed. Method and system are observable on every hand—in great things, in little things, in all details, of whatsoever size. And it is not method and system on paper, and there an end—it is method and system in practice. It has a rule for everything, and puts the rule in force; puts it in force against the poor and powerful alike, without favor or prejudice. It deals with great matters and minute particulars with equal faithfulness, and with a plodding and painstaking diligence and persistency which compel admiration—and sometimes regret. There are several taxes, and they are collected quarterly. Collected is the word; they are not merely levied, they are collected—every time. This makes light taxes. It is in cities and countries where a considerable part of the community shirk payment that taxes have to be lifted to a burdensome rate. Here the police keep coming, calmly and patiently, until you pay your tax. They charge you five or ten cents per visit after the first call. By experiment you will find that they will presently collect that money.

In one respect the million and a half of Berlin's population are like a family: the head of this large family knows the names of its several members, and where the said members are located, and when and where they were born, and what they do for a living, and what their religious brand is. Whoever comes to Berlin must furnish these particulars to the police immediately; moreover, if he knows how long he is going to stay, he must say so. If he take a house he will be taxed on the rent and taxed also on his income. He will not be asked what his income is, and so he may save some lies for home consumption. The police will estimate his income from the house-rent he pays, and tax him on that basis.

Duties on imported articles are collected with inflexible fidelity, be the sum large or little; but the methods are gentle, prompt, and full of the spirit of accommodation. The postman attends to the whole matter for you, in cases where the article comes by mail, and you have no trouble and suffer no inconvenience. The other day a friend of mine was informed that there was a package in the post-office for him, containing a lady's silk belt with gold clasp, and a gold chain to hang a bunch of keys on. In his first agitation he was going to try to bribe the postman to chalk it through, but acted upon his sober second thought and allowed the matter to take its proper and regular course. In a little while the postman brought the package and made these several collections: duty on the silk belt, 7½ cents; duty on the gold chain, 10 cents; charge for fetching the package, 5 cents. These devastating imposts are exacted for the protection of German home industries.

The calm, quiet, courteous, cussed persistence of the police is the most admirable thing I have encountered on this side. They undertook to persuade me to send and get a passport for a Swiss maid whom we had brought with us, and at the end of six weeks of patient, tranquil, angelic daily effort they succeeded. I was not intending to give them trouble, but I was lazy and I thought they would get tired. Meanwhile they probably thought I would be the one. It turned out just so.

THE GERMAN CHICAGO

One is not allowed to build unstable, unsafe, or unsightly houses in Berlin; the result is this comely and conspicuously stately city, with its security from conflagrations and breakdowns. It is built of architectural Gibraltars. The building commissioners inspect while the building is going up. It has been found that this is better than to wait till it falls down. These people are full of whims.

One is not allowed to cram poor folk into cramped and dirty tenement houses. Each individual must have just so many cubic feet of room-space, and sanitary inspections are systematic and frequent.

Everything is orderly. The fire brigade march in rank, curiously uniformed, and so grave is their demeanor that they look like a Salvation Army under conviction of sin. People tell me that when a fire alarm is sounded, the firemen assemble calmly, answer to their names when the roll is called, then proceed to the fire. There they are ranked up, military fashion, and told off in detachments by the chief, who parcels out to the detachments the several parts of the work which they are to undertake in putting out that fire. This is all done with low-voiced propriety, and strangers think these people are working a funeral. As a rule, the fire is confined to a single floor in these great masses of bricks and masonry, and consequently there is little or no interest attaching to a fire here for the rest of the occupants of the house.

There is abundance of newspapers in Berlin, and there was also a newsboy, but he died. At intervals of half a mile on the thoroughfares there are booths, and it is at these that you buy your papers. There are plenty of theaters, but they do not advertise in a loud way. There are no big posters of any kind, and the display of vast type and of pictures of actors and performance framed on a big scale and done in rainbow colors is a thing unknown. If the big show-bills existed there would be no place to exhibit them; for there are no poster-fences, and one would not be allowed to disfigure dead walls with them. Unsightly things are forbidden here; Berlin is a rest to the eye.

And yet the saunterer can easily find out what is going on at the theaters. All over the city, at short distances apart, there are neat round pillars eighteen feet high and about as thick as a hogshead, and on these the little black and white theater bills and other notices are posted. One generally finds a group around each pillar reading these things. There are plenty of things in Berlin worth importing to America. It is these that I have particularly wished to make a note of. When Buffalo Bill was here his biggest poster was probably not larger than the top of an ordinary trunk.

There is a multiplicity of clean and comfortable horse-cars, but whenever you think you know where a car is going to you would better stop ashore, because that car is not going to that place at all. The car routes are marvelously intricate, and often the drivers get lost and are not heard of for years. The signs on the cars furnish no details as to the course of the journey; they name the end of it, and then experiment around to see how much territory they can cover before they get there. The conductor will collect your fare over again every few miles, and give you a ticket which he hasn't apparently kept any record of, and you keep it til' an inspector comes aboard by and by and tears a corner off it (which he does not keep), then you throw the ticket away and get ready to buy another. Brains are of no value when you are trying to navigate Berlin in a horse-car. When the ablest of Brooklyn's editors was here on a visit he took a horse-car in the early morning, and wore it out trying to go to a point in the center of the city. He was on board all day and spent many dollars in fares, and then did not arrive at the place which he had started to go to. This is the most thorough way to see Berlin, but it is also the most expensive.

But there are excellent features about the car system, nevertheless. The car will not stop for you to get on or off, except at certain places a block or two apart where there is a sign to indicate that that is a halting-station. This system saves many bones. There are twenty places inside the car; when these seats are filled, no more can enter. Four or five persons may stand on each platform—the law decrees the number—and when these standing-places are all occupied the next applicant is refused. As there is no crowding, and as no rowdyism is allowed, women stand on the platforms as well as the men; they often stand there when there are vacant seats inside, for these places are comfortable, there being little or no jolting. A native tells me that when the first car was put on, thirty or forty years ago, the public had such a terror of it that they didn't feel safe inside of it, or outside either. They made the company keep a man at every crossing with a red flag in his hand. Nobody would travel in the car except convicts on the way to the gallows. This made business in only one direction, and the car had to go back light. To save the company, the city government transferred the convict cemetery to the other end of the line. This made traffic in both directions and kept the company from going under. This sounds like some of the information which traveling foreigners are furnished with in America. To my mind it has a doubtful ring about it.

The first-class cab is neat and trim, and has leather-cushion seats and a swift horse. The second-class cab is an ugly and lubberly vehicle, and is always old. It seems a strange thing that they have never built any new ones. Still, if such a thing were done everybody that had time to flock would flock to see it, and that would make a crowd, and the police do not like crowds and disorder here. If there were an earthquake in Berlin the police would take charge of it and conduct it in that sort of orderly way that would make you think it was a prayer-meeting. That is what an earthquake generally ends in, but this one would be different from those others; it would be kind of soft and self-contained, like a republican praying for a mugwump.

For a course (a quarter of an hour or less), one pays twenty-five cents in a first-class cab, and fifteen cents in a second-class. The first-class will take you along faster, for the second-class horse is old—

always old—as old as his cab, some authorities say —and ill-fed and weak. He has been a first-class once, but has been degraded to second class for long and faithful service.

Still, he must take you as *far* for fifteen cents as the other horse takes you for twenty-five. If he can't do his fifteen-minute distance in fifteen minutes, he must still do the distance for the fifteen cents. Any stranger can check the distance off—by means of the most curious map I am acquainted with. It is issued by the city government and can be bought in any shop for a trifle. In it every street is sectioned off like a string of long beads of different colors. Each long bead represents a minute's travel, and when you have covered fifteen of the beads you have got your money's worth. This map of Berlin is a gay-colored maze, and looks like pictures of the circulation of the blood.

The streets are very clean. They are kept so—not by prayer and talk and the other New York methods, but by daily and hourly work with scrapers and brooms; and when an asphalted street has been tidily scraped after a rain or a light snowfall, they scatter clean sand over it. This saves some of the horses from falling down. In fact, this is a city government which seems to stop at no expense where the public convenience, comfort, and health are concerned—except in one detail. That is the naming of the streets and the numbering of the houses. Sometimes the name of a street will change in the middle of a block. You will not find it out till you get to the next corner and discover the new name on the wall, and of course you don't know just when the change happened.

The names are plainly marked on the corners—on all the corners—there are no exceptions. But the numbering of the houses—there has never been anything like it since original chaos. It is not possible that it was done by this wise city government. At first one thinks it was done by an idiot; but there is too much variety about it for that; an idiot could not think of so many different ways of making confusion and propagating blasphemy. The numbers run up one side the street and down the other. That is endurable, but the rest isn't. They often use one number for three or four houses—and sometimes they put the number on only one of the houses and let you guess at the others. Sometimes they put a number on a house—4, for instance—then put 4a, 4b, 4c, on the succeeding houses, and one becomes old and decrepit before he finally arrives at 5. A result of this systemless system is that when you are at No. 1 in a street you haven't any idea how far it may be to No. 150; it may be only six or eight blocks, it may be a couple of miles. Frederick Street is long, and is one of the great thoroughfares. The other day a man put up his money behind the assertion that there were more refreshment places in that street than numbers on the houses—and he won. There were 254 numbers and 257 refreshment places. Yet as I have said, it is a long street.

But the worst feature of all this complex business is that in Berlin the numbers do not travel in any one direction; no, they travel along until they get to 50 or 60, perhaps, then suddenly you find yourself up in the hundreds—140, maybe; the next will be 139—then you perceive by that sign that the numbers are now traveling toward you from the opposite direction. They will keep that sort of insanity up as long as you travel that street, every now and then the numbers will turn and run the other way. As a rule, there is an arrow under the number, to show by the direction of its flight which way the numbers are proceeding. There are a good many suicides in Berlin; I have seen six reported in a single day. There is always a deal of learned and laborious arguing and ciphering going on as to the cause of this state of things. If they will set to work and number their houses in a rational way perhaps they will find out what was the matter.

More than a month ago Berlin began to prepare to celebrate Professor Virchow's seventieth birthday. When the birthday arrived, the middle of October, it seemed to me that all the world of science arrived with it; deputation after deputation came, bringing the homage and reverence of far cities and centers of learning, and during the whole of a long day the hero of it sat and received such witness of his greatness as has seldom been vouchsafed to any man in any walk of life in any time, ancient or modern. These demonstrations were continued in one form or another day after day, and were presently merged in similar demonstrations to his twin in science and achievement, Professor Helmholtz, whose seventieth birthday is separated from Virchow's by only about three weeks; so nearly as this did these two extraordinary men come to being born together. Two such births have seldom signalized a single year in human history.

But perhaps the final and closing demonstration was peculiarly grateful to them. This was a Commers given in their honor the other night by 1,000 students. It was held in a huge hall, very long and very lofty, which had five galleries, far above everybody's head, which were crowded with ladies—four or five hundred, I judged.

It was beautifully decorated with clustered flags and various ornamental devices, and was brilliantly lighted. On the spacious floor of this place were ranged, in files, innumerable tables, seating twenty-four persons each, extending from one end of the great hall clear to the other, and with narrow aisles between the files. In the center on one side was a high and tastefully decorated platform twenty or thirty feet long, with a long table on it behind which sat the half-dozen chiefs of the givers of the Commers in the rich medieval costumes of as many different college corps. Behind these youths a band of musicians was concealed. On the floor directly in front of this platform were half a dozen tables which were distinguished from the outlying continent of tables by being covered instead of left naked. Of these the central table was reserved for the two heroes of the occasion and twenty particularly eminent professors of the Berlin University, and the other covered tables were for the occupancy of a hundred less distinguished professors.

I was glad to be honored with a place at the table

of the two heroes of the occasion, although I was not really learned enough to deserve it. Indeed, there was a pleasant strangeness in being in such company; to be thus associated with twenty-three men who forget more every day than I ever knew. Yet there was nothing embarrassing about it, because loaded men and empty ones look about alike, and I knew that to that multitude there I was a professor. It required but little art to catch the ways and attitude of those men and imitate them, and I had no difficulty in looking as much like a professor as anybody there.

We arrived early; so early that only Professors Virchow and Helmholtz and a dozen guests of the special tables were ahead of us, and three hundred or four hundred students. But people were arriving in floods now, and within fifteen minutes all but the special tables were occupied, and the great house was crammed, the aisles included. It was said that there were four thousand men present. It was a most animated scene, there is no doubt about that; it was a stupendous beehive. At each end of each table stood a corps student in the uniform of his corps. These quaint costumes are of brilliant colored silks and velvets, with sometimes a high plumed hat, sometimes a broad Scotch cap, with a great plume wound about it, sometimes —oftenest—a little shallow silk cap on the tip of the crown, like an inverted saucer; sometimes the pantaloons are snow-white, sometimes of other colors; the boots in all cases come up well above the knee; and in all cases also white gauntlets are worn;

the sword is a rapier with a bowl-shaped guard for the hand, painted in several colors. Each corps has a uniform of its own, and all are of rich material, brilliant in color, and exceedingly picturesque; for they are survivals of the vanished costumes of the Middle Ages, and they reproduce for us the time when men were beautiful to look at. The student who stood guard at our end of the table was of grave countenance and great frame and grace of form, and he was doubtless an accurate reproduction, clothes and all, of some ancestor of his of two or three centuries ago—a reproduction as far as the outside, the animal man, goes, I mean.

As I say, the place was now crowded. The nearest aisle was packed with students standing up, and they made a fence which shut off the rest of the house from view. As far down this fence as you could see all these wholesome young faces were turned in one direction, all these intent and worshiping eyes were centered upon one spot—the place where Virchow and Helmholtz sat. The boys seemed lost to everything, unconscious of their own existence; they devoured these two intellectual giants with their eyes, they feasted upon them, and the worship that was in their hearts shone in their faces. It seemed to me that I would rather be flooded with a glory like that, instinct with sincerity, innocent of self-seeking, than win a hundred battles and break a million hearts.

There was a big mug of beer in front of each of us, and more to come when wanted. There was also a quarto pamphlet containing the words of the songs

THE GERMAN CHICAGO

to be sung. After the names of the officers of the feast were these words in large type:

"Während des Kommerses herrscht allgemeiner Burgfriede."

I was not able to translate this to my satisfaction, but a professor helped me out. This was his explanation: The students in uniform belong to different college corps; not all students belong to corps; none join the corps except those who enjoy fighting. The corps students fight duels with swords every week, one corps challenging another corps to furnish a certain number of duelists for the occasion, and it is only on this battle-field that students of different corps exchange courtesies. In common life they do not drink with each other or speak. The above line now translates itself: there is truce during the Commers, war is laid aside and fellowship takes its place.

Now the performance began. The concealed band played a piece of martial music; then there was a pause. The students on the platform rose to their feet, the middle one gave a toast to the Emperor, then all the house rose, mugs in hand. At the call "One—two—three!" all glasses were drained and then brought down with a slam on the tables in unison. The result was as good an imitation of thunder as I have ever heard. From now on, during an hour, there was singing, in mighty chorus. During each interval between songs a number of the special guests — the professors — arrived. There seemed to be some signal whereby the students on the platform were made aware that a professor had

259

arrived at the remote door of entrance; for you would see them suddenly rise to their feet, strike an erect military attitude, then draw their swords; the swords of all their brethren standing guard at the innumerable tables would flash from their scabbards and be held aloft—a handsome spectacle! Three clear bugle notes would ring out, then all these swords would come down with a crash, twice repeated, on the tables, and be uplifted and held aloft again; then in the distance you would see the gay uniforms and uplifted swords of a guard of honor clearing the way and conducting the guest down to his place.   The songs were stirring, the immense outpour from young life and young lungs, the crash of swords and the thunder of the beer-mugs gradually worked a body up to what seemed the last possible summit of excitement.   It surely seemed to me that I had reached that summit, that I had reached my limit, and that there was no higher lift desirable for me.   When apparently the last eminent guest had long ago taken his place, again those three bugle blasts rang out and once more the swords leaped from their scabbards.   Who might this late comer be?   Nobody was interested to inquire.   Still, indolent eyes were turned toward the distant entrance; we saw the silken gleam and the lifted swords of a guard of honor plowing through the remote crowds. Then we saw that end of the house rising to its feet; saw it rise abreast the advancing guard all along, like a wave.   This supreme honor had been offered to no one before.   Then there was an excited whisper at our table—"MOMMSEN!" and the whole house rose. Rose and shouted and stamped and clapped, and banged the beer-mugs. Just simply a storm! Then the little man with his long hair and Emersonian face edged his way past us and took his seat. I could have touched him with my hand—Mommsen! —think of it!

This was one of those immense surprises that can happen only a few times in one's life. I was not dreaming of him, he was to me only a giant myth, a world-shadowing specter, not a reality. The surprise of it all can be only comparable to a man's suddenly coming upon Mont Blanc, with its awful form towering into the sky, when he didn't suspect he was in its neighborhood. I would have walked a great many miles to get a sight of him, and here he was, without trouble or tramp or cost of any kind. Here he was, clothed in a Titanic deceptive modesty which made him look like other men. Here he was, carrying the Roman world and all the Cæsars in his hospitable skull, and doing it as easily as that other luminous vault, the skull of the universe, carries the Milky Way and the constellations.

One of the professors said that once upon a time an American young lady was introduced to Mommsen, and found herself badly scared and speechless. She dreaded to see his mouth unclose, for she was expecting him to choose a subject several miles above her comprehension, and didn't suppose he *could* get down to the world that other people lived in; but when his remark came, her terrors disappeared: "Well, how do you do? Have you read Howells's last book? *I* think it's his best."

The active ceremonies of the evening closed with the speeches of welcome delivered by two students and the replies made by Professors Virchow and Helmholtz.

Virchow has long been a member of the city government of Berlin. He works as hard for the city as does any other Berlin alderman, and gets the same pay—nothing. I don't know that we in America could venture to ask our most illustrious citizen to serve in a board of aldermen, and if we might venture it I am not positively sure that we could elect him. But here the municipal system is such that the best men in the city consider it an honor to serve gratis as aldermen, and the people have the good sense to prefer these men and to elect them year after year. As a result Berlin is a thoroughly well-governed city. It is a free city; its affairs are not meddled with by the state; they are managed by its own citizens, and after methods of their own devising.

CONCERNING THE JEWS

SOME months ago I published a magazine article descriptive of a remarkable scene in the Imperial Parliament in Vienna. Since then I have received from Jews in America several letters of inquiry. They were difficult letters to answer, for they were not very definite. But at last I received a definite one. It is from a lawyer, and he really asks the questions which the other writers probably believed they were asking. By help of this text I will do the best I can to publicly answer this correspondent, and also the others—at the same time apologizing for having failed to reply privately. The lawyer's letter reads as follows:

I have read "Stirring Times in Austria." One point in particular is of vital import to not a few thousand people, including myself, being a point about which I have often wanted to address a question to some disinterested person. The show of military force in the Austrian Parliament, which precipitated the riots, was not introduced by any Jew. No Jew was a member of that body. No Jewish question was involved in the *Ausgleich* or in the language proposition. No Jew was insulting anybody. In short, no Jew was doing any mischief toward anybody whatsoever. In fact, the Jews were the only ones of the nineteen different races in Austria which did not have a party—they are absolutely non-participants. Yet in your article you say that in the rioting which followed, all classes of people were unanimous only on one thing—*viz.*, in being against the Jews. Now will you kindly tell me why, in your judgment, the Jews have thus ever been, and are even now, in these days of supposed intelligence, the butt of baseless, vicious animosities? I dare say that for centuries there has been no more quiet, undisturbing, and well-behaving citizens, as a class, than that same Jew. It seems to me that ignorance and fanaticism cannot alone account for these horrible and unjust persecutions.

Tell me, therefore, from your vantage-point of cold view, what in your mind is the cause. Can American Jews do anything to correct it either in America or abroad? Will it ever come to an end? Will a Jew be permitted to live honestly, decently, and peaceably like the rest of mankind? What has become of the golden rule?

I will begin by saying that if I thought myself prejudiced against the Jew, I should hold it fairest to leave this subject to a person not crippled in that way. But I think I have no such prejudice. A few years ago a Jew observed to me that there was no uncourteous reference to his people in my books, and asked how it happened. It happened because the disposition was lacking. I am quite sure that (bar one) I have no race prejudices, and I think I have no color prejudices nor caste prejudices nor creed prejudices. Indeed, I know it. I can stand any society. All that I care to know is that a man is a human being—that is enough for me; he can't be any worse. I have no special regard for Satan; but I can at least claim that I have no prejudice against him. It may even be that I lean a little his way, on account of his not having a fair show. All religions issue bibles against him, and say the most injurious things about him, but we never hear *his* side. We have none but the evidence for the prosecution, and yet we have rendered the verdict. To my mind, this is irregular. It is un-English; it is un-American; it is French. Without this precedent Dreyfus could not have been condemned. Of course Satan has some kind of a case, it goes without saying. It may be a poor one, but that is nothing; that can be said about any of us. As soon as I can get at the facts I will undertake his rehabilitation myself, if I can find an unpolitic publisher. It is a thing which we ought to be willing to do for any one who is under a cloud. We may not pay him reverence, for that would be indiscreet, but we can at least respect his talents. A person who has for untold centuries maintained the imposing position of spiritual head of four-fifths of the human race, and political head of the whole of it, must be granted the possession of executive abilities of the loftiest order. In his large presence the other popes and politicians shrink to midges for the microscope. I would like to see him. I would rather see him and shake him by the tail than any other member of the European Concert. In the present paper I shall allow myself to use the word Jew as if it stood for both religion and race. It is handy; and, besides, that is what the term means to the general world.

In the above letter one notes these points:

1. The Jew is a well-behaved citizen.

2. Can ignorance and fanaticism *alone* account for his unjust treatment?

3. Can Jews do anything to improve the situation?

4. The Jews have no party; they are non-participants.

5. Will the persecution ever come to an **end?**

6. What has become of the golden rule?

Point No. 1.—We must grant proposition No. **1,** for several sufficient reasons. The Jew is not a disturber of the peace of any country. Even his enemies will concede that. He is not a loafer, he is not a sot, he is not noisy, he is not a brawler nor a rioter, he is not quarrelsome. In the statistics of crime his presence is conspicuously rare—in all countries. With murder and other crimes of violence he has but little to do: he is a stranger to the hangman. In the police court's daily long roll of "assaults" and "drunk and disorderlies" his name seldom appears. That the Jewish home is a home in the truest sense is a fact which no one will dispute. The family is knitted together by the strongest affections; its members show each other every due respect; and reverence for the elders is an inviolate law of the house. The Jew is not a burden on the charities of the state nor of the city; these could cease from their functions without affecting him. When he is well enough, he works; when he is incapacitated, his own people take care of him. And not in a poor and stingy way, but with a fine and large benevolence. His race is entitled to be called the most benevolent of all the races of men. A Jewish beggar is not impossible, perhaps; such a thing may exist, but there are few men that can say they have seen that spectacle. The Jew has been staged in many uncomplimentary forms, but, so far as I know, no dramatist has done him the injustice to stage him as a beggar. Whenever a Jew has real

need to beg, his people save him from the necessity
of doing it. The charitable institutions of the Jews
are supported by Jewish money, and amply. The
Jews make no noise about it; it is done quietly; they
do not nag and pester and harass us for contributions; they give us peace, and set us an example—
an example which we have not found ourselves able
to follow; for by nature we are not free givers, and
have to be patiently and persistently hunted down
in the interest of the unfortunate.

These facts are all on the credit side of the proposition that the Jew is a good and orderly citizen.
Summed up, they certify that he is quiet, peaceable,
industrious, unaddicted to high crimes and brutal
dispositions; that his family life is commendable;
that he is not a burden upon public charities; that
he is not a beggar; that in benevolence he is above
the reach of competition. These are the very
quintessentials of good citizenship. If you can add
that he is as honest as the average of his neighbors— But I think that question is affirmatively
answered by the fact that he is a successful business
man. The basis of successful business is honesty;
a business cannot thrive where the parties to it
cannot trust each other. In the matter of numbers
the Jew counts for little in the overwhelming population of New York; but that his honesty counts for
much is guaranteed by the fact that the immense
wholesale business of Broadway, from the Battery
to Union Square, is substantially in his hands.

I suppose that the most picturesque example in
history of a trader's trust in his fellow-trader was

one where it was not Christian trusting Christian, but Christian trusting Jew. That Hessian Duke who used to sell his subjects to George III. to fight George Washington with got rich at it; and by and by, when the wars engendered by the French Revolution made his throne too warm for him, he was obliged to fly the country. He was in a hurry, and had to leave his earnings behind—nine million dollars. He had to risk the money with some one without security. He did not select a Christian, but a Jew—a Jew of only modest means, but of high character; a character so high that it left him lonesome—Rothschild of Frankfort. Thirty years later, when Europe had become quiet and safe again, the Duke came back from overseas, and the Jew returned the loan, with interest added.[1]

[1] Here is another piece of picturesque history; and it reminds us that shabbiness and dishonesty are not the monopoly of any race or creed, but are merely human:

"Congress passed a bill to pay $379.56 to Moses Pendergrass, of Libertyville, Missouri. The story of the reason of this liberality is pathetically interesting, and shows the sort of pickle that an honest man may get into who undertakes to do an honest job of work for Uncle Sam. In 1886 Moses Pendergrass put in a bid for the contract to carry the mail on the route from Knob Lick to Libertyville and Coffman, thirty miles a day, from July 1, 1887, for one year. He got the postmaster at Knob Lick to write the letter for him, and while Moses intended that his bid should be $400, his scribe carelessly made it $4. Moses got the contract, and did not find out about the mistake until the end of the first quarter, when he got his first pay. When he found at what rate he was working he was sorely cast down, and opened communication with the Post Office Department. The department informed him that he must either carry out his contract or throw it up, and that if he threw it up his bondsmen would have to pay the government $1,459.85 damages. So Moses carried out his contract, walked thirty miles every weekday for a year, and carried the mail, and received for his labor $4—

268

CONCERNING THE JEWS

The Jew has his other side. He has some discreditable ways, though he has not a monopoly of them, because he cannot get entirely rid of vexatious Christian competition. We have seen that he seldom trangresses the laws against crimes of violence. Indeed, his dealings with courts are almost restricted to matters connected with commerce. He has a reputation for various small forms of cheating, and for practising oppressive usury, and for burning himself out to get the insurance and arranging for cunning contracts which leave him an exit but lock the other man in, and for smart evasions which find him safe and comfortable just within the strict letter of the law, when court and jury know very well that he has violated the spirit of it. He is a frequent and faithful and capable officer in the civil service, but he is charged with an unpatriotic disinclination to stand by the flag as a soldier—like the Christian Quaker.

Now if you offset these discreditable features by

or, to be accurate, $6.84; for, the route being extended after his bid was accepted, the pay was proportionately increased. Now, after ten years, a bill was finally passed to pay to Moses the difference between what he earned in that unlucky year and what he received."

The *Sun*, which tells the above story, says that bills were introduced in three or four Congresses for Moses' relief, and that committees repeatedly investigated his claim.

It took six Congresses, containing in their persons the compressed virtues of 70,000,000 of people, and cautiously and carefully giving expression to those virtues in the fear of God and the next election, eleven years to find out some way to cheat a fellow-Christian out of about $13 on his honestly executed contract, and out of nearly $300 due him on its enlarged terms. And they succeeded. During the same time they paid out $1,000,000,000 in pensions—a third of it unearned and undeserved. This indicates a splendid all-around competency in theft, for it starts with farthings, and works its industries all the way up to ship-loads. It may be possible that the Jews can beat this, but the man that bets on it is taking chances.

the creditable ones summarized in a preceding paragraph beginning with the words, "These facts are all
on the credit side," and strike a balance, what must
the verdict be? This, I think: that, the merits and
demerits being fairly weighed and measured on both
sides, the Christian can claim no superiority over the
Jew in the matter of good citizenship.

Yet, in all countries, from the dawn of history,
the Jew has been persistently and implacably hated,
and with frequency persecuted.

Point No. 2—"Can fanaticism *alone* account for
this?"

Years ago I used to think that it was responsible
for nearly all of it, but latterly I have come to think
that this was an error. Indeed, it is now my conviction that it is responsible for hardly any of it.
In this connection I call to mind Genesis, chapter
xlvii.

We have all thoughtfully—or unthoughtfully—
read the pathetic story of the years of plenty and
the years of famine in Egypt, and how Joseph, with
that opportunity, made a corner in broken hearts,
and the crusts of the poor, and human liberty—a
corner whereby he took a nation's money all away,
to the last penny; took a nation's land away, to
the last acre; then took the nation itself, buying
it for bread, man by man, woman by woman, child
by child, till all were slaves; a corner which took
everything, left nothing; a corner so stupendous
that, by comparison with it, the most gigantic
corners in subsequent history are but baby things,
for it dealt in hundreds of millions of bushels, and

its profits were reckonable by hundreds of millions of dollars, and it was a disaster so crushing that its effects have not wholly disappeared from Egypt to-day, more than three thousand years after the event.

Is it presumable that the eye of Egypt was upon Joseph, the foreign Jew, all this time? I think it likely. Was it friendly? We must doubt it. Was Joseph establishing a character for his race which would survive long in Egypt? And in time would his name come to be familiarly used to express that character—like Shylock's? It is hardly to be doubted. Let us remember that this was *centuries before the crucifixion.*

I wish to come down eighteen hundred years later and refer to a remark made by one of the Latin historians. I read it in a translation many years ago, and it comes back to me now with force. It was alluding to a time when people were still living who could have seen the Saviour in the flesh. Christianity was so new that the people of Rome had hardly heard of it, and had but confused notions of what it was. The substance of the remark was this: Some Christians were persecuted in Rome through error, they being *"mistaken for Jews."*

The meaning seems plain. These pagans had nothing against Christians, but they were quite ready to persecute Jews. For some reason or other they hated a Jew before they even knew what a Christian was. May I not assume, then, that the persecution of Jews is a thing which *antedates* Christianity and was not born of Christianity? I think so. What was the origin of the feeling?

MARK TWAIN

When I was a boy, in the back settlements of the Mississippi Valley, where a gracious and beautiful Sunday-school simplicity and unpracticality prevailed, the "Yankee" (citizen of the New England states) was hated with a splendid energy. But religion had nothing to do with it. In a trade, the Yankee was held to be about five times the match of the Westerner. His shrewdness, his insight, his judgment, his knowledge, his enterprise, and his formidable cleverness in applying these forces were frankly confessed, and most competently cursed.

In the cotton states, after the war, the simple and ignorant negroes made the crops for the white planter on shares. The Jew came down in force, set up shop on the plantation, supplied all the negro's wants on credit, and at the end of the season was proprietor of the negro's share of the present crop and of part of his share of the next one. Before long, the whites detested the Jew, and it is doubtful if the negro loved him.

The Jew is being legislated out of Russia. The reason is not concealed. The movement was instituted because the Christian peasant and villager stood no chance against his commercial abilities. He was always ready to lend money on a crop, and sell vodka and other necessaries of life on credit while the crop was growing. When settlement day came he owned the crop; and next year or year after he owned the farm, like Joseph.

In the dull and ignorant England of John's time everybody got into debt to the Jew. He gathered all lucrative enterprises into his hands; he was the king of commerce; he was ready to be helpful in all profitable ways; he even financed crusades for the rescue of the Sepulcher. To wipe out his account with the nation and restore business to its natural and incompetent channels he had to be banished the realm.

For the like reasons Spain had to banish him four hundred years ago, and Austria about a couple of centuries later.

In all the ages Christian Europe has been obliged to curtail his activities. If he entered upon a mechanical trade, the Christian had to retire from it. If he set up as a doctor, he was the best one, and he took the business. If he exploited agriculture, the other farmers had to get at something else. Since there was no way to successfully compete with him in any vocation, the law had to step in and save the Christian from the poorhouse. Trade after trade was taken away from the Jew by statute till practically none was left. He was forbidden to engage in agriculture; he was forbidden to practise law; he was forbidden to practise medicine, except among Jews; he was forbidden the handicrafts. Even the seats of learning and the schools of science had to be closed against this tremendous antagonist. Still, almost bereft of employments, he found ways to make money, even ways to get rich. Also ways to invest his takings well, for usury was not denied him. In the hard conditions suggested, the Jew without brains could not survive, and the Jew with brains had to keep them in good training and well sharpened up, or starve. Ages of restriction to the one tool which the law was not able to take from him—his brain—have made that tool singularly competent; ages of compulsory disuse of his hands have atrophied them, and he never uses them now. This history has a very, very commercial look, a most sordid and practical commercial look, the business aspect of a Chinese cheap-labor crusade. Religious prejudices may account for one part of it, but not for the other nine.

Protestants have persecuted Catholics, but they did not take their livelihoods away from them. The Catholics have persecuted the Protestants with bloody and awful bitterness, but they never closed agriculture and the handicrafts against them. Why was that? That has the candid look of genuine religious persecution, not a trade-union boycott in a religious disguise.

The Jews are harried and obstructed in Austria and Germany, and lately in France; but England and America give them an open field and yet survive. Scotland offers them an unembarrassed field too, but there are not many takers. There are a few Jews in Glasgow, and one in Aberdeen; but that is because they can't earn enough to get away. The Scotch pay themselves that compliment, but it is authentic.

I feel convinced that the Crucifixion has not much to do with the world's attitude toward the Jew; that the reasons for it are older than that event, as suggested by Egypt's experience and by Rome's regret for having persecuted an unknown quantity called a Christian, under the mistaken impression that she was merely persecuting a Jew. *Merely* a Jew—a skinned eel who was used to it. presumably. I am persuaded that in Russia, Austria, and Germany nine-tenths of the hostility to the Jew comes from the average Christian's inability to compete successfully with the average Jew in business—in either straight business or the questionable sort.

In Berlin, a few years ago, I read a speech which frankly urged the expulsion of the Jews from Germany; and the agitator's *reason* was as frank as his proposition. It was this: *that eighty-five per cent.* of the successful lawyers of Berlin were Jews, and that about the same percentage of the great and lucrative businesses of all sorts in Germany were in the hands of the Jewish race! Isn't it an amazing confession? It was but another way of saying that in a population of 48,000,000, of whom only 500,000 were registered as Jews, eighty-five per cent. of the brains and honesty of the whole was lodged in the Jews. I must insist upon the honesty—it is an essential of successful business, taken by and large. Of course it does not rule out rascals entirely, even among Christians, but it is a good working rule, nevertheless. The speaker's figures may have been inexact, but *the motive of persecution* stands out as clear as day.

The man claimed that in Berlin the banks, the newspapers, the theaters, the great mercantile, shipping, mining, and manufacturing interests, the big army and city contracts, the tramways, and pretty much all other properties of high value, and *also* the small businesses—were in the hands of the Jews. He said the Jew was pushing the Christian to the wall all along the line; that it was all a Christian could do to scrape together a living; and that the Jew *must* be banished, and soon—there was no other way of saving the Christian. Here in Vienna, last autumn, an agitator said that all these disastrous details were true of Austria-Hungary also; and in fierce language he demanded the expulsion of the Jews. When politicians come out without a blush and read the baby act in this frank way, *unrebuked*, it is a very good indication that they have a market back of them, and know where to fish for votes.

You note the crucial point of the mentioned agitation; the argument is that the Christian cannot *compete* with the Jew, and that hence his very bread is in peril. To human beings this is a much more hate-inspiring thing than is any detail connected with religion. With most people, of a necessity, bread and meat take first rank, religion second. I am convinced that the persecution of the Jew is not due in any large degree to religious prejudice.

No, the Jew is a money-getter; and in getting his money he is a very serious obstruction to less capable neighbors who are on the same quest. I think that that is the trouble. In estimating worldly values the Jew is not shallow, but deep. With precocious wisdom he found out in the morning of time that some men worship rank, some worship heroes, some worship power, some worship God, and that over these ideals they dispute and cannot unite —but that they all worship money; so he made it the end and aim of his life to get it. He was at

it in Egypt thirty-six centuries ago; he was at it in
Rome when that Christian got persecuted by mistake
for him; he has been at it ever since.   The cost to
him has been heavy; his success has made the whole
human race his enemy—but it has paid, for it has
brought him envy, and that is the only thing which
men will sell both soul and body to get.   He long
ago observed that a millionaire commands respect,
a two-millionaire homage, a multi-millionaire the
deepest deeps of adoration.   We all know that
feeling; we have seen it express itself.   We have
noticed that when the average man mentions the
name of a multi-millionaire he does it with that
mixture in his voice of awe and reverence and lust
which burns in a Frenchman's eye when it falls on
another man's centime.

Point No. 4.—"The Jews have no party; they are
non-participants."

Perhaps you have let the secret out and given
yourself away.   It seems hardly a credit to the race
that it is able to say that; or to you, sir, that you
can say it without remorse; more, that you should
offer it as a plea against maltreatment, injustice, and
oppression.   Who gives the Jew the right, who gives
any race the right, to sit still, in a free country,
and let somebody else look after its safety?   The
oppressed Jew was entitled to all pity in the former
times under brutal autocracies, for he was weak and
friendless, and had no way to help his case.   But
he has ways now, and he has had them for a century,
but I do not see that he has tried to make serious
use of them.   When the Revolution set him free in

France it was an act of grace—the grace of other people; he does not appear in it as a helper. I do not know that he helped when England set him free. Among the Twelve Sane Men of France who have stepped forward with great Zola at their head to fight (and win, I hope and believe [1]) the battle for the most infamously misused Jew of modern times, do you find a great or rich or illustrious Jew helping? In the United States he was created free in the beginning—he did not need to help, of course. In Austria, and Germany, and France he has a vote, but of what considerable use is it to him? He doesn't seem to know how to apply it to the best effect. With all his splendid capacities and all his fat wealth he is to-day not politically important in any country. In America, as early as 1854, the ignorant Irish hod-carrier, who had a spirit of his own and a way of exposing it to the weather, made it apparent to all that he must be politically reckoned with; yet fifteen years before that we hardly knew what an Irishman looked like. As an intelligent force, and numerically, he has always been away down, but he has governed the country just the same. It was because he was *organized*. It made his vote valuable—in fact, essential.

You will say the Jew is everywhere numerically feeble. That is nothing to the point—with the Irishman's history for an object-lesson. But I am coming to your numerical feebleness presently. In all parliamentary countries you could no doubt elect Jews to the legislatures—and even *one* member in

[1] The article was written in the summer of 1898.—EDITOR.

such a body is sometimes a force which counts.
How deeply have you concerned yourselves about
this in Austria, France, and Germany? Or even in
America for that matter? You remark that the Jews
were not to blame for the riots in this Reichsrath
here, and you add with satisfaction that there wasn't
one in that body. That is not strictly correct; if it
were, would it not be in order for you to explain it
and apologize for it, not try to make a merit of it?
But I think that the Jew was by no means in as large
force there as he ought to have been, with his
chances. Austria opens the suffrage to him on fairly
liberal terms, and it must surely be his own fault
that he is so much in the background politically.

As to your numerical weakness. I mentioned
some figures awhile ago—500,000—as the Jewish
population of Germany. I will add some more—
6,000,000 in Russia, 5,000,000 in Austria, 250,000
in the United States. I take them from memory;
I read them in the *Encyclopædia Britannica* about
ten years ago. Still, I am entirely sure of them.
If those statistics are correct, my argument is not
as strong as it ought to be as concerns America,
but it still has strength. It is plenty strong enough
as concerns Austria, for ten years ago 5,000,000
was nine per cent. of the empire's population.
The Irish would govern the Kingdom of Heaven if
they had a strength there like that.

I have some suspicions; I got them at second hand,
but they have remained with me these ten or twelve
years. When I read in the *E. B.* that the Jewish
population of the United States was 250,000, I

wrote the editor, and explained to him that I was personally acquainted with more Jews than that in my country, and that his figures were without doubt a misprint for 25,000,000.   I also added that I was personally acquainted with *that* many there; but that was only to raise his confidence in me, for it was not true.   His answer miscarried, and I never got it; but I went around talking about the matter, and people told me they had reason to suspect that for business reasons many Jews whose dealings were mainly with the Christians did not report themselves as Jews in the census.   It looked plausible; it looks plausible yet.   Look at the city of New York; and look at Boston, and Philadelphia, and New Orleans, and Chicago, and Cincinnati, and San Francisco—how your race swarms in those places!— and everywhere else in America, down to the least little village.   Read the signs on the marts of commerce and on the shops: Goldstein (gold stone), Edelstein (precious stone), Blumenthal (flower-vale), Rosenthal (rose-vale), Veilchenduft (violet odor), Singvogel (song-bird), Rosenzweig (rose branch), and all the amazing list of beautiful and enviable names which Prussia and Austria glorified you with so long ago.   It is another instance of Europe's coarse and cruel persecution of your race; not that it was coarse and cruel to outfit it with pretty and poetical names like those, but that it was coarse and cruel to make it *pay* for them or else take such hideous and often indecent names that to-day their owners never use them; or, if they do, only on official papers.   And it was the many, not the few, who got the odious names, they being too poor to bribe the officials to grant them better ones.

Now why was the race renamed? I have been told that in Prussia it was given to using fictitious names, and often changing them, so as to beat the tax-gatherer, escape military service, and so on; and that finally the idea was hit upon of furnishing all the inmates of a house with *one and the same surname*, and then holding the house responsible right along for those inmates, and accountable for any disappearances that might occur; it made the Jews keep track of *each other*, for self-interest's sake, and saved the government the trouble.[1]

If that explanation of how the Jews of Prussia came to be renamed is correct, if it is true that they fictitiously registered themselves to gain certain advantages, it may possibly be true that in America they refrain from registering themselves as Jews to fend off the damaging prejudices of the Christian customer. I have no way of knowing whether this notion is well founded or not. There may be other and better ways of explaining why only that poor little 250,000 of our Jews got into the *Encyclopædia*. I may, of course, be mistaken, but I am strongly

[1] In Austria the renaming was merely done because the Jews in some newly acquired regions had no surnames, but were mostly named Abraham and Moses, and therefore the tax-gatherer could not tell t'other from which, and was likely to lose his reason over the matter. The renaming was put into the hands of the War Department, and a charming mess the graceless young lieutenants made of it. To them a Jew was of no sort of consequence, and they labeled the race in a way to make the angels weep. As an example take these two! *Abraham Bellyache* and *Schmul Godbedamned.*— *Culled from " Namens Studien," by Karl Emil Franzos.*

of the opinion that we have an immense Jewish population in America.

Point No. 3.—"Can Jews do anything to improve the situation?"

I think so. If I may make a suggestion without seeming to be trying to teach my grandmother how to suck eggs, I will offer it. In our days we have learned the value of combination. We apply it everywhere—in railway systems, in trusts, in trade-unions, in Salvation Armies, in minor politics, in major politics, in European Concerts. Whatever our strength may be, big or little, we *organize* it. We have found out that that is the only way to get the most out of it that is in it. We know the weakness of individual sticks, and the strength of the concentrated fagot. Suppose you try a scheme like this, for instance. In England and America put every Jew on the census-book *as* a Jew (in case you have not been doing that). Get up volunteer regiments composed of Jews solely, and, when the drum beats, fall in and go to the front, so as to remove the reproach that you have few Massénas among you, and that you feed on a country but don't like to fight for it. Next, in politics, organise your strength, band together, and deliver the casting vote where you can, and, where you can't, compel as good terms as possible. You huddle to yourselves already in all countries, but you huddle to no sufficient purpose, politically speaking. You do not seem to be organized, except for your charities. There you are omnipotent; there you compel your due of recognition—you do not have to beg for it.

CONCERNING THE JEWS

It shows what you can do when you band together for a definite purpose.

And then from America and England you can encourage your race in Austria, France, and Germany, and materially help it. It was a pathetic tale that was told by a poor Jew n Galicia a fortnight ago during the riots, after he had been raided by the Christian peasantry and de poiled of everything he had. He said his vote was of no value to him, and he wished he could be exc ised from casting it, for indeed casting it was a sure *lamage* to him, since no matter which party he voted for, the other party would come straight and take its revenge out of him. Nine per cent. of the population of the empire, these Jews, and apparently they cannot put a plank into any candidate's platform! If you will send our Irish lads over here I think they will organize your race and change the aspect of the Reichsrath.

You seem to think that the Jews take no hand in politics here, that they are "absolutely non-participants." I am assured by men competent to speak that this is a very large error, that the Jews are exceedingly active in politics all over the empire, but that they scatter their work and their votes among the numerous parties, and thus lose the advantages to be had by concentration. I think that in America they scatter too, but you know more about that than I do.

Speaking of concentration, Dr. Herzl has a clear insight into the value of that. Have you heard of his plan? He wishes to gather the Jews of the world together in Palestine, with a government of their own—under the suzerainty of the Sultan, I suppose. At the convention of Berne, last year, there were delegates from everywhere, and the proposal was received with decided favor. I am not the Sultan, and I am not objecting; but if that concentration of the cunningest brains in the world was going to be made in a free country (bar Scotland), I think it would be politic to stop it. It will not be well to let that race find out its strength. If the horses knew theirs, we should not ride any more.

Point No. 5.—"Will the persecution of the Jews ever come to an end?"

On the score of religion, I think it has already come to an end. On the score of race prejudice and trade, I have the idea that it will continue. That is, here and there in spots about the world, where a barbarous ignorance and a sort of mere animal civilization prevail; but I do not think that elsewhere the Jew need now stand in any fear of being robbed and raided. Among the high civilizations he seems to be very comfortably situated indeed, and to have more than his proportionate share of the prosperities going. It has that look in Vienna. I suppose the race prejudice cannot be removed; but he can stand that; it is no particular matter. By his make and ways he is substantially a foreigner wherever he may be, and even the angels dislike a foreigner. I am using this word foreigner in the German sense—*stranger.* Nearly all of us have an antipathy to a stranger, even of our own nationality. We pile gripsacks in a vacant seat to keep him from getting it; and a dog goes further, and does as a savage would—challenges him on the spot. The German dictionary seems to make no distinction between a stranger and a fore·gner; in its view a stranger *is* a foreigner—a sour d position, I think. You will always be by ways ai·d habits and predilections substantially stranger —foreigners—wherever you are, and that will prc bably keep the race prejudice against you alive.

But you were the favorites c f Heaven originally, and your manifold and unfair prosperities convince me that you have crowded back into that snug place again. Here is an incident that is significant. Last week in Vienna a hail-storm struck the prodigious Central Cemetery and made wasteful destruction there. In the Christian part of it, according to the official figures, 621 window-panes were broken; more than 900 singing-birds were killed; five great trees and many small ones were torn to shreds and the shreds scattered far and wide by the wind; the ornamental plants and other decorations of the graves were ruined, and more than a hundred tomb-lanterns shattered; and it took the cemetery's whole force of 300 laborers more than three days to clear away the storm's wreckage. In the report occurs this remark—and in its italics you can hear it grit its Christian teeth: ". . . lediglich die *israelitische* Abtheilung des Friedhofes vom Hagelwetter *ganzlich verschont* worden war." Not a hailstone hit the Jewish reservation! Such nepotism makes me tired.

Point No. 6.—"What has become of the golden rule?"

It exists, it continues to sparkle, and is well taken care of. It is Exhibit A in the Church's assets, and we pull it out every Sunday and give it an airing. But you are not permitted to try to smuggle it into this discussion, where it is irrelevant and would not feel at home. It is strictly religious furniture, like an acolyte, or a contribution-plate, or any of.those things. It has never been intruded into business; and Jewish persecution is not a religious passion, it is a business passion.

To conclude.—If the statistics are right, the Jews constitute but *one per cent.* of the human race. It suggests a nebulous dim puff of star dust lost in the blaze of the Milky Way. Properly the Jew ought hardly to be heard of; but he is heard of, has always been heard of. He is as prominent on the planet as any other people, and his commercial importance is extravagantly out of proportion to the smallness of his bulk. His contributions to the world's list of great names in literature, science, art, music, finance, medicine, and abstruse learning are also away out of proportion to the weakness of his numbers. He has made a marvelous fight in this world, in all the ages; and has done it with his hands tied behind him. He could be vain of himself, and be excused for it. The Egyptian, the Babylonian, and the Persian rose, filled the planet with sound and splendor, then faded to dream-stuff and passed away; the Greek and the Roman followed, and made a vast noise, and they are gone; other peoples have sprung up and held their torch high for a time, but it burned out, and they sit in twilight now, or have vanished. The Jew

CONCERNING THE JEWS

saw them all, beat them all, and is now what he always was, exhibiting no decadence, no infirmities of age, no weakening of his parts, no slowing of his energies, no dulling of his alert and aggressive mind. All things are mortal but the Jew; all other forces pass, but he remains. What is the secret of his immortality?

Postscript—THE JEW AS SOLDIER

When I published the above article in HARPER'S MONTHLY, I was ignorant—like the rest of the Christian world—of the fact that the Jew had a record as a soldier. I have since seen the official statistics, and I find that he furnished soldiers and high officers to the Revolution, the War of 1812, and the Mexican War. In the Civil War he was represented in the armies and navies of both the North and the South by 10 per cent. of his numerical strength —the same percentage that was furnished by the Christian populations of the two sections. This large fact means more than it seems to mean; for it means that the Jew's patriotism was not merely level with the Christian's, but overpassed it. When the Christian volunteer arrived in camp he got a welcome and applause, but as a rule the Jew got a snub. His company was not desired, and he was made to feel it. That he nevertheless conquered his wounded pride and sacrificed both that and his blood for his flag raises the average and quality of his patriotism above the Christian's. His record for capacity, for fidelity, and for gallant soldiership in the field is as good as any one's. This is true of the Jewish private soldiers and the Jewish generals alike. Major-General O. O. Howard speaks of one of his Jewish staff-officers as being "of the bravest and best"; of another—killed at Chancellorsville— as being "a true friend and a brave officer"; he highly praises two of his Jewish brigadier-generals; finally, he uses these strong words: "Intrinsically there are no more patriotic men to be found in the country than those who claim to be of Hebrew descent, and who served with me in parallel commands or more directly under my instructions."

Fourteen Jewish Confederate and Union families contributed, between them, fifty-one soldiers to the war. Among these, a father and three sons; and another, a father and four sons.

In the above article I was not able to endorse the common reproach that the Jew is willing to feed upon a country but not to fight for it, because I did not know whether it was true or false. I supposed it to be true, but it is not allowable to endorse wandering maxims upon supposition—except when one is trying to make out a case. That slur upon the Jew cannot hold up its head in presence of the figures of the War Department. It has done its work, and done it long and faithfully, and with high approval: it ought to be pensioned off now, and retired from active service.

287

ABOUT ALL KINDS OF SHIPS

THE MODERN STEAMER AND THE OBSOLETE STEAMER

WE are victims of one common superstition—the superstition that we realize the changes that are daily taking place in the world because we read about them and know what they are. I should not have supposed that the modern ship could be a surprise to me, but it is. It seems to be as much of a surprise to me as it could have been if I had never read anything about it. I walk about this great vessel, the *Havel*, as she plows her way through the Atlantic, and every detail that comes under my eye brings up the miniature counterpart of it as it existed in the little ships I crossed the ocean in fourteen, seventeen, eighteen, and twenty years ago.

In the *Havel* one can be in several respects more comfortable than he can be in the best hotels on the continent of Europe. For instance, she has several bathrooms, and they are as convenient and as nicely equipped as the bathrooms in a fine private house in America; whereas in the hotels of the Continent one bathroom is considered sufficient, and it is generally shabby and located in some out-of-the-way corner of the house; moreover, you need to give notice so long beforehand that you get over wanting a bath by the time you get it. In the hotels there are a good many different kinds of noises, and they spoil sleep; in my room in the ship I hear no sounds. In the hotels they usually shut off the electric light at midnight; in the ship one may burn it in one's room all night.

In the steamer *Batavia*, twenty years ago, one candle, set in the bulkhead between two staterooms, was there to light both rooms, but did not light either of them. It was extinguished at eleven at night, and so were all the saloon lamps except one or two, which were left burning to help the passenger see how to break his neck trying to get around in the dark. The passengers sat at table on long benches made of the hardest kind of wood; in the *Havel* one sits on a swivel chair with a cushioned back to it. In those old times the dinner bill of fare was always the same: a pint of some simple, homely soup or other, boiled codfish and potatoes, slab of boiled beef, stewed prunes for dessert—on Sundays "dog in a blanket," on Thursdays "plum duff." In the modern ship the menu is choice and elaborate, and is changed daily. In the old times dinner was a sad occasion; in our day a concealed orchestra enlivens it with charming music. In the old days the decks were always wet; in our day they are usually dry, for the promenade-deck is roofed over, and a sea seldom comes aboard. In a moderately disturbed sea, in the old days, a landsman could hardly keep his legs, but in such a sea in our day the decks are as level as a table. In the old days the inside of a ship was the plainest and barrenest thing, and the most dismal and uncomfortable that ingenuity could devise; the modern ship is a marvel of rich and costly decoration and sumptuous appointment, and is equipped with every comfort and convenience that money can buy. The old ships had no place of assembly but the dining-room, the new ones have several spacious and beautiful drawing-rooms. The old ships offered the passenger no chance to smoke except in the place that was called the "fiddle." It was a repulsive den made of rough boards (full of cracks) and its office was to protect the main hatch. It was grimy and dirty; there were no seats; the only light was a lamp of the rancid oil-and-rag kind; the place was very cold, and never dry, for the seas broke in through the cracks every little while and drenched the cavern thoroughly. In the modern ship there are three or four large smoking rooms, and they have card-tables and cushioned sofas, and are heated by steam and lighted by electricity. There are few European hotels with such smoking-rooms.

The former ships were built of wood, and had two or three water-tight compartments in the hold with doors in them which were often left open, particularly when the ship was going to hit a rock. The modern leviathan is built of steel, and the water-tight bulkheads have no doors in them; they divide the ship into nine or ten water-tight compartments and endow her with as many lives as a cat. Their complete efficiency was established by the happy results following the memorable accident to the *City of Paris* a year or two ago.

One curious thing which is at once noticeable in

the great modern ship is the absence of hubbub,
clatter, rush of feet, roaring of orders. That is all
gone by. The elaborate mar œuvers necessary in
working the vessel into her doc< are conducted without sounds; one sees nothing of the processes, hears
no commands. A Sabbath st llness and solemnity
reign, in place of the turmoil and racket of the earlier
days. The modern ship has a spacious bridge fenced
chin-high with sail-cloth and floored with wooden
gratings; and this bridge, with its fenced fore-and-aft
annexes, could accommodate a seated audience of a
hundred and fifty men. There are three steering
equipments, each competent if the others should
break. From the bridge the ship is steered, and also
handled. The handling is not done by shout or
whistle, but by signaling with patent automatic
gongs. There are three telltales, with plainly let-
tered dials—for steering, handling the engines, and
for communicating orders to the invisible mates who
are conducting the landing of the ship or casting off.
The officer who is astern is out of sight and too far
away to hear trumpet-calls; but the gongs near him
tell him to haul in, pay out, make fast, let go, and
so on; he hears, but the passengers do not, and so
the ship seems to land herself without human help.

This great bridge is thirty or forty feet above the
water, but the sea climbs up there sometimes; so
there is another bridge twelve or fifteen feet higher
still, for use in these emergencies. The force of
water is a strange thing. It slips between one's
fingers like air, but upon occasion it acts like a solid
body and will bend a thin iron rod. In the *Havel*

it has splintered a heavy oaken rail into broom-straws instead of merely breaking it in two, as would have been the seemingly natural thing for it to do. At the time of the awful Johnstown disaster, according to the testimony of several witnesses, rocks were carried some distance on the surface of the stupendous torrent; and at St. Helena, many years' ago, a vast sea-wave carried a battery of cannon forty feet up a steep slope and deposited the guns there in a row. But the water has done a still stranger thing, and it is one which is credibly vouched for. A marlin-spike is an implement about a foot long which tapers from its butt to the other extremity and ends in a sharp point. It is made of iron and is heavy. A wave came aboard a ship in a storm and raged aft, breast high, carrying a marlin-spike point first with it, and with such lightning-like swiftness and force as to drive it three or four inches into a sailor's body and kill him.

In all ways the ocean greyhound of to-day is imposing and impressive to one who carries in his head no ship pictures of a recent date. In bulk she comes near to rivaling the Ark; yet this monstrous mass of steel is driven five hundred miles through the waves in twenty-four hours. I remember the brag run of a steamer which I traveled in once on the Pacific—it was two hundred and nine miles in twenty-four hours; a year or so later I was a passenger in the excursion tub *Quaker City*, and on one occasion in a level and glassy sea it was claimed that she reeled off two hundred and eleven miles between noon and noon, but it was probably a campaign lie. That little steamer had seventy passengers, and a crew of forty men, and seemed a good deal of a beehive. But in this present ship we are living in a sort of solitude, these soft summer days, with sometimes a hundred passengers scattered about the spacious distances, and sometimes nobody in sight at all; yet, hidden somewhere in the vessel's bulk, there are (including crew) near eleven hundred people.

The stateliest lines in the literature of the sea are these:

> Britannia needs no bulwarks, no towers along the steep—
> Her march is o'er the mountain waves, her home is on the deep!

There it is. In those old times the little ships climbed over the waves and wallowed down into the trough on the other side; the giant ship of our day does not climb over the waves, but crushes her way through them. Her formidable weight and mass and impetus give her mastery over any but extraordinary storm waves.

The ingenuity of man! I mean in this passing generation. To-day I found in the chart-room a frame of removable wooden slats on the wall, and on the slats was painted uninforming information like this

Trim-Tank	Empty
Double-Bottom No. 1	Full
Double-Bottom No. 2	Full
Double-Bottom No. 3	Full
Double-Bottom No. 4	Full

While I was trying to think out what kind of a game this might be and how a stranger might best go to work to beat it, a sailor came in and pulled out the "Empty" end of the first slat and put it back with its reverse side to the front, marked "Full." He made some other change, I did not notice what. The slat-frame was soon explained. Its function was to indicate how the ballast in the ship was distributed. The striking thing was that the ballast was water. I did not know that a ship had ever been ballasted with water. I had merely read, some time or other, that such an experiment was to be tried. But that is the modern way; between the experimental trial of a new thing and its adoption, there is no wasted time, if the trial proves its value.

On the wall, near the slat-frame, there was an outline drawing of the ship, and this betrayed the fact that this vessel has twenty-two considerable lakes of water in her. These lakes are in her bottom; they are imprisoned between her real bottom and a false bottom. They are separated from each other, thwartships, by water-tight bulkheads, and separated down the middle by a bulkhead running from the bow four-fifths of the way to the stern. It is a chain of lakes four hundred feet long and from five to seven feet deep. Fourteen of the lakes contain fresh-water brought from shore, and the aggregate weight of it is four hundred tons. The rest of the lakes contain salt-water—six hundred and eighteen tons. Upward of a thousand tons of water, altogether.

Think how handy this ballast is. The ship leaves port with the lakes all full. As she lightens forward through consumption of coal, she loses trim—her head rises, her stern sinks down. Then they spill

one of the sternward lakes into the sea, and the trim
is restored. This can be repeated right along as
occasion may require. Also, a lake at one end of the
ship can be moved to the other end by pipes and
steam-pumps. When the sailor changed the slat-
frame to-day, he was posting a transference of that
kind. The seas had been increasing, and the vessel's
head needed more weighting, to keep it from rising
on the waves instead of plowing through them;
therefore, twenty-five tons of water had been transferred to the bow from a lake situated well toward
the stern.

A water compartment is kept either full or empty.
The body of water must be compact, so that it cannot
slosh around. A shifting ballast would not do, of
course.

The modern ship is full of beautiful ingenuities,
but it seems to me that this one is the king. I
would rather be the originator of that idea than of
any of the others. Perhaps the trim of a ship was
never perfectly ordered and preserved until now.
A vessel out of trim will not steer, her speed is
maimed, she strains and labors in the seas. Poor
creature, for six thousand years she has had no comfort until these latest days. For six thousand years
she swam through the best and cheapest ballast in
the world, the only perfect ballast, but she couldn't
tell her master and he had not the wit to find it out
for himself. It is odd to reflect that there is nearly
as much water inside of this ship as there is outside,
and yet there is no danger.

MARK TWAIN

NOAH'S ARK

THE progress made in the great art of ship-building since Noah's time is quite noticeable. Also, the looseness of the navigation laws in the time of Noah is in quite striking contrast with the strictness of the navigation laws of our time. It would not be possible for Noah to do in our day what he was permitted to do in his own. Experience has taught us the necessity of being more particular, more conservative, more careful of human life. Noah would not be allowed to sail from Bremen in our day. The inspectors would come and examine the Ark, and make all sorts of objections. A person who knows Germany can imagine the scene and the conversation without difficulty and without missing a detail. The inspector would be in a beautiful military uniform; he would be respectful, dignified, kindly, the perfect gentleman, but steady as the north star to the last requirement of his duty. He would make Noah tell him where he was born, and how old he was, and what religious sect he belonged to, and the amount of his income, and the grade and position he claimed socially, and the name and style of his occupation, and how many wives and children he had, and how many servants, and the name, sex, and age of the whole of them; and if he hadn't a passport he would be courteously required to get one right away. Then he would take up the matter of the Ark:

"What is her length?"

"Six hundred feet."

"Depth?"

"Sixty-five."

"Beam?"

"Fifty or sixty."

"Built of—"

"Wood."

"What kind?"

"Shittim and gopher."

"Interior and exterior decorations?"

"Pitched within and without."

"Passengers?"

"Eight."

"Sex?"

"Half male, the others female."

"Ages?"

"From a hundred years up."

"Up to where?"

"Six hundred."

"Ah—going to Chicago; good idea, too. Surgeon's name?"

"We have no surgeon."

"Must provide a surgeon. Also an undertaker—particularly the undertaker. These people must not be left without the necessities of life at their age. Crew?"

"The same eight."

"The same eight?"

"The same eight."

"And half of them women?"

"Yes, sir."

"Have they ever served as seamen?"

"No, sir."

"Have the men?"

"No, sir."

"Have any of you ever been to sea?"

"No, sir."

"Where were you reared?"

"On a farm—all of us."

"This vessel requires a crew of eight hundred men, she not being a steamer. You must provide them. She must have four mates and nine cooks. Who is captain?"

"I am, sir."

"You must get a captain. Also a chambermaid. Also sick-nurses for the old people. Who designed this vessel?"

"I did, sir."

"Is it your first attempt?"

"Yes, sir."

"I partly suspected it. Cargo?"

"Animals."

"Kind?"

"All kinds."

"Wild, or tame?"

"Mainly wild."

"Foreign or domestic?"

"Mainly foreign."

"Principal wild ones?"

"Megatherium, elephant, rhinoceros, lion, tiger, wolf, snakes—all the wild things of all climes—two of each."

"Securely caged?"

"No, not caged.

"They must have iron cages. Who feeds and waters the menagerie?"

"We do."

"The old people?"

"Yes, sir."

"It is dangerous—for both. The animals must be cared for by a competent force. How many animals are there?"

"Big ones, seven thousand; big and little together, ninety-eight thousand."

"You must provide twelve hundred keepers. How is the vessel lighted?"

"By two windows."

"Where are they?"

"Up under the eaves."

"Two windows for a tunnel six hundred feet long and sixty-five feet deep? You must put in the electric light—a few arc-lights and fifteen hundred incandescents. What do you do in case of leaks? How many pumps have you?"

"None, sir."

"You must provide pumps. How do you get water for the passengers and the animals?"

"We let down the buckets from the windows."

"It is inadequate. What is your motive power?"

"What is my which?"

"Motive power. What power do you use in driving the ship?"

"None."

"You must provide sails or steam. What is the nature of your steering apparatus?"

"We haven't any."

"Haven't you a rudder?"

"No, sir."

"How do you steer the vessel?"

"We don't."

"You must provide a rudder, and properly equip it.   How many anchors have you?"

"None."

"You must provide six.   One is not permitted to sail a vessel like this without that protection. How many life-boats have you?"

"None, sir."

"Provide twenty-five. How many life-preservers?"

"None."

"You will provide two thousand.   How long are you expecting your voyage to last?"

"Eleven or twelve months."

"Eleven or twelve months.   Pretty slow—but you will be in time for the Exposition.   What is your ship sheathed with—copper?"

"Her hull is bare—not sheathed at all."

"Dear man, the wood-boring creatures of the sea would riddle her like a sieve and send her to the bottom in three months.   She *cannot* be allowed to go away in this condition; she must be sheathed. Just a word more: Have you reflected that Chicago is an inland city and not reachable with a vessel like this?"

"Shecargo?   What is Shecargo?   I am not going to Shecargo."

"Indeed?   Then may I ask what the animals are for?"

"Just to breed others from."

"Others?   Is it possible that you haven't enough?"

"For the present needs of civilization, yes; but the

rest are going to be drowned in a flood, and these
are to renew the supply."

"A flood?"

"Yes, sir."

"Are you sure of that?"

"Perfectly sure. It is going to rain forty days
and forty nights."

"Give yourself no concern about that, dear sir, it
often does that here."

"Not this kind of rain. This is going to cover the
mountain-tops, and the earth will pass from sight."

"Privately—but of course not officially—I am
sorry you revealed this, for it compels me to withdraw the option I gave you as to sails or steam. I
must require you to use steam. Your ship cannot
carry the hundredth part of an eleven-months' water-
supply for the animals. You will have to have condensed water."

"But I tell you I am going to dip water from outside with buckets."

"It will not answer. Before the flood reaches the
mountain-tops the fresh waters will have joined the
salt seas, and it will all be salt. You must put in
steam and condense your water. I will now bid you
good day, sir. Did I understand you to say that
this was your very first attempt at ship-building?"

"My very first, sir, I give you the honest truth. I
built this Ark without having ever had the slightest training or experience or instruction in marine
architecture.

"It is a remarkable work, sir, a most remarkable
work. I consider that it contains more features that

are new—absolutely new and unhackneyed—than are to be found in any other vessel that swims the seas."

"This compliment does me infinite honor, dear sir, infinite; and I shall cherish the memory of it while life shall last. Sir, I offer my duty and most grateful thanks. Adieu."

No, the German inspector would be limitlessly courteous to Noah, and would make him feel that he was among friends, but he wouldn't let him go to sea with that Ark.

COLUMBUS'S CRAFT

BETWEEN Noah's time and the time of Columbus naval architecture underwent some changes, and from being unspeakably bad was improved to a point which may be described as less unspeakably bad. I have read somewhere, some time or other, that one of Columbus's ships was a ninety-ton vessel. By comparing that ship with the ocean greyhounds of our time one is able to get down to a comprehension of how small that Spanish bark was, and how little fitted she would be to run opposition in the Atlantic passenger trade to-day. It would take seventy-four of her to match the tonnage of the *Havel* and carry the *Havel's* trip. If I remember rightly, it took her ten weeks to make the passage. With our ideas this would now be considered an objectionable gait. She probably had a captain, a mate, and a crew consisting of four seamen and a boy. The crew of a modern greyhound numbers two hundred and fifty persons.

ABOUT ALL KINDS OF SHIPS

Columbus's ship being small and very old, we know that we may draw from these two facts several absolute certainties in the way of minor details which history has left unrecorded. For instance: being small, we know that she rolled and pitched and tumbled in any ordinary sea, and stood on her head or her tail, or lay down with her ear in the water, when storm seas ran high; also, that she was used to having billows plunge aboard and wash her decks from stem to stern; also, that the storm racks were on the table all the way over, and that nevertheless a man's soup was oftener landed in his lap than in his stomach; also, that the dining-saloon was about ten feet by seven, dark, airless, and suffocating with oil-stench; also, that there was only about one state-room, the size of a grave, with a tier of two or three berths in it of the dimensions and comfortableness of coffins, and that when the light was out the darkness in there was so thick and real that you could bite into it and chew it like gum; also, that the only promenade was on the lofty poop-deck astern (for the ship was shaped like a high-quarter shoe)—a streak sixteen feet long by three feet wide, all the rest of the vessel being littered with ropes and flooded by the seas.

We know all these things to be true, from the mere fact that we know the vessel was small. As the vessel was old, certain other truths follow, as matters of course. For instance: she was full of rats; she was full of cockroaches; the heavy seas made her seams open and shut like your fingers, and she leaked like a basket; where leakage is, there also, of necessity, is bilge-water; and where bilge-water is, only the dead can enjoy life. This is on account of the smell. In the presence of bilge - water, Limburger cheese becomes odorless and ashamed.

From these absolutely sure data we can competently picture the daily life of the great discoverer. In the early morning he paid his devotions at the shrine of the Virgin. At eight bells he appeared on the poop-deck promenade. If the weather was chilly he came up clad from plumed helmet to spurred heel in magnificent plate armor inlaid with arabesques of gold, having previously warmed it at the galley fire. . If the weather was warm he came up in the ordinary sailor toggery of the time—great slouch hat of blue velvet with a flowing brush of snowy ostrich plumes, fastened on with a flashing cluster of diamonds and emeralds; gold-embroidered doublet of green velvet with slashed sleeves exposing under-sleeves of crimson satin; deep collar and cuff ruffles of rich limp lace; trunk hose of pink velvet, with big knee-knots of brocaded yellow ribbon; pearl-tinted silk stockings, clocked and daintily embroidered; lemon-colored buskins of unborn kid, funnel-topped, and drooping low to expose the pretty stockings; deep gauntlets of finest white heretic skin, from the factory of the Holy Inquisition, formerly part of the person of a lady of rank; rapier with sheath crusted with jewels, and hanging from a broad baldric upholstered with rubies and sapphires.

He walked the promenade thoughtfully, he noted the aspects of the sky and the course of the wind; he kept an eye out for drifting vegetation and other signs of land; he jawed the man at the wheel for pastime; he got out an imitation egg and kept himself in practice on his old trick of making it stand on end; now and then he hove a life-line below and fished up a sailor who was drowning on the quarter-deck; the rest of his watch he gaped and yawned and stretched, and said he wouldn't make the trip again to discover six Americas. For that was the kind of natural human person Columbus was when not posing for posterity.

At noon he took the sun and ascertained that the good ship had made three hundred yards in twenty-four hours, and this enabled him to win the pool. Anybody can win the pool when nobody but himself has the privilege of straightening out the ship's run and getting it right.

The Admiral has breakfasted alone, in state: bacon, beans, and gin; at noon he dines alone, in state: bacon, beans, and gin; at six he sups alone, in state: bacon, beans, and gin; at eleven P. M. he takes a night relish alone, in state: bacon, beans, and gin. At none of these orgies is there any music; the ship orchestra is modern. After his final meal he returned thanks for his many blessings, a little overrating their value, perhaps, and then he laid off his silken splendors or his gilded hardware, and turned in, in his little coffin-bunk, and blew out his flickering stencher and began to refresh his lungs with inverted sighs freighted with the rich odors of rancid oil and bilge-water. The sighs returned as snores, and then the rats and the cockroaches swarmed out in brigades and divisions and army corps and had a circus all

over him. Such was the daily life of the great discoverer in his marine basket during several historic
weeks; and the difference between his ship and his
comforts and ours is visible almost at a glance.

When he returned, the King of Spain, marveling,
said—as history records:

"This ship seems to be leaky. Did she leak
badly?"

"You shall judge for yourself, sire. I pumped the
Atlantic Ocean through her sixteen times on the
passage."

This is General Horace Porter's account. Other
authorities say fifteen.

It can be shown that the differences between that
ship and the one I am writing these historical contributions in are in several respects remarkable.
Take the matter of decoration, for instance. I have
been looking around again, yesterday and to-day,
and have noted several details which I conceive to
have been absent from Columbus's ship, or at least
slurred over and not elaborated and perfected. I
observe stateroom doors three inches thick, of solid
oak and polished. I note companionway vestibules
with walls, doors, and ceilings paneled in polished
hard woods, some light, some dark, all dainty and
delicate joiner-work, and yet every point compact
and tight; with beautiful pictures inserted, composed
of blue tiles—some of the pictures containing as
many as sixty tiles—and the joinings of those tiles
perfect. These are daring experiments. One would
have said that the first time the ship went straining
and laboring through a storm-tumbled sea those

tiles would gape apart and drop out. That they have not done so is evidence that the joiner's art has advanced a good deal since the days when ships were so shackly that when a giant sea gave them a wrench the doors came unbolted. I find the walls of the dining-saloon upholstered with mellow pictures wrought in tapestry and the ceiling aglow with pictures done in oil. In other places of assembly I find great panels filled with embossed Spanish leather, the figures rich with gilding and bronze. Everywhere I find sumptuous masses of color—color, color, color—color all about, color of every shade and tint and variety; and, as a result, the ship is bright and cheery to the eye, and this cheeriness invades one's spirit and contents it. To fully appreciate the force and spiritual value of this radiant and opulent dream of color, one must stand outside at night in the pitch dark and the rain, and look in through a port, and observe it in the lavish splendor of the electric lights. The old-time ships were dull, plain, graceless, gloomy, and horribly depressing. They compelled the blues; one could not escape the blues in them. The modern idea is right: to surround the passenger with conveniences, luxuries, and abundance of inspiriting color. As a result, the ship is the pleasantest place one can be in, except, perhaps, one's home.

A VANISHED SENTIMENT

ONE thing is gone, to return no more forever—the romance of the sea. Soft sentimentality about the sea has retired from the activities of this life, and is but a memory of the past, already remote and much faded. But within the recollection of men still living, it was in the breast of every individual; and the farther any individual lived from salt-water the more of it he kept in stock. It was as pervasive, as universal, as the atmosphere itself. The mere mention of the sea, the romantic sea, would make any company of people sentimental and mawkish at once. The great majority of the songs that were sung by the young people of the back settlements had the melancholy wanderer for subject and his mouthings about the sea for refrain. Picnic parties paddling down a creek in a canoe when the twilight shadows were gathering always sang:

> Homeward bound, homeward bound,
> From a foreign shore;

and this was also a favorite in the West with the passengers on stern-wheel steamboats. There was another:

> My boat is by the shore
> And my bark is on the sea,
> But before I go, Tom Moore,
> Here's a double health to thee.

And this one, also:

> O pilot, 'tis a fearful night,
> There's danger on the deep.

And this:

> A life on the ocean wave
> And a home on the rolling deep,
> Where the scattered waters rave
> And the winds their revels keep!

ABOUT ALL KINDS OF SHIPS

And this:

> A wet sheet and a flowing sea,
> And a wind tha follows fair.

And this:

> My foot is on my ;allant deck,
> Once more the ro' er is free!

And the "Larboard Watch '—the person referred
to below is at the masthead, or somewhere up there:

> Oh, who can tell what joy he feels,
> As o'er the foam his vessel reels,
> And his tired eyelids slumb'ring fall,
> He rouses at the welcome call,
>   Of "Larboard watch—ahoy!"

Yes, and there was forever and always some
jackass-voiced person braying out:

> Rocked in the cradle of the deep,
> I lay me down in peace to sleep!

Other favorites had these suggestive titles: "The
Storm at Sea"; "The Bird at Sea"; "The Sailor
Boy's Dream"; "The Captive Pirate's Lament";
"We are far from Home on the Stormy Main"—and
so on, and so on, the list is endless. Everybody on
a farm lived chiefly amid the dangers of the deep in
those days, in fancy.

But all that is gone now. Not a vestige of it is
left. The iron-clad, with her unsentimental aspect
and frigid attention to business, banished romance
from the war marine, and the unsentimental steamer
has banished it from the commercial marine. The

dangers and uncertainties which made sea life
romantic have disappeared and carried the poetic
element along with them.   In our day the passengers
never sing sea-songs on board a ship, and the band
never plays them.   Pathetic songs about the wanderer in strange lands far from home, once so popular
and contributing such fire and color to the imagination by reason of the rarity of that kind of wanderer,
have lost their charm and fallen silent, because everybody is a wanderer in the far lands now, and the
interest in that detail is dead.   Nobody is worried
about the wanderer; there are no perils of the sea
for him, there are no uncertainties.   He is safer in
the ship than he would probably be at home, for
there he is always liable to have to attend some
friend's funeral and stand over the grave in the sleet,
bareheaded—and that means pneumonia for him,
if he gets his deserts; and the uncertainties of his
voyage are reduced to whether he will arrive on the
other side in the appointed afternoon, or have to
wait till morning.

The first ship I was ever in was a sailing-vessel.
She was twenty-eight days going from San Francisco
to the Sandwich Islands.   But the main reason for
this particularly slow passage was that she got
becalmed and lay in one spot fourteen days in the
center of the Pacific two thousand miles from land.
I hear no sea-songs in this present vessel, but I
heard the entire lay-out in that one.   There were a
dozen young people—they are pretty old now, I
reckon—and they used to group themselves on the
stern, in the starlight or the moonlight, every eve-

ning, and sing sea-songs till after midnight in that hot, silent, motionless calm. They had no sense of humor, and they always sang "Homeward Bound," without reflecting that that was practically ridiculous, since they were standing still and not proceeding in any direction at all; and they often followed that song with "'Are we almost there, are we almost there?' said the dying girl as she drew near home."

It was a very pleasant company of young people, and I wonder where they are now. Gone, oh, none knows whither; and the bloom and grace and beauty of their youth, where is that? Among them was a liar; all tried to reform him, but none could do it. And so, gradually, he was left to himself; none of us would associate with him. Many a time since I have seen in fancy that forsaken figure, leaning forlorn against the taffrail, and have reflected that perhaps if we had tried harder, and been more patient, we might have won him from his fault and persuaded him to relinquish it. But it is hard to tell; with him the vice was extreme, and was probably incurable. I like to think—and, indeed, I do think—that I did the best that in me lay to lead him to higher and better ways.

There was a singular circumstance. The ship lay becalmed that entire fortnight in exactly the same spot. Then a handsome breeze came fanning over the sea, and we spread our white wings for flight. But the vessel did not budge. The sails bellied out, the gale strained at the ropes, but the vessel moved not a hair's-breadth from her place. The captain was surprised. It was some hours before we found

out what the cause of the detention was. It was
barnacles. They collect very fast in that part of the
Pacific. They had fastened themselves to the ship's
bottom; then others had fastened themselves to the
first bunch, others to these, and so on, down and
down and down, and the last bunch had glued the
column hard and fast to the bottom of the sea, which
is five miles deep at that point. So the ship was
simply become the handle of a walking-cane five
miles long—yes, no more moveable by wind and
sail than a continent is. It was regarded by every
one as remarkable.

Well, the next week—however, Sandy Hook is in
sight.

FROM THE "LONDON TIMES" OF 1904

I

Correspondence of the "London Times"

CHICAGO, April 1, 1904.

I RESUME by cable-telephone where I left off yesterday. For many hours, now, this vast city —along with the rest of the globe, of course—has talked of nothing but the extraordinary episode mentioned in my last report. In accordance with your instructions, I will now trace the romance from its beginnings down to the culmination of yesterday —or to-day; call it which you like. By an odd chance, I was a personal actor in a part of this drama myself. The opening scene plays in Vienna. Date, one o'clock in the morning, March 31. 1898. I had spent the evening at a social entertainment. About midnight I went away, in company with the military attachés of the British, Italian, and American embassies, to finish with a late smoke. This function had been appointed to take place in the house of Lieutenant Hillyer, the third attaché mentioned in the above list. When we arrived there we found several visitors in the room: young

313

Szczepanik;[1] Mr. K., his financial backer; Mr. W., the latter's secretary; and Lieutenant Clayton of the United States army. War was at that time threatening between Spain and our country, and Lieutenant Clayton had been sent to Europe on military business. I was well acquainted with young Szczepanik and his two friends, and I knew Mr. Clayton slightly. I had met him at West Point years before, when he was a cadet. It was when General Merritt was superintendent. He had the reputation of being an able officer, and also of being quick-tempered and plain-spoken.

This smoking-party had been gathered together partly for business. This business was to consider the availability of the telelectroscope for military service. It sounds oddly enough now, but it is nevertheless true that at that time the invention was not taken seriously by any one except its inventor. Even his financial supporter regarded it merely as a curious and interesting toy. Indeed, he was so convinced of this that he had actually postponed its use by the general world to the end of the dying century by granting a two years' exclusive lease of it to a syndicate, whose intent was to exploit it at the Paris World's Fair.

When we entered the smoking-room we found Lieutenant Clayton and Szczepanik engaged in a warm talk over the telelectroscope in the German tongue. Clayton was saying:

"Well, you know *my* opinion of it, anyway!" and he brought his fist down with emphasis upon the table.

[1]Pronounced (approximately) *Zepannik.*

"And I do not value it," retorted the young inventor, with provoking calmness of tone and manner.

Clayton turned to Mr. K., and said:

"*I* cannot see why you are wasting money on this toy. In my opinion, the day will never come when it will do a farthing's worth of real service for any human being."

"That may be; yes, that may be; still, I have put the money in it, and am content. I think, myself, that it is only a toy; but Szczepanik claims more for it, and I know him well enough to believe that he can see farther than I can—either with his telelectroscope or without it."

The soft answer did not cool Clayton down; it seemed only to irritate him the more; and he repeated and emphasized his conviction that the invention would never do any man a farthing's worth of real service. He even made it a "brass" farthing, this time. Then he laid an English farthing on the table, and added:

"Take that, Mr. K., and put it away; and if ever the telelectroscope does any man an actual service, —mind, a *real* service—please mail it to me as a reminder, and I will take back what I have been saying. Will you?"

"I will"; and Mr. K. put the coin in his pocket.

Mr. Clayton now turned toward Szczepanik, and began with a taunt—a taunt which did not reach a finish; Szczepanik interrupted it with a hardy retort, and followed this with a blow. There was a brisk fight for a moment or two; then the attachés separated the men.

The scene now changes to Chicago. Time, the autumn of 1901. As soon as the Paris contract released the telelectroscope, it was delivered to public use, and was soon connected with the telephonic systems of the whole world. The improved "limitless-distance" telephone was presently introduced, and the daily doings of the globe made visible to everybody, and audibly discussable, too, by witnesses separated by any number of leagues.

By and by Szczepanik arrived in Chicago. Clayton (now captain) was serving in that military department at the time. The two men resumed the Viennese quarrel of 1898. On three different occasions they quarreled, and were separated by witnesses. Then came an interval of two months, during which time Szczepanik was not seen by any of his friends, and it was at first supposed that he had gone off on a sight-seeing tour and would soon be heard from. But no; no word came from him. Then it was supposed that he had returned to Europe. Still, time drifted on, and he was not heard from. Nobody was troubled, for he was like most inventors and other kinds of poets, and went and came in a capricious way, and often without notice.

Now comes the tragedy. On the 29th of December, in a dark and unused compartment of the cellar under Captain Clayton's house, a corpse was discovered by one of Clayton's maid-servants. It was easily identified as Szczepanik's. The man had died by violence. Clayton was arrested, indicted, and brought to trial, charged with this murder. The evidence against him was perfect in every detail, and absolutely unassailable. Clayton admitted this himself. He said that a reasonable man could not examine this testimony with a dispassionate mind and not be convinced by it; yet the man would be in error, nevertheless. Clayton swore that he did not commit the murder, and that he had had nothing to do with it.

As your readers will remember, he was condemned to death. He had numerous and powerful friends, and they worked hard to save him, for none of them doubted the truth of his assertion. I did what little I could to help, for I. had long since become a close friend of his, and thought I knew that it was not in his character to inveigle an enemy into a corner and assassinate him. During 1902 and 1903 he was several times reprieved by the governor; he was reprieved once more in the beginning of the present year, and the execution-day postponed to March 31st.

The governor's situation has been embarrassing, from the day of the condemnation, because of the fact that Clayton's wife is the governor's niece. The marriage took place in 1899, when Clayton was thirty-four and the girl twenty-three, and has been a happy one. There is one child, a little girl three years old. Pity for the poor mother and child kept the mouths of grumblers closed at first; but this could not last forever—for in America politics has a hand in everything—and by and by the governor's political opponents began to call attention to his delay in allowing the law to take its course. These hints have grown more and more frequent of late, and more and more pronounced. As a natural result, his own party grew nervous. Its leaders began to visit Springfield and hold long private conferences with him. He was now between two fires. On the one hand, his niece was imploring him to pardon her husband; on the other were the leaders, insisting that he stand to his plain duty as chief magistrate of the State, and place no further bar to Clayton's execution. Duty won in the struggle, and the governor gave his word that he would not again respite the condemned man. This was two weeks ago. Mrs. Clayton now said:

"Now that you have given your word, my last hope is gone, for I know you will never go back from it. But you have done the best you could for John, and I have no reproaches for you. You love him, and you love me, and we both know that if you could honorably save him, you would do it. I will go to him now, and be what help I can to him, and get what comfort I may out of the few days that are left to us before the night comes which will have no end for me in life. You will be with me that day? You will not let me bear it alone?"

"I will take you to him myself, poor child, and I will be near you to the last."

By the governor's command, Clayton was now allowed every indulgence he might ask for which could interest his mind and soften the hardships of his imprisonment. His wife and child spent the days with him; I was his companion by night. He was removed from the narrow cell which he had occupied during such a dreary stretch of time, and given the chief warden's room and comfortable quarters. His mind was always busy with the catastrophe of his life, and with the slaughtered inventor, and he now took the fancy that he would like to have the telelectroscope and divert his mind with it. He had his wish. The connection was made with the international telephone-station, and day by day, and night by night, he called up one corner of the globe after another, and looked upon its life, and studied its strange sights, and spoke with its people, and realized that by grace of this marvelous instrument he was almost as free as the birds of the air, although a prisoner under locks and bars. He seldom spoke, and I never interrupted him when he was absorbed in this amusement. I sat in his parlor and read and smoked, and the nights were very quiet and reposefully sociable, and I found them pleasant. Now and then I would hear him say, "Give me Yedo"; next, "Give me Hong-Kong"; next, "Give me Melbourne." And I smoked on, and read in comfort, while he wandered about the remote under-world, where the sun was shining in the sky, and the people were at their daily work. Sometimes the talk that came from those far regions through the microphone attachment interested me, and I listened.

Yesterday—I keep calling it yesterday, which is quite natural, for certain reasons—the instrument remained unused, and that, also, was natural, for it was the eve of the execution-day. It was spent in tears and lamentations and farewells. The governor and the wife and child remained until a quarter past eleven at night, and the scenes I witnessed were pitiful to see. The execution was to take place at four in the morning. A little after eleven a sound of hammering broke out upon the still night, and there was a glare of light, and the child cried out "What is that, papa?" and ran to the window before she could be stopped, and clapped her small hands, and said: "Oh, come and see, mamma—such a pretty thing they are making!" The mother knew—and fainted. It was the gallows!

She was carried away to her lodging, poor woman, and Clayton and I were alone—alone, and thinking, brooding, dreaming. We might have been statues, we sat so motionless and still. It was a wild night, for winter was come again for a moment, after the habit of this region in the early spring. The sky was starless and black, and a strong wind was blowing from the lake. The silence in the room was so deep that all outside sounds seemed exaggerated by contrast with it. These sounds were fitting ones; they harmonized with the situation and the conditions: the boom and thunder of sudden storm-gusts among the roofs and chimneys, then the dying down into moanings and wailings about the eaves and angles; now and then a gnashing and lashing rush of sleet along the window-panes; and always the muffled and uncanny hammering of the gallows-builders in the courtyard. After an age of this, another sound—far off, and coming smothered and faint through the riot of the tempest—a bell tolling twelve! Another age, and it tolled again.

By and by, again. A dreary, long interval after this, then the spectral sound floated to us once more —one, two, three; and this time we caught our breath: sixty minutes of life left!

Clayton rose, and stood by the window, and looked up into the black sky, and listened to the thrashing sleet and the piping wind; then he said: "That a dying man's last of earth should be—this!" After a little he said: "I must see the sun again— the sun!" and the next moment he was feverishly calling: "China! Give me China—Peking!"

I was strangely stirred, and said to myself: "To think that it is a mere human being who does this unimaginable miracle—turns winter into summer, night into day, storm into calm, gives the freedom of the great globe to a prisoner in his cell, and the sun in his naked splendor to a man dying in Egyptian darkness!"

I was listening.

"What light! what brilliancy! what radiance!... This is Peking?"

"Yes."

"The time?"

"Mid-afternoon."

"What is the great crowd for, and in such gorgeous costumes? What masses and masses of rich color and barbaric magnificence! And how they *flash and glow and burn in the flooding sunlight!* What *is* the occasion of it all?"

"The coronation of our new emperor—the Czar."

"But I thought that that was to take place yesterday."

"This *is* yesterday—to you."

"Certainly it is. But my mind is confused, these days; there are reasons for it. . .'Is this the beginning of the procession?"

"Oh, no, it began to move an hour ago."

"Is there much more of it still to come?"

"Two hours of it. Why do you sigh?"

"Because I should like to see it all."

"And why can't you?"

"I have to go—presently."

"You have an engagement?"

After a pause, softly: "Yes." After another pause: "Who are these in the splendid pavilion?"

"The imperial family, and visiting royalties from here and there and yonder in the earth."

"And who are those in the adjoining pavilions to the right and left?"

"Ambassadors and their families and suites to the right; unofficial foreigners to the left."

"If you will be so good, I—"

Boom! That distant bell again, tolling the half-hour faintly through the tempest of wind and sleet. The door opened, and the governor and the mother and child entered—the woman in widow's weeds! She fell upon her husband's breast in a passion of sobs, and I—I could not stay; I could not bear it. I went into the bedchamber, and closed the door. I sat there waiting—waiting—waiting, and listening to the rattling sashes and the blustering of the storm. After what seemed a long, long time, I heard a rustle and movement in the parlor, and knew that the clergyman and the sheriff and the guard were come. There was some low-voiced talking; then a hush; then a prayer, with a sound of sobbing; presently, footfalls—the departure for the gallows; then the child's happy voice: "Don't cry *now*, mamma, when we've got papa again, and taking him home."

The door closed; they were gone. I was ashamed: I was the only friend of the dying man that had no spirit, no courage. I stepped into the room, and said I would be a man and would follow. But we are made as we are made, and we cannot help it. I did not go.

I fidgeted about the room nervously, and presently went to the window, and softly raised it—drawn by that dread fascination which the terrible and the awful exert—and looked down upon the courtyard. By the garish light of the electric lamps I saw the little group of privileged witnesses, the wife crying on her uncle's breast, the condemned man standing on the scaffold with the halter around his neck, his arms strapped to his body, the black cap on his head, the sheriff at his side with his hand on the drop, the clergyman in front of him with bare head and his book in his hand.

"I am the resurrection and the life—"

I turned away. I could not listen; I could not look. I did not know whither to go or what to do. Mechanically, and without knowing it, I put my eye to that strange instrument, and there was Peking and the Czar's procession! The next moment I was leaning out of the window, gasping, suffocating, trying to speak, but dumb from the very imminence of the necessity of speaking. The preacher could speak, but I, who had such need of words—

"*And may God have mercy upon your soul. Amen.*"

The sheriff drew down the black cap, and laid his hand upon the lever. I got my voice.

"Stop, for God's sake! The man is innocent. Come here and see Szczepanik face to face!"

Hardly three minutes later the governor had my place at the window, and was saying:

"Strike off his bonds and set him free!"

Three minutes later all were in the parlor again. The reader will imagine the scene; I have no need to describe it. It was a sort of mad orgy of joy.

A messenger carried word to Szczepanik in the pavilion, and one could see the distressed amazement dawn in his face as he listened to the tale. Then he came to his end of the line, and talked with Clayton and the governor and the others; and the wife poured out her gratitude upon him for saving her husband's life, and in her deep thankfulness she kissed him at twelve thousand miles' range.

The telelectrophonoscopes of the globe were put to service now, and for many hours the kings and queens of many realms (with here and there a reporter) talked with Szczepanik, and praised him; and the few scientific societies which had not already made him an honorary member conferred that grace upon him.

How had he come to disappear from among us? It was easily explained. He had not grown used to being a world-famous person, and had been forced to break away from the lionizing that was robbing him of all privacy and repose. So he grew a beard, put on colored glasses, disguised himself a little in other ways, then took a fictitious name, and went off to wander about the earth in peace.

Such is the tale of the drama which began with an inconsequential quarrel in Vienna in the spring of 1898, and came near ending as a tragedy in the spring of 1904.

MARK TWAIN.

II

Correspondence of the "London Times"

CHICAGO, April 5, 1904.

TO-DAY, by a clipper of the Electric Line, and the latter's Electric Railway connections, arrived an envelope from Vienna, for Captain Clayton, containing an English farthing. The receiver of it was a good deal moved. He called up Vienna, and stood face to face with Mr. K., and said:

"I do not need to say anything; you can see it all in my face. My wife has the farthing. Do not be afraid—she will not throw it away."   M. T.

III

Correspondence of the "London Times"

CHICAGO, April 23, 1904.

NOW that the after developments of the Clayton case have run their course and reached a finish, I will sum them up. Clayton's romantic escape from a shameful death steeped all this region in an enchantment of wonder and joy—during the proverbial nine days. Then the sobering process followed, and men began to take thought, and to say: "But *a man was killed*, and Clayton killed him." Others replied: "That is true: we have been overlooking that important detail: we have been led away by excitement."

The feeling soon became general that Clayton ought to be tried again. Measures were taken accordingly, and the proper representations conveyed to Washington; for in America, under the new paragraph added to the Constitution in 1899, second trials are not state affairs, but national, and must be tried by the most august body in the land—the Supreme Court of the United States. The justices were, therefore, summoned to sit in Chicago. The session was held day before yesterday, and was opened with the usual impressive formalities, the nine judges appearing in their black robes, and the new chief justice (Lemaître) presiding. In opening the case, the chief justice said:

"It is my opinion that this matter is quite simple. The prisoner at the bar was charged with murdering the man Szczepanik; he was tried for murdering the man Szczepanik; he was fairly tried, and justly condemned and sentenced to death for murdering the man Szczepanik. It turns out that the man Szczepanik was not murdered at all. By the decision of the French courts in the Dreyfus matter, it is established beyond cavil or question that the decisions of courts are permanent and cannot be revised. We are obliged to respect and adopt this precedent. It is upon prededents that the enduring edifice of jurisprudence is reared. The prisoner at the bar has been fairly and righteously condemned to death for the murder of the man Szczepanik, and, in my opinion, there is but one course to pursue in the matter: he must be hanged."

Mr. Justice Crawford said:

"But, your Excellency, he was pardoned on the scaffold for that."

"The pardon is not valid, and cannot stand, because he was pardoned for killing a man whom he had not killed. A man cannot be pardoned for a crime which he has not committed; it would be an absurdity."

"But, your Excellency, he did kill a man."

"That is an extraneous detail; we have nothing to do with it. The court cannot take up this crime until the prisoner has expiated the other one."

Mr. Justice Halleck said:

"If we order his execution, your Excellency, we shall bring about a miscarriage of justice; for the governor will pardon him again."

"He will not have the pardon. He cannot pardon a man for a crime which he has not committed. As I observed before, it would be an absurdity."

After a consultation, Mr. Justice Wadsworth said:

"Several of us have arrived at the conclusion, your Excellency, that it would be an error to hang the prisoner for killing Szczepanik, but only for killing the other man, since it is proven that he did not kill Szczepanik."

"On the contrary, it is proven that he *did* kill

Szczepanik. By the French precedent, it is plain
that we must abide by the finding of the court."

"But Szczepanik is still alive."

"So is Dreyfus."

In the end it was found impossible to ignore or
get around the French precedent. There could be
but one result: Clayton was delivered over to the
executioner. It made an immense excitement; the
state rose as one man and clamored for Clayton's
pardon and re-trial. The governor issued the pardon, but the Supreme Court was in duty bound
to annul it, and did so, and poor Clayton was
hanged yesterday. The city is draped in black, and,
indeed, the like may be said of the state. All
America is vocal with scorn of "French justice,"
and of the malignant little soldiers who invented it
and inflicted it upon the other Christian lands.

A MAJESTIC LITERARY FOSSIL

IF I were required to guess offhand, and without collusion with higher minds, what is the bottom cause of the amazing material and intellectual advancement of the last fifty years, I should guess that it was the modern-born and previously non-existent disposition on the part of men to believe that a new idea can have value. With the long roll of the mighty names of history present in our minds, we are not privileged to doubt that for the past twenty or thirty centuries every conspicuous civilization in the world has produced intellects able to invent and create the things which make our day a wonder; perhaps we may be justified in inferring, then, that the reason they did not do it was that the public reverence for old ideas and hostility to new ones always stood in their way, and was a wall they could not break down or climb over. The prevailing tone of old books regarding new ideas is one of suspicion and uneasiness at times, and at other times contempt. By contrast, our day is indifferent to old ideas, and even considers that their age makes their value questionable, but jumps at a new idea with enthusiasm and high hope—a hope which is high because it has not been accustomed to being disappointed. I make no guess as to just when this disposition was

329

born to us, but it certainly is ours, was not possessed
by any century before us, is our peculiar mark and
badge, and is doubtless the bottom reason why we
are a race of lightning-shod Mercuries, and proud of
it—instead of being, like our ancestors, a race of
plodding crabs, and proud of that.

So recent is this change from a three or four thousand year twilight to the flash and glare of open day
that I have walked in both, and yet am not old.
Nothing is to-day as it was when I was an urchin;
but when I was an urchin, nothing was much different
from what it had always been in this world. Take
a single detail, for example—medicine. Galen could
have come into my sick-room at any time during my
first seven years—I mean any day when it wasn't
fishing weather, and there wasn't any choice but
school or sickness—and he could have sat down there
and stood my doctor's watch without asking a
question. He would have smelt around among the
wilderness of cups and bottles and vials on the
table and the shelves, and missed not a stench that
used to glad him two thousand years before, nor discovered one that was of a later date. He would
have examined me, and run across only one disappointment—I was already salivated; I would have
him there; for I was always salivated, calomel was
so cheap. He would get out his lancet then; but I
would have him again; our family doctor didn't
allow blood to accumulate in the system. However,
he could take dipper and ladle, and freight me up
with old familiar doses that had come down from
Adam to his time and mine; and he could go out with

a wheelbarrow and gather weeds and offal, and build some more, while those others were getting in their work. And if our reverend doctor came and found him there, he would be dumb with awe, and would get down and worship him. Whereas if Galen should appear among us to-day, he could not stand anybody's watch; he would inspire no awe; he would be told he was a back number and it would surprise him to see that that fact counted against him, instead of in his favor. He wouldn't know our medicines; he wouldn't know our practice; and the first time he tried to introduce his own we would hang him.

This introduction brings me to my literary relic. It is a *Dictionary of Medicine*, by Dr. James, of London, assisted by Mr. Boswell's Doctor Samuel Johnson, and is a hundred and fifty years old, it having been published at the time of the rebellion of '45. If it had been sent against the Pretender's troops there probably wouldn't have been a survivor. In 1861 this deadly book was still working the cemeteries—down in Virginia. For three generations and a half it had been going quietly along, enriching the earth with its slain. Up to its last free day it was trusted and believed in, and its devastating advice taken, as was shown by notes inserted between its leaves. But our troops captured it and brought it home, and it has been out of business since. These remarks from its preface are in the true spirit of the olden time, sodden with worship of the old, disdain of the new:

If we inquire into the Improvements which have been made by the Moderns, we shall be forced to confess that we have so little Reason to value ourselves beyond the Antients, or to be tempted to contemn them, that we cannot give stronger or more convincing Proofs of our own Ignorance, as well as our Pride.

Among all the systematical Writers, I think there are very few who refuse the Preference to *Hieron, Fabricius ab Aquapendente*, as a Person of unquestion'd Learning and Judgment; and yet is he not asham'd to let his Readers know that *Celsus* among the Latins, *Paulus Aegineta* among the Greeks, and *Albucasis* among the Arabians, whom I am unwilling to place among the Moderns, tho' he liv'd but six hundred Years since, are the Triumvirate to whom he principally stands indebted, for the Assistance he had receiv'd from them in composing his excellent Book.

[In a previous paragraph are puffs of Galen, Hippocrates, and other debris of the Old Silurian Period of Medicine.] How many Operations are there now in Use which were unknown to the Antients? •

That is true. The surest way for a nation's scientific men to prove that they were proud and ignorant was to claim to have found out something fresh in the course of a thousand years or so. Evidently the peoples of this book's day regarded themselves as children, and their remote ancestors as the only grown-up people that had existed. Consider the contrast: without offense, without over-egotism, our own scientific men may and do regard themselves as grown people and their grandfathers as children. The change here presented is probably the most sweeping that has ever come over mankind in the history of the race. It is the utter reversal, in a couple of generations, of an attitude which had been maintained without challenge or interruption from the earliest antiquity. It amounts to creating man over again on a new plan; he was a canal-boat before, he is an ocean greyhound to-day. The change from reptile to bird was not more tremendous, and it took longer.

It is curious. If you read between the lines what this author says about Brer Albucasis, you detect that in venturing to compliment him he has to whistle a little to keep his courage up, because Albucasis "liv'd but six hund ed Years since," and therefore came so uncomfortably near being a "modern" that one couldn't respect him without risk.

Phlebotomy, Venesection—terms to signify bleeding—are not often heard in our day, because we have ceased to believe that the best way to make a bank or a body healthy is to squander its capital; but in our author's time the physician went around with a hatful of lancets on his person all the time, and took a hack at every patient whom he found still alive. He robbed his man of pounds and pounds of blood at a single operation. The details of this sort in this book make terrific reading. Apparently even the healthy did not escape, but were bled twelve times a year, on a particular day of the month, and exhaustively purged besides. Here is a specimen of the vigorous old-time practice; it occurs in our author's adoring biography of a Doctor Aretæus, a licensed assassin of Homer's time, or thereabouts:

In a Quinsey he used Venesection, and allow'd the Blood to flow till the Patient was ready to faint away.

There is no harm in trying to cure a headache—in our day. You can't do it, but you get more or less entertainment out of trying, and that is something;

333

besides, you live to tell about it, and that is more. A century or so ago you could have had the first of these features in rich variety, but you might fail of the other once—and once would do. I quote:

> As Dissections of Persons who have died of severe Head-achs, which have been related by Authors, are too numerous to be inserted in this Place, we shall here abridge some of the most curious and important Observations relating to this Subject, collected by the celebrated *Bonetus*.

The celebrated Bonetus's "Observation No. 1" seems to me a sufficient sample, all by itself, of what people used to have to stand any time between the creation of the world and the birth of your father and mine when they had the disastrous luck to get a "Head-ach":

> A certain Merchant, about forty Years of Age, of a Melancholic Habit, and deeply involved in the Cares of the World, was, during the Dog-days, seiz'd with a violent pain of his Head, which some time after oblig'd him to keep his Bed.
>
> I, being call'd, order'd Venesection in the Arms, the Application of Leeches to the Vessels of his Nostrils, Forehead, and Temples, as also to those behind his Ears; I likewise prescrib'd the Application of Cupping-glasses, with Scarification, to his Back: But notwithstanding these Precautions, he dy'd. If any Surgeon, skill'd in Arteriotomy, had been present, I should have also order'd that Operation.

I looked for "Arteriotomy" in this same Dictionary, and found this definition: "The opening of an Artery with a View of taking away Blood." Here was a person who was being bled in the arms, forehead, nostrils, back, temples, and behind the ears, yet the celebrated Bonetus was not satisfied, but wanted to open an artery "with a View" to insert a pump, probably. "Notwithstanding these Precautions"—he dy'd. No art of speech could more quaintly convey this butcher's innocent surprise. Now that we know what the celebrated Bonetus did when he wanted to relieve a Head-ach, it is no trouble to infer that if he wanted to comfort a man that had a Stomach-ach he disemboweled him.

I have given one "Observation"—a single Head-ach case; but the celebrated Bonetus follows it with eleven more. Without enlarging upon the matter, I merely note this coincidence—they all "dy'd." Not one of these people got well; yet this obtuse hyena sets down every little gory detail of the several assassinations as complacently as if he imagined he was doing a useful and meritorious work in perpetuating the methods of his crimes. "Observations," indeed! They are confessions.

According to this book, "the Ashes of an Ass's hoof mix'd with Woman's milk cures chilblains." Length of time required not stated. Another item: "The constant Use of Milk is bad for the Teeth, and causes them to rot, and loosens the Gums." Yet in our day babies use it constantly without hurtful results. This author thinks you ought to wash out your mouth with wine before venturing to drink milk. Presently, when we come to notice what fiendish decoctions those people introduced into their stomachs by way of medicine, we shall wonder that they could have been afraid of milk.

It appears that they had false teeth in those days. They were made of ivory sometimes, sometimes of bone, and were thrust into the natural sockets, and lashed to each other and to the neighboring teeth with wires or with silk threads. They were not to eat with, nor to laugh with, because they dropped out when not in repose. You could smile with them, but you had to practise first, or you would overdo it. They were not for business, but just decoration. They filled the bill according to their lights. ‸

This author says "the Flesh of Swine nourishes above all other eatables." In another place he mentions a number of things, and says "these are very easy to be digested; so is Pork." This is probably a lie. But he is pretty handy in that line; and when he hasn't anything of the sort in stock himself he gives some other expert an opening. For instance, under the head of "Attractives" he introduces Paracelsus, who tells of a nameless "Specific" —quantity of it not set down—which is able to draw a hundred pounds of flesh to itself—distance not stated—and then proceeds, "It happen'd in our own Days that an Attractive of this Kind drew a certain Man's Lungs up into his Mouth, by which he had the Misfortune to be suffocated." This is more than doubtful. In the first place, his Mouth couldn't accommodate his Lungs—in fact, his Hat couldn't; secondly, his Heart being more eligibly Situated, it would have got the Start of his Lungs, and, being a lighter Body, it would have Sail'd in ahead and Occupied the Premises; thirdly, you will Take Notice a Man with his Heart in his Mouth hasn't any Room left for his Lungs—he has got all he can Attend to; and finally, the Man must have had the Attractive in his Hat, and when he saw what was going to

Happen he would have Remov'd it and Sat Down on it. Indeed, he would; and then how could it Choke him to Death? I don't believe the thing ever happened at all.

Paracelsus adds this effort: ' I myself saw a Plaister which attracted as much Water as was sufficient to fill a Cistern; and by these very Attractives Branches may be torn from Trees; and, which is still more surprising, a Cow may be carried up into the Air." Paracelsus is dead now; he was always straining himself that way.

They liked a touch of mystery along with their medicine in the olden time; and the medicine-man of that day, like the medicine-man of our Indian tribes, did what he could to meet the requirement:

Arcanum. A Kind of Remedy whose Manner of Preparation, or singular Efficacy, is industriously concealed, in order to enhance its Value. By the Chymists it is generally defined a thing secret, incorporeal, and immortal, which cannot be Known by Man, unless by Experience; for it is the Virtue of every thing, which operates a thousand times more than the thing itself.

To me the butt end of this explanation is not altogether clear. A little of what they knew about natural history in the early times is exposed here and there in the Dictionary.

The Spider. It is more common than welcome in Houses. Both the Spider and its Web are used in Medicine: The Spider is said to avert the Paroxysms of Fevers, if it be apply'd to the Pulse of the Wrist, or the Temples; but it is peculiarly recommended against a Quartan, being enclosed in the Shell of a Hazlenut.

Among approved Remedies, I find that the distill'd Water of Black Spiders is an excellent Cure for Wounds, and that this was one of the choice Secrets of Sir Walter Raleigh.

The Spider which some call the Catcher, or Wolf, being beaten into a Plaister, then sew'd up in Linen, and apply'd to the Forehead or Temples, prevents the Returns of a Tertian.

There is another Kind of Spider, which spins a white, fine, and thick Web. One of this Sort, wrapp'd in Leather, and hung about the Arm, will avert the Fit of a Quartan. Boil'd in Oil of Roses, and instilled into the Ears, it eases Pains in those Parts. *Dioscorides, Lib. 2, Cap. 68.*

Thus we find that Spiders have in all Ages been celebrated for their febrifuge Virtues; and it is worthy of Remark, that a Spider is usually given to Monkeys, and is esteem'd a sovereign Remedy for the Disorders those Animals are principally subject to.

Then follows a long account of how a dying woman, who had suffered nine hours a day with an ague during eight weeks, and who had been bled dry some dozens of times meantime without apparent benefit, was at last forced to swallow several wads of "Spiders-web," whereupon she straightway mended, and promptly got well. So the sage is full of enthusiasm over the spider-webs, and mentions only in the most casual way the discontinuance of the daily bleedings, plainly never suspecting that this had anything to do with the cure.

As concerning the venomous Nature of Spiders, *Scaliger* takes notice of a certain Species of them (which he had forgotten) whose Poison was of so great Force as to affect one *Vincentinus* thro' the Sole of his Shoe, by only treading on it.

The sage takes that in without a strain, but the following case was a trifle too bulky for him, as his comment reveals:

In Gascony, observes *Scaliger*, there is a very small Spider, which, running over a Looking-glass, will crack the same by the Force of her Poison. (*A mere Fable.*)

A MAJESTIC LITERARY FOSSIL

But he finds no fault with the following facts:

Remarkable is the Enmity recorded between this Creature and the Serpent, as also the Toad: Of the former it is reported, That, lying (as he thinks securely) under the Shadow of some Tree, the Spider lets herself down by her Thread, and, striking her Proboscis or Sting into the Head, with that Force and Efficacy, injecting likewise her venomous Juice, that, wringing himself about, he immediately grows giddy, and quickly after dies.

When the Toad is bit or stung in Fight with this Creature, the Lizard, Adder, or other that is poisonous, she finds relief from Plantain, to which she resorts. In her Combat with the Toad, the Spider useth the same Stratagem as with the Serpent, hanging by her own Thread from the Bough of some Tree, and striking her Sting into her enemy's Head, upon which the other, enraged, swells up, and sometimes bursts.

To this Effect is the Relation of *Erasmus*, which he saith he had from one of the Spectators, of a Person lying along upon the Floor of his Chamber, in the Summer-time, to sleep in a supine Posture, when a Toad, creeping out of some green Rushes, brought just before in, to adorn the Chimney, gets upon his Face, and with his Feet sits across his Lips. To force off the Toad, says the Historian, would have been accounted sudden Death to the Sleeper; and to leave her there, very cruel and dangerous; so that upon Consultation it was concluded to find out a Spider, which, together with her Web, and the Window she was fasten'd to, was brought carefully, and so contrived as to be held perpendicularly to the Man's Face; which was no sooner done, but the Spider, discovering his Enemy, let himself down, and struck in his Dart, afterwards betaking himself up again to his Web; the Toad swell'd, but as yet kept his station: The second Wound is given quickly after by the Spider, upon which he swells yet more, but remain'd alive still.—The Spider, coming down again by his Thread, gives the third Blow; and the Toad, taking off his Feet from over the Man's Mouth, fell off dead.

To which the sage appends this grave remark, "And so much for the historical Part." Then he passes on to a consideration of "the Effects and Cure of the Poison."

One of the most interesting things about this tragedy is the double sex of the Toad, and also of the Spider.

Now the sage quotes from one Turner:

I remember, when a very young Practitioner, being sent for to a certain Woman, whose Custom was usually, when she went to the Cellar by Candlelight, to go also a Spider-hunting, setting Fire to their Webs, and burning them with the Flame of the Candle still as she pursued them. It happen'd at length, after this Whimsy had been follow'd a long time, one of them sold his Life much dearer than those Hundreds she had destroy'd; for, lighting upon the melting Tallow of her Candle, near the Flame, and his legs being entangled therein, so that he could not extricate himself, the Flame or Heat coming on, he was made a Sacrifice to his cruel Persecutor, who delighting her Eyes with the Spectacle, still waiting for the Flame to take hold of him, he presently burst with a great Crack, and threw his Liquor, some into her Eyes, but mostly upon her Lips; by means of which, flinging away her Candle, she cry'd out for Help, as fansying herself kill'd already with the Poison. However in the Night her Lips swell'd up excessively, and one of her Eyes was much inflam'd; also her Tongue and Gums were somewhat affected; and, whether from the Nausea excited by the Thoughts of the Liquor getting into her Mouth, or from the poisonous Impressions communicated by the nervous *Fibrillæ* of those Parts to those of the Ventricle, a continual Vomiting attended: To take off which, when I was call'd, I order'd a Glass of mull'd Sack, with a Scruple of Salt of Wormwood, and some hours after a Theriacal Bolus, which she flung up again. I embrocated the Lips with the Oil of Scorpions mix'd with the Oil of Roses; and, in Consideration of the Ophthalmy, tho' I was not certain but the Heat of the Liquor, rais'd by the Flame of the Candle before the Body of the Creature burst, might, as well as the Venom, excite the Disturbance, (altho' Mr. *Boyle's* Case of a Person blinded by this Liquor dropping from the living Spider, makes the latter sufficient;) yet observing the great Tumefaction of the Lips, together with the other Symptoms not likely to arise from simple Heat, I was inclin'd to believe a real Poison in the Case; and therefore not daring to let her Blood in the Arm [If a man's throat were cut in those old days, the doctor would come and bleed the other end of him], I did, however, with good Success, set Leeches to her Temples, which took off much of the Inflammation; and her Pain was likewise abated, by instilling into her Eyes a thin Mucilage of the Seeds of Quinces and white Poppies extracted with Rose-water; yet the Swelling on the Lips increased; upon which, in the Night, she wore a Cataplasm prepared by boiling the Leaves of Scordium, Rue, and Elder-flowers, and afterwards thicken'd with the Meal of Vetches. In the mean time, her Vomiting having left her, she had given her, between whiles, a little Draught of Distill'd Water of Carduus Benedictus and Scordium, with some of the Theriaca dissolved; and upon going off of the Symptoms, an old Woman came luckily in, who, with Assurance suitable to those People, (whose Ignorance and Poverty is their Safety and Protection,) took off the Dressings, promising to cure her in two Days' time, altho' she made it as many Weeks, yet had the Reputation of the Cure; applying only Plantain Leaves bruis'd and mixed with Cobwebs, dropping the Juice into her Eye, and giving some Spoonfuls of the same inwardly, two or three times a day.

So ends the wonderful affair. Whereupon the sage gives Mr. Turner the following shot—strengthening it with italics—and passes calmly on:

I must remark upon this History, that the Plantain, as a Cooler, was much more likely to cure this Disorder than warmer Applications and Medicines.

How strange that narrative sounds to-day, and how grotesque, when one reflects that it was a grave contribution to medical "science" by an old and reputable physician! Here was all this to-do—two weeks of it—over a woman who had scorched her eye and her lips with candle grease. The poor wench

is as elaborately dosed, bled, embrocated, and otherwise harried and bedeviled as if there had been
really something the matter with her; and when a
sensible old woman comes along at last, and treats
the trivial case in a sensible way, the educated
ignoramus rails at her ignorance, serenely unconscious of his own. It is pretty suggestive of the
former snail-pace of medical progress that the spider
retained his terrors during three thousand years, and
only lost them within the last thirty or forty.

Observe what imagination can do. "This same
young Woman" used to be so affected by the strong
(imaginary) smell which emanated from the burning
spiders that "the Objects about her seem'd to turn
round; she grew faint also with cold Sweats, and
sometimes a light Vomiting." There could have
been Beer in that cellar as well as Spiders.

Here are some more of the effects of imagination:
"*Sennertus* takes Notice of the Signs of the Bite or
Sting of this Insect to be a Stupor or Numbness upon
the Part, with a sense of Cold, Horror, or Swelling
of the Abdomen, Paleness of the Face, involuntary
Tears, Trembling, Contractions, a (. . .), Convulsions, cold Sweats; but these latter chiefly when the
Poison has been received inwardly," whereas the
modern physician holds that a few spiders taken inwardly, by a bird or a man, will do neither party any
harm.

The above "Signs" are not restricted to spider
bites—often they merely indicate fright. I have
seen a person with a hornet in his pantaloons exhibit
them all.

As to the Cure, not slighting the usual Alexipharmics taken internally, the Place bitten must be immediately washed with Salt Water, or a Sponge dipped in hot Vinegar, or fomented with a Decoction of Mallows, Origanum, and Mother of Thyme; after which a Cataplasm must be laid on of the Leaves of Bay, Rue, Leeks, and the Meal of Barley, boiled with Vinegar, or of Garlick and Onions, contused with Goat's Dung and fat Figs. Meantime the Patient should eat Garlick and drink Wine freely.

As for me, I should prefer the spider bite. Let us close this review with a sample or two of the earthquakes which the old-time doctor used to introduce into his patient when he could find room. Under this head we have "Alexander's Golden Antidote," which is good for—well, pretty much everything. It is probably the old original first patent-medicine. It is built as follows:

Take of Afarabocca, Henbane, Carpobalsamum, each two Drams and a half; of Cloves, Opium, Myrrh, Cyperus, each two Drams; of Opobalsamum, Indian Leaf, Cinnamon, Zedoary, Ginger, Coftus, Coral, Cassia, Euphorbium, Gum Tragacanth, Frankincense, Styrax Calamita, Celtic, Nard, Spignel, Hartwort, Mustard, Saxifrage, Dill, Anise, each one Dram; of Xylaloes, Rheum, Ponticum, Alipta Moschata, Castor, Spikenard, Galangals, Opoponax, Anacardium, Mastich, Brimstone, Peony, Eringo, Pulp of Dates, red and white Hermodactyls, Roses, Thyme, Acorns, Penyroyal, Gentian, the Bark of the Root of Mandrake, Germander, Valerian, Bishops Weed, Bay-berries, long and white Pepper, Xylobalsamum, Carnabadium, Macodonian, Parsley-seeds, Lovage, the Seeds of Rue, and Sinon, of each a Dram and a half; of pure Gold, pure Silver, Pearls not perforated, the Blatta Byzantina, the Bone of the Stag's Heart, of each the Quantity of fourteen Grains of Wheat; of Sapphire, Emerald, and Jasper Stones, each one Dram; of Haslenut, two Drams; of Pellitory of Spain, Shavings of Ivory, Calamus Odoratus, each the Quantity of twenty-nine Grains of Wheat; of Honey or Sugar a sufficient Quantity.

Serve with a shovel. No; one might expect such an injunction after such formidable preparation; but it is not so. The dose recommended is "the Quantity of an Haslenut." Only that; it is because there is so much jewelry in it, no doubt.

Aqua Limacum. Take a great Peck of Garden-snails, and wash them in a great deal of Beer, and make your Chimney very clean, and set a Bushel of Charcoal on Fire; and when they are thoroughly kindled, make a Hole in the Middle of the Fire, and put the Snails in, and scatter more Fire amongst them, and let them roast till they make a Noise; then take them out, and, with a Knife and coarse Cloth, pick and wipe away all the green froth: Then break them, Shells and all, in a Stone Mortar. Take also a Quart of Earth-worms, and scour them with Salt, divers times over. Then take two Handfuls of Angelica and lay them in the Bottom of the Still; next lay two Handfuls of Celandine; next a Quart of Rosemary-flowers; then two Handfuls of Bearsfoot and Agrimony; then Fenugreek; then Turmerick; of each one Ounce: Red Dock-root, Bark of Barberry-trees, Wood-sorrel, Betony, of each two Handfuls.—Then lay the Snails and Worms on the top of the Herbs; and then two Handfuls of Goose Dung, and two Handfuls of Sheep Dung. Then put in three Gallons of Strong Ale, and place the pot where you mean to set Fire under it: Let it stand all Night, or longer; in the Morning put in three Ounces of Cloves well beaten, and a small Quantity of Saffron, dry'd to Powder; then six Ounces of Shavings of Hartshorn, which must be uppermost. Fix on the Head and Refrigeratory, and distil according to Art.

There. The book does not say whether this is all one dose, or whether you have a right to split it and take a second chance at it, in case you live. Also, the book does not seem to specify what ailment it was for; but it is of no consequence, for of course that would come out on the inquest.

Upon looking further, I find that this formidable nostrum is "good for raising Flatulencies in the

Stomach"—meaning *from* the stomach, no doubt. So it would appear that when our progenitors chanced to swallow a sigh, they emptied a sewer down their throats to expel it. It is like dislodging skippers from cheese with artillery.

When you reflect that your own father had to take such medicines as the above, and that you would be taking them to-day yourself but for the introduction of homeopathy, which forced the old-school doctor to stir around and learn something of a rational nature about his business, you may honestly feel grateful that homeopathy survived the attempts of the allopathists to destroy it, even though you may never employ any physician but an allopathist while you live.

AT THE APPETITE CURE

THIS establishment's name is Hochberghaus. It is in Bohemia, a short day's journey from Vienna, and being in the Austrian Empire is, of course, a health resort. The empire is made up of health resorts; it distributes health to the whole world. Its waters are all medicinal. They are bottled and sent throughout the earth; the natives themselves drink beer. This is self-sacrifice, apparently—but outlanders who have drunk Vienna beer have another idea about it. Particularly the Pilsener which one gets in a small cellar up an obscure back lane in the First Bezirk—the name has escaped me, but the place is easily found: You inquire for the Greek church; and when you get to it, go right along by—the next house is that little beer-mill. It is remote from all traffic and all noise; it is always Sunday there. There are two small rooms, with low ceilings supported by massive arches; the arches and ceilings are whitewashed, otherwise the rooms would pass for cells in the dungeons of a bastile. The furniture is plain and cheap, there is no ornamentation anywhere; yet it is a heaven for the self-sacrificers, for the beer there is incomparable; there is nothing like it elsewhere in the world. In the first room you will find twelve or fifteen ladies and gentlemen of civilian quality; in the other one a dozen generals and ambassadors. One may live in Vienna many months and not hear of this place; but having once heard of it and sampled it the sampler will afterward infest it.

However, this is all incidental—a mere passing note of gratitude for blessings received—it has nothing to do with my subject. My subject is health resorts. All unhealthy people ought to domicile themselves in Vienna, and use that as a base, making flights from time to time to the outlying resorts, according to need. A flight to Marienbad to get rid of fat; a flight to Carlsbad to get rid of rheumatism; a flight to Kaltenleutgeben to take the water cure and get rid of the rest of the diseases. It is all so handy. You can stand in Vienna and toss a biscuit into Kaltenleutgeben, with a twelve-inch gun. You can run out thither at any time of the day; you go by the phenomenally slow trains, and yet inside of an hour you have exchanged the glare and swelter of the city for wooded hills, and shady forest paths, and soft, cool airs, and the music of birds, and the repose and peace of paradise.

And there are plenty of other health resorts at your service and convenient to get at from Vienna; charming places, all of them; Vienna sits in the center of a beautiful world of mountains with now and then a lake and forests; in fact, no other city is so fortunately situated.

There are abundance of health resorts, as I have said. Among them this place—Hochberghaus. It stands solitary on the top of a densely wooded mountain, and is a building of great size. It is called the Appetite Anstalt, and people who have lost their appetites come here to get them restored. When I arrived I was taken by Professor Haimberger to his consulting-room and questioned:

"It is six o'clock. When did you eat last?"

"At noon."

"What did you eat?"

"Next to nothing."

"What was on the table?"

"The usual things."

"Chops, chickens, vegetables, and so on?"

"Yes; but don't mention them—I can't bear it."

"Are you tired of them?"

"Oh, utterly. I wish I might never hear of them again."

"The mere sight of food offends you, does it?"

"More, it revolts me."

The doctor considered awhile, then got out a long menu and ran his eye slowly down it.

"I think," said he, "that what you need to eat is—but here, choose for yourself."

I glanced at the list, and my stomach threw a handspring. Of all the barbarous layouts that were ever contrived, this was the most atrocious. At the top stood "tough, underdone, overdue tripe, garnished with garlic"; half-way down the bill stood "young cat; old cat; scrambled cat"; at the bottom stood "sailor-boots, softened with tallow—served raw." The wide intervals of the bill were packed with dishes calculated to insult a cannibal. I said:

"Doctor, it is not fair to joke over so serious a case as mine. I came here to get an appetite, not to throw away the remnant that's left."

He said, gravely, "I am not joking; why should I joke?"

"But I can't eat these horrors."

"Why not?"

He said it with a naïveté that was admirable, whether it was real or assumed.

"Why not? Because—why, doctor, for months I have seldom been able to endure anything more substantial than omelettes and custards. These unspeakable dishes of yours—"

"Oh, you will come to like them. They are very good. And you *must* eat them. It is the rule of the place, and is strict. I cannot permit any departure from it."

I said, smiling: "Well, then, doctor, you will have to permit the departure of the patient. I am going."

He looked hurt, and said in a way which changed the aspect of things:

"I am sure you would not do me that injustice. I accepted you in good faith—you will not shame that confidence. This appetite cure is my whole living. If you should go forth from it with the sort of appetite which you now have, it could become known, and you can see, yourself, that people would say my cure failed in your case and hence can fail in other cases. You will not go; you will not do me this hurt."

I apologized and said I would stay.

"That is right. I was sure you would not go; it would take the food from my family's mouths."

"Would they mind that? Do they eat these fiendish things?"

"They? My family?" His eyes were full of gentle wonder. "Of course not."

"Oh, they don't! Do you?"

"Certainly not."

"I see. It's another case of a physician who doesn't take his own medicine."

"I don't need it. It is six hours since you lunched. Will you have supper now—or later?"

"I am not hungry, but now is as good a time as any, and I would like to be done with it and have it off my mind. It is about my usual time, and regularity is commanded by all the authorities. Yes, I will try to nibble a little now—I wish a light horse-whipping would answer instead."

The professor handed me that odious menu.

"Choose—or will you have it later?"

"Oh, dear me, show me to my room; I forgot your hard rule."

"Wait just a moment before you finally decide. There is another rule. If you choose now, the order will be filled at once; but if you wait, you will have to await my pleasure. You cannot get a dish from that entire bill until I consent."

"All right. Show me to my room, and send the cook to bed; there is not going to be any hurry."

The professor took me up one flight of stairs and showed me into a most inviting and comfortable apartment consisting of parlor, bedchamber, and bath-room.

The front windows looked out over a far-reaching spread of green glades and valleys, and tumbled hills clothed with forests—a noble solitude unvexed by the fussy world. In the parlor were many shelves filled with books. The professor said he would now leave me to myself; and added

"Smoke and read as much as you please, drink all the water you like. When you get hungry, ring and give your order, and I will decide whether it shall be filled or not. Yours is a stubborn, bad case, and I think the first fourteen dishes in the bill are each and all too delicate for its needs. I ask you as a favor to restrain yourself and not call for them."

"Restrain myself, is it? Give yourself no uneasiness. You are going to save money by me. The idea of coaxing a sick man's appetite back with this buzzard fare is clear insanity."

I said it with bitterness, for I felt outraged by this calm, cold talk over these heartless new engines of assassination. The doctor looked grieved, but not offended. He laid the bill of fare on the commode at my bed's head, "so that it would be handy," and said:

"Yours is not the worst case I have encountered, by any means; still it is a bad one and requires robust treatment; therefore I shall be gratified if you will restrain yourself and skip down to No. 15 and begin with that."

Then he left me and I began to undress, for I was dog-tired and very sleepy. I slept fifteen hours and woke up finely refreshed at ten the next morning. Vienna coffee! It was the first thing I thought of— that unapproachable luxury—that sumptuous coffee-house coffee, compared with which all other European coffee and all American hotel coffee is mere fluid poverty. I rang, and ordered it; also Vienna bread, that delicious invention. The servant spoke through the wicket in the door and said—but you know what he said. He referred me to the bill of fare. I allowed him to go—I had no further use for him.

After the bath I dressed and started for a walk, and got as far as the door. It was locked on the outside. I rang and the servant came and explained that it was another rule. The seclusion of the patient was required until after the first meal. I had not been particularly anxious to get out before; but it was different now. Being locked in makes a person wishful to get out. I soon began to find it difficult to put in the time. At two o'clock I had been twenty-six hours without food. I had been growing hungry for some time; I recognized that I was not only hungry now, but hungry with a strong adjective in front of it. Yet I was not hungry enough to face the bill of fare.

I must put in the time somehow. I would read and smoke. I did it; hour by hour. The books were all of one breed—shipwrecks; people lost in deserts; people shut up in caved-in mines; people starving in besieged cities. I read about all the revolting dishes that ever famishing men had stayed their hunger with. During the first hours these things nauseated me; hours followed in which they did not so affect me; still other Hours followed in which I found myself smacking my lips over some tolerably infernal messes. When I had been without food forty-five hours I ran eagerly to the bell and ordered the second dish in the bill, which was a sort of dumplings containing a compost made of caviar and tar.

It was refused me. During the next fifteen hours I visited the bell every now and then and ordered a dish that was further down the list. Always a refusal. But I was conquering prejudice after prejudice, right along; I was making sure progress; I was creeping up on No. 15 with deadly certainty, and my heart beat faster and faster, my hopes rose higher and higher.

At last when food had not passed my lips for sixty hours, victory was mine, and I ordered No. 15:

"Soft-boiled spring chicken—in the egg; six dozen, hot and fragrant!"

In fifteen minutes it was there; and the doctor along with it, rubbing his hands with joy. He said with great excitement:

"It's a cure, it's a cure! I knew I could do it. Dear sir, my grand system never fails—never. You've got your appetite back—you know you have; say it and make me happy."

"Bring on your carrion—I can eat anything in the bill!"

"Oh, this is noble, this is splendid—but I knew I could do it, the system never fails. How are the birds?"

"Never was anything so delicious in the world; and yet as a rule I don't care for game. But don't interrupt me, don't— I can't spare my mouth, I really can't."

Then the doctor said:

"The cure is perfect. There is no more doubt nor danger. Let the poultry alone; I can trust you with a beefsteak now."

The beefsteak came—as much as a basketful of it—with potatoes, and Vienna bread and coffee; and I ate a meal then that was worth all the costly preparation I had made for it. And dripped tears of gratitude into the gravy all the time—gratitude to the doctor for putting a little plain common sense into me when I had been empty of it so many, many years.

II

Thirty years ago Haimberger went off on a long voyage in a sailing-ship. There were fifteen passengers on board. The table-fare was of the regulation pattern of the day: At seven in the morning, a cup of bad coffee in bed; at nine, breakfast: bad coffee, with condensed milk; soggy rolls, crackers, salt fish; at 1 P.M., luncheon: cold tongue, cold ham, cold corned beef, soggy cold rolls, crackers; 5 P.M., dinner: thick pea-soup, salt fish, hot corned beef and sauerkraut, boiled pork and beans, pudding; 9 till 11 P.M., supper: tea, with condensed milk, cold tongue, cold ham, pickles, sea-biscuit, pickled oysters, pickled pig's feet, grilled bones, golden buck.

At the end of the first week eating had ceased,

nibbling had taken its place. The passengers came to the table, but it was partly to put in the time, and partly because the wisdom of the ages commanded them to be regular in their meals. They were tired of the coarse and monotonous fare, and took no interest in it, had no appette for it. All day and every day they roamed the ship half hungry, plagued by their gnawing stomachs, moody, untalkative, miserable. Among them were three confirmed dyspeptics. These became shadows in the course of three weeks. There was also a bedridden invalid; he lived on boiled rice; he could not look at the regular dishes.

Now came shipwreck and life in open boats, with the usual paucity of food. Provisions ran lower and lower. The appetites improved, then. When nothing was left but raw ham and the ration of that was down to two ounces a day per person, the appetites were perfect. At the end of fifteen days the dyspeptics, the invalid and the most delicate ladies in the party were chewing sailor-boots in ecstasy, and only complaining because the supply of them was limited. Yet these were the same people who couldn't endure the ship's tedious corned beef and sauerkraut and other crudities. They were rescued by an English vessel. Within ten days the whole fifteen were in as good condition as they had been when the shipwreck occurred.

"They had suffered no damage by their adventure," said the professor. "Do you note that?"

"Yes."

"Do you note it well?"

MARK TWAIN

"Yes—I think I do."

"But you don't. You hesitate. You don't rise to the importance of it. I will say it again—with emphasis—*not one of them suffered any damage.*"

"Now I begin to see. Yes, it was indeed remarkable."

"Nothing of the kind. It was perfectly natural. There was no reason why they should suffer damage. They were undergoing Nature's Appetite Cure, the best and wisest in the world."

"Is that where you got your idea?"

"That is where I got it."

"It taught those people a valuable lesson."

"What makes you think that?"

"Why shouldn't I? You seem to think it taught you one."

"That is nothing to the point. I am not a fool."

"I see. Were they fools?"

"They were human beings."

"Is it the same thing?"

"Why do you ask? You know it yourself. As regards his health—and the rest of the things—the average man is what his environment and his superstitions have made him; and their function is to make him an ass. He can't add up three or four new circumstances together and perceive what they mean; it is beyond him. He is not capable of observing for himself. He has to get everything at second hand. If what are miscalled the lower animals were as silly as man is, they would all perish from the earth in a year."

"Those passengers learned no lesson, then?"

"Not a sign of it. They went to their regular meals in the English ship, and pretty soon they were nibbling again—nibbling, appeti eless, disgusted with the food, moody, miserable, ha f hungry, their outraged stomachs cursing and swearing and whining and supplicating all day long. And in vain, for they were the stomachs of fools."

"Then, as I understand it, yo r scheme is—"

"Quite simple. Don't eat ill you are hungry. If the food fails to taste good, fails to satisfy you, rejoice you, comfort you, don't eat again until you are *very* hungry. Then it will rejoice you—and do you good, too."

"And I observe no regularity, as to hours?"

"When you are conquering a bad appetite—no. After it is conquered, regularity is no harm, so long as the appetite remains good. As soon as the appetite wavers, apply the corrective again—which is starvation, long or short according to the needs of the case."

"The best diet, I suppose—I mean the wholesomest—"

"All diets are wholesome. Some are wholesomer than others, but all the ordinary diets are wholesome enough for the people who use them. Whether the food be fine or coarse, it will taste good and it will nourish if a watch be kept upon the appetite and a little starvation introduced every time it weakens. Nansen was used to fine fare, but when his meals were restricted to bear-meat months at a time he suffered no damage and no discomfort, because his appetite was kept at par through the difficulty of getting his bear-meat regularly."

"But doctors arrange carefully considered and delicate diets for invalids."

"They can't help it. The invalid is full of inherited superstitions and won't starve himself. He believes it would certainly kill him."

"It would weaken him, wouldn't it?"

"Nothing to hurt. Look at the invalids in our shipwreck. They lived fifteen days on pinches of raw ham, a suck at sailor-boots, and general starvation. It weakened them, but it didn't hurt them. It put them in fine shape to eat heartily of hearty food and build themselves up to a condition of robust health. But they did not perceive that; they lost their opportunity; they remained invalids; it served them right. Do you know the tricks that the health-resort doctors play?"

"What is it?"

"My system disguised—covert starvation. Grape-cure, bath-cure, mud-cure — it is all the same. The grape and the bath and the mud make a show and do a trifle of the work—the real work is done by the surreptitious starvation. The patient accustomed to four meals and late hours—at both ends of the day—now consider what he has to do at a health resort. He gets up at six in the morning. Eats one egg. Tramps up and down a promenade two hours with the other fools. Eats a butterfly. Slowly drinks a glass of filtered sewage that smells like a buzzard's breath. Promenades another two hours, but alone; if you speak to him he says anxiously, 'My water!—I am walking off my water!—please don't interrupt,' and goes stumping along again. Eats a candied rose-leaf. Lies at rest in the silence and solitude of his room for hours; mustn't speak, mustn't read, mustn't smoke. The doctor comes and feels of his heart, now, and his pulse, and thumps his breast and his back and his stomach, and listens for results through a penny flageolet; then orders the man's bath—half a degree, Réaumur, cooler than yesterday. After the bath, another egg. A glass of sewage at three or four in the afternoon, and promenade solemnly with the other freaks. Dinner at six—half a doughnut and a cup of tea. Walk again. Half past eight, supper—more butterfly; at nine, to bed. Six weeks of this régime —think of it. It starves a man out and puts him in splendid condition. It would have the same effect in London, New York, Jericho—anywhere."

"How long does it take to put a person in condition here?"

"It ought to take but a day or two; but in fact it takes from one to six weeks, according to the character and mentality of the patient."

"How is that?"

"Do you see that crowd of women playing football, and boxing, and jumping fences yonder? They have been here six or seven weeks. They were spectral poor weaklings when they came. They were accustomed to nibbling at dainties and delicacies at set hours four times a day, and they had no appetite for anything. I questioned them, and then locked them into their rooms, the frailest ones to starve nine or ten hours, the others twelve or fifteen. Before long they began to beg; and indeed they suffered a good deal. They complained of nausea, headache, and so on. It was good to see them eat when the time was up. They could not remember when the devouring of a meal had afforded them such rapture—that was their word. Now, then, that ought to have ended their cure, but it didn't. They were free to go to any meals in the house, and they chose their accustomed four. Within a day or two I had to interfere. Their appetites were weakening. I made them knock out a meal. That set them up again. Then they resumed the four. I begged them to learn to knock out a meal themselves, without waiting for me. Up to a fortnight ago they couldn't; they really hadn't manhood enough; but they were gaining it, and now I think they are safe. They drop out a meal every now and then of their own accord. They are in fine condition now, and they might safely go home, I think, but their confidence is not quite perfect yet, so they are waiting awhile."

"Other cases are different?"

"Oh, yes. Sometimes a man learns the whole trick in a week. Learns to regulate his appetite and keep it in perfect order. Learns to drop out a meal with frequency and not mind it."

"But why drop the entire meal out? Why not a part of it?"

"It's a poor device, and inadequate. If the stomach doesn't call vigorously—with a shout, as you may say—it is better not to pester it, but just give it a real rest. Some people can eat more meals than others, and still thrive. There are all sorts of people, and all sorts of appetites. I will show you a man presently who was accustomed to nibble at eight meals a day. It was beyond the proper gait of his appetite by two. I have got him down to six a day, now, and he is all right, and enjoys life. How many meals do you effect per day?"

"Formerly—for twenty-two years—a meal and a half; during the past two years, two and a half: coffee and a roll at nine, luncheon at one, dinner at seven-thirty or eight."

"Formerly a meal and a half—that is, coffee and a roll at nine, dinner in the evening, nothing between—is that it?"

"Yes."

"Why did you add a meal?"

"It was the family's idea. They were uneasy. They thought I was killing myself."

"You found a meal and a half per day enough, all through the twenty-two years?"

"Plenty."

"Your present poor condition is due to the extra meal. Drop it out. You are trying to eat oftener than your stomach demands. You don't gain, you lose. You eat less food now, in a day, on two and a half meals, than you formerly ate on one and a half."

"True—a good deal less; for in those old days my dinner was a very sizable thing."

"Put yourself on a single meal a day, now—dinner—for a few days, till you secure a good,

sound, regular, trustworthy appetite, then take to
your one and a half permanently, and don't listen to
the family any more. When you have any ordinary
ailment, particularly of a feverish sort, eat nothing
at all during twenty-four hours. That will cure it.
It will cure the stubbornest cold in the head, too.
No cold in the head can survive twenty-four hours
on modified starvation.''

"I know it. I have proved it many a time."

SAINT JOAN OF ARC

CHAPTER I

THE evidence furnished at the Trials and Rehabilitation sets forth Joan of Arc's strange and beautiful history in clear and minute detail. Among all the multitude of biographies that freight the shelves of the world's libraries, *this is the only one whose validity is confirmed to us by oath.* It gives us a vivid picture of a career and a personality of so extraordinary a character that we are helped to accept them as actualities by the very fact that both are beyond the inventive reach of fiction. The public part of the career occupied only a mere breath of time—it covered but two years; but what a career it was! The personality which made it pos-

NOTE.—The Official Record of the Trials and Rehabilitation of Joan of Arc is the most remarkable history that exists in any language; yet there are few people in the world who can say they have read it: in England and America it has hardly been heard of.

Three hundred years ago Shakespeare did not know the true story of Joan of Arc; in his day it was unknown even in France. For four hundred years it existed rather as a vaguely defined romance than as definite and authentic history. The true story remained buried in the official archives of France from the Rehabilitation of 1456 until Quicherat dug it out and gave it to the world two generations ago, in lucid and understandable modern French. It is a deeply fascinating story. But only in the Official Trials and Rehabilitation can it be found in its entirety.—M. T.

sible is one to be reverently studied, loved, and marveled at, but not to be wholly understood and accounted for by even the most searching analysis.

In Joan of Arc at the age of sixteen there was no promise of a romance. She lived in a dull little village on the frontiers of civilization; she had been nowhere and had seen nothing; she knew none but simple shepherd folk; she had never seen a person of note; she hardly knew what a soldier looked like; she had never ridden a horse, nor had a warlike weapon in her hand; she could neither read nor write: she could spin and sew; she knew her catechism and her prayers and the fabulous histories of the saints, and this was all her learning. That was Joan at sixteen. What did she know of law? of evidence? of courts? of the attorney's trade? of legal procedure? Nothing. Less than nothing. Thus exhaustively equipped with ignorance, she went before the court at Toul to contest a false charge of breach of promise of marriage; she conducted her cause herself, without any one's help or advice or any one's friendly sympathy, and won it. She called no witnesses of her own, but vanquished the prosecution by using with deadly effectiveness its own testimony. The astonished judge threw the case out of court, and spoke of her as "this marvelous child."

She went to the veteran Commandant of Vaucouleurs and demanded an escort of soldiers, saying she must march to the help of the King of France, since she was commissioned of God to win back his lost kingdom for him and set the crown upon his head. The Commandant said, "What, you? You are only a child." And he advised that she be taken back to her village and have her ears boxed. But she said she must obey God, and would come again, and again, and yet again, and finally she would get the soldiers. She said truly. In time he yielded, after months of delay and refusal, and gave her the soldiers; and took off his sword and gave her that, and said, "Go—and let come what may." She made her long and perilous journey through the enemy's country, and spoke with the King, and convinced him. Then she was summoned before the University of Poitiers to prove that she *was* commissioned of God and not of Satan, and daily during three weeks she sat before that learned congress unafraid, and capably answered their deep questions out of her ignorant but able head and her simple and honest heart; and again she won her case, and with it the wondering admiration of all that august company.

And now, aged seventeen, she was made Commander-in-Chief, with a prince of the royal house and the veteran generals of France for subordinates; and at the head of the first army she had ever seen, she marched to Orleans, carried the commanding fortresses of the enemy by storm in three desperate assaults, and in ten days raised a siege which had defied the might of France for seven months.

After a tedious and insane delay caused by the King's instability of character and the treacherous counsels of his ministers, she got permission to take the field again. She took Jargeau by storm; then Meung; she forced Beaugency to surrender; then—

in the open field—she won the memorable victory of
Patay against Talbot, "the English lion," and broke
the back of the Hundred Years' War. It was a
campaign which cost but seven weeks of time; yet
the political results would have been cheap if the
time expended had been fifty years. Patay, that
unsung and now long-forgotten battle, was the Mos-
cow of the English power in France; from the blow
struck that day it was destined never to recover. It
was the beginning of the end of an alien dominion
which had ridden France intermittently for three
hundred years.

Then followed the great campaign of the Loire,
the capture of Troyes by assault, and the triumphal
march past surrendering towns and fortresses to
Rheims, where Joan put the crown upon her King's
head in the Cathedral, amid wild public rejoicings,
and with her old peasant father there to see these
things and believe his eyes if he could. She had restored the crown and the lost sovereignty; the King
was grateful for once in his shabby poor life, and
asked her to name her reward and have it. She
asked for nothing for herself, but begged that the
taxes of her native village might be remitted forever.
The prayer was granted, and the promise kept for
three hundred and sixty years. Then it was broken,
and remains broken to-day. France was very poor
then, she is very rich now; but she has been collecting
those taxes for more than a hundred years.

Joan asked one other favor: that now that her
mission was fulfilled she might be allowed to go back
to her village and take up her humble life again with

her mother and the friends of her childhood; for she had no pleasure in the cruelties of war, and the sight of blood and suffering wrung her heart. Sometimes in battle she did not draw her sword, lest in the splendid madness of the onset she might forget herself and take an enemy's life with it. In the Rouen Trials, one of her quaintest speeches—coming from the gentle and girlish source it did—was her naïve remark that she had "never killed any one." Her prayer for leave to go back to the rest and peace of her village home was not granted.

Then she wanted to march at once upon Paris, take it, and drive the English out of France. She was hampered in all the ways that treachery and the King's vacillation could devise, but she forced her way to Paris at last, and fell badly wounded in a successful assault upon one of the gates. Of course her men lost heart at once—she was the only heart they had. They fell back. She begged to be allowed to remain at the front, saying victory was sure. "I will take Paris now or die!" she said. But she was removed from the field by force; the King ordered a retreat, and actually disbanded his army. In accordance with a beautiful old military custom Joan devoted her silver armor and hung it up in the Cathedral of St. Denis. Its great days were over.

Then, by command, she followed the King and his frivolous court and endured a gilded captivity for a time, as well as her free spirit could; and whenever inaction became unbearable she gathered some men together and rode away and assaulted a stronghold and captured it.

At last in a sortie against the enemy, from Compiègne, on the 24th of May (when she was turned eighteen), she was herself captured, after a gallant fight. It was her last battle. She was to follow the drums no more.

Thus ended the briefest epoch-making military career known to history. It lasted only a year and a month, but it found France an English province, and furnishes the reason that France is France to-day and not an English province still. Thirteen months! It was, indeed, a short career; but in the centuries that have since elapsed five hundred millions of Frenchmen have lived and died blest by the benefactions it conferred; and so long as France shall endure, the mighty debt must grow. And France is grateful; we often hear her say it. Also thrifty: she collects the Domremy taxes.

CHAPTER II

JOAN was fated to spend the rest of her life behind bolts and bars. She was a prisoner of war, not a criminal, therefore hers was recognized as an honorable captivity. By the rules of war she must be held to ransom, and a fair price could not be refused if offered. John of Luxembourg paid her the just compliment of requiring a prince's ransom for her. In that day that phrase represented a definite sum—61,125 francs. It was, of course, supposable that either the King or grateful France, or both, would fly with the money and set their fair young benefactor free. But this did not happen. In five and a half months neither King nor country stirred a hand nor offered a penny. Twice Joan tried to escape. Once by a trick she succeeded for a moment, and locked her jailer in behind her, but she was discovered and caught; in the other case she let herself down from a tower sixty feet high, but her rope was too short, and she got a fall that disabled her and she could not get away.

Finally, Cauchon, Bishop of Beauvais, paid the money and bought Joan—ostensibly for the Church, to be tried for wearing male attire and for other impieties, but really for the English, the enemy into whose hands the poor girl was so piteously anxious not to fall. She was now shut up in the dungeons of the Castle of Rouen'and kept in an iron cage, with her hands and feet and neck chained to a pillar; and from that time forth during all the months of her imprisonment, till the end, several rough English soldiers stood guard over her night and day—and not outside her room, but in it. It was a dreary and hideous captivity, but it did not conquer her: nothing could break that invincible spirit. From first to last she was a prisoner a year; and she spent the last three months of it on trial for her life before a formidable array of ecclesiastical judges, and disputing the ground with them foot by foot and inch by inch with brilliant generalship and dauntless pluck. The spectacle of that solitary girl, forlorn and friendless, without advocate or adviser, and without the help and guidance of any copy of the charges brought against her or rescript of the complex and voluminous daily proceedings of the court to modify the crushing strain upon her astonishing memory, fighting that long battle serene and undismayed against these colossal odds, stands alone in its pathos and its sublimity; it has nowhere its mate, either in the annals of fact or in the inventions of fiction.

And how fine and great were the things she daily said, how fresh and crisp—and she so worn in body, so starved, and tired, and harried! They run through the whole gamut of feeling and expression—from scorn and defiance, uttered with soldierly fire and frankness, all down the scale to wounded dignity clothed in words of noble pathos; as, when her patience was exhausted by the pestering delvings and gropings and searchings of her persecutors to find out what kind of devil's witchcraft she had employed to rouse the war spirit in her timid soldiers, she burst out with, "What I said was, '*Ride these English down*'—and I did it myself!" and as, when insultingly asked why it was that *her* standard had place at the crowning of the King in the Cathedral of Rheims rather than the standards of the other captains, she uttered that touching speech, "*It had borne the burden, it had earned the honor*"—a phrase which fell from her lips without premeditation, yet whose moving beauty and simple grace it would bankrupt the arts of language to surpass.

Although she was on trial for her life, she was the only witness called on either side; the only witness summoned to testify before a packed jury commissioned with a definite task: to find her guilty, whether she was guilty or not. She must be convicted out of her own mouth, there being no other way to accomplish it. Every advantage that learning has over ignorance, age over youth, experience over inexperience, chicane over artlessness, every trick and trap and gin devisable by malice and the cunning of sharp intellects practised in setting snares for the unwary—all these were employed against her without shame; and when these arts were one by one defeated by the marvelous intuitions of her alert and penetrating mind, Bishop Cauchon stooped to a final baseness which it degrades human speech to describe: a priest who pretended to come from the region of her own home and to be a pitying friend and anxious to help her in her sore need was smuggled into her cell, and he·misused his sacred office to steal her confidence; she confided to him the things sealed from revealment by her Voices, and which her prosecutors had tried so long in vain to trick her into betraying. A concealed confederate set it all down and delivered it to Cauchon, who used Joan's secrets, thus obtained, for her ruin.

Throughout the Trials, whatever the foredoomed witness said was twisted from its true meaning when possible, and made to tell against her; and whenever an answer of hers was beyond the reach of twisting it was not allowed to go upon the record. It was upon one of these latter occasions that she uttered that pathetic reproach—to Cauchon: "Ah, you set down everything that is against me, but you will not set down what is for me."

That this untrained young creature's genius for war was wonderful, and her generalship worthy to rank with the ripe products of a tried and trained military experience, we have the sworn testimony of two of her veteran subordinates—one, the Duc d'Alençon, the other the greatest of the French generals of the time, Dunois, Bastard of Orleans; that her genius was as great—possibly even greater—in the subtle warfare of the forum we have for witness the records of the Rouen Trials, that protracted exhibition of intellectual fence maintained with credit against the master-minds of France; that her moral greatness was peer to her intellect we call the Rouen Trials again to witness, with their testimony to a fortitude which patiently and steadfastly endured during twelve weeks the wasting forces of captivity, chains, loneliness, sickness, darkness, hunger, thirst, cold, shame, insult, abuse, broken sleep, treachery, ingratitude, exhausting sieges of cross-examination, the threat of torture, with the rack before her and the executioner standing ready: yet never surrendering, never asking quarter, the frail wreck of her as unconquerable the last day as was her invincible spirit the first.

Great as she was in so many ways, she was perhaps even greatest of all in the lofty things just named—her patient endurance, her steadfastness, her granite fortitude. We may not hope to easily find her mate and twin in these majestic qualities; where we lift our eyes highest we find only a strange and curious contrast—there in the captive eagle beating his broken wings on the Rock of St. Helena.

CHAPTER III

THE Trials ended with her condemnation. But as
she had conceded nothing, confessed nothing, this
was victory for her, defeat for Cauchon. But his
evil resources were not yet exhausted. She was persuaded to agree to sign a paper of slight import, then
by treachery a paper was substituted which contained a recantation and a detailed confession of
everything which had been charged against her during the Trials and denied and repudiated by her
persistently during the three months; and this false
paper she ignorantly signed. This was a victory for
Cauchon. He followed it eagerly and pitilessly up
by at once setting a trap for her which she could not
escape. When she realized this she gave up the long
struggle, denounced the treason which had been
practised against her, repudiated the false confession, reasserted the truth of the testimony which she
had given in the Trials, and went to her martyrdom
with the peace of God in her tired heart, and on her
lips endearing words and loving prayers for the cur
she had crowned and the nation of ingrates she had
saved.

When the fires rose about her and she begged for
a cross for her dying lips to kiss, it was not a friend
but an enemy, not a Frenchman but an alien, not

a comrade in arms but an English soldier, that answered that pathetic prayer. He broke a stick across his knee, bound the pieces together in the form of the symbol she so loved, and gave it her; and his gentle deed is not forgotten, nor will be.

CHAPTER IV

TWENTY-FIVE years afterward the Process of Rehabilitation was instituted, there being a growing doubt as to the validity of a sovereignty that had been rescued and set upon its feet by a person who had been proven by the Church to be a witch and a familiar of evil spirits. Joan's old generals, her secretary, several aged relations and other villagers of Domremy, surviving judges and secretaries of the Rouen and Poitiers Processes—a cloud of witnesses, some of whom had been her enemies and persecutors —came and made oath and testified; and what they said was written down. In that sworn testimony the moving and beautiful history of Joan of Arc is laid bare, from her childhood to her martyrdom. From the verdict she rises stainlessly pure, in mind and heart, in speech and deed and spirit, and will so endure to the end of time.

She is the Wonder of the Ages. And when we consider her origin, her early circumstances, her sex, and that she did all the things upon which her renown rests while she was still a young girl, we recognize that while our race continues she will be also the *Riddle* of the Ages. When we set about accounting for a Napoleon or a Shakespeare or a Raphael or a Wagner or an Edison or other extraordinary person, we understand that the measure of his talent will not explain the whole result, nor even the largest part of it; no, it is the atmosphere in which the talent was cradled that explains; it is the training which it received while it grew, the nurture it got from reading, study, example, the encouragement it gathered from self-recognition and recognition from the outside at each stage of its development: when we know all these details, then we know why the man was ready when his opportunity came. We should expect Edison's surroundings and atmosphere to have the largest share in discovering him to himself and to the world; and. we should expect him to live and die undiscovered in a land where an inventor could find no comradeship, no sympathy, no ambition-rousing atmosphere of recognition and applause—Dahomey, for instance. Dahomey could not find an Edison out; in Dahomey an Edison could not find himself out. Broadly speaking, genius is not born with sight, but blind; and it is not itself that opens its eyes, but the subtle influences of a myriad of stimulating exterior circumstances.

We all know this to be not a guess, but a mere commonplace fact, a truism. Lorraine was Joan of Arc's Dahomey. And there the Riddle confronts us. We can understand how she could be born with military genius, with leonine courage, with incomparable fortitude, with a mind which was in several particulars a prodigy—a mind which included among its specialties the lawyer's gift of detecting traps laid by the adversary in cunning and treacherous arrangements of seemingly innocent words, the orator's gift of eloquence, the advocate's gift of presenting a case in clear and compact form, the judge's gift of sorting and weighing evidence, and finally, something recognizable as more than a mere trace of the statesman's gift of understanding a political situation and how to make profitable use of such opportunities as it offers; we can comprehend how she could be born with these great qualities, but we cannot comprehend how they became immediately usable and effective without the developing forces of a sympathetic atmosphere and the training which comes of teaching, study, practice—years of practice—and the crowning and perfecting help of a thousand mistakes. We can understand how the possibilities of the future perfect peach are all lying hid in the humble bitter-almond, but we cannot conceive of the peach springing directly from the almond without the intervening long seasons of patient cultivation and development. Out of a cattle-pasturing peasant village lost in the remotenesses of an unvisited wilderness and atrophied with ages of stupefaction and ignorance we cannot see a Joan of Arc issue equipped to the last detail for her amazing career and hope to be able to explain the riddle of it, labor at it as we may.

It is beyond us. All the rules fail in this girl's case. In the world's history she stands alone—quite alone. Others have been great in their first public exhibitions of generalship, valor, legal talent, diplomacy, fortitude; but always their previous years and associations had been in a larger or smaller degree a preparation for these things. There have been no

SAINT JOAN OF ARC

exceptions to the rule. But Joan was competent in a law case at sixteen without ever having seen a law-book or a court-house before; she had no training in soldiership and no associations with it, yet she was a competent general in her first campaign; she was brave in her first battle, yet her courage had had no education—not even the education which a boy's courage gets from never-ceasing reminders that it is not permissible in a boy to be a coward, but only in a girl; friendless, alone, ignorant, in the blossom of her youth, she sat week after week, a prisoner in chains, before her assemblage of judges, enemies hunting her to her death, the ablest minds in France, and answered them out of an untaught wisdom which overmatched their learning, baffled their tricks and treacheries with a native sagacity which compelled their wonder, and scored every day a victory against these incredible odds and camped unchallenged on the field. In the history of the human intellect, untrained, inexperienced, and using only its birthright equipment of untried capacities, there is nothing which approaches this. Joan of Arc stands alone, and must continue to stand alone, by reason of the unfellowed fact that in the things wherein she was great she was so without shade or suggestion of help from preparatory teaching, practice, environment, or experience. There is no one to compare her with, none to measure her by; for all others among the illustrious *grew* toward their high place in an atmosphere and surroundings which discovered their gift to them and nourished it and promoted it, intentionally or unconsciously. There have been

379

other young generals, but they were not girls; young generals, but they had been soldiers before they were generals: she *began* as a general; she commanded the first army she ever saw; she led it from victory to victory, and never lost a battle with it; there have been young commanders-in-chief, but none so young as she: she is the only soldier in history who has held the supreme command of a nation's armies at the age of seventeen.

Her history has still another feature which sets her apart and leaves her without fellow or competitor: there have been many uninspired prophets, but she was the only one who ever ventured the daring detail of naming, along with a foretold event, the event's precise nature, the special time-limit within which it would occur, and the place—*and scored fulfilment.* At Vaucouleurs she said she must go to the King and be made his general, and break the English power, and crown her sovereign—"at Rheims." It all happened. It was all to happen "next year" —and it did. She foretold her first wound and its character and date a month in advance, and the prophecy was recorded in a public record-book three weeks in advance. She repeated it the morning of the date named, and it was fulfilled before night. At Tours she foretold the limit of her military career —saying it would end in one year from the time of its utterance—and she was right. She foretold her martyrdom—using *that word*, and naming a time three months away—and again she was right. At a time when France seemed hopelessly and permanently in the hands of the English she twice asserted in her prison before her judges that within seven years the English would meet with a mightier disaster than had been the fall of Orleans: it happened within five—the fall of Paris. Other prophecies of hers came true, both as to the event named and the time-limit prescribed.

She was deeply religious, and believed that she had daily speech with angels; that she saw them face to face, and that they counseled her, comforted and heartened her, and brought commands to her direct from God. She had a childlike faith in the heavenly origin of her apparitions and her Voices, and not any threat of any form of death was able to frighten it out of her loyal heart. She was a beautiful and simple and lovable character. In the records of the Trials this comes out in clear and shining detail. She was gentle and winning and affectionate; she loved her home and friends and her village life; she was miserable in the presence of pain and suffering; she was full of compassion: on the field of her most splendid victory she forgot her triumphs to hold in her lap the head of a dying enemy and comfort his passing spirit with pitying words; in an age when it was common to slaughter prisoners she stood dauntless between hers and harm, and saved them alive; she was forgiving, generous, unselfish, magnanimous; she was pure from all spot or stain of baseness. And always she was a *girl;* and dear and worshipful, as is meet for that estate: when she fell wounded, the first time, she was frightened, and cried when she saw her blood gushing from her breast; but she was Joan of Arc! and when presently she found that her generals were sounding the retreat, she staggered to her feet and led the assault again and took that place by storm.

There is no blemish in that rounded and beautiful character.

How strange it is!—that almost invariably the artist remembers only one detail—one minor and meaningless detail of the personality of Joan of Arc: to wit, that she was a peasant girl—and forgets all the rest; and so he paints her as a strapping middle-aged fishwoman, with costume to match, and in her face the spirituality of a ham. He is slave to his one idea, and forgets to observe that the supremely great souls are never lodged in gross bodies. No brawn, no muscle, could endure the work that their bodies must do; they do their miracles by the spirit, which has fifty times the strength and staying-power of brawn and muscle. The Napoleons are little, not big; and they work twenty hours in the twenty-four, and come up fresh, while the big soldiers with the little hearts faint around them with fatigue. We know what Joan of Arc was like, without asking —merely by what she did. The artist should paint her *spirit*—then he could not fail to paint her body aright. She would rise before us, then, a vision to win us, not repel: a lithe young slender figure, instinct with "the unbought grace of youth," dear and bonny and lovable, the face beautiful, and trans-figured with the light of that lustrous intellect and the fires of that unquenchable spirit.

Taking into account, as I have suggested before, all the circumstances—her origin, youth, sex, illiteracy, early environment, ånd the obstructing conditions under which she exploited her high gifts and made her conquests in the field ariḍ before the courts that tried her for her life—she i. easily and by far the most extraordinary person the human race has ever produced.

IN MEMORIAM

OLIVIA SUSAN CLEMENS

DIED AUGUST 18, 1896; AGED 24

IN a fair valley—oh, how long ago, how long ago!
Where all the broad expanse was clothed in vines
And fruitful fields and meadows starred with flowers,
And clear streams wandered at their idle will,
And still lakes slept, their burnished surfaces
A dream of painted clouds, and soft airs
Went whispering with odorous breath,
And all was peace—in that fair vale,
Shut from the troubled world, a nameless hamlet
    drowsed.

Hard by, apart, a temple stood;
And strangers from the outer world
Passing, noted it with tired eyes,
And seeing, saw it not:
A glimpse of its fair form—an answering momentary
    thrill—
And they passed on, careless and unaware.

They could not know the cunning of its make;
They could not know the secret shut up in its heart;
Only the dwellers of the hamlet knew:
They knew that what seemed brass was gold;

IN MEMORIAM

What marble seemed, was ivory.
The glories that enriched the milky surfaces—
The trailing vines, and interwoven flowers,
And tropic birds awing, clothed all in tinted fire—
They knew for what they were, not what they
    seemed:
Incrustings all of gems, not perishable splendors of
    the brush.
They knew the secret spot where one must stand—
They knew the surest hour, the proper slant of sun—
To gather in, unmarred, undimmed,
The vision of the fane in all its fairy grace,
A fainting dream against the opal sky.

    And more than this. They knew
That in the temple's inmost place a spirit dwelt,
Made all of light!

    For glimpses of it they had caught
Beyond the curtains when the priests
That served the altar came and went.

    All loved that light and held it dear
That had this partial grace;
But the adoring priests alone who lived
By day and night submerged in its immortal glow
Knew all its power and depth, and could appraise
    the loss
If it should fade and fail and come no more.

    All this was long ago—so long ago!
The light burned on; and they that worshiped it,
And they that caught its flash at intervals and held
    it dear,

Contented lived in its secure possession.   Ah,
How long ago it was!   .
                        And then when they
Were nothing fearing, and God's peace was in the air,
And none was prophesying harm—
The vast disaster fell:
Where stood the temple when the sun went down,
Was vacant desert when it rose again! .
     Ah, yes!   'Tis ages since it chanced!
                              So long ago it was,
That from the memory of the hamlet-folk the Light
     has passed—
They scarce believing, now, that once it was,
Or, if believing, yet not missing it,
And reconciled to have it gone.

     Not so the priests!   Oh, not so
The stricken ones that served it day and night,
Adoring it, abiding in the healing of its peace:
They stand, yet, where erst they stood
Speechless in that dim morning long ago;
And still they gaze, as then they gazed,
And murmur, "It will come again;
It knows our pain—it knows—it knows—
Ah, surely it will come again."
                              S. L. C.

LAKE LUCERNE, August 18, 1897.

MARK TWAIN

A BIOGRAPHICAL SKETCH

By Samuel E. Moffett

IN 1835 the creation of the Western empire of America had just begun. In the whole region west of the Mississippi, which now contains twenty-one million people—nearly twice the entire population of the United States at that time—there were less than half a million white inhabitants. There were only two states beyond the great river, Louisiana and Missouri. There were only two considerable groups of population, one about New Orleans, the other about St. Louis. If we omit New Orleans, which is east of the river, there was only one place in all that vast domain with any pretension to be called a city. That was St. Louis, and that metropolis, the wonder and pride of all the Western country, had no more than ten thousand inhabitants.

It was in this frontier region, on the extreme fringe of settlement "that just divides the desert from the sown," that Samuel Langhorne Clemens was born, November 30, 1835, in the hamlet of Florida, Missouri. His parents had come there to be in the thick of the Western boom, and by a fate for which no lack of foresight on their part was to blame, they found themselves in a place which succeeded in accumulating one hundred and twenty-five inhabitants in the next sixty years. When we read of the westward sweep of population and wealth in the United States, it seems as if those who were in the van of that movement must have been inevitably carried on to fortune. But that was a tide full of eddies and back-currents, and Mark Twain's parents possessed a faculty for finding them that appears nothing less than miraculous. The whole Western empire was before them where to choose. They could have bought the entire site of Chicago for a pair of boots. They could have taken up a farm within the present city limits of St. Louis. What they actually did was to live for a time in Columbia, Kentucky, with a small property in land, and six inherited slaves, then to move to Jamestown, on the Cumberland plateau of Tennessee, a place that was then no farther removed from the currents of the world's life than Uganda, but which no resident of that or any other part of Central Africa would now regard as a serious competitor, and next to migrate to Missouri, passing St. Louis and settling first in Florida, and afterward in Hannibal. But when the whole map was blank the promise of fortune glowed as rosily in these regions as anywhere else. Florida had great expectations when Jackson was President. When John Marshall Clemens took up eighty thousand acres of land in Tennessee, he thought he had established his children as territorial magnates. That phantom vision of wealth furnished later one of the motives of *The Gilded Age.* It conferred no other benefit.

If Samuel Clemens missed a fortune, he inherited good blood. On both sides his family had been settled in the South since early colonial times. His father, John Marshall Clemens, of Virginia, was a descendant of Gregory Clemens, who became one of the judges that condemned Charles I. to death, was excepted from the amnesty after the Restoration in consequence, and lost his head. A cousin of John M. Clemens, Jeremiah Clemens, represented Alabama in the United States Senate from 1849 to 1853.

Through his mother, Jane Lampton (Lambton), the boy was descended from the Lambtons of Durham, whose modern English representatives still possess the lands held by their ancestors of the same name since the twelfth century. Some of her forebears on the maternal side, the Montgomerys, went with Daniel Boone to Kentucky, and were in the thick of the romantic and tragic events that accompanied the settlement of the "Dark and Bloody Ground," and she herself was born there twenty-nine years after the first log cabin was built within the limits of the present commonwealth. She was one of the earliest, prettiest, and brightest of the many belles that have given Kentucky such an enviable reputation as a nursery of fair women, and her vivacity and wit left no doubt in the minds of her friends concerning the source of her son's genius.

John Marshall Clemens, who had been trained for the bar in Virginia, served for some years as a magistrate at Hannibal, holding for a time the position of county judge. With his death, in March, 1847, Mark Twain's formal education came to an end, and his education in real life began. He had always been a delicate boy, and his father, in consequence, had been lenient in the matter of enforcing attendance at school, although he had been profoundly anxious that his children should be well educated. His wish was fulfilled, although not in the way he had expected. It is a fortunate thing for literature that Mark Twain was never ground into smooth uniformity under the scholastic emery wheel. He has made the world his university, and in men, and books, and strange places, and all the phases of an infinitely varied life, has built an education broad and deep, on the foundations of an undisturbed individuality.

A BIOGRAPHICAL SKETCH

His high school was a village printing-office, where his elder brother Orion was conducting a newspaper. The thirteen-year-old boy served in all capacities, and in the occasional absences of his chief he reveled in personal journalism, with original illustrations hacked on wooden blocks with a jack-knife, to an extent that riveted the town's attention, "but not its admiration," as his brother plaintively confessed. The editor spoke with feeling, for he had to take the consequences of these exploits on his return.

From his earliest childhood young Clemens had been of an adventurous disposition. Before he was thirteen, he had been extracted three times from the Mississippi, and six times from Bear Creek, in a substantially drowned condition, but his mother, with the high confidence in his future that never deserted her, merely remarked: "People who are born to be hanged are safe in the water." By 1853 the Hannibal tether had become too short for him. He disappeared from home and wandered from one Eastern printing-office to another. He saw the World's Fair at New York, and other marvels, and supported himself by setting type. At the end of this *Wanderjahr*, financial stress drove him back to his family. He lived at St. Louis, Muscatine, and Keokuk until 1857, when he induced the great Horace Bixby to teach him the mystery of steamboat-piloting. The charm of all this warm, indolent existence in the sleepy river towns has colored his whole subsequent life. In *Tom Sawyer, Huckleberry Finn, Life on the Mississippi*, and *Pudd'nhead Wilson*, every phase of that vanished estate is lovingly dwelt upon.

Native character will always make itself felt, but one may wonder whether Mark Twain's humor would have developed in quite so sympathetic and buoyant a vein if he had been brought up in Ecclefechan instead of in Hannibal, and whether Carlyle might not have been a little more human if he had spent his boyhood in Hannibal instead of in Ecclefechan.

A Mississippi pilot in the later fifties was a personage of imposing grandeur. He was a miracle of attainments; he was the absolute master of his boat while it was under way, and just before his fall he commanded a salary precisely equal to that earned at that time by the Vice-President of the United States or a Justice of the Supreme Court. The best proof of the superlative majesty and desirability of his position is the fact that Samuel Clemens deliberately subjected himself to the incredible labor necessary to attain it—a labor compared with which the efforts needed to acquire the degree of Doctor of Philosophy at a university are as light as a summer course of modern novels. To appreciate the full meaning of a pilot's marvelous education, one must read the whole of *Life on the Mississippi*, but this extract may give a partial idea of a single feature of that training—the cultivation of the memory:

"First of all, there is one faculty which a pilot must incessantly cultivate until he has brought it to absolute perfection. Nothing short of perfection will do. That faculty is memory. He cannot stop with merely thinking a thing is so and so; he must *know* it; for this is eminently one of the exact sciences. With what scorn a pilot was looked upon, in the old times, if he ever ventured to deal in that feeble phrase 'I think,' instead of the vigorous one 'I know'! One cannot easily realize what a tremendous thing it is to know every trivial detail of twelve hundred miles of river, and know it with absolute exactness. If you will take the longest street in New York, and travel up and down it, conning its features patiently until you know every house, and window, and door, and lamp-post, and big and little sign by heart, and know them so accurately that you can instantly name the one you are abreast of when you are set down at random in that street in the middle of an inky black night, you will then have a tolerable notion of the amount and the exactness of a pilot's knowledge who carries the Mississippi River in his head. And then, if you will go on until you know every street-crossing, the character, size, and position of the crossing-stones, and the varying depth of mud in each of those numberless places, you will have some idea of what the pilot must know in order to keep a Mississippi steamer out of trouble. Next, if you will take half of the signs in that long street and *change their places* once a month, and still manage to know their new positions accurately on dark nights, and keep up with these repeated changes without making any mistakes, you will understand what is required of a pilot's peerless memory by the fickle Mississippi.

"I think a pilot's memory is about the most wonderful thing in the world. To know the Old and New Testaments by heart, and be able to recite them glibly, forward or backward, or begin at random anywhere in the book and recite both ways, and never trip or make a mistake, is no extravagant mass of knowledge, and no marvelous facility, compared to a pilot's massed knowledge of the Mississippi, and his marvelous facility in handling it. . . .

"And how easily and comfortably the pilot's memory does its work; how placidly effortless is its way; how *unconsciously* it lays up its vast stores, hour by hour, day by day, and never loses or mislays a single valuable package of them all! Take an instance. Let a leadsman say: 'Half twain! half twain! half twain! half twain! half twain!' until it becomes as monotonous as the ticking of a clock; let conversation be going on all the time, and the pilot be doing his share of the talking, and no longer consciously listening to the leadsman; and in the midst of this endless string of half twains let a single 'quarter twain!' be interjected, without emphasis, and then the half-twain cry go on again, just as before: two or three weeks later that pilot can describe with precision the boat's position in the river when that quarter twain was uttered, and give you such a lot of head marks, stern marks, and side marks to guide you that you ought to be able to take the boat there and put her in that same spot again yourself! The cry of 'Quarter twain!' did not really take his mind from his talk, but his trained faculties instantly photographed the bearings, noted the change of depth, and laid up the important details for future reference without requiring any assistance from him in the matter.''

Young Clemens went through all that appalling training, stored away in his head the bewildering mass of knowledge a pilot's duties required, received the license that was the diploma of the river university, entered into regular employment, and regarded himself as established for life, when the outbreak of the Civil War wiped out his occupation at a stroke, and made his weary apprenticeship a useless labor. The commercial navigation of the lower Mississippi was stopped by a line of fire, and black, squat gunboats, their sloping sides plated with railroad iron, took the place of the gorgeous white side-wheelers, whose pilots had been the envied aristocrats of the river towns. Clemens was in New Orleans when Louisiana seceded, and started North the next day. The boat ran a blockade every day of her trip, and on the last night of the voyage the batteries at the Jefferson Barracks, just below St. Louis, fired two shots through her chimneys.

Brought up in a slaveholding atmosphere, Mark Twain naturally sympathized at first with the South. In June he joined the Confederates in Ralls County, Missouri, as a second lieutenant under General Tom Harris. His military career lasted for two weeks. Narrowly missing the distinction of being captured by Colonel Ulysses S. Grant, he resigned, explaining that he had become "incapacitated by fatigue" through persistent retreating. In his subsequent writings he has always treated his brief experience of warfare as a burlesque episode, although the official reports and correspondence of the Confederate commanders speak very respectfully of the work of the raw countrymen of the Harris Brigade. The elder Clemens brother, Orion, was *persona grata* to the Administration of President Lincoln, and received in consequence an appointment as the first Secretary of the new Territory of Nevada. He offered his speedily reconstructed junior the position of private secretary to himself, "with nothing to do and no salary." The two crossed the plains in the Overland coach in eighteen days—almost precisely the time it will take to go from New York to Vladivostok when the Trans-Siberian Railway is finished.

A year of variegated fortune-hunting among the silver-mines of the Humboldt and Esmeralda regions followed. Occasional letters written during this time to the leading newspaper of the territory, the Virginia City *Territorial Enterprise*, attracted the attention of the proprietor, Mr. J. T. Goodman, a man of keen and unerring literary instinct, and he offered the writer the position of local editor on his staff. With the duties of this place were combined those of legislative correspondent at Carson City, the capital. The work of young Clemens created a sensation among the lawmakers. He wrote a weekly letter, spined with barbed personalities. It appeared every Sunday, and on Mondays the legislative business was obstructed with the complaints of members who rose to questions of privilege, and expressed their opinion of the correspondent with acerbity. This encouraged him to give his letters more individuality by signing them. For this purpose he adopted the old Mississippi leadsman's call for two fathoms (twelve feet)—"Mark Twain."

At that particular period dueling was a passing fashion on the Comstock. The refinements of Parisian civilization had not penetrated there, and a Washoe duel seldom left more than one survivor. The weapons were always Colt's navy revolvers—distance, fifteen paces; fire and advance; six shots allowed. Mark Twain became involved in a quarrel with Mr. Laird, the editor of the Virginia *Union*, and the situation seemed to call for a duel. Neither combatant was an expert with the pistol, but Mark Twain was fortunate enough to have a second who was. The men were practising in adjacent gorges, Mr. Laird doing fairly well, and his opponent hitting everything but the mark. A small bird lit on a sagebush thirty yards away, and Mark Twain's second fired and knocked off its head. At that moment the enemy came over the ridge, saw the dead bird, observed the distance, and learned from Gillis, the humorist's second, that the feat had been performed by Mark Twain, for whom such an exploit was nothing remarkable. They withdrew for consultation, and then offered a formal apology, after which peace was restored, leaving Mark Twain with the honors of war.

However, this incident was the means of effecting another change in his life. There was a new law which prescribed two years' imprisonment for any one who should send, carry, or accept a challenge. The fame of the proposed duel had reached the capital, eighteen miles away, and the governor wrathfully gave orders for the arrest of all concerned, announcing his intention of making an example that would be remembered. A friend

A BIOGRAPHICAL SKETCH

of the duelists heard of their danger, outrode the officers of the law, and hurried the parties over the border into California.

Mark Twain found a berth as city editor of the San Francisco *Morning Call*, but he was not adapted to routine newspaper work, and in a couple of years he made another bid for fortune in the mines. He tried the "pocket-mines" of California, this time, at Jackass Gulch, in Calaveras County, but was fortunate enough to find no pockets. Thus he escaped the hypnotic fascination that has kept some intermittently successful pocket-miners willing prisoners in Sierra cabins for life, and in three months he was back in San Francisco, penniless, but in the line of literary promotion. He wrote letters for the Virginia *Enterprise* for a time, but, tiring of that, welcomed an assignment to visit Hawaii for the Sacramento *Union* and write about the sugar interests. It was in Honolulu that he accomplished one of his greatest feats of "straight newspaper work." The clipper *Hornet* had been burned on "the line," and when the skeleton survivors arrived, after a passage of forty-three days in an open boat on ten days' provisions, Mark Twain gathered their stories, worked all day and all night, and threw a complete account of the horror aboard a schooner that had already cast off. It was the only full account that reached California, and it was not only a clean "scoop" of unusual magnitude, but an admirable piece of literary art. The *Union* testified its appreciation by paying the correspondent ten times the current rates for it.

After six months in the islands, Mark Twain returned to California, and made his first venture upon the lecture platform. He was warmly received, and delivered several lectures with profit. In 1867 he went East by way of the Isthmus, and joined the *Quaker City* excursion to Europe and the Holy Land, as correspondent of the *Alta California*, of San Francisco. During this tour of five or six months the party visited the principal ports of the Mediterranean and the Black Sea. From this trip grew *The Innocents Abroad*, the creator of Mark Twain's reputation as a literary force of the first order. *The Celebrated Jumping Frog of Calaveras County* had preceded it, but *The Innocents* gave the author his first introduction to international literature. A hundred thousand copies were sold the first year, and as many more later.

Four years of lecturing followed—distasteful, but profitable. Mark Twain always shrank from the public exhibition of himself on the platform, but he was a popular favorite there from the first. He was one of a little group, including Henry Ward Beecher and two or three others, for whom every lyceum committee in the country was bidding, and whose capture at any price insured the success of a lecture course.

The *Quaker City* excursion had a more important result than the production of *The Innocents Abroad*. Through her brother, who was one of the party, Mr. Clemens became acquainted with Miss Olivia L. Langdon, the daughter of Jervis Langdon, of Elmira, New York, and this acquaintance led, in February, 1870, to one of the most ideal marriages in literary history.

Four children came of this union. The eldest, Langdon, a son, was born in November, 1870, and died in 1872. The second, Susan Olivia, a daughter, was born in the latter year, and lived only twenty-four years, but long enough to develop extraordinary mental gifts and every grace of character. Two other daughters, Clara Langdon and Jean, were born in 1874 and 1880, respectively, and still live (1899).

Mark Twain's first home as a man of family was in Buffalo, in a house given to the bride by her father as a wedding present. He bought a third interest in a daily newspaper, the Buffalo *Express*, and joined its staff. But his time for jogging in harness was past. It was his last attempt at regular newspaper work, and a year of it was enough. He had become assured of a market for anything he might produce, and he could choose his own place and time for writing.

There was a tempting literary colony at Hartford; the place was steeped in an atmosphere of antique peace and beauty, and the Clemens family were captivated by its charm. They moved there in October, 1871, and soon built a house which was one of the earliest fruits of the artistic revolt against the mid-century Philistinism of domestic architecture in America. For years it was an object of wonder to the simple-minded tourist. The facts that its rooms were arranged for the convenience of those who were to occupy them, and that its windows, gables, and porches were distributed with an eye to the beauty, comfort, and picturesqueness of that particular house, instead of following the traditional lines laid down by the carpenters and contractors who designed most of the dwellings of the period, distracted the critics, and gave rise to grave discussions in the newspapers throughout the country of "Mark Twain's practical joke."

The years that followed brought a steady literary development. *Roughing It*, which was written in 1872, and scored a success hardly second to that of *The Innocents*, was, like that, simply a humorous narrative of personal experiences, variegated by brilliant splashes of description; but with *The Gilded Age*, which was produced in the same year, in collaboration with Mr. Charles Dudley Warner, the humorist began to evolve into the philosopher. *Tom Sawyer*, appearing in 1876, was a veritable manual of boy nature, and its sequel, *Huckleberry Finn*, which was published nine years later, was not only an advanced treatise in the same science, but a most moving study of the workings of the untutored human soul, in boy and man. *The Prince and the Pauper* (1882), *A Connecticut Yankee at King Arthur's Court* (1890), and *Pudd'nhead Wilson* (firs published serially in 1893–94), were all alive with a comprehensive and passionate sympathy to which their humor was quite subordinate, although Mark Twain never wrote, and probably never will write, a book that could be read without laughter His humor is as irrepressible as Lincoln's, and like that, it bubbles out on the most solemn occasions; but still, again like Lincoln's, it has a way of seeming, in spite of the surface incongruity, to belong there. But it was in the *Personal Recollections of Joan of Arc*, whose anonymous serial publication in 1894–95 betrayed some critics of reputation into the absurdity of attributing it to other authors, notwithstanding the characteristic evidences of its paternity that obtruded themselves on every page, that Mark Twain became most distinctly a prophet of humanity. Here, at last, was a book with nothing ephemeral about it—one that will reach the elemental human heart as well among the flying-machines of the next century as it does among the automobiles of to-day, or as it would have done among the stage-coaches of a hundred years ago.

And side by side with this spiritual growth had come a growth in knowledge and in culture. The Mark Twain of *The Innocents*, keen-eyed, quick of understanding, and full of fresh, eager interest in all Europe had to show, but frankly avowing that he "did not know what in the mischief the Renaissance was," had developed into an accomplished scholar and a man of the world for whom the globe had few surprises left. The Mark Twain of 1895 might conceivably have written *The Innocents Abroad*, although it would have required an effort to put himself in the necessary frame of mind, but the Mark Twain of 1869 could no more have written *Joan of Arc* than he could have deciphered the Maya hieroglyphics.

In 1873 the family spent some months in England and Scotland, and Mr. Clemens lectured for a few weeks in London. Another European journey followed in 1878.

A Tramp Abroad was the result of this tour, which lasted eighteen months. *The Prince and the Pauper, Life on the Mississippi*, and *Huckleberry Finn* appeared in quick succession in 1882, 1883, and 1885. Considerably more amusing than anything the humorist ever wrote was the fact that the trustees of some village libraries in New England solemnly voted that *Huckleberry Finn*, whose power of moral uplift has hardly been surpassed by any book of our time, was too demoralizing to be allowed on their shelves.

395

All this time fortune had been steadily favorable, and Mark Twain had been spoken of by the press, sometimes with admiration, as an example of the financial success possible in literature, and sometimes with uncharitable envy, as a haughty millionaire, forgetful of his humble friends. But now began the series of unfortunate investments that swept away the accumulations of half a lifetime of hard work, and left him loaded with debts incurred by other men. In 1885 he financed the publishing-house of Charles L. Webster & Co. in New York. The firm began business with the prestige of a brilliant *coup*. It secured the publication of the Memoirs of General Grant, which achieved a sale of more than 600,000 volumes. The first check received by the Grant heirs was for $200,000, and this was followed a few months later by one for $150,000. These are the largest checks ever paid for an author's work on either side of the Atlantic. Meanwhile, Mr. Clemens was spending great sums on a type-setting machine of such seductive ingenuity as to captivate the imagination of everybody who saw it. It worked to perfection, but it was too complicated and expensive for commercial use, and after sinking a fortune in it between 1886 and 1889 Mark Twain had to write off the whole investment as a dead loss.

On top of this the publishing-house, which had been supposed to be doing a profitable business, turned out to have been incapably conducted, and all the money that came into its hands was lost. Mark Twain contributed $65,000 in efforts to save its life, but to no purpose, and, when it finally failed, he found that it had not only absorbed everything he had put in, but had incurred liabilities of $96,000, of which less than one-third was covered by assets.

He could easily have avoided any legal liability for the debts, but as the credit of the company had been based largely upon his name, he felt bound in honor to pay them. In 1895–96 he took his wife and second daughter on a lecturing tour around the world, wrote *Following the Equator*, and cleared off the obligations of the house in full.

The years 1897, 1898, and 1899 were spent in England, Switzerland, and Austria. Vienna took the family to its heart, and Mark Twain achieved such a popularity among all classes there as is rarely won by a foreigner anywhere. He saw the manufacture of a good deal of history in that time. It was his fortune, for instance, to be present in the Austrian Reichsrath on the memorable occasion when it was invaded by sixty policemen, and sixteen refractory members were dragged roughly out of the hall. That momentous event in the progress of parliamentary government profoundly impressed him.

Mark Twain, although so characteristically American in every

A BIOGRAPHICAL SKETCH

fiber, does not appeal to Americans alone, nor even to the English-speaking race. His work has stood the test of translation into French, German, Russian, Italian, Swedish, Norwegian, and Magyar. That is pretty good evidence that it possesses the universal quality that marks the master. Another evidence of its fidelity to human nature is the readiness with which it lends itself to dramatization. *The Gilded Age, Tom Sawyer, The Prince and the Pauper*, and *Pudd'nhead Wilson* have all been successful on the stage.

In the thirty-eight years of his literary activity Mark Twain has seen generation after generation of "American humorists" rise, expand into sudden popularity , and disappear, leaving hardly a memory behind. If he has not written himself out like them, if his place in literature has become every year more assured, it is because his "humor" has been something radically different from theirs. It has been irresistibly laughter-provoking, but its sole end has never been to make people laugh. Its more important purpose has been to make them think and feel. And with the progress of the years Mark Twain's own thoughts have become finer, his own feelings deeper and more responsive. Sympathy with the suffering, hatred of injustice and oppression, and enthusiasm for all that tends to make the world a more tolerable place for mankind to live in, have grown with his accumulating knowledge of life as it is. That is why Mark Twain has become a classic, not only at home, but in all lands whose people read and think about the common joys and sorrows of humanity.

THE END